ANOTHER MAN'S KISSES

Ladro pulled Aeneva to him, holding her close, breathing in the clean, warm scent of her body. He kissed the top of her head, stroking her soft, silky hair. He knew it was wrong to hold her like this; he knew he was taking advantage of her but he couldn't help himself. He wanted her; he wanted her more than he had ever wanted anyone in his life. He lifted her face up and kissed her, enjoying the softness of her lips, the sweetness of her mouth, the warmth of her body. He knew in his heart that he was taking another man's wife, a child's mother, but still he could not stop himself. He could only think of Aeneva and having her to himself.

"You will not leave me, Ladro?"

"I won't leave you, Aeneva. I won't ever leave you unless you want me to." Ladro kissed Aeneva passionately, unable to control the desire that had welled up inside of him . . .

SAVAGE FURY

SWEET MEDICINE'S PROPHECY
#4

BY KAREN A. BALE

ZEBRA BOOKS
KENSINGTON PUBLISHING CORP.

ZEBRA BOOKS

are published by

Kensington Publishing Corp.
475 Park Avenue South
New York, NY 10016

Second printing: October, 1989

Printed in the United States of America

To my children, Courtney and Brandon—
you make my heart soar like an eagle.

Acknowledgments

A special thanks to Kathleen Duey—friend, colleague, and editor *extraordinaire*. Thanks for the help. I hope I can do the same for you someday.

Chapter I

Aeneva walked across the open prairie, her robe wrapped around her shoulders. She breathed deeply, admitting the fresh, sweet air into her lungs. She looked around her, smiling. The hills stood up in the distance as majestic warriors, ever-present, ever-watching. The sun was beginning its ascent in the east. She heard the deep snorts of the buffalo bulls nearby as the sun woke them. As Aeneva looked at everything that surrounded her, she felt that when she died she would become a part of this land, watching over her people and the animals who lived here. She felt at peace, yet as her eyes scanned the familiar land she knew that all was not well.

"Aeneva."

Aeneva turned when she heard the voice of her husband. She held her arms out to him. "I did not expect to see you out here."

"You know I can't sleep when you're not there." He put his arms around her. "I worry when you're not close to me."

"Oh, Trenton," she said softly, reaching up and touching her husband's face, the face she knew so well. She admired his striking looks—the blond hair, the deep blue eyes, the dark skin—and she loved him with all her heart. She took his hand and put it on her stomach. "Do you feel it? Do you feel the life moving within me?" She watched as a smile spread across his face. "This life makes me feel so strong. It makes me feel as if I could do anything."

"You have done too much already." He smiled, a light coming into his eyes.

"What do you mean?" she asked in mock anger.

"I lived through all of the years when you were a warrior and you fought with the men. You were foolish, but no one could stop you. When Crooked Teeth stole you away from me, I was afraid I would never see you again. Then there were the Shoshonis . . ."

Aeneva put her hand over Trenton's mouth. "I do not need to hear about my past. I know all that I have done. What is most important to me now is the future with you and Nathan and the baby."

The sun moved up higher in the early morning sky, casting a golden glow over the prairie. Aeneva and Trenton watched as one of the huge buffalo rolled in its wallow, refreshing itself, enlivening itself for a new day. Far off beyond the herds of buffalo a small cloud of dust arose. Aeneva put her arm around Trenton's waist, her body tensing. "Trenton, look."

"I see them."

"What are hunters doing on Cheyenne land?

10

Crows would not be so foolish to come on to our land and hunt in the daylight."

"I don't think they're Crows. Maybe they're hunters from the camp north of us."

"Perhaps."

"Don't worry. I'll ride out and see who they are. Come on."

Dogs barked furiously as Aeneva and Trenton entered the camp. Smoke filled the air from the campfires as the women began cooking their morning meals. Trenton and Aeneva walked to the lodge of Brave Wolf, Aeneva's brother.

"Haahe, Brave Wolf. May Aeneva and I enter?"

Brave Wolf came to the lodge flap. "Haahe, sister and brother. What is it you want so early in the morning?"

"We saw riders out beyond the buffalo herds. Hunters I think."

Brave Wolf nodded. "I will tell Coyote Boy and some of the others. We will meet you by the horses, brother."

Aeneva and Trenton walked back to their lodge and went inside. Aeneva watched Trenton buckle his gunbelt and check his rifle. Aeneva waited for him by the lodge flap.

"I don't want you going with me, Aeneva."

She nodded. "I will walk with you to the horses."

They hurried to the horses. Aeneva watched as the men quickly mounted up, riding out of the camp. Brave Wolf was on his magnificent stallion. She smiled as he rode past her. She turned and walked back toward camp, folding her arms across her

11

slightly swollen belly.

"Haahe, Aeneva. Why do you look so sad this day?"

Aeneva looked up at Little Deer, Brave Wolf's wife. They had been married only a short time, but already Aeneva had grown to love Little Deer. "I am not sad, Little Deer. Why do you ask me such a thing?"

"I know you, Aeneva. What is it?"

"I watched the men ride out just now. It reminded me of the times when I rode as a warrior. It took me a long time before I gained respect."

"You still miss it?"

"There are times when I would like to ride off with the men instead of staying here to cook the meals and tan the hides."

"I would not know what to do if I had to ride with the men. I would die of fright."

"You would not, Little Deer. You would learn if you had to."

"I do not think so, Aeneva. I am not like you. You are very brave."

"You do not know that, Little Deer."

"I have heard the stories. Even though I did not grow up in this band, I have heard the stories of you and your brothers. We all know how brave you were as a woman warrior. We all know of the way you were kidnapped by the Crow, Crooked Teeth, and how you managed to survive. You have done many brave things, Aeneva."

"Please, Little Deer, do not make me out to be something I am not. We are all brave when we must be." She patted Little Deer on the arm and smiled. She glanced up at the blue sky. "I wonder what

12

Nathan is doing right now."

"You miss him."

"Yes, although he is not the child of my body, he is the child of my heart. I yearn for him." She smiled. "But I will see him soon at the gathering."

"Yes, soon spring will be here."

"I must go now, Little Deer. I have medicines to prepare before I can do my work."

"Do not worry about the evening meal. I will do that for you."

"Thank you, Little Deer."

Aeneva walked back to her lodge, the sweet smell of herbs coming from it as it always had. Aeneva wondered if the smell of her herbs clung to her own clothing as it had to her grandmother's. This was the lodge she had grown up in. When her grandparents had died, she had brought Trenton and Nathan into the lodge and they tended it with the same loving care that her grandparents had. This spring, as she had done every year, Aeneva would carefully repaint the large yellow sun and the black horse on the outside of the lodge. Sun Dancer and Stalking Horse. They had been the only parents Aeneva had ever known. In her heart, this was still their lodge.

She selected the medicines she would need this day, placing them in the same large basket her grandmother had used. She lifted the basket, recalling how heavy it had seemed when she followed her grandmother as a child, always complaining that she would rather be with her brothers. She smiled at the memory and walked to the lodge of Rain Flower. Rain Flower had been injured in a fall from her horse.

"Haahe, Snake Man."

Snake Man came to the lodge door. "Please come in, Aeneva."

"How is Rain Flower today?"

"She seems better, but her skin is still hot."

"That is good. Her body is fighting off the sickness." Aeneva knelt next to Rain Flower, putting her hand on the girl's forehead. "How do you feel today, Rain Flower?"

Rain Flower stared up at Aeneva. "Better, I think, but my head hurts greatly."

"I will look at it." Aeneva removed the cloth she had tied around Rain Flower's head the day before and examined the gash. It was still swollen, but the color of the skin was pink. "You will be fine, Rain Flower. It is healing well. Your head will be tender for a few days. I will leave some more medicine with Snake Man. If you have much pain, drink some of the tea."

"Thank you, Aeneva. It is good of you to help me."

"That is what I am here for."

"I would like to send something home with you."

"I need nothing, Rain Flower. I will see you tomorrow." She smiled at Snake Man as she walked out. "The wound is healing well. She should be completely well soon."

"Thank you, Aeneva."

Aeneva waved to Snake Man and headed across the camp. She heard riders come into camp. She followed the other people to see what had happened. Trenton was not among the riders. Brave Wolf dismounted, addressing his people.

"We have seen riders. They came here for buffalo.

We do not know who they are. Some of them are Indian, the others . . ." Brave Wolf shrugged his shoulders. "We are posting guards. I want no one to leave the camp."

Aeneva went forward to her brother. "Is Trenton all right?"

"He is fine, little sister. He is checking the tracks, trying to determine how many men there are."

"You said some were Indians. Who are the others?"

"I do not know. White men maybe."

"Soldiers?"

"I do not think so. They appeared to be a strange group."

Aeneva glanced past her brother. "You are sure Trenton is all right?"

"Would it make you feel better if I went back for him?"

"Yes."

"You know he will not like this."

"I do not care. He is my only husband, the only one I ever intend to have. I do not want to lose him."

Brave Wolf shook his head. "Such a stubborn girl, always so stubborn. Even when you were a little girl you would always have things your own way no matter what."

"I cannot help it, Brave Wolf. It is my way."

"Do not act so coy with me, Aeneva. It is your way because you want it to be your way." He kissed her on the forehead. "I will look for your husband."

"Thank you, Brave Wolf." He mounted and turned his magnificent appaloosa. This stallion was important to Brave Wolf not only because he was so rare and beautiful, but also because he was the grandson of the appaloosa that their grandfather had given to their grandmother. That stallion had sired many foals. They had grown to be fine horses but the prized appaloosa coloring had not reappeared until this generation. It was fitting that her brother should ride such a horse.

Aeneva picked up her basket and returned to her work. Many people needed her help and advice. On her way back to her own lodge, she heard horses approaching and looked up. Trenton and Brave Wolf pulled their mounts to a stop. She ran to her husband, smiling her thanks to her brother as he rode past.

They went to their lodge. Trenton put his arm around Aeneva, but he didn't speak.

"What is it, Trenton? What did you find?"

"I found the tracks of some Indian ponies, but there were about ten horses with shoes."

"Soldiers?"

"I don't think so. Soldiers wouldn't do what they did."

"What did they do?"

"They left eight buffalo carcasses out there to rot. They shot each one, cut some meat, and left them. The bastards didn't even take the best parts of the animals." He shook his head slowly. "I don't like this. An Indian wouldn't do this, at least not an Indian who hadn't gone completely renegade."

"But you said there were only a few Indian ponies. Who are they?"

"I don't know, but I have a feeling. There are groups of men who ride further south who call themselves Comancheros. They took the name from

16

the Comanche tribe because they trade with the Comanches, some of the few people who can."

"What do these Comancheros do?"

"Just about anything for money. They steal, rob, and murder."

"They are horse thieves?"

"No, worse, they steal people, women and children usually. They take them down south to Mexico to sell as slaves."

"You mean they make these people into slaves like Joe was?"

"Yes, but in Mexico things are a lot worse." He stood up, walking to the lodge flap. "I've never heard of Comancheros this far north. I'm going to talk to Brave Wolf. I think we should double the guard around the camp."

"But if there are only a few of them . . ."

"I don't know for sure how many there are, Aeneva. That may have just been a hunting party. There could be a lot more somewhere around here."

"The people wanted to gather around the big fire tonight. Spring is almost here, they wish to celebrate. Should we not do it?"

"It will probably be all right as long as we have plenty of guards." Trenton went to her, taking her in his arms. "Don't worry. It's probably nothing. I just don't want to lose you again." He kissed her deeply.

"You will not lose me, my husband. I will never leave you again."

He smiled. "That's good news, especially since we have a child on the way." He patted her rounded belly lovingly. "I'll be back later."

*   *   *

As the sun went down, there were sounds of merriment in the camp, although the sounds were more subdued than in years past. Joe leaned close to Aeneva, his black skin glistening in the firelight.

"Wait until this one is over. Your fool brother talked me into helping him act out the bear story. Want to guess who gets to be the bear?"

"You know Coyote Boy. He always likes to be the brave warrior." Aeneva laughed loudly. As Coyote Boy and Joe acted out the bear story the people around the great fire clapped and called good-natured taunts. When the men had finished, Coyote Boy sat down next to Aeneva.

"Well, what did you think, little sister? Am I not the best storyteller in the camp?"

"Yes, Coyote Boy, you are the best."

"What about me, girl? It wasn't easy acting with this savage."

Aeneva and the others laughed in delight. "You were both good except I am not sure that a warrior could kill a grizzly so easy, my brother."

"Not any warrior can, little sister. I was talking about myself, of course."

"Of course," Aeneva agreed, smiling at Trenton.

Joe winked. "Aren't you going to dance tonight, girl?"

"I do not think the people of the camp want to see a woman with a swollen belly dance, Joe. I will wait until next year."

"Yes, next year her stomach will be flat again." Trenton reached out and touched his wife's stomach. "What do you think, a boy or a girl?"

Brave Wolf spoke from behind them. "I hope for

your sake it is a boy, brother. Boys are easier to handle than girls."

"How would you know, Brave Wolf? You have no children of your own yet."

"I know because I am your older brother, Aeneva. I had to go through life trying to keep you out of trouble."

"And it was so easy with Coyote Boy." Aeneva narrowed her dark eyes. "I remember the time that Grandfather punished you for knocking down someone's lodge. You were not allowed to speak to anyone for a whole moon."

"Do not laugh." Coyote Boy grimaced at the memory. "It was the worst punishment I have ever received."

"Ah, Coyote Boy, I remember that once you forgot and you got angry with me. Grandfather made you eat the fire weed."

"And you liked it, did you not, brother? But you were made to suffer, also."

"What happened?" Joe asked impatiently.

"My little brother put one of the large prickly burrs under my saddle blanket one day. My horse went crazy and I fell to the ground, yelling as I landed." Brave Wolf smiled sheepishly. "Grandfather made me eat the fire weed also."

Laughter rang out. Aeneva raised her hand to silence them. "It is time for a story. Tell us one about Naxane Jean, Brave Wolf. It is nights like these that I miss him most."

"I will tell a story about Naxane Jean and Grandfather," Brave Wolf said. "We all know of the time Naxane Jean saved my grandfather's life but I will tell you a funny story. When Naxane Jean decided to stay here, Grandfather wanted to take him into the sweat lodge. Grandfather tried to warn him about it, but Naxane would have none of it. He said he would do it and it would not bother him. But it is said that once he got inside the lodge he never stopped yelling. Grandfather told him to quiet himself and save his strength, but Naxane said things to Grandfather that could never be repeated. It is said Naxane cursed in ten languages that night." Brave Wolf waited until the laughter subsided. Silence spread to the people sitting close to him. All of the Cheyennes loved stories about Stalking Horse and Naxane Jean. A voice came from the darkness outside the firelight.

"Is it true Naxane Jean took you and Coyote Boy and Aeneva to one of the white man's cities?"

"Yes. It was a strange place, this city. All of the lodges were of wood and another hard material. They were built in straight lines next to each other with no open spaces." A hush was heard around the campfire.

"And the women wear things such as you have never seen," Aeneva said. "They are strange things that go around their waists and then are pulled tightly to make them small in here." She put her hands on her waist. "Naxane Jean said that the women can hardly breathe with them on."

The people around the fire whispered and talked to each other, smiling and nodding. Brave Wolf stood up, waiting for silence.

"Spring will soon be here. We have much to be thankful for. The Great Father continues to smile down upon us." Everyone nodded their heads in agreement. "Soon we will go south, as will our people further north, and we will meet with our other bands and those of the Arapahos."

Voices swelled at the outer edge of the camp. Brave Wolf stopped, looking into the darkness. One of the camp guards stepped into the firelight. "Brave Wolf, this is Long Knife from our brothers to the north. He must speak to you."

Brave Wolf stepped forward, feeling the eyes of his people on him. "Come, Long Knife. What is it you have to tell me?"

"Our band has been attacked. There were men, many men. I have never seen them before. They attacked us a few days ago. They took some of our women and children. They were coming this way, Brave Wolf."

Brave Wolf glanced at Trenton and Coyote Boy who had come to stand next to him. "Do you know how many there were, Long Knife?"

"We do not know. It seemed like only a few at first and then more came later. Many of our men were killed. We need help to get the rest of our band joined with yours."

"Rest, Long Knife. We will help you." Brave Wolf turned to his people, their merriment long since stopped. "We must gather our things. I am sending the women and children south to the Arapahos. They will be guarded by some of our braves. The rest of us will help our people to the north. Go now. Ready yourselves." He turned to Trenton. "Perhaps you will be able to track them down." Trenton nodded, looking at Aeneva.

"Brave Wolf, I can guard the women and children."

"Thank you, Joe. I will send some braves with you."

Joe gripped Trenton's shoulder. "I'll see you later, boy. Take care of yourself. See you down south."

"Take care, Joe."

Trenton and Aeneva hurried back to their lodge. Aeneva quickly packed some of her things in her bags and began taking down the lodge poles.

"Leave them, Aeneva. We don't have time." Trenton went to her, giving her one of the rifles. "You have your knife?"

"Yes." Aeneva's eyes searched Trenton's. "It is those same men. You knew they would come here."

"I had a feeling." He held her close to him. "I want you to listen to me, Aeneva. No matter what happens, I want you to save yourself. Do anything you can to stay away from these men."

"Trenton . . ."

"Hurry up. Joe and the others are waiting. I'll see you soon."

"Be careful, Trenton. I love you."

Aeneva ran to the horses. Joe and some of the other men were already waiting. Little Deer handed her the reins to her mount. Aeneva heard a child whimper, but it was quickly hushed. Aeneva swung up on her horse, looking over at the warrior who was next to her. It was Broken Foot. "I am glad you are coming with us, Broken Foot."

"Thank you, Aeneva." He turned to help a woman calm her horse.

Joe raised his voice. "Is everyone here?"

"We are ready," Broken Foot replied calmly.

They rode through the night, surrounded by an eerie silence. Joe rode in front, the other warriors on the edges and behind, forming a protective circle around the frightened women. They rode steadily, not pushing the horses, until the sun rose. When it was light enough Joe picked up the pace. They rode hard until sunset, stopping near the base of a rocky bluff. Mothers lifted weary children to the ground. They took food from their packs and ate in silence.

Aeneva sat close to Joe. "Have I told you that I value our friendship?"

"You don't have to tell me that. I know how you feel."

"But I wanted to say it. Sometimes I worry . . ."

"Nothing's going to happen. We'll get you all to safety and everything will be fine."

"It's not me I am worried about, Joe."

"Trenton and your brothers can take care of themselves."

Aeneva tore a piece of jerky. "Sometimes I think I will lose everyone I have ever known."

"That's not going to happen."

"My parents were killed by Crows when I was just a little girl. I never got to know them. I was told that my mother was a gentle woman who loved my brothers and me very much. She was called Little Flower. My father was called Young Eagle and he was good and brave."

"I'm sorry, Aeneva."

"I just wish I had known them. I wish they could have known me."

Joe put his arm around Aeneva's shoulders.

"They'd be real proud of you, girl. Real proud. I bet they're looking down at you right now."

"Yes, with my grandparents and Naxane Jean."

"Don't be so sad. They're all up there having a good old time. They're not sad, so you shouldn't be. Why, I bet my ma is up there with them."

"You are so good." Aeneva leaned her head against Joe's shoulder. "I hope you never leave us, Joe. I would miss you if you did."

"I don't plan on going anywhere soon. Your people don't seem to notice the color of my skin and that means a lot to a man who was raised as a slave." Joe patted Aeneva on the back. "You better get yourself some rest."

Aeneva spread her mat and lay down, covering herself with her blanket. She closed her eyes, willing her body to relax. It seemed as though she had just fallen asleep when Joe gently shook her, telling her it was time to leave. She quickly gathered her things and mounted her horse. She took another woman's child and held the boy against her chest, thankful that Nathan was safe with the Arapahos. At least she didn't have to worry about him.

The sun had barely risen the next day when they heard riders. Fear showed on the faces around Aeneva. Mothers clutched their children tightly.

"Ride!" Joe shouted. "Broken Foot, get them to those rocks."

Aeneva's horse leaped forward with the others, but she jerked it around, riding toward Joe. Broken Foot cut her off before she got halfway there.

"Let me go, Broken Foot. I can help."

24

"You cannot help, Aeneva. Go with the other women."

"I want to help Joe." She attempted to ride around Broken Foot, but he blocked her way, leaning over to grab her reins.

"I promised your brother that I would take care of you and I will."

Aeneva watched silently and with great anguish as Broken Foot led her horse away from the skirmish. She looked back and the last thing she saw was Joe falling. A man with a rifle stood over him. She closed her eyes, her shoulders slumping forward. She had lost so many people in her lifetime and now she had lost Joe.

The sun shone brightly on the small band, but it was only a false brightness. They were weary, tired from endless days of traveling in the heat with little food and water. Aeneva never complained and kept up with the others; it would have gone against her grain to use her pregnancy as an excuse to rest. As nighttime neared they stopped in some rocks, looking for a safe place to camp for the night. As the darkness enclosed them, they all sought its safety as another night of freedom offered itself to them.

Aeneva lay back against one of the rocks. She closed her eyes, feeling the strength flow out of her. She wondered how she, who had once been a woman warrior of the proud Cheyenne tribe, had been forced to flee for her life with the women and children of her band, while the men had stayed to fight. She

25

wondered, too, about Joe. Had he died quickly or had he suffered? And what about Nathan? Was he really safe with the Arapahos or had the Comancheros attacked them also?

"Aeneva, are you asleep?"

She heard the voice of Little Deer and she opened her eyes and smiled, grateful for the brief respite from her thoughts. "No, I am not asleep, Little Deer. I am just thinking."

"Are you feeling all right? I worry for you."

"Do not worry, I am fine. I am strong and the child inside of me is also strong."

Little Deer leaned closer. "Brave Wolf told me that Nathan looks much like your husband did when he was a small boy."

"Yes, Trenton was tall and strong with brown skin and hair the color of corn and eyes the color of the sky. I had never seen a boy like him before. I loved him from the first, I think."

"Yes, I have heard the stories from Brave Wolf. He said that you and Trenton and Coyote Boy would spend the days roaming the prairie. It must have been a wonderful time."

"It was." Aeneva nodded slightly, wishing more than ever that she could be with Trenton. "His mother called him Swiftly Running Deer. He could run faster than any boy I had ever seen."

"His white blood did not slow him down then."

Aeneva laughed. "No, I think his white blood has served him well."

"You should sleep now, Aeneva. Tomorrow will be another long day. You will need your strength."

"It will be better, Little Deer, we will reach the Arapahos soon. Then we will be safe."

"I hope so, Aeneva. I sometimes fear that I will never see Brave Wolf again." Her voice had dropped to a whisper.

Aeneva took Little Deer's hand. "You will see Brave Wolf again, I promise you." Aeneva looked up at the sky, then closed her eyes. She prayed silently, but she was hoping her grandmother would hear her. She felt that Sun Dancer watched over her and her family. "Go now, Little Deer, you must also rest. We will travel far tomorrow."

"All right, Aeneva. Call me if you need anything in the night."

"I will, sister. Sleep well." Aeneva watched as Little Deer walked away, and she wondered if any of them would see their families again.

The hot spring sun was relentless and Aeneva felt the sweat drip down her neck. The added weight of the child inside her made walking that much more difficult. It seemed as though her fate was always to be torn away from her husband.

Aeneva stopped for a moment. She rubbed her back and wiped the sweat from her face. She shaded her eyes and looked into the endless distance. The yellowed stalks of last year's wild grassses were bent from the winter winds. Seedlings, fragile and green, were just beginning to break through the soil. Would they ever reach the Arapahos, she wondered? The rest of the band passed her slowly, and again she followed. She concentrated on putting one foot in front of the other, trying not to feel the heaviness of the child in her stomach. She fixed her eyes on a line of trees at the base of some hills on the horizon and

27

did not allow herself to stop again until she stood beneath them. Broken Foot told them to wait there while he climbed high enough to see beyond the hills. Aeneva watched him as he limped away. She had seen him defend their camp many times with the others, but he had been forbidden to go with the men on raids when they had to go on foot; he was only allowed to stay with the horses. She had seen him ridiculed as a child and still hold his head high and now she watched as he took on the role of leader and she felt proud for him. One of the women grumbled, "We would do better following a real warrior." A few of the women murmured agreement. But Aeneva told them to quiet themselves and wait until Broken Foot returned. They listened to her as they always did. They respected her word as a warrior and as the sister of the leader of their band. Aeneva rested, but after some time had passed, she followed Broken Foot, finding him on a rocky outcrop, looking southward across the prairie. The sun was lower now, glaring. Aeneva crouched beside him.

"What is it, Broken Foot? What have you seen?"

Broken Foot glanced at her, his face impassive. "I do not know, Aeneva, but it is something. I feel it in the ground. There are people somewhere, riding closer."

"We should hide in these rocks until you are sure," Aeneva said quietly. He nodded without looking at her.

"Go back and tell the others to come here. We will stay until I am sure it is safe."

Aeneva hurried back to the small band and led them to the rocks where Broken Foot was waiting.

"We will rest here for a while," Broken Foot told the women and children. "Keep quiet. We must make no sound." He pulled Aeneva along with him to a higher vantage point. He pointed into the distance. "Look out there. Riders. Many riders."

Aeneva squinted her eyes against the bright sunlight and saw the dust from the horses. Her breath caught . . . there were at least twenty riders. "They are not Indians," Aeneva said quietly.

Broken Foot nodded. "Soldiers, perhaps. There is a fort somewhere in Arapaho territory."

Aeneva looked again, but could not shake the uneasy feeling which suddenly seized her. "I do not think they are soldiers, Broken Foot."

They watched as the riders approached, and Aeneva motioned to the women to hide and keep the children quiet. As the riders passed in a thundering cloud of dust, Aeneva watched them closely.

They were a ragged group, none of them dressed the same. Many of them were dark of skin but they were not Indians, and many had hair on their faces. Some wore large round hats and colorful blankets around their waists.

"Who are they?" Broken Foot whispered to Aeneva as the riders passed by.

Aeneva shook her head. "Trenton told me they might be men who band together to kill and rob people. They come from Mexico and raid different tribes, then return to Mexico where they are free from any laws. He told me they sometimes steal women and children and take them there to sell."

Broken Foot nodded his head. "That would explain the dark skin on some of them. Some of them are Mexicans. But I do not understand why they are this far north."

"I think we should stay here until darkness and travel tonight. They might come back." Aeneva forced calmness into her voice.

Broken Foot looked at her steadily. "Yes, that is my feeling also. We will travel as far as we can tonight and hopefully find some shelter by the morning."

While it was difficult to sleep in the waning heat of day, the women knew it was essential to be rested for the night travel, and they were tired. When the sun had barely set, Aeneva and Broken Foot awakened everyone and again they set off southward onto the open prairie. Aeneva walked with a renewed sense of urgency, sometimes touching her swollen belly. She kept remembering the stories Trenton had told her of those men. Comancheros he had called them, and she knew she was truly frightened. It seemed that they did not respect human life at all, and honor was not a word that they knew.

When any of the women slowed down, Aeneva made sure that they kept up their pace. She helped with crying children and found strength in chanting. And all the while she marveled at Broken Foot—the man with the misshapen foot, the man who was never truly treated as a respected warrior—and she admired the way he limped along at a hurried pace, making sure that no one slowed down. It was obvious that he felt these women were his responsibility and he intended to take care of them. The dusty grass muffled their footsteps and the small, exhausted sounds of the children as the band moved on.

By sunrise they had covered many miles and

Broken Foot and Aeneva pushed the small group further. Still, as the sun rose again the next day, they were caught in the middle of the prairie. With little or no shelter, they would be helpless victims if the Comancheros were anywhere near.

As the group struggled to go on, Aeneva felt a growing ache in her stomach. The ache soon gave way to pain and fear as she realized that something was wrong with the child inside her. She clasped her stomach and tried to make the stabbing pains go away. She struggled to keep up with the group, but it was soon apparent that something was very wrong. Instead of having the group stop or leave Aeneva behind, Broken Foot picked her up in his arms and carried her.

Aeneva tried to struggle. "No, Broken Foot, leave me. I will only slow you and the others down. Please, take the others to safety."

"I will not leave you here alone to die, Aeneva. We will find shelter."

"Please." Aeneva tried to protest, but another wave of pain overcame her and she groaned. She knew now that she would lose the baby; pains like this did not forebode good. She tried to relax, but her fear for her unborn child made the pain even worse. She felt a warm wetness between her legs and she could feel the very life of the child flowing out of her. "Put me down, Broken Foot. Leave me here," she said sadly, a cold emotionless tone coming into her voice.

"I know what is happening, Aeneva, and I will not leave you here. If you lose this child there will be others; you must think of your husband and his son."

She looked up at the man who held her so firmly

while he tried valiantly to keep an even stride. No one had even known of the pain he had endured in his lifetime yet he never complained of it. Aeneva reached up and touched Broken Foot's face.

"You are a good man. I thank you."

"Do not thank me yet, Aeneva, because I have not yet gotten us to safety."

"You have been an honorable man and a friend to me, Broken Foot. I will not forget it."

Broken Foot nodded his head slightly, his face calm and still. He pushed the band forward. Midmorning, with the children crying softly and even the strongest of the women faltering, Broken Foot led the way down a steep bank cut into the prairie by an eternity of springs rains. There was a small grove of trees at the bottom, giving them shade and a place to hide. Broken Foot carried Aeneva to a small clearing apart from the others and laid her down. He called for Little Deer and she came quickly.

"I think she is losing the child," Broken Foot said solemnly.

Little Deer nodded and took one of Aeneva's hands. "It will be all right, Aeneva. I will help you."

Aeneva looked up at Broken Foot. "Thank you, my friend." Aeneva watched Broken Foot as he nodded and limped away. "I am losing my child, Little Deer," Aeneva said softly, finally shifting her eyes away from Broken Foot. She sat up suddenly, clutching her stomach with her arms. Blood ran down her legs and she saw the fear in Little Deer's eyes. Aeneva knew she would have to be brave. "Little Deer, please leave me. There is nothing you can do for me now."

"I cannot leave you alone like this. I cannot."

"I must do this alone; I do not need you now."

"But I want to help."

"Bring me my bags. There is a healing tea you can brew for me. It will help with the pain after it is over."

Little Deer rushed to do Aeneva's bidding and returned with her sister-in-law's bag. "Here they are, Aeneva."

Aeneva sat up slowly, rummaging through the bags until she found the one she wanted. She handed the small buckskin bag to Little Deer. "Put just a few of these leaves into a kettle and let it boil for a while. I will need some soon." Little Deer hurried away. Aeneva crossed her arms over her stomach. The cramps had increased to such intensity that she thought she would scream, but she did not. She chanted to bring herself courage, using one of her grandmother's favorite chants. As she felt the life of her child tear from her, she had to fight to keep from screaming. She had wanted this child so desperately. What if she were never to see Trenton again? Or Nathan? This child would have been the only reminder of the love she had shared with her husband. When Little Deer returned, Aeneva was pale and covered with sweat. She reached out for Little Deer's hand. "I will need your help now, sister. You must help me deliver this child."

Little Deer understood. Aeneva squatted, pushing as hard as she could. At last, Little Deer helped to pull the dead child from her straining body. Little Deer moved away as Aeneva fell forward onto her hands, gasping for breath. "Please take it away, Little Deer. I do not want to see it. I do not want to see its face."

Little Deer turned silently and laid the small body on the ground. When she returned, she found Aeneva lying on her side, her knees pulled up to her chest. She helped Aeneva to a sitting position and forced her to drink the tea. When Aeneva refused to drink it all, Little Deer made her finish the bowl. Without speaking, she brought water and gently cleansed Aeneva and helped her into a clean dress, taking the other to bury the child in. Then she covered Aeneva with a heavy robe and bade her sleep.

Broken Foot approached cautiously. Upon seeing Aeneva asleep on the ground, he went to Little Deer. "It is over?"

"Yes. I buried the child. It was such a small thing."

"Aeneva is brave. She did not cry out."

"She would not," Little Deer responded proudly.

Broken Foot nodded. "We will rest here until night. We will travel as much as we can in the darkness."

"But Aeneva will not be able to travel by this night. She is very weak."

"I will carry her," Broken Foot said quietly.

As darkness approached, Aeneva was still very weak, but she was determined to walk. She didn't get very far before she collapsed and Broken Foot picked her up. She didn't have the strength to argue with him and she laid her head against his shoulder and slept. Broken Foot kept the group going, nagging the slow ones and urging the children on with kind words. He knew if they could only reach the safety of the Arapaho camp they would have nothing to fear.

By sunrise they had reached a river, wide and shallow. Broken Foot bade them all rest and relax for a time. The river's shady banks gave them shelter from the sun and hid them from the enemy. And it was a constant source of food and water.

Aeneva was strong enough to wade into the cool water and bathe. She felt cleansed and she tried to put her dead child from her mind; she knew it would do her no good to grieve. Nathan was her only child now and she would be with him soon. Aeneva ate and drank, then slept deeply. She wanted to regain as much strength as possible so that Broken Foot would not have to carry her. When she awakened, she sought Broken Foot and found him by the river, soaking his feet in the cool water. She sat down next to him.

"Your feet are bad?"

Broken Foot did not turn to face Aeneva. "They are as always."

"Perhaps I can help."

"You cannot help, Aeneva. My feet have always been like this."

"I know that, Broken Foot, but I think I can make walking more comfortable for you. Will you let me help you as you helped me?"

Broken Foot shrugged and Aeneva ran off for her bags and returned quickly. She withdrew a pasty substance and told Broken Foot to dry his feet. She rubbed the paste on his feet.

"What is this? It smells worse than a dead buffalo!" Broken Foot tried to pull his foot away, but Aeneva held firm.

"Do not be so frightened of such a silly thing, Broken Foot."

"I am not frightened, I just do not like the smell."

"Then you will have to get used to the smell because you are going to keep using this on your feet. Hold still!" Aeneva took out some soft deerskin leggings and cut them into strips, carefully wrapping them around Broken Foot's feet. "Now put your moccasins back on," she ordered.

Broken Foot complied and when he was finished he stood up and scowled. "Nothing feels different. My feet still burn, only now they smell terrible."

"They will feel differently after you have walked for a time. I learned this from my grandmother, Sun Dancer, and she was one of the best healers in all the Cheyenne bands."

Broken Foot did not seem impressed. "I will try it for a while, but if it doesn't work I will rip the wrappings off and wash the stench from my feet."

Aeneva smiled in amusement as she watched Broken Foot walk away. Even if the medicine helped he would probably not admit it. Her grandmother had often told her that men did not like to be treated by women healers; it made them feel less strong, less noble. But her grandmother had earned great respect from all men of her tribe, as well as from her teacher, the great healer, Horn.

"How are you feeling, Aeneva?"

Aeneva turned to see Little Deer carrying a basket. "I am much better, Little Deer. What have you there?"

"Berries. They are delicious and sweet. They are growing wild everywhere."

36

Aeneva reached into the basket and took a handful, stuffing them into her mouth. It brought to mind the many times she and her brothers had gone berry-picking and had eaten so many that they had gotten sick. "They are wonderful. I have never tasted anything so sweet."

"Are you well enough to travel, Aeneva? If you are not, I will stay here with you until you are strong. We can follow the others later."

"No, Little Deer, I cannot let you do that. I will keep up. Somehow I will keep up."

"I worry about you. You are weak and you should rest."

"I will get stronger," Aeneva said confidently, but she knew how really weak she was. She had lost a great deal of blood and she needed to rebuild her strength. She wasn't sure if she could keep up with the others, but she would not let herself slow them down.

"Broken Foot says that we will leave in a short time. He says we will travel along the river."

"He is right. The river is the safest way."

"Please, Aeneva . . ."

"Do not argue with me, Little Deer. I will be ready to travel when it is time." Aeneva turned away and tried to help the women preparing food, but they gently pushed her away. She sat apart, leaning against the rough trunk of an ancient cottonwood tree.

Aeneva rested until Broken Foot broke camp. She refused help from Broken Foot, walking along at her own slow pace until midmorning. Then Broken Foot told the women to make camp again—that they would travel no more until the next morning. The weary women set about their work with gladness, talking quietly. The next morning Aeneva was stronger. The children ran into the water, laughing. Smiles came to the women's lips. It was good to walk again in daylight.

The land became greener around them as the days passed. Broken Foot's decision to travel in daylight upon reaching the river had seemed like a wise one. Although still weak in body, they all seemed stronger in spirit as they neared the safety of the land of the Arapahos. Even Aeneva recovered her strength quickly and she was well enough to bother Broken Foot about the treatments she had prescribed for his feet.

"You do not seem to limp so much now, Broken Foot," Aeneva said offhandedly as they walked along the river.

"It is easier walking here. The ground is softer."

"I see. So your feet feel just the same at the end of the day? They have the same burning, the same pain?"

"They are better. The burning is not so bad."

"Only because of the soft ground near the river," Aeneva responded dryly.

"Of course." Broken Foot walked faster.

Aeneva matched his pace. "Broken Foot."

"What is it?"

"I am glad that you are better," Aeneva said simply and continued walking. Broken Foot caught at her arm and turned her to face him.

"Wait, Aeneva. I should thank you for helping me. But it is not easy. All of my life I have walked alone with my pain. It is not easy for me to accept help."

"But it is easy for you to give it? You saved my life, Broken Foot."

"I did not save your life. I only carried you until you were able to walk again."

Aeneva smiled. "I cannot carry you, Broken Foot, but at least I can help you walk with more ease."

Broken Foot nodded slowly. "Why is it none of the healers gave this medicine to me when I was young?"

"I do not think many of them knew of it. My grandmother mixed her own medicines, sometimes certain medicines for certain people. This one has no name. From now on, I shall call this medicine 'Broken Foot Medicine'."

Broken Foot extended his arm and Aeneva clasped it tightly. "You are my friend, Aeneva, and I will not forget what you have done for me."

"Nor will I forget what you have done for me, Broken Foot."

He looked at her steadily for a moment. "I think we should reach the big bend in the river soon. We will surely see some sign of Arapahos there."

"And soon we will be with our people again. My husband and brothers will come for us and I will be sure to tell them of your courage and strength."

"I do not need for you to speak for me, Aeneva."

"But I will do so anyway. Courage should always be spoken of."

By late afternoon they saw signs of old campfires and they knew they were close to finding the Arapahos. They camped by the river and felt safer than they had in many weeks. Early the next morning they were awakened by a group of Arapaho hunters and were led back to the tribe. Aeneva's joy knew no boundaries when she saw Nathan. He stood out among the other children, blond and dark-skinned. He ran to her when he saw her and she picked him up, holding him against her.

"Oh, Nathan. I have missed you so."

"And I have missed you, Mother. Where is Pa?"

"He will come soon. You look well. Have you enjoyed your time here?"

"Yes, I have learned many things. But it's good to be with you, Mother." He clasped his arms tightly around Aeneva's neck.

"It is good to be with you, my son." Safe among her husband's people, Aeneva could see by the way they looked at her and Nathan how they loved Trenton.

Trenton's mother had been an Arapaho, his father a white tracker. They met, fell in love, and married. After Trenton's birth they had spent part of their time in a cabin in the mountains and part of their time with the Arapahos. In the lodge of Trenton's grandparents, Aeneva felt immediately welcome. The long days were full. Trenton's grandfather had great dignity and a quiet good nature. He told Aeneva many stories of Trenton when he was a young boy. She took care of Nathan and she helped the healer of the tribe as he went about his various tasks and she even helped him mix the medicine for a boy whose feet were deformed. Her account of Broken Foot's bravery brought him glances of respect from the Arapaho warriors.

Weeks passed and Aeneva grew restless and a yearning for her own people overcame her. She raged inwardly when she thought of Joe. Her dear friend was gone. She had to find out what had happened to Trenton, her brothers, and the rest of her people. She rode farther from the camp each day, searching the northern horizon for riders. If they did not come soon, she would go to find them. The Arapahos were good people, but her heart was aching for her own tribe. She chanted, sometimes, when thoughts of Trenton or Joe hurt too much to bear.

Aeneva rode out of camp early the next morning. A feeling of urgency pushed her along. She found a low rise and rode her horse to the top and reined the mare in. The horse stood, blowing, as she shielded her eyes from the sun to get a better look. A smile came over her face. There was dust in the distance. The dust of many riders. Aeneva dug her heels into the mare's sides, and she rode to greet the oncoming riders. She could see Trenton galloping toward her. When they had barely met he jumped from his horse and swept her down from hers, encompassing her in his arms. He laughed and pulled her close against him, then held her away for a moment.

"Oh, God, you look good." He kissed Aeneva deeply, hugging her even more fiercely.

Aeneva spoke, her lips against his skin. "Joe is gone. They killed him."

"Joe, dead? I can't believe it," Trenton murmured absently. "What happened?"

Aeneva looked up, grateful to see her brothers among the riders. "We were attacked. Joe and the others stayed to fight, while Broken Foot led us to safety."

"Did you actually see Joe get killed?"

"No, but I saw him on the ground, a man with a

rifle standing over him."

Trenton glanced at Brave Wolf and Coyote Boy. "I don't think he's dead, Aeneva. We found your people, but we didn't find Joe's body."

"You think he is alive? But where is he?"

"They probably took him with them. They can sell him in Mexico."

"But why? Why, Joe?"

"They'll probably sell him to a mine owner. He'll wind up digging for metal in tunnels under the ground."

"No," Aeneva protested. "That will kill him. He is a free man."

"Not down there he's not."

"And our people to the north?"

Brave Wolf shook his head. "Many died fighting these men but most of them are safe. They are on their way here."

"Some good news at least."

Brave Wolf's eyes went to Aeneva's stomach, but he said nothing when he saw her shake her head slightly. "I will go to Little Deer now. You and I will talk later."

She tried to smile. "Let me feel that you are really alive." She put her arms around her brother and hugged him to her.

"And what of me, little sister, am I not also important?"

"You know that you are, Coyote Boy. Without you to stick up for me against Brave Wolf I would have never made it through childhood." She hugged him and kissed him on the cheek. "You are a good brother."

Coyote Boy smiled widely and motioned the other warriors onward. He and Brave Wolf mounted their horses.

"We will meet you back at camp," Brave Wolf told Aeneva and Trenton as they rode away.

Trenton turned to Aeneva, taking her in his arms. "You look beautiful. But something . . ." He put his hand on her stomach and looked into her eyes. "What happened?"

"I lost our child, Trenton. I do not know if it was a boy or girl; I did not wish to see."

"I'm so sorry." He pulled her to him, stroking her hair softly. "I was afraid something like this would happen."

"It was not anybody's fault."

"It wouldn't have happened if you weren't forced to walk hundreds of miles."

"It is over. My sorrow has ended. We must go on."

Trenton nodded wearily. "Yes, we must go on. We must always go on." He sat down on the ground, running his hands through the dirt, picking it up in his hands and letting it fall through. "It is not how I imagined it would be, Aeneva."

Aeneva sat next to Trenton. "What is not as you imagined it?"

"Everything. I thought that growing up would be exciting, an adventure of sorts. I thought living among the Indians would be the perfect life for me, as it was for my father."

"But it is not."

"There is too much hardship and pain, Aeneva. It's not like it was when our grandparents were growing up in this land."

43

"Nothing is ever as we would like it to be, Trenton. Was it so easy in the white world?"

"No."

"What is it you want, Trenton?"

Trenton turned to Aeneva, surprised at her question. "I don't want anything." He stood up, walking away from her, looking out at the vast prairie.

Aeneva went to him, putting her arm through his. "Perhaps you should go off by yourself for a time."

Trenton turned to Aeneva, an angry look clouding his face. "How can I go anywhere when my friend is gone?"

Aeneva lowered her head, remembering how Joe had fought. "At least he is alive."

Trenton shook his head angrily. "What good will that do him if he is forced into slavery again?"

Aeneva raised her head. "I don't understand. That is not possible. How can they make a slave of a free man?"

"Comancheros have no honor. They'll sell anyone for a price."

"Mexico. That is the place to the south that you have told me about. Uncle Jean once said that the people there are very different from us."

"Very different. Joe will be treated like dirt. If he can't escape, Aeneva, his spirit will die."

"Joe's spirit will never die, Trenton. Never."

"He told me once that if he ever became a slave again he would kill himself. Freedom is too important to him."

"Then we must find him as soon as we can."

"I've looked for over three weeks for the Comancheros, but there haven't been any traces of them. It's like they have disappeared."

"I saw those men, those Comancheros."

Trenton turned, anger and excitement blazing in his eyes. "When? When did you see them?"

"It was about two weeks ago. Broken Foot saw them; he knew that they were dangerous. We hid in some rocks as they rode by."

"Did they have prisoners?"

"I don't think so. Maybe Joe has escaped."

Trenton shook his head. "He would know to come here. I have a bad feeling about this, Aeneva. I know Joe; he won't go with them willingly."

"You think they will kill him?"

"Maybe not, but they have other ways to make prisoners behave."

"We have to find him."

"No, *I* have to find him. I want you to stay here."

"I will not stay. I can help you."

"I don't want to argue about it now; I'm tired. Let's get to camp and we'll talk about it later."

"All right."

They mounted their horses and rode in silence back to the Arapaho camp. Trenton was greeted joyously by his relatives, but especially by Nathan who leapt into his arms. He was fed and brought a bowl for washing. Aeneva watched in amusement as the Arapaho women hovered around him like he was a golden god; indeed, she could see that he could easily have five or six wives in this camp.

Aeneva decided it was not time to pursue their earlier conversation, and seeing that Nathan was firmly ensconced in his father's lap, she went off

45

alone, trying to figure out a way they could rescue Joe. She had always loved walking at night; it was a good time for her to think. She walked a little way and found a clearing. The voices in the camp were muted and distant. She sat down, picking at the wild grass that grew in front of her. She absently braided three strands together. There had to be a way she could help Joe.

"What are you doing out here all alone?"

Aeneva smiled to herself, feeling the warmth of Trenton's voice as he spoke, still hidden in the shadows. He crossed the clearing and sat next to her, taking the grass from her hands. "I was trying to gather my thoughts. I thought you would be too busy with all of the women to notice that I had gone."

He stuck the grass in his mouth, chewing on the tip. "Arapaho women are beautiful, there is no doubt." He reached out for her hand, and pressing the palm to his mouth, he kissed it gently. "But it is said that Cheyenne women are the most beautiful and the most intelligent."

"Is that what is said?" She smiled, freeing her hand and pulling the grass from Trenton's mouth. "You could have many wives here; you could have your pick."

"I suppose that I could." Trenton agreed. A smile touched his lips.

"Would you be happy with many wives?"

"What do you think?"

"Why must you answer me with a question?"

"I learned how to do that from you."

"You are still evading my question."

46

"It was a foolish question to begin with. You know that I don't want any other woman but you."

"Sometimes I do not know . . ."

"You don't know what?"

"I do not know why you and I ever got married. It seems we have spent most of our lives trying to be together and yet we have been apart."

"But the times we've been together have been worth it, haven't they?" Trenton reached for Aeneva, cupping her face in his large hand. "You are so beautiful. I can't imagine my life without you." He covered her mouth with his, gently kissing her lips. "I love you, Aeneva. You are my life." He pulled her to him, tightening his arms around her.

"And you are mine, my husband, but it seems we are always apart. I do not want to live like that."

"We won't. We'll never be . . ."

Aeneva's fingers came up to Trenton's mouth. "No, don't say we will never be parted again because you cannot make that promise to me. It has happened too many times before. Let us just enjoy our time together." She pulled him down to her, holding him tightly. They kissed passionately, their mouths locked together. Trenton undressed, reaching for Aeneva's dress and pulling it up over her head. He stared in admiration at her long, brown body, then he held her, kissing her deeply. "I love you, Aeneva," he said gently. Their bodies became entwined as they rolled across the wild grass that served as their bed on this night. Aeneva felt alive as she felt her husband inside her, urging her to press herself against him until they both could no longer contain their love

47

and excitement. Aeneva cried out and Trenton covered her mouth with his. They lay in each other's arms until the cool of the night forced them to dress. When they stood up, still holding on to each other, they began to walk back to their camp. Neither said a word but nothing needed to be said now. Their love was enough.

Chapter II

Aeneva stared obstinately at her brothers and her husband, refusing to back down. "My plan is good. Why is it that none of you can accept it?"

"Because it is too dangerous!" Coyote Boy stood up, not cowed by his sister's angry glares.

"I thought you would stick up for me, Coyote Boy. You know how well I can fight; I fought next to you many times."

"But this is different; this is crazy!"

"It is a good idea. It is the best any of you have come up with."

"Aeneva," Brave Wolf said tenderly, "I cannot believe that you would willingly do this again."

"I would do it for Joe."

While the others argued back and forth, Trenton was silent, drawing on the ground with a stick. He knew his wife and he knew there was no easy way of dissuading her from doing something when she had her mind set to it. Brave Wolf turned to him.

"Trenton, my brother, you have not yet spoken

your mind. What have you to say about your wife's plan?"

Trenton looked up at the group. "Aeneva is right, it is the best plan."

"You see, my own husband agrees with me."

"I am not finished, Aeneva. It is a good plan. But have you already forgotten that the last time you had an idea like this you were a captive of the Crows for over a year?"

Aeneva stared into Trenton's eyes and she saw for the first time that he was frightened for her. "I have not forgotten."

"Then how can you think of doing this, sister?" Coyote Boy demanded.

"It will be different this time."

Trenton stood up, walking over to his wife. "How will it be different, Aeneva? I saw you after you had been a captive of Crooked Teeth's. You were like a helpless, wounded animal. You were frightened and you had lost all will to live. Do you want to take a chance on that happening again?"

"It will not happen again. I will be prepared this time."

"Jesus, woman!" Trenton kicked at the ground in frustration. "If you want to do this, then do it. But I won't be a part of it. If you want to go off and get yourself killed, go do it."

"Wait!" Aeneva shouted angrily. "Why is it that if *you* go after Joe and our people it is a good plan, but if *I* want to do it, it is a bad plan?"

"Because you are a woman."

"Because I am a woman? You know of my abilities; you know that I am as able as any man here."

"I know that, Aeneva. But what good did all that do you when you were tied up in a Crow camp and made to do the chief's bidding whenever he desired you? You are still a woman and you are bound by certain limitations just because you are a woman. If you could carry your knife and fight, I wouldn't worry. But you will be tied up and again you will be a captive. And what do we know of these Comancheros? The things we have heard make them sound worse than the Crows."

"Aeneva, Trenton is right. It is too dangerous. We will find another way."

"No. You must all consider my idea. It will be different this time. You will be following me; if I get into trouble you can help me."

Trenton looked at her. "God, Aeneva, you're crazy. Do you think these men are going to be nice to you until they take you to Mexico to sell you? What do you think they are going to do?"

"Nothing, if we tell them that I am the daughter of a great chief and I have never before been touched by a man. My worth will be great then. They will keep me safe out of greed."

Trenton looked at Brave Wolf and Coyote Boy, shaking his head. "You two try and talk some sense into her; she's your sister."

"Yes, but she is your wife, brother," Coyote Boy replied in amusement.

Trenton glared at him. "This is not funny, Coyote Boy. I don't want to lose Aeneva again to someone like Crooked Teeth." He turned to look at all of them, his deep blue eyes traveling from one to the other. "Do any of you really know about the

Comancheros? Do you know where the name comes from?"

"It comes from the Comanches," Aeneva replied.

"But do you know why?" Trenton held her eyes.

"Because the Comanches are fierce warriors."

"And because they will stop at nothing to get what they want. These men, these Comancheros, took their name from the Comanches. They are outlaws, killers, slavers, who will do anything for money. They love to torture their victims just for fun; I've heard stories of what they've done to women. Just because we tell them not to touch Aeneva it doesn't mean that they won't. We can't trust them."

"And how else are we to get our people back?"

"We track them, just as we have done in the past."

"And we may never find them, Trenton. What do you know of this place called Mexico?"

"I know enough, Aeneva, and I can find out more. The important thing is that I know you are safe."

"And what about Joe?"

"I will find Joe."

"But I want to help and this is the best way. These men will lead us right into Mexico and possibly to where they have traded Joe or some of our people."

"I can't let you do it, don't you understand?"

Aeneva walked to Trenton, putting her hands on his chest. "I do understand, but I also understand how much you love Joe and I think this is the best way to find him. I will be safe. You just said these men will do anything for money, so you sell me to them. You follow me. You are the best tracker I know, Trenton. You won't lose me again."

Trenton shook his head. "I still don't like it."

52

"But it is a good idea, is it not?"

Trenton looked at Brave Wolf and Coyote Boy. "What do you think?"

"I, too, do not want my sister with these men, but if she is willing and there is a good chance it will help us find our people and your friend, then I think we should take the chance."

"You mean she should take the chance."

"It may be the only chance, brother," Coyote Boy said evenly. "We will have our eyes on her at all times. We will not let her be hurt."

"I have to think about it some more." Trenton looked at Aeneva for a moment and walked away, an angry look on his face.

"He is afraid for you, little sister. Perhaps you should listen to him."

"I understand how he feels, Brave Wolf, and I know why he is afraid. He thinks I will be destroyed like I almost was by Crooked Teeth. But that will not happen this time. My spirit is stronger now. I know that you will be following me and you will help me if I need help."

"We could just follow them without pretending to sell you to them as Trenton said."

Aeneva shook her head adamantly. "No, it will not be the same. If I can go into their camp as a captive, perhaps I can overhear something about where Joe or some of our people are. If we just follow them, they might just go to the border of Mexico, sell their captives, and return for more. These men know where our people are and we must find out from them."

"Then I think we should attack them," Coyote Boy

said angrily. "Why follow them when together with our Arapaho brothers we can capture them and make them tell us where they have sold our people."

"I do not know, Coyote Boy. These men are very dangerous and I have heard that they do not fear torture or death."

"Then what are we to do? Send our little sister into their camp as a slave and let them do what they will with her before they sell her? No, I agree with Trenton; it is a bad plan."

Brave Wolf nodded. "I am sorry, little sister, but my brothers are right; we will not send you into their camp. We will find another way."

Aeneva looked at them both and turned away not masking her anger. She was not willing to give up on Joe so easily.

The Comancheros had been in Cheyenne and Arapaho territory long enough and they were anxious to get as many women and children as they could and head back to Mexico. With the help of some renegade Crows and Pawnees, they were ready to make one more raid. The Cheyennes they had already captured were being held captive in a secluded camp. The Comancheros had been watching the Cheyennes and Arapahos for days now and they knew that the time to strike was in the early morning before sunrise. The combined forces of the Cheyennes and the Arapahos was only about two hundred people, and over half of them were women and children. And the Comancheros knew from the Crows that the Cheyennes and Arapahos would not meet up with their own tribes until later in the spring. The timing was perfect.

Ladro sat chewing on a piece of grass, thinking of the money he would make this time. He had promised Cortez at least twenty Cheyenne women but he would be coming back with probably thirty or more. And he had many children as well. After this raid he could go back to Mexico and find his sister. He'd been searching a long time for her and now Cortez knew where she was. He had promised Ladro the two things that would end his search; Larissa's whereabouts and enough money to buy her freedom. And all it would take was just one Cheyenne woman beautiful enough to please Cortez. He glanced at the women and children as he rode out of the camp that night; fear was evident in all of their faces. He forced them from his mind. He would do whatever he had to do to find his sister and nothing would stop him, not even innocent women and children.

Aeneva could not sleep. She could not stop thinking about Joe and her people and how frightened they must be. She remembered what it was like when she was a captive of the Crows; she had never been more frightened in her life. She sat up, trying to still the tears in her eyes.

"What is it?" Trenton sat up next to Aeneva in the dark lodge. "Are you all right?"

"I cannot stop thinking about Joe. I want to do something to help him."

"We will find a way."

"What way? Attack the Comancheros and lose

more men? And what of Joe? What if he gets hurt during the battle?"

"It's the only way, Aeneva. I can't let you go into their camp. I can't lose you too."

"You will not lose me, Trenton. I will be all right. I would not do it if I did not believe that I would come out of it alive."

Trenton brushed his hand through his thick blond hair. "I don't want to argue with you about it, Aeneva. I won't let you go into their camp."

Aeneva looked at her husband, her eyes almost glowing with anger in the darkness. "But you cannot stop me." She stood up, quickly pulling on her dress.

"I'll tie you up if I have to. It's foolish to even think you could go in there and come out alive and unhurt."

"And it is foolish for you to believe that I will give up so easily." She walked to the flap of the lodge. "I will find a way to get Joe back, Trenton, and there is nothing you can do to stop me."

Trenton watched as Aeneva walked out of the lodge and into the night. Part of him knew that she was right, but the other part could not forget the Aeneva he had seen when he had ridden into Crooked Teeth's camp and had seen her tied like an animal, forced to grovel at the feet of the Crows. He would never forget the look that had been in her eyes; he would never forget that he had almost lost her. Trenton stood up, determined to find a way to convince Aeneva there was some other way to get Joe back.

*　　*　　*

Aeneva had walked silently from the camp, into the hills above the river. She loved the time right before sunrise. The sky was starting to go from black to blue and the stars were slowly disappearing. The air smelled fresh and there was a slight breeze as she looked around her. She loved this country and the way she and her people lived with it and respected it. She had not returned to the lodge because she was still angry with Trenton, but she did understand why he refused to let her go into the Comancheros' camp. She was frightened, too, but she was more frightened for Joe and all of the other people who had been taken captive. Nothing else mattered but them; there had to be a way to find them.

Aeneva looked up at the sky and stretched, reaching her hands up as far as she could. She closed her eyes and slowly moved her head around in a circle to relieve the tension from sitting all night. She thought about Trenton and she smiled, thinking of all the times they had fought and all the times they had found a way back to each other. She heard silent footsteps and her smile broadened; she knew Trenton had followed her tracks into the hills to talk to her and to make love. She waited for the gentle pressure of his strong hands but what she felt was something totally different. Strong hands picked her up off the ground and struck her across the face before she could do anything. She struggled to get up but a dirty hand covered her mouth.

"Be quiet, squaw, or you'll be dead real fast. Understand?"

Aeneva nodded slightly. The Comancheros had come into their camp. Now it was too late to do anything.

Before she realized it, the man stuffed a dirty cloth into her mouth and tied her hands behind her back. There was nothing she could do but follow him as he dragged her down the hill and across the river. She tried to resist, but he pulled her along as though she weighed nothing. When they crossed the river she was given to another man and put astride a horse with him. As they started to ride away, she heard the screams of the others in the camp and she tried to jump from the horse. The man wrestled her back into the saddle, cursing in a language that was strange to her. His hot breath stank and he wrenched her to one side. She saw his arm go back but her hands were tied too tightly. The pain exploded and spread from her temple to her jaw, bringing with it a curious soft blackness that engulfed her in silence.

Trenton had come back to his lodge, angry at Aeneva. She had known he couldn't track her until sunrise. Maybe by then she'd come to her senses. He drifted into uneasy sleep. But soon, screams brought him running from his lodge with his gun. He fired into the air, but it was too late. The Comancheros had gotten into the camp and stolen many of the women and children. His heart pounded furiously as he ran through the confused and angry Arapahos, looking for Aeneva. But he couldn't find her. The angry voices of the warriors rose. By the time they had come out of their lodges the Comancheros had already gotten away with their captives. Trenton went back into the lodge and quickly packed food, extra shells, and an extra rifle. He would find the bastards if it took him the rest of his life.

"Trenton, have you seen Aeneva?" Brave Wolf ran into the lodge.

"No, but I'm going after her. They won't get away with this."

"Maybe she is still somewhere around, perhaps the river."

"She's not here, Brave Wolf. They've taken her."

"We will be ready to ride soon. They have taken Little Deer also."

"How did they get into the camp? You had extra guards."

"They managed to kill all of the guards. They even killed many of the dogs to keep them quiet. They went into the lodges, killed the men, and took the women."

"How many men did we lose?"

"Fifteen. And they took at least that many women and probably more."

"And how did they get Little Deer without killing you?"

"She must have gone outside. They must have taken her then."

"The same with Aeneva. She went out for a walk. Damn it, I should have known this would happen."

"Let us see how many are gone. Then we will ride."

The men searched the camp and the surrounding area. Twenty women had been taken, as well as ten children.

While they searched, Trenton rode out following the Comancheros' trail until it abruptly stopped. He followed the river and doubled back on the other side, but there was no trail. Then he rode back to the area where the trail stopped and he studied the ground. His father had taught him that even people adept at hiding a trail could not disappear into thin air. Jim Hawkins had been one of the best trackers the army ever saw and he taught his son everything he knew. Trenton tried to think logically, tried to think as the hunted and not the hunter. He tried to keep his mind from Aeneva because he knew if he thought too much about her he would go crazy with anger. He looked around, squinting in the early morning sunlight. The Comancheros had taken their captives and ridden to this point and seemingly disappeared, but where had they gone? Trenton walked around the area looking for signs in the brush, but his eyes caught something else. He found tracks he hadn't seen before, tracks leading back the way they had come. Then he knew that the Comancheros hadn't really come this way at all. The main group had taken the captives and gone along the river, while the rest of them had led a false trail to this point and then backtracked. Trenton rode hard back to the Arapaho camp. He knew the Comancheros would eventually head toward Mexico to sell their captives. He resolved to follow them. If he couldn't find the trail he would just head south. Once he got to Mexico he figured he could find out where Indians had been sold.

When Brave Wolf and Coyote Boy returned, Trenton told them about the false trail.

"That is impossible!" Coyote Boy protested.

"It's the truth, Coyote Boy. There is no other explanation."

60

"We have underestimated our enemies."

"They're different from most enemies you have known, Brave Wolf. They are very smart, very cunning, like the fox."

"Then we must ride now to track them."

"We won't find them, Brave Wolf."

"How do you know that? We must try."

"We will try but we must think like they think, not like an Indian thinks."

"But Indians are the best trackers I have ever known. To think like the enemy would be to think like ourselves."

"No, Coyote Boy, there is a difference."

"And what is that?"

"These men care about nothing or no one and so they are afraid of nothing. That makes them more dangerous than anyone you have ever before encountered."

"I will do anything to find my sister."

"I know that." Trenton turned to Brave Wolf. "I think you should call a meeting. You will need to plan who will come with us and who will stay. Our group should be small. Leave enough men here to guard the camp. We will not let this happen again."

"We will ride before the hour is gone."

Aeneva awakened in the cold darkness of the night. Her head throbbed, but when she reached to rub it she found that she couldn't move because her hands were tied behind her. She tried to stretch, but her legs were tied as well. She couldn't see anything in the darkness. Her head ached unmercifully as she tried to recall how she had come to be here. She heard soft crying somewhere around her, but the darkness hid everything. Afraid to speak, she tried to remember something, *anything* of how she came to be in this place. She could remember nothing, not even her own name. Not only was the night black and empty, so was her memory. Her confusion scared and wearied her. After a time she slept again.

In the gray light before dawn, Little Deer whispered to Aeneva, trying to get her to respond. "Aeneva, please talk to me. I am so frightened."

Aeneva turned to the pretty young woman. "Who . . . who are you? Where are we?"

"My name? My name is Little Deer."

"Little Deer," Aeneva repeated softly. "Do I know you, Little Deer?" Her eyes seemed unfocused and strange.

Little Deer saw the blood on Aeneva's face. "Of course you know me. I am married to your brother, Brave Wolf. You have been hurt. You will soon remember."

"But I cannot remember anything. I am not even able to remember my own name. Please, Little Deer, tell me what happened. Tell me who I am. It frightens me not to know. Please."

"We are women of the Cheyenne tribe. We were staying with our friends, the Arapahos. Some terrible men, men who are called Comancheros, came to our camp in darkness and took many of our women and children. I have heard it said we will be taken to Mexico."

"Mexico? It is a place?"

"Yes, a place far south of here. It is said the people there are fierce."

"Do the people there look like us?"

"They are said to be browner of skin, dark of hair."

"Then they are like us?"

"I do not know. I have just heard that they are cruel to people like us."

"You are married to my brother. And what of me? Do I have family?"

"Yes, you have two older brothers, Brave Wolf and Coyote Boy. And you have a husband, Trenton, and a son, Nathan."

"A husband and a son? Do I love them?"

"You love them with all your heart, Aeneva."

"How, then, could I forget them? I do not understand this."

"Have patience, sister, you are hurt."

"But how is it that I can forget people that I love so much?"

"You must not worry about that now. You must set your mind to getting well. Listen, Aeneva, I will tell you some things about yourself and perhaps it will help you. You fought may times as a warrior. You are very able with a lance, shield, bow and arrow, and a rifle. You are also a healer. You learned the art of healing from your grandmother, Sun Dancer. Sun Dancer was well known in the Cheyenne tribe. She and your grandfather, Stalking Horse, were well respected. You are very close to your brothers. You love them and they love you very much."

"And my husband?"

"Your husband is a white man. He has hair the color of corn and eyes the color of the sky. His mother's people are Arapaho but his father was a white man. You have loved each other since you were children."

"And our son?"

"His name is Nathan and he is really your husband's son. He looks like your husband."

"Is my son here?"

"No, I think he is safe. But they took other children."

"But what do they want with the children?"

"Children can be sold to other tribes or as slaves in Mexico."

"My son . . . Little Deer, it frightens me to remember nothing." Aeneva looked around. The rough blankets spread on the ground were colored brightly. The women and children lay in exhausted sleep. Two of the Comancheros stood easily at the edge of the camp, their guns held loosely, but ready. Aeneva leaned closer to Little Deer. "Is there any way for us to escape these men?"

"I do not think so. Even if we got untied, we would have to get past the guards. We will have to be patient until our husbands come for us."

"And if they don't come for us?"

"They will, Aeneva. Believe that they will."

"It is hard to believe anything right now, Little Deer." Aeneva again tried to stretch, attempting to loosen her ropes, but they were tied too tightly. "I am frightened like this, remembering nothing. But we must find a way to escape. If these men are as bad as you say, we will be killed or sold into slavery."

"You are hurt badly, Aeneva. We will wait for Brave Wolf to come."

Aeneva nodded slowly. "I am hurt, but I cannot wait here, Little Deer. I will try to escape if it is possible."

The Comancheros kept to the river, traveling where their tracks could not be easily followed. They pulled the women and children along with ropes tied together in groups of five, dragging them if they couldn't keep up. One woman and two small children died during the grueling walk; they were cut free of the ropes and left where they fell.

Despite Little Deer's warnings to Aeneva about the Comancheros' cruelty to women, these men showed few signs of it. They kept the captives moving quickly during the day and part of the night, and had no mercy for the weak. But the rest of the time the men stayed to themselves. Aeneva constantly looked for ways to escape. Her empty mind filled with her desperate resolve to be free. She managed to loosen her ropes a little, but they were never left alone, not even when they had to relieve themselves. Little Deer was moved to replace one of the women who died, leaving Aeneva alone. Other women sometimes spoke to her, but she ignored them, ashamed of her fear and confusion. The women tied to her were worn to exhaustion, moving like wooden dolls when the Comancheros jerked the ropes each morning.

Words came into Aeneva's mind sometimes. At first they frightened her because they rose unbidden through the black emptiness where her memories had been. But the words spoke of honor and courage, so she clung to them, and raised her head as she walked.

The Comancheros spoke loudly among themselves sometimes, in a language she could not understand. Once, one of them pointed at a heavyset woman and laughed loudly. The woman turned to hide her full breasts and the Comanchero laughed louder. Aeneva glared at the grinning men, her head held high. They were too busy with their crude joking to notice her, except for one man, who stood a little apart from the others. He was tall and lean, younger than the rest. She had heard his name. Ladro looked at her with unreadable black eyes until they moved on.

Instead of heading south, they followed the river west and continued in that direction for a few days. Aeneva walked, ignoring Little Deer's cautions. Trying to remember confused and frightened her. Held by the eerie silence of her lost memories, she remained alert to only one thing: a chance for escape.

While they were walking along the riverbank, some of the women slipped, falling into the water. Because they were tied together, when one woman fell, the others were dragged down. It had happened before, but this time the Comanchero rode closer, jerking at the rope in fury. The frantic women screamed and thrashed. The Comanchero's horse reared away from the water that splashed into its face. Aeneva saw her chance to escape. While the Comancheros tried to get the other women out of the water, Aeneva worked at her loosened ropes until her hands were free. Hardly daring to breathe, she backed into the woods. The other women moved closer together. She ran for as long as she could until she found a good tree. It would be impossible to outdistance men on horses. She wiped out her tracks with some branches and climbed the tree, hiding in its thick branches. She stilled her breathing when she heard the crash of branches in the woods and the voices of the men as they came closer. Two passed beneath her and went on, but one stopped below the tree, looking at the ground. He was the one called Ladro. He walked around the area, checking the ground, looking at the broken branches, then he looked upward. Aeneva was unsure whether or not he could see her, but she remained still. The two Comancheros who had passed came back, cursing.

"Have you seen her, Ladro?"

Ladro looked around, slowly moving his head. "No."

"But we must find her. She is exactly what the *Patrón* is looking for."

"We have others. We must not waste too much time on one Cheyenne woman."

"But such a beauty, eh? The *Patrón* would pay highly for one such as her. She is brave, too. I say we search for her."

Ladro shrugged his shoulders. "If you think she is so important I will search for her a while. You two go back and make sure no others escaped. I will catch up with you."

Aeneva watched in horrified silence as the men hurried away and as Ladro walked over to the tree. "Come down, girl." He spoke in Cheyenne.

Aeneva still did not move, hoping that the man couldn't see her.

"Come down, girl, or I will come up after you."

Sensing that Ladro was not a man to toy with, Aeneva slowly made her way down the tree. She stood in front of him, looking at the black eyes and the long black hair that hung from beneath his dark hat. He stared at her, but for some reason Aeneva was not afraid.

"Do you speak English?" He used words different from the other Comancheros.

"Yes," Aeneva replied, surprised that she understood him.

"Good. My command of the Cheyenne tongue is limited." He put his hand on her upper arm and led her deeper into the woods. "We will wait here until they have gone."

They sat on a fallen tree, Ladro rolling a cigarette, Aeneva confused yet strangely unafraid. Ladro looked at her.

"I am going to take you to Mexico."

"I know."

"Do you know anything about Mexico?"

"I know only what I have heard."

"What have you heard?"

"I have heard that the people are of dark skin and hair, like you, and that they are cruel."

"Mexican people are not cruel. Many of them are fine, gentle people."

"Then why is it they pay men like you to take women and children away from their families just so that they can have slaves?"

"Not all Mexicans do that, just some."

"The rich ones?"

Ladro puffed on his cigarette, picking the errant tobacco from his teeth. "How do you know of money, girl? I did not think Indians knew of such things."

"I know enough about rich white people to know that they are not good. Are these Mexican people like that also?"

"Some."

"You do not answer clearly. I want to know what will happen to me when I get to this place."

"You will be much more fortunate than the others."

"What is fortunate?"

"Lucky."

"I am lucky to be sold as a slave and to live in a place to which I have never been?"

"You won't be a slave."

"How do you know this? What are you taking me there for?"

"I am taking you there for another reason."

"And what is that?"

"To become the wife of Senor Emiliano Cortez."

"What? I do not understand . . ."

"There is no need for you to understand."

"But I am already married; I already have a husband."

"That doesn't matter."

"It matters to me!"

"It doesn't matter to me or to Senor Cortez. He wants a beautiful Indian wife and you are the one."

"Why would a man do such a thing? Why would he marry a woman who is already married?"

"There are reasons. Perhaps one day he will tell you."

"And why are you doing this?"

"For money, what other reason is there?"

"You do not seem like a cruel man, please . . ."

"Don't fool yourself, girl, I can be very cruel if I must be. We are talking right now because I enjoy talking to someone other than the idiots I ride with. But do not make the mistake of believing that I am a kind man. I am not. Do as I say and I will get you to Mexico alive. Try to escape again, I will shoot you. Do you understand?"

Aeneva stared into the black eyes and she nodded. She would do as he said.

"Good. I will not hurt you unless you force me to."

"And I will never see my husband or son again?"

Ladro stared at Aeneva as if looking straight through her. "They are not my concern. My concern is getting you to Mexico and getting my money. Let's go." He stood up, taking her tightly by the arm. "Remember what I said—do not try to escape again."

They made their way slowly back to the bank. Ladro's horse was waiting for him. He mounted and pulled Aeneva up behind him. "Don't try to get one of my guns; I can feel the slightest movement."

Aeneva felt at ease for the first time in weeks. She wasn't quite sure why. She was with a man who admittedly would shoot her if she tried to escape, yet she felt safer with him than she had with any of the others. Maybe it was because he talked to her, made her feel as if she were a human being again. Perhaps if she talked to him enough, she could change his mind.

They rode well into the night before Ladro stopped. He led his horse away from the river and into some shrubs. He didn't build a fire. He offered

Aeneva dried fruit and meat, which she ate hungrily; then he told her to sleep.

During the night Aeneva awoke suddenly, startled by something in her dream. It was the face of a man, an Indian man. His teeth were crooked and he had a scar on his face. His face was the face of absolute evil. Aeneva looked around her in the darkness.

"Ladro?"

"I am here."

"Do you never sleep?"

"I sleep, but my ears do not. I heard you move."

Aeneva thought it a strange thing to say but she didn't respond. Everything about this man seemed strange. He looked mean yet he was kind to her. He seemed educated, or at least traveled; and he seemed unafraid of anything. Aeneva lay back down on the hard ground, trying to summon up the face of the man who was her husband. But try as she might, she could not see it. She wondered if she ever would again.

Trenton examined the ground. "They split up here. The main group has all of the captives. But there is one lone rider who is following."

"We need not be concerned with the lone rider. We need to find the large group."

"But why would one of them be following behind? And look at the tracks, they are deeper than the others. The horse is carrying two riders."

"You think this person has one of our women or children?"

"It's possible."

"We will keep following."

"Yes, we'll keep following, but I want to know about this lone rider. I have a feeling it means something."

"Then let us ride, brother."

Ladro and Aeneva watched as the Comancheros and their captives headed south. Aeneva wanted to ask Ladro why they weren't going to ride with the others, but she already knew. Ladro would make more money if he sold her and didn't have to split the money with anyone else. Aeneva knew that Ladro cared only about money and that is what she had to remember, no matter how safe she felt with him.

They rode for endless days and nights, traveling an alternate route from the others. Aeneva kept wondering if her husband or brothers were looking for her or if they had long ago given up. She wished they would find her, but even then, she realized, she would not be happy. How could she be when she didn't remember anyone from her past?

It was while they were riding through Comanche territory that Aeneva became the most uneasy. The land was bleak and Aeneva felt a sense of foreboding. Ladro told her that the Comancheros had taken their name from the Comanches.

"The Comanches are fierce fighters," he told her as they rode.

"Better than the Cheyennes?"

"I have heard many stories about each. The Comanches are supposed to be the fiercest fighters, unafraid of anything. The Cheyennes are supposed to be the best horsemen on the plains. You should know. You tell me."

Aeneva hesitated. How could she tell this man that she couldn't remember her people or anything about them? "I want to know what you think. You know the Comanches better than I."

"No one knows the Comanches well. They are fiercely territorial and they will do anything to keep people out of their land. Just like your people."

Aeneva couldn't remember. The dark void where her memories should have been ached inside her. "If these Comanches are so fierce, why do they let men like you come into their camps? Why do they trade with you?"

"Because we give them things that they want. And because we show no fear."

"That is important to you? Showing no fear?"

"It's important to every man. You are Cheyenne, you should know about that."

"I know only that it is difficult to keep from showing fear when you are frightened to your very soul."

Ladro stopped the horse, turning slightly to look at Aeneva. "You have done a good job; you haven't shown your fear."

"You tell me you do this for money, Ladro, but I feel there is another reason. What is it?"

Ladro's dark eyes narrowed as he looked at Aeneva. "I heard some of the woman say things about you. Maybe they are true."

"What is it you have heard?"

"You are the granddaughter of Sun Dancer, Cheyenne healer. It was said she could foretell the future. Is it true?"

Aeneva shrugged her shoulders. "All people believe what they want to." She struggled to keep her face impassive. The words of courage that had come into her mind as if by magic . . . could they have come from Sun Dancer?

Ladro nodded his head, a semblance of a smile appearing on his face. "You did not answer my question. What is your name, girl?"

"I am called Aeneva."

"Winter. That is a good name."

"And *Ladro*, what does that mean in your language?"

"It comes from the word *ladrón*." He reached into one of his saddlebags, offering Aeneva a piece of dried meat. "It means thief."

Aeneva smiled slightly. "It fits you, I think."

"Yes, I think it fits. Are you ready, Winter?"

"Yes, Thief, I am ready."

Ladro kneed his mount and they rode furiously across the open prairie. Aeneva looked about her, feeling the wind in her face, and she felt alive for the first time in a long while. She could remember nothing, not even the people who loved her, but she was with a man whom she thought of as a guarded friend. It was a strange relationship. This man put no pressure on her and if he did sell her when he got to Mexico, she would face that when it happened. For now, she was satisfied just to be alive.

Chapter III

Ladro knew he would have problems with Aeneva in the Comanche camp. He knew how the Comanches felt about the Cheyennes; he also knew that Cheyenne women were greatly desired for their beauty. But he had no choice. He was traveling through Comanche territory and rather than chance an attack, he decided to go to the camp of Long Bow. He had known Long Bow for many years and he knew that the chief would treat him fairly in return for some kind of payment.

As they rode into the Comanche camp, Aeneva drew stares from everyone. She sat straight and tall, trying not to let the stares of the strangers frighten her. She returned the glares of the Comanche women and looked at the men with equal disdain. She knew that to show these people fear would be to give them the advantage. Ladro stopped the horse in front of a lodge. He dismounted and offered Aeneva his hand.

"Do not be frightened. They will offer to buy you, but I am going to tell Long Bow that you are

75

my woman."

Aeneva nodded and followed Ladro as he went to the lodge. "I will wait outside and take care of the horse." She also knew somehow that to enter the chief's lodge was forbidden her. She went to Ladro's horse, removing the saddle and blanket. She rubbed the horse for a time, then led him to where the Comanche horses were grazing. When she returned to the lodge, a group of Comanche women were standing around staring at her. Aeneva sat down, silent, her arms crossed in front of her. The women came closer, looking at her, touching her clothes, poking at her. Aeneva kept calm, refusing to let them frighten her. Ladro came out of the lodge in a few minutes, laughing loudly.

"We'll stay here the night," he said in English. "The chief will give us his protection."

Aeneva looked at the curious people who surrounded her. "I am not sure if I want this kind of protection."

"But we'll need it if my friends catch up with us. You are valuable and I stole you from them. They won't be too happy about it."

She looked up at him. "I should hate you, Ladro. But I do not."

"And I shouldn't care about you, but I do." He took her arm. "Come, they have a lodge for us. You better get some food ready."

While Ladro played cards with some of the Comanche men, Aeneva proceeded to make a stew from the meat that Long Bow had given them. When Ladro returned to the lodge Aeneva gave him a bowl of stew, then she served herself.

"This is the best stew I've had in a long time."

"Thank you. It is not too difficult to make stew."

"Tell me something, Aeneva. Why is it you don't seem to miss your people?"

Aeneva put her hands around her bowl, feeling the warmth. She didn't look at Ladro when she spoke. "I do not miss my people because I cannot remember them. I was hurt." She touched the tender part of her scalp.

"But you told me that you're married."

"My sister, Little Deer, told me things about myself that I could not remember."

Ladro shook his head. "Do you think your husband will follow you?"

"I cannot remember my husband, but Little Deer told me that he would never give up searching for me. She told me that once he searched over a year for me when I was kidnapped by the Crows."

"Is he Cheyenne?"

"No, he is a white man."

Ladro's eyes narrowed. "A white man. He must love you very much."

Aeneva shrugged her shoulders. "It is strange not to remember something so important as my husband, but I cannot. Little Deer told me that we love each other very much."

Ladro threw his bowl on the ground. "This doesn't change anything. I am taking you to Mexico to marry Cortez. With the money he is going to give me for you, I can travel anyplace I want."

"But why *me*, Ladro? What is so special about me that this Cortez would pay so much money?"

"You are young, beautiful, and Cheyenne. He

likes Cheyenne women because they are strong and they don't complain. He also likes them because they don't talk much. He might not like the fact that you use your brain well."

"I still do not understand why he would pay money for a woman he has never before seen."

"Cortez is from a large family in Mexico. His grandfather, Francisco, owns all of the land where Cortez is now living. He has let Cortez live there and work the ranch for many years, but now he has decided he wants Cortez to marry. The old man's health is failing and he wants Emiliano to marry and produce an heir or he will not give him the land. It is very simple—Cortez needs you for the land, the money, and the power that the land will bring him."

"Why not a Mexican woman? Surely there are many who would like to be married to such a rich and powerful man."

"Yes, there are many, but the ones from good families will not allow their daughters to associate with Cortez. He does not have a good reputation."

"What do you mean? I do not understand."

"It is well known that Senor Cortez has made most of his money illegally. He sends men like me up here to bring captives back and he sells them for a lot of money."

"And who buys Indian women and children?"

"Many of the Mexican landowners buy the women to work in their haciendas and they keep the children to work as laborers."

"It is not unlike the black men of the south then?"

"No, I guess it's not much different." Ladro

stretched out his long legs, putting his hands behind his head. "You better get some rest now. We're leaving early in the morning."

"All right." Aeneva cleaned the bowls and lay down on one of the mats in the lodge. It was terrible, she thought, to be sold to a man she did not even know, to become his wife. She had no fear, only a strange calmness inside her. She knew that she would never be anyone's slave; that much she knew about herself. But she would be patient and she would not be foolish. When the time came, whether it was with Ladro or with Cortez, she would find a way to escape and find her way back to the Cheyenne people and her past.

Trenton and Brave Wolf waited patiently, watching as the activity in the small camp died down. They could see the women and children tied together.

"I count fifteen men." Trenton spoke silently.

"Fifteen that we can see. There are probably more surrounding the camp."

"We'll take them when they're asleep."

"We will be as silent as the fox who steals the egg from the bird's nest."

Trenton smiled to himself. "You used to say that when we were children and we pretended to raid the enemy camp."

"It was good practice."

"Yes." Trenton stared down at the rocks below. He tried to make out the faces of the women, but the light from the campfires was very dim and he couldn't see. "I can't see Aeneva."

"It is dark, brother. Do not worry, we will get Aeneva."

"I have a strange feeling, Brave Wolf."

"The lone rider?"

"Yes. I think he has Aeneva."

"Why Aeneva?"

"I don't know." He shook his head. "Maybe I'm just tired."

"Do not worry. My sister is strong. She will survive until we find her."

"I hope so, Brave Wolf." But as he spoke the words, Trenton didn't truly believe them. His gut told him that something was wrong and he knew it had something to do with the lone rider.

Brave Wolf stepped on the large rock, carefully trying to avoid loosening any smaller rocks. He watched the man below him walk back and forth. The man held a rifle crosswise in his arms; he was relaxed and Brave Wolf knew that he would be unprepared. Brave Wolf stepped to a lower rock and waited, his body tense and ready. As the man walked underneath the rock, Brave Wolf jumped, knocking him to the ground. The man struggled, but Brave Wolf slit his throat. He took the man's rifle and climbed back up the rocks. He ran around the periphery of the camp until he saw Trenton, who was already waiting for him.

"What of Red Bull and Spotted Elk?"

"Here they come now."

"Spotted Elk, bring the others to this place. Trenton and I will go down by the women and children. When we reach them, be ready to attack. We don't want any of our people hurt." Brave Wolf turned to Red Bull. "You will come with us, Red Bull. Watch the Comancheros. If any of them move, shoot them."

Trenton and Brave Wolf moved quietly into the camp, pulling the women and children to their feet, while Red Bull looked on. Brave Wolf whispered to the women, telling them to keep the children quiet, but one child, frightened by the confusion, cried out for his mother. One of the Comancheros turned, his pistol in his hand. Red Bull fired, awakening the other Comancheros.

Trenton ran to one side, drawing fire away from the captives while Brave Wolf pushed them to the ground. Trenton fell to the ground, rolling. He fired in the direction of the Comancheros. The flash of the answering shot gave him a target and he made his second shot count. The man's scream was lost in gunfire as Trenton ran again. War cries shattered the night, seeming to come from every direction. The Comancheros froze for an instant, then one broke, running for the trees. A single shot dropped him. Trenton's voice filled the silence.

"Don't move. You're surrounded. Drop your weapons by the fire."

One by one, the Comancheros moved to the fire, dropping their weapons to the ground. They stood, staring uneasily into the darkness.

"On your bellies, hands behind your backs," Trenton ordered. Cautiously Trenton moved forward, his rifle ready. The Indians came into the clearing with their weapons raised.

Trenton kicked at the embers of the campfire, stirring a small flame. He pulled a log from the stack of dry wood and threw it on. He stared into the flames for a moment, then turned back toward the darkness.

"Aeneva isn't there, is she, Brave Wolf?" Trenton knew before the answer came that she wasn't. Since they had been children, he had been able to sense her presence. He kicked at the fire again, sending a shower of sparks into the night. A glint of polished metal caught his eye and he raised his rifle, pointing it in the direction of one of the Comancheros. He moved silently, stopping when he was close enough to press the barrel of his rifle into the man's back.

"What're you hiding?"

The man tried to raise his head, but Trenton shoved it into the dirt. He pushed his rifle harder into the man's spine and bent down. The Comanchero lay still as Trenton pulled a rifle from beneath him. The inlaid stock and silver trigger plate shone in the firelight.

"How did scum like you end up with a weapon like this?" When the man didn't answer, Trenton dragged him over to the fire. "I've heard you men aren't afraid of much, is that true?"

"It's true." The man's black eyes reflected the flames.

"What's your name?"

"Luis."

"Well, Luis, if that's true then let's see how you feel about fire. I've seen a lot of people who said they weren't afraid of things suddenly get afraid real fast." Trenton pulled Luis closer to the hot coals. "Feel warm yet?"

"What do you want, senor?"

"You and these bastards stole my wife and I want to know where she is."

Luis gestured around the campfire. "Looks to me like you already got all the women."

"My wife isn't here. I want you to tell me where she is."

The man looked at Trenton and started to laugh. "Are you crazy? What do I care about some Indian bitch for? They're all the same anyway. They fornicate like dogs, they smell like pigs, and they all deserve to die as far as I'm concerned."

Trenton punched Luis hard, knocking him into the hot coals. He screamed and tried to roll out of the fire ring, but Trenton put his foot on his chest. "You better talk fast, or you're going to cook."

"All right, I'll tell you. Just let me out of here!"

Trenton lifted his foot, pulling Luis out of the fire. He rolled on the ground, groaning in agony, but Trenton stopped him. "You better tell me real quick about my wife or you're gonna be dead and I'll move on to the next man."

"All right. What'd she look like?"

"She's very tall, very beautiful. She tried to escape by the river a few days ago."

"I don't know . . ." Luis tried to stall.

Trenton dragged him back over the fire ring, pushing his head over the hot coals. "One more time or you're dead."

"All right. She's with a man called Ladro."

"Is he one of you?"

"Not really. Ladro goes his own way."

"Why did he take her?"

"Because she's worth a lot of money in Mexico. She tried to escape and we searched for her, but Ladro said he'd find her. He never came back. He found her, probably, and he'll take her south."

"You're sure they're still alive?"

"Ladro wants the money real bad. They're alive all right."

"What kind of money are we talking about?"

"Thousands."

"Who'd pay that kind of money for an Indian woman?"

"Lots of wealthy men in Mexico. They keep them for a while if they're pretty enough or they force them into prostitution."

"Do you know who this Ladro plans to sell my wife to?"

"Yeah, I know."

Trenton put the rifle next to the man's throat. "I think you better speak up real fast. I'm losing my patience."

"A man named Cortez, Emiliano Cortez."

"Tell me about Cortez."

"He's rich, he's the man who gave me the rifle. I don't know anything else."

Trenton pulled the hammer back on the rifle. "You have two seconds."

The man put his hands up. "All right, senor, don't shoot. Cortez lives on a big rancho outside of Matamoros. His grandfather owns all of the land. Cortez will lose all of it if he doesn't marry and produce an heir."

"So this Ladro is taking my wife to Cortez?"

"*Sí*, she's a real beauty that one. Cortez wanted a

beautiful Cheyenne woman."

"Why doesn't he marry a Mexican woman?"

"Because none of them will have him. His hands are too dirty, if you know what I mean."

"No, I don't know, so why don't you tell me." Trenton pressed the rifle into the man's throat. "My finger's getting a cramp in it."

"Cortez has made most of his money from prostitution, slaves, and bringing illegal goods into Mexico. He owns a number of ships and it's well known that he uses them for bringing in slaves." Luis shook his head. "The man gets what he wants. Women and horses. He had three men killed once just to get a stallion he wanted."

Trenton put his foot on Luis's chest and shoved. "And you were planning to sell my wife to this bastard?"

"Look, senor, I told you what you wanted to know."

"You and your friends here are scum," Trenton said softly, pressing the rifle to the man's head. "You don't deserve to live."

"No, wait! You can use me. I can lead you to Cortez. Riders guard every part of his rancho. Even the men I don't know have heard of my rifle. They will let us through."

"Then why do I need you, Luis?" Trenton bent down and picked up the rifle. He stared at Luis for a second and then slammed the rifle into his jaw. "I don't need you for a damn thing. In fact, I think the world would be a whole lot better off without your kind."

"Wait, senor, you can't just kill us."

Trenton turned around and looked at Brave Wolf and the other Cheyennes and Arapahos. "What do you think, Brave Wolf? Should we kill them?"

Brave Wolf looked solemn. "You decide, brother. We will do as you say."

Trenton walked around the camp, eyeing each of the men. "I don't like to kill men in cold blood, but I also don't like men who steal women and children and sell them for profit." He walked over to the men who were lying on their bellies. "I'm giving all of you fair warning right now—if any of you show your faces in Cheyenne or Arapaho territory again, I'll see to it personally that you're all skinned alive and that you feel every painful second of it. Now stand up and strip. Everything off."

When the men had done as Trenton ordered, they threw their clothes, boots, and personal belongings onto a pile. "Now, I want all of you on your bellies again." When the men lay down, Trenton and the Indians tied their hands behind their backs, connecting them all with one rope.

"You can't leave us like this," Luis protested. "We'll die out here without any clothes or weapons. We'll never make it."

"You have a chance. It's more than you deserve."

Luis looked disdainfully at Trenton. "You might not make it through Comanche territory. Sometimes you get lucky, sometimes you don't. The best way to be with them is to show no fear. I'd like to be there if they get ahold of you." He nodded his head toward Brave Wolf and the others. "I'll tell you one thing for sure, they won't take kindly to your friends there. You'll probably be shot before you can even talk."

"We'll take our chances." Trenton walked away, the others following behind. Luis shouted after them.

"Hey, senor, you may be going to a lot of trouble for nothing. Your woman may not be worth much when you find her."

Trenton didn't stop, but the words had struck home; the very same thought had occurred to him.

"I am proud of you, my brother." Brave Wolf put his hand on Trenton's shoulder. "It would have been easy to kill those men. Grandfather would also have been proud of you."

"I wanted to kill them all, Brave Wolf, but what good would it have done?" Trenton shrugged his shoulders. "Luis was right about something; you and the others can't come with me."

"Of course we will come with you. Do you think we will let you ride into Comanche territory alone?"

"I'll have a better chance of getting through on my own. The Comanches hate you; they hate any other Indians. I might pass for a Comanchero."

"You will be taking too big of a chance to go alone."

"It's the way it has to be, Brave Wolf. You must get the women and children back to the Arapaho camp. I will find Aeneva and Joe. And maybe I can find out where some of the others have been sold. This man, Cortez, he seems to be the one with all the answers. I find him and I'll probably find out a lot."

"I am worried for you, my brother. I do not like letting you go off alone. I should be with you." Brave Wolf paused a moment. "The Comanchero said Cortez values horses. The rifle might get you past the guards, but having something Cortez wants will get you farther. Take my stallion."

"Thank you, Brave Wolf. I will bring him back to you if I can."

"Just bring my sister back."

"I'll do what I have to do to find her and Joe."

Brave Wolf grasped Trenton's shoulders tightly. "Go safely then, brother. May the Great Spirit guide you."

"Thank you, Brave Wolf. I'll return when I can."

Ladro bought a horse from the Comanches for Aeneva and she could barely believe how happy it made her. She felt so at home on the animal, so free. She kept up with Ladro, often surprising him by her endurance. She didn't complain about the heat or the long, seemingly endless ride. To Aeneva, it was the first time since losing her memory that she was able to feel whole.

The Comanches who rode with them stayed apart. They were like outriders, ready to defend them if it was necessary but not willing to ride with them. Aeneva thought them to be a very sullen, serious people.

Each night after they had eaten, Ladro and Aeneva talked. There grew between them a kind of bond, and Ladro grew to respect Aeneva's courage, endurance, and intelligence. He began teaching her Spanish and was astonished by how quickly she learned. Soon they used Spanish as much as English when they stopped to make camp.

"You are full of surprises, Aeneva. It is a shame I

have to sell you."

"What would you do with me if you did not sell me, Ladro?"

"I'd keep you with me, I guess. You're definitely better than most of the people I ride with." The firelight glinted in his dark eyes.

"Then do not sell me to this Cortez, Ladro. I will be your companion."

"I told you I can't do that. I need the money and Cortez will pay a lot for you."

"I understand. You need the money to travel and see places which you have never before seen. I suppose that is worth a woman's life."

"Don't try to make me feel guilty, woman, because it won't work. You're lucky I've treated you as well as I have. Those Comancheros would have had their way with you by now and you'd be half dead."

"Am I to be grateful to you then?"

Ladro stared across the small fire at the beautiful woman. "No, Aeneva. Because I should have let you stay in that tree in the woods. I should never have made you come down."

"What made you, Ladro? Was it only the money?"

Ladro stared into the fire. "I watched you from the first; you were so different from the others. You were a fighter and you weren't afraid. When you tried to escape that day I admired you for it." He looked up at her. "But I didn't want you to get away."

"Why?"

"I don't know why. Maybe . . ." Ladro shook his head. "Rest now. The riding will get harder from here on in."

Aeneva lay down, wrapping her blanket around

89

her. "Do not worry, Ladro. After you have sold me to Cortez, you will be free of me. Then you can travel and do as you please."

"Yes," Ladro repeated softly. He wondered about this woman and the white man who loved her. And what right did he have to sell her to Cortez? He told himself that none of it mattered, only the money. He had to have the money. He couldn't think of anyone but his sister right now, not even the beautiful Indian woman who slept across from him every night.

Ladro had the uneasy feeling they had been watched all day; the Comanches felt it too. He had never really seen anyone, but his gut told him that they were being followed. He made Aeneva stay close to him and he checked his rifle to make sure it was loaded. The Comanches had moved in a tighter circle around them; they too were ready.

They rode until sunset, but they didn't see anyone. They stopped by rocks, leaving the horses down below while they climbed to the top. If anyone came they would see them from a distance. They ate in silence and Ladro told Aeneva to rest. She tried, although she found it difficult to relax. She knew Ladro wouldn't sleep; she knew he would stay awake all night if necessary.

The night passed uneventfully and they started out early the next morning. Aeneva found herself looking at Ladro, watching him. He was restless and she wanted to know why. The Comanches still kept their distance, but there was no doubt that they would protect Ladro and Aeneva if the need arose.

They were riding through vast, arid plains, different from the land they had come from. Aeneva watched the horizons tensely, straining to see in the glaring sun. For the first time since she'd been taken from her people she was frightened. She was frightened that she would be taken away from Ladro, the only person she knew in this vast Comanche land, the only person she could trust.

The second day passed. Aeneva could see that Ladro was still uneasy. When he told her to go to sleep that night she took her blanket and sat next to him.

"If something happens I want to thank you for treating me well, Ladro."

Ladro stared at Aeneva in the darkness, unable to really see her face. "You are a strange woman. I have kidnapped you, I am going to sell you to a man you don't know, and now you're thanking me. Why?"

"Because you could have treated me badly and you have not. I saw the way the other men treated the women; you did not do that. Now I will ask you why?"

He was silent for a moment, and when he spoke his voice was gentle. "I don't believe in hurting women or children. I am a thief, but I don't find pleasure in cruelty."

Aeneva was silent. Ladro watched her face, trying to read the thoughts that she refused to speak.

"Aeneva, what is it?"

"Nothing. I will go to sleep now." Aeneva lay down, wrapping herself in the blanket. She looked up at the stars, trying to imagine what her past had been like, but she could picture only what Little Deer had told her. The images were blurred, incomplete, and she drifted into sleep.

Ladro was still for a long time, thinking about Aeneva, wondering why he *had* taken her. Her breathing had become even and soft. He reached out, feeling her dark shining hair. He stroked it for a second, then pulled his hand back. He wouldn't allow this to happen; he couldn't.

The attack came on the third day, when the sun was high overhead. Ladro and the Comanches heard the horses approaching. Instantly they broke into a full gallop. In open land the only way for them to get away was to outrun their enemies. Aeneva rode as swiftly as the others, not thinking of the men behind them, but only of the safety that was ahead. They had ridden only two miles when the horses slowed, flecked with sweat. The men who followed them had fresher horses, and began to gain ground. The Comanches stopped suddenly, turning their horses to face their pursuers. They waved Ladro on, but he reined in, whirling his horse to face Aeneva.

"You go on," he shouted. "You'll have a chance if we stay here and fight them."

She shook her head, her hair whipping around her face. "I can help. Give me a rifle or a knife, anything. I can fight."

"No!" Ladro leaned out and slapped the flank of Aeneva's horse. The startled animal leaped into a gallop. Aeneva fought him to a stop and jerked him around. She couldn't see how many men had chased them, but it was a band of Indians, probably Kiowas.

The sounds of battle cries tightened her stomach. She wouldn't have much of a chance alone in Comanche territory; she would die or be killed before she could make it back to her people. Her horse pawed at the ground nervously. Aeneva freed a rope from her blanket-roll, feeling a strange calm. She was going back to fight. She had no proper weapon so she would use what she had. She dug her heels into her horse's sides and he pounded into a gallop. One of the Kiowas saw her coming and faced her with a lance. Aeneva swung the rope high in the air and kneed her horse hard to one side at the last moment. The rope caught around the Kiowa's neck. He fell under his horse's hooves, screaming. Aeneva jumped from her horse. She grabbed the man's lance and took his knife. Spinning around, she remounted and rode into the fight, the lance raised and poised to throw. From somewhere behind her, a Kiowa jumped from his horse, slamming her to the ground. Aeneva struggled to move, but the man had her pinned. He freed one hand to pull his knife from his belt. He stared at Aeneva a moment, a cruel smile appearing on his face, then he raised the knife. A rifle shot sounded and the man fell on top of her. His cruel smile collapsed in death. Aeneva heaved the man's weight aside and rolled free. She stood, drawing her knife, and saw Ladro. He threw the reins of her horse to her.

"Go!" Ladro yelled.

"I will not," Aeneva cried out. She swung onto her horse, breathing hard. A Kiowa rode toward Ladro, his lance drawn and ready. Aeneva cried out in warning, but the Kiowa threw hard, hitting Ladro in

93

the side. He slumped across his horse but held on. Aeneva drew her knife and threw hard. The blade sank deep into the Kiowa's chest. One of the Comanches rode close and jerked it free. A Kiowa lance struck him in the shoulder.

Aeneva spun her horse, leaning to catch Ladro's slackened reins. The lance hung from his side. She pulled it free and he bent over the neck of his horse. Aeneva led his horse away from the battle as fast as she dared. Ladro straightened up, but he did not speak or try to take the reins from her. His hands were tangled in the horse's mane and his dark face was pale and sweaty.

"Keep south and we'll hit a watering hole." Ladro spoke with great effort. Aeneva kept the horses moving. The sounds of battle dimmed behind them.

It was almost sunset when they reached water. Aeneva helped Ladro from his horse, putting his arm around her shoulders. He almost fell to the ground. The horses made their way to the spring, reins dragging. Ladro raised his head.

"Leave me here, Aeneva. They'll be coming after us."

Aeneva didn't answer. She went to the water and scooped some in her hands. When she had drunk, she helped Ladro to the water. He drank greedily and fell back, breathing hard. Aeneva moved close to him and pulled his bloody shirt up.

"I want to look at the wound."

Ladro pushed Aeneva away. "No, leave me alone. Ride. Now. You can probably get away from the Kiowas."

"I cannot get away without your help. You must

94

get back onto your horse."

Ladro shook his head. "God, woman, would you listen to me. I can't ride; I can't even get back on my horse. I don't want you to die; I've done enough to you already."

"Ladro, please, if you want me to live you must come with me. I will not have a chance in this country without you. I cannot remember anything, so how will I find my way back to my own people? I will die without you."

Ladro breathed deeply, pulling his shirt out of his pants. "All right, but look at the wound later. Help me back on the horse now."

Aeneva pulled Ladro up from the ground, supporting him as he walked to his horse. Once Ladro was mounted, he couldn't sit up.

"You're going to have to tie me on, Aeneva. I'll fall off if you don't."

Aeneva got up in front of Ladro. "Put your arms around me." He didn't move. "Please hold on to me, Ladro." She felt his arms close around her waist.

Aeneva leaned down and grabbed the reins of her horse and turned Ladro's horse toward the south. She felt Ladro's weight against her back as they rode, but he held on. She looked back countless times, but she couldn't see any sign of the Kiowas. They rode until she found shelter, a formation of rocks with many outcroppings. Aeneva found an area completely surrounded by rocks. She led the horses inside, helping Ladro from his horse and holding on to him as they went into a small cave. She covered him with a blanket, then went outside and erased their tracks. She climbed to the top of the rocks to see if the Kiowas were coming, but still she could not see a sign of them.

Aeneva went back to Ladro. He was lying back against a rock, his eyes closed. She unbuttoned his shirt and examined the wound. Instinctively she knew he would be all right. The wound was deep, but it was clean. She took some water from her bag and cleansed the wound. She got up and walked around, searching the area for something with which to make a poultice. Little Deer had told Aeneva she was a healer, but Aeneva couldn't remember what kinds of plants she had used. Still she searched, passing dusty gray sages and dark-leaved plants that smelled pungent. She passed a tall shrub, then turned back to it and pulled some leaves. She crushed them with a smooth rock and mixed them with some clay dirt and water. She applied it to Ladro's wound and covered it with a piece of cloth ripped from his shirt. Ladro didn't wake up. Aeneva sat back on her heels. All of the riding, the nights without sleep, and the wound had made him so weak that all he needed now was sleep.

She took Ladro's rifle and went back up to the top of the rocks to keep watch. She sat very still, alert and relaxed. To stay alive she needed Ladro. She needed to keep them both hidden from the Kiowas until he grew stronger.

As the sun set, Aeneva stared at the brilliant orange sky and she felt an incredible peace inside. She became immersed in the colors, feeling that she was a part of them. She didn't know why she felt so at peace watching the sunset, but she felt that it must have something to do with her past. Perhaps she had watched the sunset many times with her husband. Her husband. Where was he now? Would he come looking for her again as he had once before? Did he still love her? She ached to know something about him, anything about him. But no matter how hard she tried to remember the face of her husband, the only face that came to mind was Ladro's strong, dark face. He was the only man in her life. She would do everything in her power to make him care for her. Her own life depended on it.

Trenton had already decided to ride straight for Mexico, to the rancho of Emiliano Cortez. The only way he could find out about Aeneva or Joe would be to go to Cortez himself. But to confront Cortez and try to force the information from him might prove impossible. Powerful men used their money to buy guards. Deception was foreign to Trenton, but it was the only way. He would go to Cortez and say he wanted to work for him. He would tell him that Indians had killed all of his family and he hated them all. He would tell Cortez that he would bring him as many Indians as he wanted. Trenton knew he would have to prove himself to Cortez in order for Cortez to trust him. Then maybe when he had gained Cortez's trust, he could find out what he wanted to know.

Trenton tried to put Aeneva and Joe from his mind as he rode. To think of them suffering made him sick inside. Joe, he knew, could take care of himself, and when the opportunity arose, Joe would try to escape. But Aeneva would probably not have such a chance. He remembered all too clearly how Aeneva had suffered at the hands of Crooked Teeth. When he had finally found her, he barely had been able to recognize her. She had been dirty, weak, and spiritless, totally unlike the woman he had known. It had taken him a long time to reach her; it had taken her a long time to forget all of the things that Crooked Teeth had done to her. If the same thing happened again, he might never get her back. Aeneva was too proud to live through such a thing again. The horrible thoughts made him urge his tired horse even faster across the dusty plain. He thought only of Emiliano Cortez, the man who would help him find Aeneva, whether he wanted to or not. And God be with him, Trenton thought, if he does anything to hurt her.

Aeneva gently took the cloth from Ladro's wound. He flinched and opened his eyes.

"Where are we?"

"We are hiding from the Kiowas. I found some shelter. You needed to rest."

"We should have kept going."

"The horses also needed to rest. It will do us no good to ride them to death."

Ladro tried to sit up, but it was too painful. "What smells? Did you put something on this?"

"Yes, I put some medicine on it that should make it heal quickly."

"I thought you couldn't remember anything. How can you remember what plants are good for healing?"

"I cannot."

"Then this could be something poisonous. You could be trying to kill me!"

Aeneva smiled. "Yes, I could be doing that."

Ladro examined the wound, turning his nose away in disgust. "You Indians are all alike."

"Why do you say that?"

"Because you all use things that smell uglier than my horse to put on wounds or, even worse, you make people *drink* them."

Aeneva smiled. "Does it matter so much that it has a bad odor if it helps you to heal?"

"I'd rather try healing on my own."

"If you wish." Aeneva reached for a wet cloth to wipe the wound clean, but Ladro took her hand.

"Leave it. I trust you."

"Of course you trust me. You know there is nothing I can do alone. You know that I need you."

"You don't really believe that."

"If I did not, I would not still be here with you."

"If your memory returned right now, would you leave me?"

"You mean, would I leave you here to die?" She pushed her hair back. "Truly, Ladro, I do not know. It would depend."

"On what?"

"On how sick you were. If you were dying, I do not believe that I could leave you alone."

"Why?"

"Because it would not be honorable." Aeneva ignored Ladro's stare and cleaned his wound, reapplying the medicine. When she had covered it and closed his shirt, she brought him some food.

"Here is some fresh meat. Rabbit. You will have to

eat it raw. I did not think it wise to build a fire."

"Did you use the rifle to kill the rabbit?"

Aeneva looked at Ladro, an impatient look on her face. "I may not have my memory, Ladro, but I am not stupid. Do you think I would go to all this trouble just to place us in danger by shooting a rabbit for our meal?"

Now it was Ladro's turn to smile. "I take it back."

"Take what back?"

"All Indians aren't alike. You're different. Very different."

"I am just me. That is all I know right now."

"You know how to fight like a man, you ride as well as anyone I've ever seen, and you have a good mind."

"It is as good as it can be for someone who has no memory."

"I have a feeling you have done a lot in your lifetime."

"I do not know, but sometimes I have a feeling that something is just right. When I went to look for a healing plant for you, I did not know which one to choose. But inside I knew that I had found the right one." Aeneva offered Ladro some more meat and she leaned back against a rock, chewing on hers. "Tell me what you have heard about my grandmother. Little Deer told me that she raised me and my brothers. She also said that my grandmother was a very strong, loving person. I think I must have loved her very much."

"It is said that she was very beautiful, more beautiful than you even." Ladro stopped for a second, acknowledging Aeneva's smile. "She and your grandfather loved each other from the time they were children. It is said he paid one hundred horses for your grandmother."

"Is that a lot of horses?"

"Most bands don't own that many horses all together. He went after the horses himself. He stole them from the Kiowas."

"He stole them?"

"Yes. It was quite a feat that your grandfather got the wedding horses for his bride from the enemy."

Aeneva sat up straighter, excitement apparent in her face. "My grandfather must have been a wonderful man. I am sure he was handsome too."

"I don't know that, but I do know some things about him too. He was a great warrior but a very honorable man. He was one of the most respected chiefs of any tribe. And there's something else."

"What is it?"

"He had a friendship with a white man, a French trapper, for over thirty years. They had a friendship that was unbreakable."

"How did they become friends?"

"That has come to be a legend. They went hunting and your grandfather was attacked by a bear, a giant of a beast. It almost killed your grandfather, but the Frenchman fought him off with a lance. He made a travois and pulled your grandfather for three days."

"Three days, that is a long time. He must have loved my grandfather."

"They came upon a war party of Crows and when they saw the Frenchman carrying the Cheyenne they couldn't understand why. The Frenchman told them that your grandfather was his brother. And the Crows let them pass."

"How is it you know so much about my family?"

"A man hears many things in his travels. You have a very honorable family, Aeneva."

Aeneva's pleasure gradually turned to sadness. "I do not think I want to hear anymore."

"Why? I thought you'd be pleased to learn you had such an honorable family. Honor is very important to your people."

"You do not think it sad that I have had such a family and I cannot remember any of them?" Aeneva stood up. "I do not want to hear any more about my family." Aeneva hurried out of the shelter and climbed up the rocks. The day was almost over and again she watched the magnificent sky as the sun prepared to set. But this time she found no joy in the beauty, only pain. Her entire life had been taken away from her and she was afraid she would never get it back. The man in the cave below was her only friend and he was going to sell her to another man. She looked out across the vast prairie and wondered if she should ride away. Would it really matter if she got killed? What did she have now that was worth living for? She had nothing. She looked up at the sky and saw the faint glimmerings of stars.

"Help me, Grandmother. Please, help me. I cannot remember you, but if you loved me as much as it is said that you did, please help me to remember. I will have no life if I cannot remember you or Grandfather or my husband or brothers. What is a person without a memory, Grandmother? A person is made up of what she has experienced in life, and with no memory, I have experienced nothing, and that means I have not lived. I want to live, Grandmother, but it is so hard to continue. My heart tells me to keep trying, but my brain tells me it does not matter if I do." The sky was dark now and the stars sparkled brightly in the new night sky. "I know you are watching me, Grandmother, so guide me. Please help me to find the courage to go on." Aeneva climbed back down the rocks and quietly found her way back into the cave. She lay down, pulling her blanket over her. All she wanted to do was sleep; she wanted to still the restless feelings inside. But she knew that peace would not come that easily.

Sun Dancer appeared to Aeneva in her dream. She was just as beautiful as Ladro had described her. Aeneva watched as Sun Dancer and Stalking Horse raced along the banks of a river and as they dove into the water and swam. They laughed together and it was apparent by their faces that they loved each other very much. Aeneva tried to speak to them, but she could only watch. When Sun Dancer and Stalking Horse disappeared she was frightened until she saw four small children running through the prairie grass, chasing rabbits. There were two Indian boys, an Indian girl, and a white boy with hair the color of the sun. They ran and laughed and they were happy. Aeneva watched as the boy with golden hair and the Indian girl walked together, talking and laughing with each other. It looked like they too were in love. They looked up at the sky, watching as an eagle soared in wide circles. Aeneva tried to speak to these children, but they too disappeared. She called after them but they were gone.

"Aeneva, wake up. Wake up."

Aeneva heard a voice and, reluctantly, she opened her eyes. She saw Ladro. "What is it?"

"You were saying something in Cheyenne. I couldn't understand you. You seemed frightened."

"I lost them."

"Lost who?"

"The children. I lost the children."

"Are you all right?"

Aeneva tried to think of the people in her dream, but they quickly were becoming just a memory. A memory. She smiled. "Yes, I am all right now."

"Were you dreaming about your people?"

"I was dreaming about my grandmother. You are right; she was beautiful. Very beautiful."

"More beautiful than you?"

"I do not know what I look like, so I cannot answer that. But I do not think there could be a woman more beautiful than she."

"You are also beautiful, Aeneva."

Aeneva tried to see his eyes in the darkness. "That is good for you then, is it not?"

"What do you mean?"

"The more beautiful I am, the more money you will get when you sell me, is that not true?"

Ladro moved back to his blanket without answering Aeneva's question.

"Do not worry, Ladro, once you have your money you can ride away and forget that I ever existed." The hardness in her voice matched Ladro's.

Ladro looked over at Aeneva. If she only knew how

104

hard it would be for him to forget her. But he had no choice. No matter how much he cared for Aeneva, he had to sell her. She would survive, somehow. She was strong. But Ladro couldn't forget the fact that she had saved his life and, in return, he was going to sell her into slavery. His hands closed into fists. The fact was that he would ruin her; she might not survive living with Cortez. She was too good and too free; she would die if she were enslaved. But he knew that he had to. He could not justify what he had to do to Aeneva. But he was so close now. So close, after so many years. Cortez knew where Larissa was. And nothing would stop him from finding out. Nothing.

Chapter IV

Emiliano Cortez surveyed his land from high atop his favorite hill. He nodded his head. One day soon all of this land would be legally his. All he had to do was convince his grandfather that he had married. He wondered anew at the idiotic decree that he marry a woman of the Cheyenne tribe, if one would have him willingly. It had always puzzled him why his grandfather had made this stipulation until one day he had finally explained.

Francisco Cortez had arrived from Spain at the age of seventeen, eager and hungry for adventure. Francisco accompanied a group of explorers into the plains country north of the Rio Grande. They came upon many tribes of Indians, barely making it out of Comanche territory alive. They kept traveling north, exploring and learning about the northern plains tribes. When they were attacked by a band of Utes, everyone in the party was killed, but Francisco, who, badly wounded, managed to escape. He was found days later by a hunting party of Cheyennes who took him back to their band. They cared for Francisco until he was well, teaching him many of their customs. He came to admire and respect these people, especially the women, who were strong yet gentle.

Francisco had fallen in love with a Cheyenne woman who had taken care of him and he had wanted to marry her. But he could not. He was already betrothed to a Mexican girl from a very important family, a family who would give the young Spaniard the roots and kind of power he needed in the new world.

Bitterly disappointed by Emiliano's reckless amorality, Francisco had demanded that his grandson marry and produce an heir or lose his inheritance to distant relatives in Spain. And to be sure that the woman would be strong enough to influence his wastrel grandson, he had decreed that Cortez marry a woman of the Cheyenne tribe.

Emiliano knew his grandfather. The old man thought it would be impossible for him to find such a woman. He laughed. He would have his Cheyenne woman soon and he could not wait to see his grandfather's face. There was no doubt in his mind that Ladro would be back soon. The man was obsessed with the search for his sister. Cortez intended to pay Ladro well and to tell him where Larissa was. What he didn't intend to tell him was that he himself had owned Larissa since she was a child. And when Ladro paid for her, the money would only come back to him.

Emiliano took one last glance around the land that was soon to be his. It was all going to work out just as he had planned it.

*   *   *

Aeneva had talked very little in the previous week. She knew that it was best if she did not grow too attached to Ladro. Soon they would be at their destination and Ladro would sell her. She would never see him again. She was saddened at the thought and somewhat frightened, but she wouldn't let him know it.

For his part, Ladro wanted desperately to take Aeneva and ride as far away from Mexico as possible. But he couldn't do that. Cortez would pay him and pay him well for Aeneva, and then he would tell Ladro where his sister was and Ladro would buy her back. And maybe after he found Larissa, he could take her to a safe place and go back for Aeneva. Yes, it was a possibility. He looked over at Aeneva as she rode. God, she was beautiful. He wondered what it would be like to take her in his arms and hold her . . . Ladro shook his head and pushed the thought from his mind. Larissa was all that counted now, and after he had her then he could think about Aeneva.

But Ladro couldn't get his mind off Cortez. He had heard of Cortez's reputation with women. He'd heard that he beat many of his prostitutes and treated them like animals. What would he do to a woman like Aeneva who was so willful and strong? He would probably wind up killing her before long.

"Is that the big river of which you spoke?" Aeneva's voice broke through Ladro's thoughts.

"Yes, that's the Rio Grande. Once we cross it we will be in Mexico."

Aeneva's face became very still and she didn't speak. Ladro fixed his eyes on the river.

"It has traveled as far as we have, and it will go

109

farther, all the way to the ocean."

Ladro was relieved when Aeneva's blank face was touched by a smile. "What is an ocean?"

Ladro shook his head. "Never mind. Instead of explaining it to you, I will show you someday."

"No, Ladro, you will not." The calm resignation in her voice stabbed at him.

"Never mind. Let's get going. We have a ways to go to find a part of the river we can cross over."

They rode until they came to a shady stand of trees. Before he could stop her, Aeneva dismounted and ran into the water. Her brown skin flashed in the sunlight. Ladro tied the horses, then sat, watching her. His mind flinched at the sudden thought of Cortez watching Aeneva like this.

Aeneva broke the surface and tossed her wet hair. "Aren't you coming in, Ladro? It's wonderful!"

Ladro took off his gunbelt and boots and followed Aeneva into the water. "It's a little cold."

Her laughter was warm, teasing. "I thought you were a brave man, Ladro. Are you going to let a little cold water frighten you?" Aeneva swam closer and splashed water on him.

"Don't, Aeneva. Don't do that."

"Come, Ladro, come swim. You will enjoy it." Aeneva splashed water on Ladro again. An anger he couldn't explain rose in him.

"I told you not to do that!" He swam out after Aeneva, but she dove and he had to stop, watching the surface. She was like a fish; first here then there. Ladro turned back toward shore. Halfway there, Aeneva came up close by and started to swim away again. He grabbed her foot and pulled her toward him. She was laughing, her teeth white and even. He pulled her closer, his feet touching the bottom. Aeneva's laughter stopped and she struggled against him.

"Do not do that. Please."

"Do what?"

"Hold me like this. I do not like it." Aeneva squirmed in Ladro's arms, the water just above her breasts.

"Are you sure?" Ladro leaned down and kissed Aeneva on the mouth, barely touching her lips. The warmth of her skin beneath the cool wetness startled him. He let her go abruptly.

Aeneva stared at him, then wiped her hand across her mouth. "You should not have done that."

"You're right." Ladro turned and waded out, furious with himself. He unstrapped a bag from his horse and began setting up camp.

When Aeneva came out of the water, she didn't look at Ladro but went straight to her horse and grabbed her blanket. She disappeared into the trees and came back with the blanket wrapped around her and her wet dress and moccasins in her hand.

"Can we build a small fire so I can dry these?"

Ladro nodded, not looking directly at her. After he had built the fire, he went into the woods and returned with his blanket wrapped around his waist.

Aeneva looked up as Ladro came back to the camp. She admired his dark, lean body and she saw him as she had never seen him before. He was a handsome man and he was strong, and Aeneva knew that he was good. He was going to sell her to Cortez, but she had a feeling that he didn't want to do it. She didn't want to

111

believe that he was bad.

Ladro laid his clothes out on sticks that Aeneva had set up. "You're a clever woman. You've made a tanning rack."

"It just seemed like the right thing to do with the sticks."

"I think you'll get your memory back, Aeneva. And when you do . . ."

"What? I will just run away from Cortez and ride hundreds and hundreds of miles through hostile territory alone and find my people and my husband and everything will be as it was before?" Aeneva pushed over one of the racks. The anger that surged into her voice was uncontrollable. "I hate you, Ladro! You know that this is wrong."

Aeneva ran from the camp. She sat down and stared at the ripples in the water until they calmed her. It felt right to sit here, just as it had felt right to watch the sun set while sitting high on the rocks.

"Aeneva." Ladro walked up next to her. "I want to talk to you."

"Do as you please. You will anyway."

"Aeneva, I want to tell you something. I don't expect you to understand and I don't expect it to change your hatred for me, but I just want you to know." Ladro reached for a stick and scratched it into the ground. "I grew up in Mexico. My mother was Mexican, my father part Indian and Mexican. We had a large family—five boys and three girls. We were farmers. My father worked hard from the time he was a boy to save enough money to buy a farm of his own. He and my mother bought a small place when my older brothers were still small. Over the years, as the

112

rest of us were born, my father and mother added on to the house. It was a good house, strong and warm, and it had three bedrooms for all of us children. My father sold his crop in the city, and my mother made clothes for some of the wealthy women. They worked hard so that all of us could have a good life. We were all happy for a very long time, but it ended suddenly." Ladro smashed his stick into the bank, the muscles in his forearm rigid. "One night while we were asleep, a group of men rode into our yard. While we slept, they broke into our house. They killed my mother and father instantly; shot them in the head. They raped my two older sisters and dragged them away, and they took my little sister with them. My older brothers tried to fight them but they could not. They were all killed. I was the only one who survived."

"Why did they not kill you?"

"Because my oldest brother made me leave. My brothers and I slept in one room. When we were awakened by the noise, my brother pushed me out of the window and told me to run for help. I didn't want to go; I knew how to use a rifle. But Miguel told me to run through the fields. I think he knew there was no chance; our nearest neighbor lived over a mile away. But I ran. And I brought back men to help. But it was too late. By the time we got back our house was burned down. There was nothing left, only the bodies of my parents, brothers, and one of my sisters."

Aeneva shook her head silently, imagining what he had lost.

"I almost went crazy with grief, but I decided then

113

that I would find my two sisters if it took me the rest of my life."

"Did you ever find them?"

"Finally. First, I found two of the men who had taken them. I was only sixteen. They laughed at me, but I killed them. I learned where one of my sisters was from them before they died. But I couldn't go to her for a long time."

"Why?"

"Even men like those have friends. I had to run. For almost five years I lived in a place called El Circulo. It is a place where those who have to run understand each other. There is an old man there. Ignacio taught me much about being a man."

"But you found your sister?"

"I found my oldest sister, but it was too late. She didn't know me anymore; she didn't want to know me. She had been a prostitute for so long and had become so bitter that she didn't even think about what had happened to her."

"And what of your little sister?"

"Larissa? My older sister, Manuela, knew that Larissa had been taken to work on the hacienda of a wealthy man. I went there but she was gone."

"How old was Larissa when they took her?"

"She was only ten years old. I myself was only fifteen. Larissa is twenty-two years old now."

"She is still alive then?"

Ladro nodded, his eyes on the river. "She is somewhere in Mexico. She is a slave."

"And you know who owns her?"

"No, but I will be told."

Aeneva now understood. "You will be told where

114

your sister is when you deliver me to Cortez."

Ladro nodded without looking at Aeneva. "And I will earn the money to buy her freedom. I am sorry, Aeneva, but I have worked ten years to find Larissa. Perhaps after I find my sister I can come back for you."

Aeneva touched Ladro's arm. "It is all right, Ladro. You must do what you have to do to find your sister. I understand."

"I almost wish you didn't; it would make it a lot easier."

Aeneva glanced at him, then looked out at the water again. "Ladro, if Cortez knows where your sister is, why can't you force the information out of him?"

"Because he's always protected. It's impossible to get near him. Even when I do business with him, I can't take any weapons into his house. He has guards all around him. There is no way to get to Cortez."

"What about me?"

"What?"

"If I can get you the information, will you take me with you?"

Ladro shook his head, but she went on.

"Please, listen a moment. Deliver me and collect your money. Pretend to be on your way but don't leave. Hide someplace on the rancho. I will try to find out where your sister is and then you and I can leave together."

"Cortez won't let you out of his sight. You will always be guarded."

"Then I will find a way to get a message to you. Surely everyone who works for Cortez is not loyal to

115

him. I will find someone to help me."

"No, it's too dangerous. I won't let you do it."

Aeneva sat still for a moment. She felt as if she had been pulled back in time and someone else was telling her the same thing. But who?

"Aeneva?" Ladro's voice drew her out of her reverie.

"You have already told me what kind of man Cortez is; I will be in danger just by being in the same house with him."

"But if you try to find out something that you're not supposed to know, he'll kill you. He's ruthless, Aeneva. Once he has what he wants, you won't matter."

"And he wants a child, does he not?"

"Yes. That's the only way his grandfather will give him the land."

"Then he won't hurt me until I give him a child."

Ladro stared in amazement at Aeneva. "How can you say that? Do you know what you just said?"

"Yes."

"How can you be so calm when you talk about having this man's child? God, Aeneva, the man is a murderer!"

"I will do what I must to stay alive, Ladro. I did not say I would enjoy it."

"No, you can't do this. *I* can't do this." Ladro stood up. "I won't sell you to Cortez."

Aeneva stood up next to Ladro, touching his arm. "But if it is the only way to get your sister back . . ."

"No, it's not the only way."

"What do you mean?"

"I'll figure something out. I won't leave you with

Cortez, Aeneva. I won't do it." Ladro's arms encircled Aeneva and he pulled her to him. It felt good to have her in his arms.

"Aeneva."

"Yes."

"I can't promise you anything. I can't even promise you that I'll love you. I'm not sure I know how to do that anymore."

"I am not asking you for your love, Ladro. Your companionship is enough."

Ladro hugged Aeneva fiercely. He did love her, but he was afraid that he would lose her, like he had lost so many of his loved ones. It would be enough for now just to have her near him. He would worry about love later.

Trenton had ridden hard. When he reached Cortez's rancho he looked much like a Comanchero. His blond hair was shoulder length and shaggy. He had grown a beard and his clothes were dirty and torn. He hadn't taken a bath in the Rio Grande, but he had washed the stallion and rubbed his coat until it shone. There was no way Cortez would be able to resist this animal.

Trenton saw riders in the distance. He gripped the lead rope of Brave Wolf's stallion. The stallion pranced, scenting the horses. So much depended on getting past the outriders, getting close to Cortez.

The riders fanned out, circling him. *"Buenos días, señor.* Where are you going?"

"I want to see Cortez." He jerked his head toward the stud. "I have something he wants. And I have a message from Luis." He slid the rifle forward, cocked and ready. Two of the Comancheros put their hands on their guns. The inlaid stock of the rifle glinted in the sun.

"That is Luis's rifle. He is dead?"

Trenton shrugged. "The message is for Cortez. I will give it to him." He looked straight into the man's eyes, ignoring the riders behind him.

The lead rider looked at the rifle, then back at Trenton. The stallion reared. Trenton pulled him down without taking his eyes from the man's face. "All right, you ride along with us. But give me your guns, *señor*."

Trenton shook his head. "I can't do that."

The leader spat into the dust. "You will give them up before you see Cortez, gringo. No one goes near him armed."

Trenton nodded. "But I carry them until we get there. Unless you are afraid I might shoot you all before we reach the rancho." He let a slow grin shape his mouth.

The lead rider glared at him, then threw his head back and laughed. "I could like you, gringo. We will take you to Cortez. He will want Luis's message. And the horse, perhaps. I have never seen one like him. Ride, gringo." He turned his horse and kicked it into a gallop. Trenton followed, hearing the other riders spread out behind him. He had been right to show no fear. But the guns would be gone soon enough. He would face Cortez with no weapon, but at least it looked like he would live to face him.

They rode over rolling hills. Thousands of cows grazed on the land. The cattle were sleek and many of the cows were nursing calves. Trenton saw green fields farther east. If all this belonged to Cortez, he was a vastly wealthy man.

It took them almost two hours to reach the hacienda. For some reason, Trenton had expected an old wooden rancho. Instead he saw a beautifully whitewashed adobe hacienda built around a courtyard. It was completely surrounded by flowers and the fields alongside the barns were green with corn and fruit trees. It was a much more civilized place than Trenton had expected of someone with Cortez's reputation.

The lead rider reined in. "Here, *señor*. Your guns will be safe with Pedro."

"I will take Luis's rifle with me."

Pedro glanced at the lead rider. He was talking to a man in the courtyard.

"Unload it, of course."

Trenton nodded. "Of course." He freed the bullets from the chamber and handed his revolver and the shells to Pedro. Another man stepped from the courtyard with a revolver pointed at Trenton's chest.

"Come with me, gringo."

Trenton walked ahead of the guard into a courtyard. A fountain splashed softly, filled with water lilies. They passed through an archway to a huge oak door that was intricately carved with battle scenes. The guard pulled on the bell twice, his eyes never leaving Trenton. Almost instantly, an old Indian woman appeared.

"*Buenos días*, Maria. Tell the *Patrón* a gringo is here. He says he has a message from Luis. He carries

Luis's rifle and will speak to no one else."

The old woman nodded imperceptibly and led Trenton and the man through a long hallway and into an open entryway. While Maria knocked on double wooden doors, Trenton surveyed the richness of the hacienda. He didn't know a lot about art but he guessed that the marble statues in the entryway were expensive. No wonder Cortez dealt in slaves, Trenton thought. He had to find a way to keep himself in all this luxury.

A voice was heard from inside the doors and Maria opened them. She went in, closing the doors behind her.

"Pardoname, señor, but I have a man here who wants to see you."

Cortez did not turn away from his desk as he was writing. "Who is this man, Maria?"

"I don't know, *señor.* But I think you should speak with him."

"And why is that?"

"He brings a message from Luis. I saw the rifle. There cannot be two like it."

Cortez turned slowly from the desk. "Bring him in."

Maria turned silently and opened the doors. The guard motioned Trenton forward.

"You have his weapons?" Cortez asked impatiently.

"Sí. The rifle is empty."

"Then I will be fine. Wait outside the door." Cortez picked up a revolver from his desk. "This *is* loaded, *señor,* so please don't think I am helpless. You can sit down in that chair and tell me what

120

message you have."

Trenton stood still, not even glancing at the chair. "Luis may be a little late returning with your women."

"What women?"

Trenton moved closer, an angry scowl on his face. "Look, Cortez, don't waste my time. I know you buy women the same way you buy horses. I can bring you more of both, and better ones than Luis ever did."

"Relax, gringo, I just wanted to see what kind of man I am dealing with." Cortez picked up a glass and sipped from it. "Tell me about the women."

"Luis told me you buy women and horses for a good price."

"That is true but only if they are worth paying for."

"These will be. I can get women and I brought a horse with me, one finer than any you have."

"And where is this horse, gringo?"

"At the gate of your hacienda. You've never seen anything like this stallion."

Cortez stood up. "Let's have a look at him. You interest me, gringo. If I like your horse, we will talk other business." He motioned with the gun and Trenton led the way back through the courtyard. He heard the guard follow with Cortez. The outriders had gone, but two guards had appeared from somewhere. They carried rifles. Trenton ignored them and unlooped the stallion's rope from the saddle horn. The big animal threw his head, dancing as far as the rope would allow. The white on his hindquarters flashed in the sun. Cortez swore softly.

Trenton remained impassive, watching. Cortez

circled the stallion, disbelief and greed on his face. His hands rose to touch the stallion's sleek coat, the lace cuffs of his shirt falling open. The man's lips were parted, an ugly, nearly lustful expression in his eyes.

Trenton wanted to punch this foppish bastard in the face, but he remained calm. "He comes from the north, Cortez. And he is going to cost you plenty." Trenton's words were chilling and he was startled at the viciousness that seeped into his voice. But Cortez answered as though he hadn't heard it.

"I have heard of such horses. But the Indians who breed them will die before they give them up. Who did you kill, gringo, to get this one?"

"That's my business. Just like where I plan to raid for more women." Trenton tied the stallion and walked toward Cortez, ignoring the guards. "Luis told me a little bit about your business, Cortez. He didn't really want to, but he talked."

Cortez raised his pistol. "Luis is dead?"

Trenton shrugged. "Maybe. Maybe not. Why don't you put that pistol away, Cortez. I come to sell you a horse and talk a little business."

Trenton reached out quickly, pulling a knife from his shirt before the guards could react. He pressed the blade to Cortez's throat, knocking the gun from his hand. "Tell the guards to go back inside."

"They will kill you for this, gringo. I have only to order them."

"I'll have your blood all over that lace shirt before you get the words out."

The sweat on Cortez's face was beginning to run in little rivulets down his rigid jaw. "All right, gringo,

take it easy. Alfredo—take the others and go inside."
The guards moved away slowly, their faces dark and angry.

"That's not all I want, Cortez," Trenton said quietly.

"You want money, gringo?"

"I want money, but not like you think. I'm not a thief."

Cortez tried to wipe the sweat from his eyes, but Trenton pushed the knife into his skin. Cortez swallowed hard.

"I haven't finished talking yet."

"*Sí*, gringo, whatever you say."

"I want to work for you, Cortez. I want to help run your whorehouses, I want to make sure the women are worth the price you pay, and I want to make sure I get some of the profits."

"I choose men who will be loyal to me, gringo. Will you be loyal?"

"Why not? There's good money in it, lots of pretty women, and someday with your help, I'll be able to buy a place like this. You can use someone like me, Cortez. I'm smart, I'm not afraid of anyone, and after today you'll know you can trust me better than anyone else."

"And why is that, gringo?"

"Because I'm not going to kill you."

Cortez gave a cracked little laugh. "I am glad to hear that, gringo."

"Yes, I bet you are. So, what do you think about my little proposition, *Señor* Cortez?"

Cortez was silent a moment. "If you kill me, you are a dead man, gringo. And you knew it, but you

123

took the chance. It is true I could use someone like you."

Trenton lowered the knife, but he held it ready. Cortez put a hand to his throat.

"There are many times when I have to travel to Mexico City to see my grandfather, the *cabrón*, and I don't like leaving Alfredo in charge. He is a good man but not too smart, if you know what I mean. I need someone who can handle anything that comes up." He looked at Trenton again, this time his look changing from one of fear to one of genuine interest. "You might be just what I need, *señor*. Soon I will have all of this land and the land in Mexico City, when the old man dies. I will need a *mayordomo* I can trust."

"You will be able to trust me, Cortez, because you know what I want. I want money, land, some power, but you can have the rest. And maybe a woman someday."

"An Indian one perhaps?" Cortez had an ugly smile on his face.

Trenton shook his head, hiding the disgust he felt. "I don't care much for the dark-skinned ones. I want one with light hair and light skin. One with skin like milk."

"That is a shame, gringo. You do not know what you are missing with the Indian women. I have had many and I swear that they are the very best. They know how to really please a man."

"Well, who knows, maybe my tastes will change while I'm here." Trenton put the knife into his shirt. He extended his hand to Cortez. "So, we have a deal then?"

Cortez took Trenton's hand and shook it loosely. "Yes, gringo, we have a deal. A deal which will prove very profitable for both of us."

Trenton lay awake in the soft bed, his body clean for the first time in over a month. Learning Cortez's business was filthy work. But Cortez was smart enough to know that the ranchhands and the Comancheros wouldn't easily accept a white man's authority unless he proved himself first. So Trenton had spent long, hot days riding the grazing lands, learning how to work cattle. And he had learned that Cortez's holdings were even more vast than he had thought at first. The man had wealth beyond imagining. He had paid Trenton's price for the stallion without balking. And he had spent even more money for the special, high-spirited mares that were pastured with him. Cortez did everything big. Even his whorehouses boasted the most beautiful women.

Trenton was tired and he ached all over but he couldn't sleep. He kept thinking about Aeneva. And he wondered about this man Ladro. Cortez had talked about him.

"I am somewhat concerned about a man."

"What man?"

"His name is Ladro. He is very dangerous. He thinks I know where his sister is and he will do anything to find her."

"Do you know where his sister is?"

"Of course, but I will not tell him for nothing, eh, gringo? First he has promised to do something

125

for me."

"What?"

"I simply told him to bring me back the most beautiful Cheyenne woman he could find and I would pay him two thousand dollars and tell him where his sister is so he can buy her back." Cortez began to laugh, but there was only cruelty in the sound.

"What's so funny?"

"I am sorry, but it is too ironic. You see, I have owned Ladro's sister since she was very young. In fact, I myself taught her many of the things she knows. Then when I grew tired of her, I put her in one of my houses. I have told Ladro that the man there is the one who owns her. Ladro will pay this man for his sister and I will get my money back. Ladro will be gone and all will be well again."

"And what will prevent Ladro's sister from telling him about you?"

"She will not do that."

"Why not?"

"Because she has learned many times now to keep her mouth shut. She knows if she says anything about me to anyone she will have her tongue cut out."

Trenton's thoughts came back to the present and to Ladro. He didn't even know the man, but he admired him somewhat. He was a man who was doing what he had to do to save someone he loved; much like Trenton was doing now. He only hoped that this Ladro was not as cruel as he sounded and that he didn't hurt Aeneva. Because if he did, he would pay dearly. He forced himself to sleep. In the morning he would leave for the coast, to tour Cortez's shipping concerns.

Ladro rode confidently up to the hacienda. Every one of Cortez's men knew him by now, and no one dared stop him. He couldn't wait to see the expression on Cortez's face when he told him he had the woman but he wanted the money first. Cortez would be furious but he would pay. He would do anything to have his precious land.

Ladro dismounted and walked through the courtyard and up to the front door. He nodded curtly at the guards, pulling the bell once. Maria appeared at once, as usual not looking at him but leading him to the study. She knocked on the heavy doors and Cortez bade her enter. Ladro waved Maria away and he entered the room, closing the doors after him.

"What is it, Maria?" Cortez said without looking up. "Did you bring me my sweet?"

Ladro shook his head, disgusted at the effeminate man in front of him. But there was no denying the man's power or the fact that he alone knew where Larissa was. He had to be careful.

"Hello, Cortez."

Cortez turned around, quickly lifting up the ever-present pistol from the desk. "Ladro! It's about time. Do you have her? Where is she?"

"I have her. She is a real beauty, Cortez. The granddaughter of a chief."

Cortez could hardly contain his impatience. He stood up, brandishing the pistol as he walked toward Ladro. "Why do you have your guns on? You know you are not supposed to enter this hacienda with any weapons! Where is Alfredo?"

"I don't know where Alfredo is. Look, Cortez, I came to talk to you about the woman."

"You take your guns off first."

Ladro casually undid his belt buckle and dropped his gunbelt to the floor. "All right?"

"Not quite." Cortez went to the double doors, yelling for Maria. When the old woman appeared, she looked frightened. "Tell Alfredo to get in here immediately!" Cortez walked up behind Ladro, pulling back the hammer on his pistol. "We will wait until Alfredo is here."

When the guard entered, Cortez slapped him. "Where have you been? I should have you shot for letting this man in here with guns. Do you know he could have killed me? The gringo would not have let this happen."

"I am sorry, *señor*. I was in my quarters. The guards in the courtyard did not think Ladro posed any danger to you."

"They did not think? *You* did not think! It is your job to be where I need you. If you ever make such a mistake again, I will shoot you myself! Do you understand?"

"*Sí, señor.*"

"Good. Now wait by the doors but leave them open so you can see inside." Cortez walked back to his desk chair, sitting down and relaxing a little. "So, Ladro, tell me. Tell me about my wife."

Ladro's gut twisted, but his expression remained the same. "I told you I have the most beautiful Cheyenne woman I have ever seen. She is tall, strong, and she is smart. She has a good mind."

"Well, I don't care about her mind, Ladro. How is her body? Is it good?"

Ladro tried with great difficulty to mask his disgust. "Yes, very good. Even you will be surprised, Cortez."

"Well." Cortez stood up. "I want to see her."

"She's not here."

Cortez's face went cold.

"What do you mean she's not here? Are you playing games with me, Ladro?"

"Things have changed a little since we last talked."

"What do you mean?"

"I want my money now, and I want to know where my sister is."

Cortez stared at Ladro in amazement, then he broke into laughter. "You are playing games with me, Ladro. And that is stupid."

Ladro stood up, picking his gunbelt off the floor. "Alfredo!"

The guard stepped inside, but Ladro ignored him and buckled his gunbelt. "Look, Cortez, I don't like you and I don't like the way you play with people's lives. You're not going to do it with mine. Either you give me what I came for or I take the woman somewhere else. Considering how beautiful she is, I don't think I'll have much trouble selling her. And your time is about up, isn't it? How is your grandfather, Cortez? In good health?"

"Sit down, Ladro. We'll talk." He waved Alfredo back to the door. "All right, I'll pay you the money now. But I want the Indian before I tell you where your sister is. That's fair, Ladro. You can't expect more from me."

Ladro stood up. "Then tell me where my sister is first, and pay me after you see the woman."

Cortez smiled slightly, waving his index finger back and forth. "You are a sly one, Ladro. Do you think I am as stupid as that? If I tell you where your sister is now, you'll take the Cheyenne woman, sell her, get your sister, and I'll be without a wife. Ladro, I am not that stupid."

Ladro thought for a moment. He had hoped to bluff the payment from Cortez. He didn't want to put Aeneva in danger. But she would be ready and waiting as they had planned, in case the bluff didn't work. "All right, the money now."

Cortez nodded. "Where is she?"

"She's someplace safe."

"You're not going to bring her here?"

"No."

"Why not?"

"Because I trust you about as much as you trust me."

Cortez laughed, nodding. "True enough. What do you have in mind, then?"

"I'll take you to her, Cortez, but you have to come alone."

Cortez shook his head. "You know I never go anywhere alone. There are too many people around here who would like to kill me. Maybe even you, Ladro."

"Then you can bring Alfredo, but if anyone follows us, you'll never see her. One guard, Cortez, no more."

130

"You are not thinking clearly, Ladro . . ."

Ladro stood up, his anger and impatience showing. "I am thinking more clearly than ever and if you don't do this my way you'll never see this woman."

"I could kill you right here, Ladro."

Ladro stared at the pistol Cortez was holding. "You could but you won't. You're too greedy, Cortez. I have something you want. You'll never find another woman like this one. Not soon enough to please your grandfather. If you want her badly enough you'll do it my way."

Cortez lowered the pistol. "All right, all right. Fredo and I will come with you. But no surprises, Ladro, or you will never see your sister."

"No surprises, Cortez. I just want what's owed me."

"Of course." Cortez stood, smiling.

Ladro followed Cortez out of the study, wondering how a man like him was able to have so much power. He despised Cortez and everything he stood for. Cortez didn't deserve to be alive, and the thought of him even touching Aeneva made Ladro's insides squirm. There was no way Cortez would ever get close enough to touch Aeneva, let alone sleep in the same bed with her. As soon as Ladro found out where Larissa was, the three of them would leave Mexico and never return. Emiliano Cortez would pay for everything he had ever done to hurt anyone.

Chapter V

The brush thickened as they started downhill toward the river. Ladro knew Aeneva would be able to see them now. He remembered the calm strength in her face and the way she had fought the Kiowas. She would need that courage now. He watched Cortez as they rode; he could see the man's look of impatience and anticipation. He didn't even want Cortez to see Aeneva but he couldn't find out what he had to know any other way.

"Where are we going, Ladro?"

"You'll see, Cortez."

Cortez looked behind at Alfredo. The guard rode with his hand on his gun. "Ladro, I hope you don't plan to play any tricks on me. You will not live long if you try. Alfredo is very good with that pistol."

"What do you think I'm going to do, Cortez, try to sell you a fat, light-haired, fair-skinned woman instead of an Indian?"

Cortez laughed. "You're right, even you would not be so stupid." Ladro stopped suddenly. "What are you doing?"

"We dismount here and walk the rest of the way. The woman is there—in those trees."

Cortez shook his head. "Ladro, you make things so tiresome." He dismounted. "Alfredo, Ladro says we must walk. Draw your weapon."

"*Sí, señor.*"

They followed Ladro downhill to the edge of the trees. Ladro quickly disappeared into them, but Cortez stopped.

"Ladro, where is the woman? Bring her here."

Ladro positioned himself carefully where Cortez could see him. Aeneva stood against a tree. She nodded and smiled.

"Over here, Cortez," Ladro shouted.

Cortez started forward slowly, drawing his gun. Alfredo followed, glancing behind and to both sides. They saw Aeneva standing in a clearing. She was dressed in her buckskins, her shiny black hair hanging straight down to her waist. She held her hands behind her back as if she were tied up. Alfredo stopped close to Ladro, alert and tense. Cortez walked up to Aeneva, reaching out to her.

"Don't touch her, Cortez."

Cortez turned around. "I am getting a little tired of your orders, Ladro."

"I said don't touch her."

"What do you mean don't touch her? She's mine, isn't she?"

"Is she? I haven't seen any money yet."

Cortez holstered his gun and reached into his jacket. In that instant Aeneva leaped forward, a knife flashing in her hand. Ladro slammed the barrel of his

134

gun on Alfredo's wrist. Alfredo screamed, doubling over. Ladro hit him again, in the head, and he fell. Aeneva was circling Cortez, the knife poised to throw.

Ladro stepped out into the clearing, his gun pointed at Cortez. "Throw the money over here, Cortez. Then take off your gunbelt and come over here. Hurry up." Cortez cursed and threw the pouch at Ladro's feet. He unbuckled his gunbelt and let it fall.

"You won't get off my land alive, Ladro." Ladro motioned with his gun and Cortez moved closer. Aeneva brought rope. Ladro tied Cortez securely.

"You're in no place to threaten anyone, Cortez. Tell me where my sister is."

"Or what? You'll kill me? I don't think so, Ladro, or you'll never find out where she is. I think you better do as I say."

Ladro hit Cortez across the face with the rifle. "I think you better do as I say, Cortez, or I'll kill you right now. I hate your guts, you bastard, and I'd rather kill you than fool around with you."

Cortez gingerly touched the bleeding wound on his chin. "She's in a town called Guadalupe del Sol."

"Where is she in the town?"

"She is living in a house."

"With a man?"

"With a man and several women." Cortez laughed, shaking his head. "She's in a whorehouse, Ladro. From what I understand, she's been there for a number of years."

Ladro raised the gun to hit Cortez again but stopped himself. "Shut up."

135

Cortez stared at Ladro. "I told you where your sister is and I gave you the money, Ladro. But I have no wife. You have as much honor as a rattlesnake."

"I'm going to leave you alive, Cortez. But if you keep talking I may change my mind." He bent and tied Alfredo's limp hands. "Somebody will find you in a couple days."

"My men will catch you, Ladro, and when they do . . ."

Ladro raised his gun and Cortez closed his mouth. "Aeneva, get the horses. Theirs, too." Ladro waited silently, fighting the urge to just kill Cortez. But when Aeneva returned he mounted and they rode away without looking back. After a few miles he stopped and took the saddles and bridles off the horses they led. He threw the tack into some thick brush and slapped the horses' rumps. Then he remounted and they rode hard until sunset.

After they had made camp, Aeneva walked up to Ladro. "Are you all right?"

Ladro shook his head. "I knew that something like this could have happened to Larissa, but I didn't want to hear it. Especially not from him."

"You're still going after her, aren't you?"

"Of course, even though she may not want to come with me."

"She will want to go with you, Ladro. You are her brother."

"But she hasn't seen me in twelve years. She won't even recognize me."

"You do not know that for sure. You must go after her. She may have been waiting for you all of these years. She knows that you are the only one of her brothers who got away. You cannot let her down, Ladro."

Ladro looked at Aeneva, cupping her chin in his hand. "You have a good heart, Aeneva, and you are braver than most men. When this is over and I find Larissa, I am going to take you back to your people."

Aeneva caught her breath and turned away.

"What is it, Aeneva?"

"I do not want to go back to my people. I do not even know who my people are. I do not belong there anymore."

"But your husband, what about him, and your son?"

"I do not know." Aeneva turned to face Ladro. "I only know that I do not want to leave you, Ladro. I feel safe with you." She slowly, tentatively wrapped her arms around him. "You are all I have now."

Ladro pulled Aeneva to him, holding her close, breathing in the clean, warm scent of her body. He kissed the top of her head, stroking her soft, silky hair. He knew it was wrong to hold her like this; he knew he was taking advantage of her, but he couldn't help himself. He wanted her; he wanted her more than he had ever wanted anyone in his life. He lifted her face up and kissed her, enjoying the softness of her lips, the sweetness of her mouth, the warmth of her body. He knew in his heart that he was taking another man's wife, a child's mother, but still he could not stop himself. He could only think of Aeneva and having her to himself. They fell to their knees in the clearing, each holding on to the other as if they were afraid to let go.

"You will not leave me, Ladro?"

"I won't leave you, Aeneva. I won't ever leave you unless you want me to." Ladro kissed Aeneva passionately, unable to control the desire that had welled up inside him. "I will never hurt you again. Never." Ladro lay down on the ground and pulled Aeneva to him, running his hands the length of her body. He had never felt anything so graceful or lovely in his life. The surge of protectiveness he felt almost frightened him. It swelled, mixed with his desire.

Ladro undressed Aeneva, then sat up. As he undressed, he felt her eyes unashamedly looking at him. When he came to her, she was eager with desire and her eyes expressed delight at his touch. When he made love to her, his passion grew as never before.

"I love you, Aeneva," Ladro said gently, surprising even himself with the words.

Aeneva put her arms around Ladro as he made love to her, knowing that somewhere she had a husband. But if there was a face beneath the golden hair, she no longer knew it. She was holding the only person she really knew anything about in her life. She loved Ladro and that was enough.

Trenton was amazed at the extent of Cortez's power. The man not only owned his own ships, he owned many of the stores to which the supplies went. As Trenton investigated Cortez's holdings, he found out that the man's power spread through several cities, and in those cities Cortez owned not only stores and warehouses, but whorehouses as well. Trenton played his role well—he was the brash, right-hand man of Cortez who was overseeing the workings of many of his houses. He checked each one, hoping to find Aeneva or any of their Indian friends, but he could find none. Whatever Cortez had done with the women, they weren't in *his* houses.

Trenton was in Guadalupe del Sol. Cortez's biggest house was here. Trenton was appalled at the number of young girls Cortez had working here and he wondered how many Cortez had tried out for himself. After going over the financial records with Ramon, he looked around the house. The women smiled at him and blew him kisses, motioning him toward their rooms. Trenton shook his head, smiling good-naturedly. He walked out, going through the well-kept garden. A beautiful young woman sat against the trunk of a tree reading a book. Trenton stopped to look at her; for some reason she reminded him of Aeneva. She really looked nothing like Aeneva other than the fact that she had long dark hair, but still he stared at her. She looked up and quickly looked back down at the book she was reading. Trenton was intrigued; she seemed different from the others. He walked over to her.

"Buenos días, señorita."

"Buenos días."

"Habla usted inglés?"

She looked up with large, round, dark eyes. "Yes, I speak English."

"What is your name?"

"My name is Larissa. Why?"

Trenton shook his head slightly. "I just wondered. What are you reading?"

Larissa quickly closed the book and set it in her lap. "It's nothing important. I must go now." She

139

started to get up but Trenton took her hand.

"Don't go yet, please."

"*Señor,* I know who you are. You work for Cortez, so if you want me I cannot say no. But if you want nothing else, please, will you leave me alone. This is the only time I have to myself."

"So you know I work for Cortez?"

"Everyone knows who you are. Word spreads quickly in these places."

"And what do people say?"

"They say that Cortez has sent another bastard to do his dirty work." Larissa's dark eyes glared at Trenton.

"Do you believe that's why I have come here?"

"What else am I to believe, *señor?*"

Trenton rubbed his beard thoughtfully, wondering what he looked like. He looked at Larissa. "Do you have a razor around here?"

"Yes, of course."

"Can you give me a shave?"

Larissa looked puzzled. "I suppose so."

"Good. If you shave me and give me a haircut I'll give you the night off."

"But Ramon never lets me take a night off. I make too much money for this place."

"Ramon has nothing to say about it while I'm here. Will you do it?"

For the first time, Larissa smiled. "Yes, I will do it."

"Good." Trenton stood up, putting out his hand to help Larissa. "When we're done, perhaps we can go for a walk somewhere."

Again Larissa looked puzzled. "We are not

permitted to leave these grounds during the day. It offends certain people of the town."

"Well, it's time certain things were changed around here, don't you think, Larissa?"

"Oh, yes, *señor*, I have not been on a long walk during the day in so long, I have almost forgotten what it is like."

"Well, then, the sooner you finish with me the sooner we can take that walk."

Trenton stared in the mirror, but he didn't see the boyish clean-cut face that stared back at him. Larissa's gentle touch had aroused feelings in him that made him think of Aeneva. The thought of her made him ache.

"You look very handsome, *señor*. Like a young boy."

Trenton turned to Larissa, almost forgetting her presence. "Thank you. It feels good to have it gone. Are you ready for our walk now?"

"Oh, yes." Larissa grabbed a shawl from the back of a chair and followed Trenton out of the small room and down the stairs. Ramon was waiting for them at the bottom of the stairs.

"She is not allowed to leave here. You know the rules."

"Well, I'm changing the rules. A walk is good for everyone. If you want your women to be happy, Ramon, you should give them a little freedom."

"That's just what they shouldn't have. *Señor* Cortez says they are to be guarded at all times."

"What's the matter, Ramon, don't you trust me?

141

Do you think I'm going to let this little thing get away from me?"

"No, *señor,* but she is one of *Señor* Cortez's favorites. If something should happen . . ."

"Nothing will happen. You worry too much, Ramon. We'll be back later. Larissa is taking the evening off."

"But, *señor,* she has regular customers who come here just to see her. If she is not here they will be angry."

"Then you handle it, Ramon. That's your job."

"*Señor* Cortez will not like this."

"*Señor* Cortez sent me here to look after things, which is what I'm doing right now. All of these women need a little time to themselves or they won't be working for you for very long. We'll talk later, Ramon."

Trenton took Larissa's arm and they walked out of the door, leaving Ramon to stare after them in mute silence.

"I cannot believe you talked to Ramon like that. He does not take that from anyone."

"That's because he's not used to taking it from anyone. You girls should learn to speak up. There are more of you than there are of him."

"You are strange, *señor.* I do not understand you."

"There's nothing to understand. I'm just doing what's best for all of you."

They walked by a small flower stand and Trenton stopped. He bought a small bouquet of flowers and handed them to Larissa.

"*Señor.*" Larissa smelled the flowers, breathing in their sweet odor. "I have never had flowers before."

142

"Tell me about yourself, Larissa."

"I do not like to talk about myself."

"Are you hungry?"

"I am always hungry, *señor*. I can never get enough to eat."

"I'll buy some cheese and bread and we'll have a picnic, all right?"

"I would like that very much."

Trenton purchased bread, cheese, wine, and fruit and he and Larissa walked outside of town, to a secluded place under some oak trees. He cut bread and cheese and handed the pieces to Larissa, who was still holding on to her flowers.

"Now, tell me about yourself."

"Please, *señor*. If you really work for Cortez, then you should know all about me."

"I want you to tell me."

Larissa took a bite of her bread and cheese and chewed slowly, staring down at the ground. "I lived with my parents and brothers and sisters on a small farm here in Mexico. I had five brothers and three sisters. I was the youngest and they all spoiled me. They let me have anything I wanted." She smiled at the memory. "I was closest to the youngest brother. He was only five years older than I and we did everything together. No matter what our older brothers and sisters told us to do, we would do the opposite. I loved him so, and it seemed as though we had a new adventure every day." Larissa lifted the cheese and bread to her mouth but she didn't take a bite. "Then one night some men came to our farm. They broke in and killed my parents as they slept. They raped my two older sisters, killing the oldest

143

as she reached for a knife to defend herself. All of my older brothers came from the room to help Manuela and me, but they too were killed."

"And the youngest boy?"

"I never saw him."

"What happened to him?"

"I think that my brothers might have sent him for help. He would not have just run away. I know he is alive somewhere. I feel it."

"And what about you and Manuela?"

"After the men looted our home and burned it to the ground, they took Manuela and me away. They used Manuela as their woman and I was their slave. I was made to take care of the horses, fix and serve the food, and stay out of the way. After about a week, some of the men took Manuela and rode away, while the rest took me."

"Where did they take you, Larissa?" Trenton heard the gentleness in his voice.

Larissa smiled sadly at him. "They took me to Cortez's rancho. They sold me to him."

"But why? How old were you at the time?"

"I was only ten years old at the time, but Cortez was willing to wait. At first he used me as a house servant and then as I grew up, he made me his whore." Larissa threw the bread onto the ground, tears welling in her dark eyes. "I hate him as I have never hated anyone on this earth. I was just a child and he forced me to do things that I did not even understand. He told me he loved me and that he would never let me go."

"But he did."

"He heard that my brother was looking for me and

144

he was afraid, I think, so he sent me here. I was to earn money for him, as well as be his woman when he came to visit."

"Does he still come?"

"Yes, at least once a month. He says that he will never let me go. He says I will always be with him."

"Why doesn't he take you home with him?"

"Because my brother is still looking for me. I knew he would. And he will find me someday, too. I knew Ladro would never give up."

Trenton froze at Larissa's words. Ladro. That was the name that Luis had given him, the name of the man who had taken Aeneva and who was going to sell her to Cortez. Larissa was the sister Ladro was searching for.

He kept his voice steady. "Ladro, that is an unusual name."

"Yes, it comes from the word *ladrón,* thief. My older brothers called him that because he always took their things when he was little. But he is brave and has a kind heart. And I know he will not give up searching for me."

"Do you know anything about your brother now? Do you know what he's doing?"

"Not really, although I have heard rumors. I have heard that he works for Cortez." Larissa laughed. "I could never believe such a thing of my own brother."

"But so many years have passed, Larissa, maybe your brother has to work for Cortez. Maybe he needs the money."

"If that were true then he would have come for me a long time ago. Don't you see how silly this is, *señor?* If he worked for Cortez he would surely know about me."

Not if Cortez valued his life, Trenton thought, and he did. He would never tell Ladro that he had made his little sister into a whore. He could just send him on various leads all over Mexico looking for Larissa and Ladro would never know that Cortez had Larissa. Indeed, had had her the entire time.

"I need your help, Larissa. I need you to trust me."

Larissa looked at Trenton's boyish face and his clear blue eyes. "You do not really work for Cortez, do you, *señor*?"

Trenton shook his head. "I just made him believe that. I made him believe that he could trust me."

"Why? What is it you want from him?"

"It's a long story, but I think he has my wife somewhere."

"Your wife? You are married?"

"Yes, to a Cheyenne Indian. She was kidnapped from our camp and taken here to Mexico by some Comancheros. One of them took her away from the others and they were headed here to Mexico. He was going to sell her to Cortez. But I don't think Cortez has seen her yet or else he has her hidden someplace."

"He could have her in any of his houses, *señor*. I am sorry."

"I don't think so. I think the man who brought her to Mexico still has her."

"Why do you think that?"

"Because the man wants something from Cortez."

"Of course, he wants money."

"No, Larissa, he wants something else. He wants you."

"I do not understand, *señor*."

"The man who has my wife is called Ladro. He is your brother, Larissa."

"Ladro." Tears filled Larissa's eyes as she said the name. "I knew he would not give up on me."

"But he has my wife, Larissa. I don't want him to hurt her."

"Ladro would never do such a thing."

"Larissa, it has been over twelve years since you've seen your brother. He's a grown man now, not the young boy you remember. He has worked for Cortez many times in the past, bringing Indian women and children into Mexico to sell."

"No, I do not believe it. Not Ladro."

"Maybe he has a good reason. Maybe Cortez keeps telling him that if he brings in more women he'll tell him where you are. But I think this time your brother won't play Cortez's game."

"Why?"

"Ladro and my wife haven't come yet. And Cortez is desperate. He needs a wife and an heir in order to inherit his land. He is hoping my wife will be the woman he can marry."

"Why your wife?"

"Because she is Cheyenne."

Larissa nodded, a look of disdain on her face. "Your wife is Cheyenne," she repeated quietly. "Of course, I remember now. Emiliano's grandfather demands that he marry a Cheyenne woman. It is the only way he can gain his inheritance."

"Why?"

"I don't know. His grandfather traveled in your land once and the Cheyennes helped him. He thought they were good people. Maybe he thinks

147

some of their goodness will rub off on Emiliano."

"I don't want my wife to get hurt in any way."

"Ladro will not hurt your wife, *señor*. I know many years have passed and my brother is now a man, but I do not think he would change so much. I know that he is still good or he would not be looking for me. I do not think he will hurt your wife." She shrugged her shoulders. "He will probably treat her well."

Trenton looked at Larissa in surprise. "What do you mean?"

"Perhaps he has come to care for her, in some way. They have been together a long while now, haven't they?"

Trenton nodded his head numbly. That had never occurred to him. And if that was possible, it was possible that Aeneva cared for Ladro.

"*Señor*, do not worry. Ladro will take care of your wife and then he will come looking for me. I am sure of it."

Trenton didn't respond. He wasn't sure if it was easier knowing that Ladro cared for Aeneva or if it was easier assuming that Ladro was a cold-blooded killer who had taken Aeneva for the money. For the first time, Trenton was scared of losing Aeneva in a way he had never thought possible. He was afraid of losing her to another man.

Ladro ran his hand along the smooth skin of Aeneva's back, leaning over to kiss her. She stirred slightly, turning her head with a smile as she did so. Ladro pulled her next to him, feeling the warmth of her naked body next to his. He had waited all of his life for someone like Aeneva and he would never let her go now that he had found her. For a brief moment he thought of Aeneva's husband, but he deliberately pushed the thought from his mind. He could not think about the man; he would not.

"I like it here under the trees," Aeneva said lazily.

"No one will find us here. I don't think Cortez will even send anyone after us. He won't want to marry you now, little warrior."

Aeneva smiled. "What will we do when we find your sister, Ladro?"

"Maybe we'll go back to my parents' land. Maybe we'll rebuild the farm and live there."

"Is it very beautiful there?"

"Yes, it is. It's in the foothills and the mountains in the winter look down on us like great white giants."

"Will your sister like me, Ladro? Perhaps she will want you all to herself. She has not seen you in so many years."

"She will love you, just as I do." Ladro pulled Aeneva on top of him, holding her so tightly she was forced to wrap her hands around his neck. She smiled as he kissed her and quickly he rolled over, almost crushing her. He stared at her and he saw that her eyes reflected the love and passion she felt at that moment, and suddenly he was making love to her, his hands touching her everywhere, his mouth devouring hers. When he entered her, she wrapped her legs around him, holding on to him, whispering his name as he consumed her with passion.

"Ladro, I love you. I love you." Aeneva closed her eyes and felt warm tears run down her face. She couldn't explain why she was crying; all she knew was that she felt such joy and fulfillment that she wanted to explode.

"Are you all right?" Ladro spoke softly, kissing away Aeneva's tears.

"Yes." She held him tightly around the neck. "Don't ever leave me, Ladro. Please, don't ever leave me." And as she spoke the words she again had the strange sensation that she had been pulled backward in time, and was speaking them to someone else. She pushed the feeling away. Ladro was here. Ladro was real.

"I won't leave you, Aeneva. I love you."

Aeneva held on to Ladro as if he were her only tie to life and to let him go would be to lose touch with everything she knew. She had lost one man, she didn't want to lose another.

In the morning Aeneva and Ladro walked down from the rocks to a stream that ran in the valley. Ladro watched Aeneva bathing. He was happier than he thought he could be. Then he saw the dust in the distance. He shouted to Aeneva. "Riders. Maybe Cortez. We should've left here last night when we had the cover of darkness, but I was so sure he'd be glad to be rid of us. They're tracking us."

"Can we outride them?"

"No, by the time we get back to the horses they'll be too close. We have to go upstream. Maybe they'll lose our trail if we stay in the water. I've got my guns. Here, you carry this one. I have some food in my bag. If we can't get back to the horses later, we'll just have to walk until we find some more. Come on."

Ladro took Aeneva's hand and ran. Once or twice Aeneva thought she heard horses behind them, but Ladro kept her moving. It seemed as though they had run for miles when they came to a circle of steep hills. The stream rose from a spring in their base. Ladro shook his fist at the rocky slopes.

"Damn it, how could I have been so stupid!"

Aeneva stood close to him, breathing hard.

"We're trapped, Aeneva. The only way out is back toward Cortez or up over those hills."

"Then we will climb the hills."

"They're taller than they look, and once we get over them there are more just like them."

"But it will give us time, will it not?"

Ladro nodded, squeezing Aeneva's hand. "Yes, it will give us time. Come on." He led the way, holding on to her hand as he started climbing. At first, as Aeneva had said, the hills didn't seem so hard to climb, but they were steep and the rocks slid underneath their feet. They were only about halfway up the side of the hill when they heard Cortez.

"Stop, Ladro. Or I will shoot the woman."

Ladro turned and looked. Cortez was a few hundred yards away. It would take a lucky shot from that distance. "Climb, Aeneva, I will follow."

Aeneva climbed as quickly as she could, but it was difficult to find footholds. Halfway up she lost her footing and fell, sliding into Ladro. He caught her, breaking her fall.

"Ladro, I'm sorry."

"Try, Aeneva. They're coming." Ladro pushed her upward, then turned to fire down at the men below him. "Get going. I'll catch up with you. Use your fingers."

Aeneva dug her fingers into the dirt and this time she was able to make it all the way to the top. She turned, firing, keeping Cortez and his men out of range. "Ladro! Come on."

As Ladro started his ascent, Aeneva took careful aim with the pistol, shooting at one of Cortez's men. He screamed, clutching his shoulder. When Ladro reached the top, he took Aeneva's hand.

"I don't think they can get a horse up here. They'll probably ride around. We'll slide down this side. It'll leave a helluva trail, but it'll save time. Be careful of the rocks."

Ladro pulled Aeneva after him as he slid down the hill, half sitting, half rolling. When they got to the bottom, Aeneva was barely able to stand up before Ladro took her hand and began running. It seemed as if the entire day continued on that way, climbing up hills, sliding down others, until finally they had put some distance between themselves and Cortez. When Ladro was sure they were safe, he took some food out of the saddlebags and gave some to Aeneva. They ate in silence, listening for any sound of riders. When they finished eating, Aeneva lay down next to Ladro. He put his arm protectively across her as she slept.

The next day continued on much as the previous day had, only the hills had turned into mountains. They had only seen Cortez and his men once that day and that was in the early morning. Ladro knew that Cortez could never keep up the pace; he would send his men to do his work for him. They walked until dark, slept for a few hours, and then continued on in

152

darkness. Ladro was not willing to take any chances with Aeneva's life.

By the third day, they had not seen any sign of Cortez's men, but Ladro still kept up the pace. Cortez was one who was never to be underestimated. It took them a week to make it over the mountains and they were both totally exhausted by the time they descended the last slope. Below they found a stream and drank greedily, and continued on. Later in the day they came upon a small farm. They found a man, woman, and their four small children working in the fields, and they walked up to them.

"Buenos días." Ladro spoke in a friendly tone, aware of how dirty and ragged they looked.

The man looked first at Ladro and then at Aeneva. *"Buenos días.* What is it you want, *señor?"*

"My wife and I have been traveling for a long time now and we are tired and hungry. We wonder if you have a place for us to sleep, just until we have rested. We will work for our keep."

The man looked at them both again, studying them intently. "Why is it you have been running, *señor?* The truth please."

Ladro realized there was not reason to lie. "We are being chased."

"For what reason?"

"A man, a man with much money, wants my wife. And I will not let him have her."

The man looked once more at Aeneva and he lifted his straw hat for a moment to wipe the sweat from his brow. "You may stay in our barn. It is small, but it will serve your needs."

"Gracias, señor. Is there work we can do for you?"

153

"No, you both rest now. Tomorrow you can help."

Ladro nodded his thanks and took Aeneva's hand. They walked slowly across the field of corn to the yard. The barn was indeed small, but it had a loft, full of clean, sweet hay. He pulled the ladder over and Aeneva climbed up. Ladro followed her, moving the ladder against the wall once they were up. He crawled across the loft to the small window that looked out over the fields and the mountains beyond. He knew that Cortez would follow and that eventually he would find them. Ladro knew he had to find a way to keep Aeneva safe. He reached for Aeneva's hand, but she was lying on the hay, already asleep. He touched her hair and leaned down, kissing her head.

"He'll never hurt you." Ladro lay next to Aeneva, pulling her close to him. He wondered about the white man who searched for Aeneva and again he felt sorry for the man he did not know. He knew what it was like to love Aeneva and he couldn't imagine what it would be like to lose that love. But he wouldn't give her up to anyone, not even her own husband. He listened to Aeneva's deep, even breathing until sleep took him.

Aeneva saw him walk toward her and she was frightened. His hair shone like gold in the sunlight, and his eyes were clear and blue like the sky on a summer day. He was tall and his skin was dark. She tried to move, but her legs wouldn't carry her. He came closer still and when she tried to yell for help no words would come from her mouth. He continued to

154

walk slowly toward her until he stood directly in front of her, staring into her eyes.

"I have missed you, Aeneva."

She stared at him, puzzled by his words. He reached out and touched her cheek, the barest touch, like the flick of a butterfly's wings. She closed her eyes. Her stomach felt uneasy, as if she were going to be sick, only she wasn't. It was more a feeling of excitement. She opened her eyes again, but he was walking away. She reached out to him but she couldn't reach him.

"Wait, please." But it was too late. He was almost gone. The only sign that he was there was the sun shining on his golden hair. "Don't go. Please!" She looked after him, but he was gone. She touched her cheek and she could almost feel his gentle touch. "Who are you?" she asked herself, but she felt someone shaking her and she turned around. All she could see was a hand, a hand that was leading her out of her dream.

"Wake up, Aeneva. You were dreaming again."

Aeneva opened her eyes to the darkness. "Where are we?"

"We're in a barn. We've been sleeping since the afternoon."

Aeneva sat up, rubbing her eyes. "What was I dreaming about? What did I say?"

"You told someone to wait. You asked them not to go. Do you remember who you were dreaming about?"

Aeneva recalled vividly the man with the golden hair and the eyes the color of the sky. "No, I don't remember." She moved next to Ladro, putting her arms around his waist. "I am frightened, Ladro. I feel as though something is going to happen."

"Don't worry, we will be all right. Cortez won't look for us forever. There are other Indian women around and he needs to find one soon."

"It's not just Cortez."

"What then?"

"I do not know. It's just a feeling."

"Your husband?"

Aeneva felt a stabbing pain in her chest at those words: her husband. "What will we do if he finds us, Ladro? I am his wife."

"Don't worry about it now, Aeneva. We will deal with it if it happens."

But Aeneva was worried about the golden-haired man she had seen in her dream. Was he her husband? Was he the man whom Little Deer said she had loved since she was a little girl? And what would happen if she regained her memory and found out she loved not only her husband, but Ladro, too? She lay down again, snuggling into the soft hay. She felt Ladro's arm come around her and she felt safe. She would not think of anything else now. She closed her eyes again, praying that this time she wouldn't dream.

Aeneva felt a hand go over her mouth. For an instant she thought it was Ladro, but she knew instinctively that it wasn't. She opened her eyes, about to scream, but she saw the pistol that was pointed at Ladro's head. The gunman waved her over to the edge of the loft and the ladder. Aeneva did as she was told, barely making a sound as she crawled to the ladder. Ladro stirred for a second and turned, not noticing her absence. The gunman roughly took her arm, pulling her the rest of the way to the ladder. Once she stepped onto the first rung, he moved aside and waved her down. She looked below and saw all of the men waiting for her. She did not see Cortez. She wanted to yell, to warn Ladro, but she knew the gunman would shoot if she opened her mouth. When she reached the bottom, one of the men grabbed her and jerked her toward the door of the barn. He gagged her and tied her hands together. The man at the top of the ladder waved another of the men to climb up into the loft. Both of them aimed their guns at Ladro. Aeneva watched helplessly.

"Ladro, wake up!"

Ladro opened his eyes. He turned his head, looking for Aeneva. She was gone. He sat up slowly.

"Throw the gun and rifle over here, Ladro. No use looking for the woman. She's down here with us."

"Well, Alfredo, I should have known Cortez would send you."

"You owe me, Ladro. Cortez has made my life hell since you got into his hacienda with your weapons." Alfredo smiled. "He wants you dead, Ladro."

"Don't hurt her, Alfredo . . ."

"I don't think you're in a position to threaten me, Ladro. In fact, you're in no position at all to be saying anything."

Ladro sat up slowly, talking softly. "Where's Cortez? Had to send you to do his dirty work, eh, Alfredo? I can't believe you still work for the bastard."

"It seems to me you did a lot of work for him, Ladro."

157

"But I always got the best end of the deal."

"Well, it looks like this time something went wrong, eh, *compadre?* You didn't get the best end of the deal this time. Cortez wants you dead."

Ladro shrugged nonchalantly. "Cortez is a coward. I've always scared him because I always stood up to him. He couldn't stand that. But someone like you, Alfredo, Cortez knows he can control you. He puts fear into you."

"You're a fool, Ladro. I do not fear Cortez."

"Prove it. Let me and the woman go."

"You know I can't do that."

"You said you weren't afraid of Cortez, Alfredo. Here's your chance to prove it."

"I need the money, Ladro. Cortez will pay a lot of money if I bring her back. You know that. You also know that if I do this job well, Cortez will pay me extra."

"What, for killing me?"

Alfredo nodded. "I am sorry, Ladro. I have no choice."

"There is always a choice, Alfredo." Ladro looked down at the hay. "At least take the woman out when you do it. I don't want her to see it."

Alfredo thought a moment, glancing down. "Take her outside," he hissed at the man who held Aeneva. But as he turned back, Ladro threw hay in his face. Alfredo fired wildly, backing toward the ladder. He felt his way down, bracing his pistol against the wood. Ladro moved forward, kicking at the ladder. It went backward with Alfredo clutching at it for life. Ladro spun to the window, squeezing himself through the small opening. He climbed on to the roof, crawling along slowly, trying to see the men on the ground. Some of them rode away at a gallop and he knew they had Aeneva. He had to get to her. There was no way down. He stood up, walking to the lowest part of the roof, ready to jump to the ground. A shot fired, hitting Ladro in the shoulder. He fell, rolling to the edge of the roof, trying desperately to hold on, but his strength finally gave way. He fell to the ground, fighting the blackness that swam in his mind. He couldn't move. There was pain in his leg and wrist, but it seemed distant. Cortez's men ran up but he couldn't fight, couldn't even move.

Alfredo kicked at him once. "He's dead. Let's go."

Ladro heard the voices through his pain and rage.

"You'd better be sure, Alfredo. Cortez will kill you if he is alive."

"He is dead, I tell you. Now mount up." Alfredo bent down next to Ladro, whispering as he did so. "Do not return to the rancho, Ladro, or I will have to kill you next time. I let you live to prove you wrong. Cortez does not scare me." He stood up and moved away. Hoof beats shook the ground, then there was silence.

Ladro tried to sit up, groaning. He had broken his right leg, he was sure, and possibly one of his wrists. He'd been lucky; he could have been dead.

"Let me help you, *señor*." The farmer bent down next to Ladro, putting his arm around his neck. "Lean on me. We will try to get you into the house." He called for his wife, who appeared instantly at the door of the small house. She stood on the other side of Ladro, helping him inside. They led him to their own bed.

"Lie down here, *señor*. My wife will see to your injuries."

Ladro lay back on the bed, his body weak. He felt as though he could sleep for weeks. But he couldn't. He had to get to Aeneva. He tried to sit up.

"I have to go," he groaned, leaning on his elbow.

"You are not going anywhere, *señor*, not until you heal."

"But my wife . . ."

"I think she will be all right, *señor*. They did not go to all this trouble just to kill her, eh?"

"But you don't understand. She needs me. She has lost her memory . . ." Ladro realized that he was rambling and he lay back on the bed. There was no way he could help Aeneva now, he was too weak. He'd have to wait until he was stronger and his bones had healed.

"You rest, *señor*. I will see to your wounds." The farmer's wife worked quickly, cleaning the bullet wound and then setting the breaks in Ladro's leg and arm. He was unconscious before she was finished. She turned to her husband.

"He will need to rest for a long time now."

"Yes, he has been through much, I think."

"He loves his wife very much. I don't know what he'll do when he realizes she is gone."

"I think he already knows she is gone," the farmer responded quietly, watching Ladro as he slept. "Sleep is his only escape right now, but when he wakes up, he will have to face reality." The farmer nodded. "He will find the men who took his woman."

*　　　*　　　*

160

Aeneva looked out the window to the mountains beyond, the same mountains that she and Ladro had crossed alone. Tears came to her eyes when she thought of Ladro. He was dead. He had died trying to help her. Again, she was all alone. She looked around the room. She hated this place already. It was her prison and there was no escape. The windows were barred and the door was only unlocked when food was brought to her. She couldn't understand why Cortez hadn't been in to see her. If he had gone to all the trouble to kidnap her, why hadn't he come to see her? By her counting, it had been eight days since they had put her into this room and locked the door. Again her thoughts went to Ladro. She hoped that he hadn't suffered. He had been good to her; he had loved her in his own way. But in the end it was not enough to keep them together. It seemed that she was not meant to be with anyone she loved.

Aeneva sat by the window until the sky grew dark. She didn't touch the food that was sent in on a tray; she had no desire for anything but her freedom. She lay down on the bed, curling up on her side. She wished that she had been killed with Ladro. Perhaps that would have given her some peace. The doorknob turned and the door opened. Aeneva assumed it was the old woman coming to take the tray of food away.

"Well, I hear you haven't been eating. That's not very good for a bride-to-be, is it? You must keep your strength up."

Aeneva sat up, finally getting to see Cortez face to face. She noticed that his bodyguard was in the doorway. "Is Ladro dead?"

"Of course he's dead. You don't think I'd leave him alive after what he did to me, do you?"

"But perhaps he wasn't killed during the fall. Perhaps . . ."

"My dear, Alfredo checked to make sure. I assure you your valiant captor is dead." He walked closer to Aeneva, pulling her chin up so he could look at her face. "You really are beautiful, you know. Ladro did know exactly what I wanted."

Aeneva jerked her chin away. "Ladro didn't want you to keep me."

"Yes, I know, that's why this is all the more delightful, don't you agree?" Cortez laughed loudly.

Aeneva stared at the man before her. He was short in stature, not much taller than she, and very thin, almost frail looking. He had long, thin fingers, and he wore his hair slicked back away from his face. He appeared young, almost boylike, but there was no mistaking the cruelty in his face.

"Well, well, what do you think of your room? Do you like it?"

"It is not bad for a prison."

"That's very good, my dear. You could be just what I need around here."

"You do not need me, *señor*. Why not marry someone else? All I want to do is go back to my people."

"I am sorry, but I can't permit you to do that. I suppose I should explain myself." Cortez walked to the window and looked out. "This land extends as far as you can see and beyond, and someday it will all be mine. You see, my grandfather is from Spain and he believes that the family name should not die with me.

162

The only thing that will satisfy him is if I produce an heir." He turned to her. "An heir of a Cheyenne woman."

"Why a Cheyenne?"

"It's a long story. There is no need to bore you with the details, my dear."

"Surely there are many babies born on your rancho. Why not show him one of those and tell him it is yours?"

"Yes, I thought of that myself, but my grandfather has many spies here. He wants to know that I am married, legally, and that I have produced a child out of this marriage. That is the only thing that will make him happy."

"But why me? I do not understand."

Cortez walked back over to Aeneva, staring into her face with a cruel look. "Because I want you and that is all that matters. It also makes it better that Ladro wanted you so much."

"Why did you hate Ladro?"

"Because he was dangerous to me. I couldn't trust him." Cortez waved his hand in the air. "Enough about Ladro. He is dead and we are alive, very much alive, my dear. You and I will be married tomorrow, and tomorrow night I will make love to you and every night after that until you carry my child. If you do as I say, I will treat you well. You will have everything you could ever wish for. As long as you give me the child I ask for, that is."

"And if I cannot?"

"Then I will probably have to kill you. What use would I have for a woman who cannot give me a child?" He walked back over to the window. "It is going to be a lovely evening. I suggest you get some rest. Tomorrow is your wedding day, after all."

Aeneva watched Cortez as he walked out and she lay back down on the bed. The thought of sleeping with the man made her physically ill, but she knew she would do whatever it took to survive. She would not give up easily. She would play Cortez's game for a while, and when she could, she would find a way to escape. Her life was her own and no one would take it from her.

Aeneva stood motionless as the woman dressed her. Her Indian clothes had been taken from her and she had been bathed in a strange sort of tub. The woman dressed her in many layers of clothing, all of them extremely uncomfortable to Aeneva. She wore a white lace dress with button-up shoes. She had never worn shoes in her life and when she tried to stand she almost fell over. Her long hair was pulled up and pinned, covered with a long lace mantilla. She was taken downstairs into a large room, where Cortez and two other people were waiting for her.

Cortez held out his hand to Aeneva. "Ah, my dear, you look lovely, just as I knew you would. This is Father Ramirez. Father, this is Aeneva."

"Buenos días, señorita. You do indeed look lovely today."

"Thank you," Aeneva responded quietly.

The witnesses consisted of Maria and Alfredo. The ceremony was quick; it was over in minutes. Aeneva stood in a daze as Cortez laughed with the priest, acting all the while as if nothing were wrong. He smiled at her occasionally, playing the part of the new groom with intensity. At one point, he even walked over to Aeneva and put his arm around her.

They sat down for a large meal, but Aeneva was in no mood for food. She felt as though her entire life were slipping away from her and there was nothing she could do.

"You must eat, my dear. You'll need your strength tonight." Cortez laughed as he leaned over and whispered something to the priest.

Aeneva picked at her food, occasionally putting a bite into her mouth. Nothing appealed to her, especially not the man who sat across the table from her. When the meal was over, Aeneva was taken back to her room while Cortez went off with the priest. Once inside her room, Aeneva tore off the constricting clothes and threw them on the bed. She wrapped herself in a robe and sat down in front of the window, waiting. It was like a death sentence waiting for Cortez; every time she heard a noise she was sure it was Cortez. She fell asleep in the chair, her arms resting on the windowsill. She barely moved when Estella, Alfredo's wife, woke her.

"*Señora*, it is time to get ready."

Aeneva stared at the woman.

"Do you understand me, *señora?* It is time to get ready."

Aeneva nodded. She understood all too clearly. Thanks to Ladro she understood Spanish. Oh, Ladro, she thought, feeling an ache too deep to control.

"Come, *señora*, we must get you ready for your husband. He has something special he wants you to wear." Estella went to the cupboard and took out a sheer white nightgown. She motioned for Aeneva to stand up. "Please, *señora*, the *Patrón* will get angry with me if you do not put this on."

Aeneva consented, unwillingly putting on the flimsy piece of cloth. She felt naked and reached for the robe, but Estella shook her head.

"No, *señora*, this goes over it." She reached into the closet and came out with another sheer white piece of cloth.

"But this will not cover me. I cannot wear this." Aeneva spoke for the first time.

"I am sorry, *señora*, but this is what the *Patrón* wishes you to wear." Estella lowered her eyes. "I am sorry for you."

"Why? Why are you sorry for me?"

Estella quickly walked away from Aeneva, picking up the clothes around the room and putting them away. "It does not matter. Please, *señora*, forget that I said anything."

Aeneva walked to Estella. "What is your name?"

"Estella, *señora*."

"Estella, please, you must know that I did not want to marry *Señor* Cortez. Is there not some way that I can escape from here?"

Estella's eyes grew large. "I must go now, *señora*. Please, do not say anything to the *Patrón*."

"But Estella . . ." Aeneva followed Estella to the door, but it was shut and locked before she could say anything. The woman was afraid of Cortez. Perhaps she could find a friend and ally in Estella, if she went slowly.

Aeneva tried to relax, but she could not. The day

166

was dragging on and she knew as soon as the sun set, Cortez would be in to claim his rights as her husband. She paced the room, walking back and forth, her arms crossed in front of her to shield herself from her own nakedness. She hated these clothes and she hated herself in them. She wanted only to get out of them. Just as she had suspected, Cortez appeared right after sunset, followed by Maria with a tray of food.

"You must be starving, my dear wife. Eat while I change. I will be back soon."

Aeneva watched him as he walked out, wanting to slap the smile from his face. She almost threw the tray of food on the floor until she saw the fork. She touched the prongs with her fingers. It wasn't very sharp but if used on the right part of the body . . . She put the fork under her pillow and sat on the bed. She decided to eat. Cortez was right about one thing—she would need her strength if she was to survive this ordeal. When she was finished, she put the tray of food at the end of the bed and waited. Maria came in and took the tray. Aeneva heard voices in the hallway. The door opened and Cortez came in.

"Where is the fork?"

Aeneva froze. "What fork? I don't eat with a fork."

Cortez walked over to the bed, taking Aeneva's face in his long, thin fingers. He squeezed her chin tightly. "Do not play games with me, Aeneva. There was a fork on this tray and you took it. Give it to me."

"There was no fork."

Cortez nodded slightly, almost as if he agreed with Aeneva. He struck her hard across the face. She fell back against the bed and when she tried to get up, he struck her again.

"Where is the fork?"

"I don't . . ." Before she could get the words out, Cortez's fingers were around her throat, squeezing the very life out of her. She tried to pry his fingers away from her neck, but he was deceptively strong. When he let go, Aeneva fell back against the bed, coughing and gasping for air.

"I will only ask you one more time. Where is the fork?"

Aeneva reached under the pillow and handed it to Cortez. He studied it a moment, then very slowly and precisely, he lowered it to her neck, pressing it against her flesh.

"How does it feel, Aeneva? Is it sharp? Is this what you hoped to do to me?" He pressed even harder for an instant, then abruptly put it into the pocket of his velvet jacket. He ran his fingers over the bruise on her neck. "You are beautiful, Aeneva. I will make you very happy."

Aeneva smiled slowly, staring rapturously into Cortez's eyes. "No man will ever make me as happy as Ladro did. No man." Cortez struck Aeneva again.

"No one talks to me that way, especially not a woman! You are my wife and you will do as I say. Do you understand?"

Aeneva stared at Cortez, but she didn't reply. She knew she was playing a dangerous game, but she didn't care.

Cortez put both hands around Aeneva's neck. "Do you understand?"

This time Aeneva nodded, knowing that she must stay alive. "I understand."

"Good. Now, I am tired. It has been a long day for

me. We shall continue this tomorrow night. Make sure that you are ready for me then." Cortez left the room, slamming the door behind him.

Aeneva walked to the small wash bowl and cleaned herself. She didn't want Cortez's touch on her; she wanted to be completely free of him. She stripped off the nightclothes and wrapped herself in the robe. She crawled into bed and turned down the lamp. She knew she had to think of something. She couldn't let Cortez touch her. She thought of Estella and an idea began to form. With Estella's help, she could succeed in making Cortez leave her alone, at least for a while. And at this point, she was willing to do anything.

Trenton lay next to Larissa, his hands clasped behind his head, staring up at the ceiling.

"What are you thinking about?"

Trenton felt Larissa's hand run over his chest. "It doesn't matter."

"You are thinking about her. About your wife."

"Yes."

"And what are you thinking about her? You are wondering if she has fallen in love with my brother?"

"No, I wasn't thinking that," Trenton responded, almost too quickly. "I was just wondering if she was all right."

"Then why don't you go back to Cortez's rancho and see if she is there? Then you will know for sure."

"I can't go back yet. If she's not there, Cortez will wonder why I've come back so soon. I'm supposed to be looking after things for him, remember? I need Cortez right now."

"If you gain his trust, you can find out where your wife is, yes?"

"Yes."

"If he marries her, then it will be very easy to find her." Larissa propped herself up on one elbow and studied Trenton's face. "What will you do if they are together? Will you just take her?"

"I don't know. He has the place so well guarded. That's why I've got to get him to trust me. If he trusts me, he won't suspect that I'm taking Aeneva away from him."

"Yes, I suppose you are right." Larissa laid her head on Trenton's chest. "It has been good since you have come, Trenton. You have made me happy for the first time in a long time."

Trenton put his arm around Larissa. "You've helped me too. I've been lonely."

"Trenton, what if you don't find your wife? What will you do?"

"I can't think like that. I have to believe that I'll find her. And I have a friend to search for too."

"Will you never give up searching for these people? I do not understand you."

Trenton turned Larissa to face him. "I thought you of all people would understand why I have to keep searching. Your own brother has been doing the same thing for over twelve years. You should understand."

Larissa kissed Trenton's chest, rubbing her cheek next to it. "I suppose it is difficult for me to understand men like you and my brother. The men I have known in my life have been cruel and distrustful of everyone. They have never cared for anyone; they will never care for anyone but themselves. I am glad for men like you and Ladro, but I do not understand you."

Trenton pulled Larissa up so that her face was close to his. "I suppose you don't have to understand us, Larissa. Just know that we do what we do out of love." He touched her young face and pulled her head down to his. He kissed her passionately, enjoying the feel of her youthful body next to his. It reminded him of . . . He turned his head away.

"Please do not turn away from me, Trenton."

"I'm sorry, Larissa, I can't do this. I'm not really making love to you, I'm making love to Aeneva."

"That is all right, don't you see? It is all right to make believe that I am someone else. That is what men do with me all the time."

"I can't use you like that."

"You are not using me. I want you to make love to me, Trenton."

"But I'm not making love to you."

"Yes, you are. You might believe you are making love to your wife but you are making love to me, to my body. You and I are the ones who are together." She leaned down, kissing him softly, moving her mouth against his until she felt his arms go around her.

Trenton made love to Larissa, reveling in the pure physical pleasure he felt from it, but also feeling guilty because he could so easily make love to another woman. He kissed Larissa as she lay sleeping. She looked much more like an innocent child than an experienced whore. But what did it matter, as long as she understood that he didn't love her. They fulfilled a mutual desire and need in each other, and it could never be more than that. Because as long as he lived, there would only be one woman for him. And he would find Aeneva no matter how long it took.

Chapter VI

Ladro limped onto the porch, easing himself into the old chair. He watched as Gonzalo and Elena toiled in the fields. Even the children helped; no one lived a life of leisure here. The wound in his shoulder had closed cleanly and his leg was healing well. It was the inside that was not healing well. Ladro missed Aeneva more than he thought possible; he ached when he thought of her in Cortez's house, or worse yet, in Cortez's bed. Many times he had been tempted to ride to Cortez's rancho to rescue Aeneva, but he knew it was impossible. Until he was stronger, there was no way he could help her. He had to believe that she was strong enough to survive until he could free her.

He rested his head back on the chair, closing his eyes. He felt the heat of it literally pressed against him. The very stillness was almost stifling. He put his bad leg up on the stool that Gonzalo had made for him and he thought about Aeneva. He wondered if he would ever see her again; he wondered if this was his punishment for taking her away from her husband and son who loved her. He often wondered about the white man who loved her so strongly that he had searched Crow territory for her for over a year until he found her. He wondered where the man was now and if he had found Aeneva.

"Better with him than Cortez. I hope he has found her," he said aloud to himself, but the words brought a stab of pain. He tried to clear his mind of all thoughts of Aeneva.

Gonzalo's children were shouting at Ladro over the rows of corn. They were laughing. He waved at them and smiled, thinking back to when he and his brothers used to run through the fields, hiding from their sisters. Their father was always reminding them to do their work. At night, when they had finished with their chores, their mother would always give them a sweet treat she had baked during the day, and they would all run outside together and play games. It was a good childhood, the kind of childhood he hoped to give his own children some day.

He remembered the noise when the bandits had broken into their house. He had heard his sisters screaming and had tried to run out of the room, but his brothers had held him back. Against his own will, they had pushed him out of the bedroom window, telling him to run for help. He remembered running into the night, hearing the screams of his sisters and the gunshots that had killed his parents and brothers. He had looked back only once and seen the fire.

"No!" He started to run back to his home but remembered what his brothers had told him. They were depending on him for help. So, against every

174

instinct that told him to return to his family, he ran across the fields for help.

"Wake up, *señor*. Wake up. You were dreaming again."

Ladro opened his eyes. Gonzalo was standing over him, his hand on Ladro's shoulder. "I'm sorry, Gonzalo. I seem to be reliving too many things these days."

"It is all right, *señor*. It takes time for all wounds to heal."

Elena walked into the house and came out carrying a cup of water. "Drink this, *señor*. You need liquid inside of you."

Ladro accepted the cup, drinking greedily from it. "I'm sorry. I wish I could do something to help around here."

"We do not ask for your help, *señor*. We only ask that you get well. You need to be strong inside as well as outside to find your wife."

Ladro nodded slightly. "She is not my wife, Gonzalo."

Gonzalo exchanged glances with his wife. She and the children took their lunch under a shade tree near the barn. Gonzalo watched them go. "But you love her very much, *señor*. And she loved you, I think. She seemed content with you."

"She lost her memory. I was riding with some Comancheros and we kidnapped some Cheyenne women to sell here in Mexico. I fell in love with her along the way and, I think, she with me. But she already has a husband and a son somewhere. She is married, Gonzalo."

Gonzalo took the straw hat from his head,

wiping the sweat from his brow with a swipe of his forearm. "Can you forget about this woman, *señor?*"

"No, Gonzalo, I can't. You saw the men who took her. They work for a man named Cortez."

"I have heard of this Cortez and all that I have heard is bad. It surprises me that you would work for a man like this."

"I have to, Gonzalo. He knows where my sister is. I've been searching for her for a long time. I can't give up now."

"Do not trust him to tell you where your sister is, *señor*. Men like Cortez use people. It comes easily to them."

Ladro nodded his head. Gonzalo was right. Cortez had never intended to tell him where Larissa was. He had been using him all along. And how many innocent women and children had suffered because he had believed Cortez? He slammed his fist into the porch railing.

"What will you do, *señor?*"

"I will leave as soon as I can ride."

"And then?"

Ladro rubbed his leg, his dark eyes staring out at some distant place. "I will make Cortez pay for what he's done to my sister and to Aeneva. He'll never hurt another person again."

Larissa looked out of her window into the garden below. She could see Trenton and Ramon and she wondered what they were talking about. She knew that Cortez would be here soon. It was as if he couldn't stay away from her. She watched Trenton as he walked, admiring the way he held himself, noticing the way the sun shone on his golden hair. She had never met a man like him before and she didn't want to let him go.

She turned away from the window and walked to the small dresser. From the back of the bottom drawer she pulled out a small box. She opened it and looked inside, admiring all of the jewels Cortez had given her over the years. She had a small fortune here, enough to take her and Trenton far away, to all of the places she had read about. She had enough to keep them in luxury for a long time. She shut the box and put it back in its hiding place.

Cortez would kill her if she dared to speak such thoughts to him. The man was perverse in his thinking. He had owned her since she was ten years old; indeed, had sexually initiated her at the age of fourteen. She had been his to do with as he pleased. She had hated him at first, but she grew to rely on him and eventually care for him in a way. And he had seemed to care for her. He had always given her gifts and even after he had sent her here, he had given specific orders that she was only to be with the most important and richest of men. When Cortez came to visit, he always brought her a gift, usually jewelry, and she always thanked him in the way he liked best. She was sure that she alone knew his secret pleasure, the thing that delighted him more than anything in the world.

There was a knock on the door and Larissa ran her hands through her hair and walked across the room. She opened it.

"Are you all right? You look sad."

Larissa stared at Trenton, a feeling unlike she had ever known tearing at her stomach. "I am fine. I was just thinking about my brother. Come in." She walked to the window and looked out. "I think he would have come for me by now, Trenton. It's been so many years, perhaps he has just given up."

Trenton went to Larissa, putting his hands on her shoulders. "He hasn't given up, Larissa. He'll come for you."

She turned to face Trenton, putting her hands on his chest. "And if he does not come, what then? Shall I stay in this place forever and do Cortez's bidding?" She shook her head furiously. "I won't do that. I am going to run away."

"You can't do that, Larissa. He would find you. As long as you stay here, there's a chance your brother will come for you."

"And a chance that you can find out where your wife is from him, isn't that so?" Larissa walked to the other side of the room. "You are using me, Trenton, just as Cortez uses me. Just as all men use me."

Trenton walked across the room, taking a reluctant Larissa into his arms. "Maybe I have used you, but not in the way you think. At first I used you to help me forget my wife and my loneliness, but then I liked being with you. I don't like the thought of other men being with you."

Larissa threw her arms around Trenton. "I want to leave this place, Trenton. Please, take me away. Cortez will be here soon. He makes me do things that I do not like to do with him. I can't say no to him, Trenton. I don't know how."

"You must learn to say no, Larissa. No man has

the right to make you do things you don't want to do."

"But he does. He forces me in a way that does me no physical harm. He forces me with his mind and emotions. He has known me since I was a child. He bought me from the man who kidnapped me. He fed me and clothed me and educated me . . . He made me into a woman."

"And then he put you here when he grew tired of you."

"No, that's not true. He never grew tired of me; he never will grow tired of me. He only put me here for my safety."

"You mean so that he would have you to himself and make money off of you at the same time. God, Larissa, I can't believe you are actually defending this man."

"He put me here because my brother was searching for me."

"And you thank him for that?"

"Yes." Larissa walked away from Trenton, returning to the window. "I asked him to send me away, Trenton. I did not want my brother to find me. I did not want him to see what had happened to me. Now I . . ."

"Larissa, your brother would never blame you for what happened. It wasn't your fault. You were an innocent child."

"I started out as an innocent child, but I grew to like being with Cortez. I liked pleasing him because I knew that by pleasing him I would continue to be safe."

"And you wouldn't feel safe with your brother?"

"I don't know." She made a little sound, deep in her throat. "I haven't seen my brother in twelve years; we are strangers to each other now. How can I feel safe with a stranger?"

Trenton walked to Larissa, gently running his fingers through her hair. "I am a stranger and you feel safe with me, don't you?"

Larissa turned, her large eyes filling with tears. "You are not a stranger, Trenton." She laid her head against his chest, listening to the steady beat of his heart. His arms went around her and she felt as if she could stay with him forever. "Take me away before Cortez comes. Please."

"I can't do that, Larissa. You know I have to stay here."

"Yes, I know." She pulled away from him, walking to her small dresser and picking up her brush. She slowly ran the brush through her long hair, as if mesmerized by the feel of it. "Don't worry, I won't cause any trouble for you. When Cortez arrives, I'll be the dutiful whore he has always known."

"Larissa, don't."

"Don't what?" She turned around, throwing the brush on the dresser. "Don't cause you any problems but be there to sleep with you if you need me?" She walked up to Trenton, her dark eyes flashing as she confronted him. "Do you want me to find out about your wife from Cortez? Is that what you want?"

"You know that's not what I want."

"But it would make things easier for you, wouldn't it?"

Trenton walked to the door. "I'll come back later when you've cooled down."

Larissa ran to Trenton, pulling his arm. "Wait, I want to ask you something. Please be honest with me."

Trenton turned around. "I'll be as honest as I can be."

"If you find that your wife is dead or if she has run away with Ladro, what will you do?"

"I don't know, I haven't even thought about that. I can only go on the assumption that she is alive."

"But if you can't find her?"

"I don't know."

She held on to his hands. "I want to be with you if your wife cannot. Please don't say no right now. I want you to think about it. I can help you and I'll make sure that you are never lonely again." She stood up on her tiptoes, kissing him passionately. "Just think about it, please."

Larissa watched as Trenton went out the door. She knew what she had to do. She knew that Cortez would help her because he would have no choice, just as she had no choice. She couldn't help the fact that she loved Trenton and she would do anything to keep him. Even if it meant lying to him.

Cortez felt better already. Trenton had done a good job. He'd cleaned up the place and the women seemed happier, more content. Even Ramon's mood was tolerable, and the receipts showed that the customers were extremely pleased. He'd done the right thing by trusting Trenton. And then there was Larissa.

It seemed that every time he saw Larissa, she grew

more beautiful. She was like a flower that never died, only bloomed more lovely each day. He puffed on his cigar as he leaned his head back on the rim of the tub. The warm water relaxed his muscles and made him feel alive again. He couldn't wait to go to Larissa's room for dinner. He especially couldn't wait for dessert. He laughed to himself as he thought of the evening in front of him. And then he thought of Aeneva and his anger grew. The woman was driving him crazy. She was a real beauty, but she didn't listen to reason. He had had to punish her several times and he enjoyed that more than anything. It frightened her, he knew, and that was the best part.

There was something that fascinated him about the woman. No other woman had ever been so openly defiant of him and it threw him off guard. He was used to having women do as he said; he was used to getting his own way. He was the master, they were the slaves. But with this one it was different; he got the distinct impression that she would stab him in the back if given the chance.

He thought of Larissa. She was so different. She knew how to treat a man; she knew how to make a man feel like the master. But then he had taught her. The door opened and Larissa walked in looking as fresh as a spring flower. She smiled at him and he held out his hand to her.

"You look more lovely each time I see you," he said sincerely.

Larissa knelt next to the tub, sticking her hands into the water. She rubbed her hands softly along Cortez's back, gently massaging the muscles. "Would you like me to bathe you?"

"No, Larissa. I would like to talk to you." Cortez stood up, waiting for her to bring him a towel. Larissa wrapped the towel around Cortez and he stepped out of the tub, walking over to the bed. He held out his hand and she sat down next to him. "I have heard rumors, Larissa."

"There are always rumors in a place like this, Emiliano." Larissa decided not to play games with Cortez; he was too smart. She looked him in the eyes. "What have you heard?"

"That you have been with my man."

"That is true. Isn't that part of my job?"

"You don't normally sleep with my hired hands, do you? What is so special about this one?"

Larissa shrugged her shoulders nonchalantly. "There is nothing special about him. He asked to have me and I complied. He said he was your assistant. How could I refuse?"

"I suppose that you could not." Cortez reached out and stroked Larissa's hair. "Have you heard about your brother?"

"What about my brother? He is not coming here, is he?"

"No, my sweet Larissa. Your brother is dead."

"No," Larissa responded in a small voice. She could not believe he was dead. Not Ladro. "What happened?"

"He was killed by some men."

"By *your* men, you mean." Larissa stared into Cortez's eyes.

"Yes, by my men."

"But why? You promised me that you would never hurt him as long as I stayed away from him. You promised me, Emiliano." Larissa turned away, but Cortez pulled her back to face him.

"It could not be helped. He was trying to escape with the Indian woman that I had bought. He tried to deceive me and he had to pay the price."

"Did you have to kill him?"

"I had no other choice."

"And what of this Indian woman? Is she dead also?"

"Dead? Of course not, she is my wife."

Larissa stared at Cortez. "She is your wife? You have married her?"

"Why do you act so surprised? You knew of my plan all along. As soon as she gives me a child, I will get rid of her."

"What is she like?"

"Are you jealous?" Cortez tipped Larissa's chin up. "Is my little flower jealous?"

"I am not jealous, I just want to know what she is like."

"She is quite beautiful really, but not my type. She has too much senseless spirit. That is probably why your brother cared for her."

"Ladro cared for the woman?"

"Yes, he died trying to save her. And she, the silly woman, was in love with him." Cortez shook his head impatiently. "Actually, the two of them belonged together. They deserved each other."

"Is the woman with child yet?"

"She has only been with me a few weeks."

"That does not sound like you, Emiliano. Does she frighten you?"

"Don't be ridiculous. Of course not. I am in the

184

process of teaching her her role right now. When she has learned her place, then I will make her my woman."

"You mean you are punishing her."

"Call it what you like, but by the time I return from this little trip, she will be more than willing to do as I say."

"And Trenton, will you take him back with you?"

"Yes, I intend to train him in his duties on the rancho. I need to have someone who can be in charge when I am in Mexico City. Someone I can trust."

"And you think you can trust this man?"

"As much as I can trust anyone. I will never let him know all of my secrets, but I will let him think I trust him. He will make things easier for me."

"Do you never get tired of using people, Emiliano?"

Cortez took Larissa's hair in his hand and jerked it back roughly. "I never get tired of using people, Larissa, especially if it suits my purpose." He saw the frightened look in her eyes and ripped her robe open. "You will always be mine, Larissa. Always." Cortez forced Larissa down onto the bed. She fought him this time, not playing the game he so enjoyed. The more she fought him, the more he liked it. When Larissa screamed for him to stop, he laughed, forcing her to do all the things he wanted her to do, knowing that she would never be free of him.

Later, as Cortez slept, Larissa put on her robe and walked to Trenton's room. She knocked quietly on the door and opened it. She went to the bed and sat down, tentatively reaching out to touch him. He took her hand, kissing her fingers. She lay down next to him, her head on his chest.

"Please hold me, Trenton." With his arms securely around her, Larissa knew that no matter who she hurt, she had to have this man. She could not go back to the life she had led all these years now that she had met Trenton. He had made all the difference in the world. She would never let him go now that she had found him.

Larissa saw Cortez smile as she walked up to him in the garden. "I want to talk to you, Emiliano."

"Yes, what is it, my dear? A new dress or some jewelry? You know that you can have anything you want."

"Anything?"

Cortez looked at Larissa. "What do you want, Larissa?"

"I want Trenton."

Cortez waved his hand in an impatient gesture. "It will pass."

"No, it won't."

"Don't tell me that you're in love with this man? Do you actually think he loves you, a whore?"

Larissa's voice was cold and hard when she spoke. "I do not care what you think, Emiliano, but I think you had better listen to me."

"And if I do not?"

"I will tell Trenton that you had his wife kidnapped and now have her locked up in your rancho."

Cortez looked shocked. "What are you talking about?"

"The woman you have at your rancho is his wife. He was following Ladro and her into Mexico. He is only working for you so that he can find her."

"I don't believe this. It's impossible." Cortez stood up. "The woman at my rancho was in love with Ladro, not with this white man."

"I do not know what happened. Perhaps she came to depend on Ladro and she fell in love with him. I only know that the woman who was traveling with Ladro is Trenton's wife."

"And how does he feel about her?"

"He loves her very much. He will do anything to get her back."

"Including killing me, I suppose."

Larissa nodded her head. "But if we can make him believe that she is dead, then I can take him away from here. He cares for me; he has told me that."

Cortez thought a moment. "I could have him killed; that would be the easiest way."

Larissa grabbed Cortez's shoulders. "No! You must not do that. I love him, Emiliano. He will not bother you if you make him believe that his wife is dead."

"And if I don't?"

"I will tell him that she is at your rancho. Then he will be your problem."

"I don't like threats, Larissa," Cortez said under his breath, squeezing Larissa's arm tightly. "You know what I do to people who threaten me."

"Do not hurt me, Emiliano, or I will scream. Trenton will be down here and I will tell him the truth." She nodded her head toward one of the upstairs windows. "Look, he is watching us. I told him I was frightened of you; I told him to watch out for me."

Cortez glanced up at the window, letting go of Larissa's arm. "I don't like this, Larissa."

"But you don't have a choice." Larissa looked at Cortez, angry and desperate. "Emiliano, you once told me that you cared for me, really cared for me. If that is true, please let me have this man. I don't want anything else from you."

"And if he still asks to work for me?"

"Have him work here or in one of your other places. He does not have to be at your rancho. This will help to solve your problems, Emiliano, and it will help me. Please."

Cortez looked at Larissa, shaking his head. "I never could say no to you, could I, my little flower?" He leaned down and kissed her cheek. "You are so beautiful. I do not like the thought of giving you up to another man."

"My soul will always be yours, Emiliano. Always." She threw her arms around Cortez's neck. "Just please give me this one thing. Please."

Cortez held Larissa to him. "All right, Larissa. You will have this man if you want him. But he is to believe that his wife is dead. He is never to know that she is living with me. Do you understand?"

"He will never find out the truth from me. Thank you, Emiliano. Thank you."

"Just remember, Larissa, you are never to tell him anything about the woman. Make up any story you want, just make sure he believes it. His life depends on it. And so does yours."

*　　　*　　　*

Trenton walked into Ramon's cantina, his eyes scanning the room for Cortez. He walked to the table where Cortez was sitting.

"I want to talk, Cortez."

Cortez motioned to the chair. "Sit down, gringo. Have a drink."

Trenton waited while Cortez poured him a drink and pushed the glass to him. "Everything is running smoothly here, Cortez. You don't need me here anymore. I think it's time I head back to your rancho. There's a lot there I have to learn." Trenton tried to sound casual, but he wanted desperately to be at the rancho when Ladro and Aeneva got there.

Cortez leaned back in his chair, studying his glass. "Perhaps so, gringo. I want you to know everything there is to know about my business. But there is a job I want you to do first. It seems I picked the wrong man the first time."

"What're you talking about?"

Cortez's eyes went past Trenton to the stairs. "We will talk business later. Larissa is coming and I fear it is not me she looks at these days. I will leave the two of you alone." Cortez stood up and left the room.

Larissa walked to Trenton, glancing after Cortez. "Did he tell you?"

"Tell me what?"

Larissa sat down next to Trenton, her face betraying her sadness. "We've lost everything, Trenton. You and I have lost everything that matters to us."

"What're you talking about?"

"My brother is dead. And so is your wife."

Trenton stared at her. "What happened?" He picked up the drink Cortez had poured for him. He downed the fiery liquid, trying to still the tremor in his hands.

Tears welled in Larissa's eyes. "Ladro had no intention of taking your wife to Cortez. He wanted to keep her for himself."

"How do you know that?"

"He saw Cortez once, demanding to know where I was. But he refused to sell the woman."

"How were they killed?"

"Cortez's men followed them for two days, but when they finally caught up to them, they were already dead. *Bandidos* attacked them while they slept." She shook her head. "He was all the family I had left."

"Did anyone see the woman? Are you sure it was Aeneva?"

"Alfredo led the riders. He said the woman was very beautiful. The *bandidos* took everything of value. Alfredo found only one bag of dried herbs."

The glass in Trenton's hand shattered. He stared at the bloody hand, too numb to speak. From somewhere outside the silence that engulfed him he could hear Larissa's voice.

"I am so sorry, Trenton. I know what you are feeling. I am feeling it too." She took his bloodied hand, wrapping her handkerchief around it. "We have no one but each other now."

Larissa held Trenton tightly, but Trenton knew that no one could ever fill the emptiness that was already beginning to eat away at him.

* * *

Aeneva paced around the room. Since the time Cortez had brought her to his rancho, she had not been allowed out of the room. At first, she thought she would go mad, but she knew that was exactly what he wanted. He thrived on her fear. She became cold and sullen, showing little emotion when he touched her. It made him angry and frustrated him, but it gave her more time. As long as she didn't show any fear she knew she had a chance to survive. The man was sick. She would use his sickness to defeat him. She would find a way to escape.

She was standing at the window looking out into the yard the day Cortez and his men returned from their trip. She tried to prepare herself for his onslaught; she knew he would be coming to her soon. He had already wasted too much time. He needed an heir soon.

She sat down on the bed, forcing herself to be calm, waiting for Cortez to come to her room. She grew sleepy and lay back on the bed. Her mind drifted into sleep and again she saw the man with the golden hair and blue eyes. He was laughing at her. It made her angry. She had fallen into a creek and she stood wet, her hair hanging in her face, her dress clinging to her body. He reached out to her and she took his hand. He pulled her up on the bank, enclosing her in his arms. She didn't protest; she stared into his eyes. She felt warm and safe as he held her; she felt at home. When she looked up again, his mouth touched hers and she felt something she had never felt with any other man, not even with Ladro. Ladro. Where was he?

The key turned in the lock and Cortez walked into the room. "Wake up, my dear, your husband is home. Don't you want to greet him?"

Aeneva opened her eyes, staring at the stranger who kept her a prisoner in his house. "I was hoping you might have fallen from your horse and been killed," Aeneva said dryly.

Cortez laughed, turning to Alfredo. "Isn't she funny, Alfredo? I love her sense of humor." Cortez's face instantly changed from one of laughter to one of anger. He walked to Aeneva, taking her arms tightly in his. "Tonight will be the night, my dear. Tonight you will conceive my child. And when you give me the child I want, I will have no more use for you." Cortez spat out the words as he walked from the room, locking the door behind him. Aeneva tried to control her fear but it threatened to engulf her. She had to find a way to keep Cortez away from her. It was time to try the only thing left to her. She hoped that Estella would help her because if she did not, there would be no escaping the man.

When Cortez walked into the room, he found Aeneva lying across the bed. He touched her arm but she groaned and turned away from him.

"What is the matter with you, woman?" When Aeneva didn't respond, Cortez called Estella. "Estella, what is wrong with the *señora?*"

"I do not know, *señor.*" Estella rubbed her hands in her apron, looking at the floor.

Cortez stepped forward. "Come, Estella, if you know something, I want you to tell me. You know that I expect loyalty from you and Alfredo."

"*Sí, señor.*"

"Do not be afraid to tell me. Has she eaten bad food? Has she been like this while I was gone? What sort of sickness is this?"

"I do not think the *señora* is sick, *señor.*"

"Then what is the matter with her?"

Estella fumbled with her apron, looking from the bed to Cortez. "Do not be angry with me, *señor.*"

"Angry about what?"

"I think the *señora* is with child."

"What!"

"*Sí.* Ever since you left she has been sick and unable to eat."

"Did she tell you she is with child?"

"No, *señor,* I have observed this for myself. She has tried to hide it from me but I know about such things. I have had five children of my own."

Cortez looked back at the bed and he led Estella outside into the hall. "You are sure she is pregnant, Estella?"

"I think so, *señor.* Why else would she be sick at the sight of food. And I have seen her holding her stomach and staring out of the window as if she were dreaming. Maybe I am wrong, *señor,* but I do not think so."

Cortez nodded, a smile spreading across his face. "You may go now, Estella."

"You are not angry, *señor?*"

"No, Estella. In fact you shall have a little reward for being such a loyal servant. *Gracias.*" Cortez shut the door behind Estella and walked over to the bed. "Pregnant," he said softly, hardly able to contain the

193

relief inside him. He would have an heir much sooner than he had expected, even if the heir wasn't his. She had been trying to hide it from him. Why? Cortez nodded thoughtfully. Of course, the child had to be Ladro's and she didn't want him to know. Cortez shrugged his shoulders. What did it matter to him if he raised another man's child as long as he had a child. When his grandfather died, he could send the child away somewhere and he would be free. Aeneva moved on the bed and Cortez sat down, touching her arm.

"You are beautiful," Cortez said aloud. "I could teach you some things." He bent down next to her, kissing her neck. Aeneva groaned and tried to pull away but Cortez held her. "Why didn't you tell me you are going to be a mother, my dear?" Cortez whispered into Aeneva's ear.

Aeneva turned her head, looking at Cortez. "What are you talking about?"

"Estella tells me you are with child. Is that true?"

"Of course it is not true. She is lying." Aeneva pulled away from Cortez and sat up. "How could I be with child?"

"You tell me. You were the one who was with Ladro all of that time." Cortez ran his fingers up and down Aeneva's bare arm. "Was he the man he appeared to be?"

Aeneva pulled her arm away. "Stop it! I do not want to hear any more about Ladro."

"Why, Aeneva? Did you love him so much?"

"I was afraid what you would do when you found out it was Ladro's child. I know how much you

194

hated him."

"It makes no difference to me whose child it is, just as long as I have an heir to present to my grandfather." He cupped Aeneva's chin in his hand. "Are you all right? You look pale."

"I have been locked up in this room too long."

Cortez stared at Aeneva thoughtfully. "Perhaps you are right, my dear, perhaps what you need is some fresh air. Tomorrow you may go riding with Alfredo. If you show me that you can be trusted, then I will give you more freedom. Who knows, perhaps we can even grow to like each other."

In spite of her hatred of the man, Aeneva turned to face him. "Perhaps."

Cortez smiled. "Good. Well, it is late and I've had a long day. I will see you at breakfast."

"Breakfast?"

"Yes, from now on you will dine with me. You must keep your health up now that you are going to have a child." He walked over to Aeneva. "Estella is the only one who knows and she will be sworn to secrecy. As far as anyone else around here knows, the child will be mine."

Aeneva continued playing the part. "All right, I'll do as you say. I am tired of fighting you. I want to make this child strong. I will do anything you want me to do."

"Good, good, I'm glad to hear you say that. Now, you get some rest. I'll see you in the morning." Cortez bent down, kissing Aeneva on the cheek. She forced herself to accept the proffered gesture and she didn't move until Cortez left. She smiled. He believed her—

he actually believed that she was pregnant with Ladro's child. Now she had some time to plan. She had to get away from Cortez and back to her people. She didn't know what it would be like when she reached the Cheyennes—if she reached the Cheyennes—but it would be better than being with Cortez.

Chapter VII

Aeneva felt the wind blow through her hair. She enjoyed her daily rides with Alfredo. Alfredo had come to be a friend to her. He seemed to realize that she wanted only to get away from Cortez and the hacienda. He was patient with her and let her ride as long as she wished.

"I will trust you, *señora*. But please remember that if you try to escape, the *Patrón* will take it out on me and my family."

"You can trust me, Alfredo. I only want to ride."

And from then on, Aeneva had a silent alliance with Alfredo, as well as with Estella, who had helped her to convince Cortez that she was pregnant. It helped to know that she had two people who cared for her, even if they did work for Cortez.

Aeneva rode to the top of a knoll, stopping to look down on Cortez's land. It was beautiful; she could understand why Cortez would do anything to keep it. Things were as good as they could be right now except that she wasn't really pregnant. What would

Cortez do when he found out she was lying? He would probably kill her. She dismounted, walking over to pick some wildflowers. She looked out across the pastures. At the foot of the hill a beautiful stallion was walking proudly from a stand of trees. He was midnight black except for his back and rump. There he was white, splashed with spots of ink-black. His mane and tail hung long. Aeneva felt a stab of confusion.

The stallion tossed his head and whickered. A dozen mares came from the trees behind him, their bodies muscled and sleek-coated. The stallion led them downhill, toward a stream.

Aeneva stood transfixed, images reeling through her mind; close, yet just out of touch. A tall man with long black hair, smiling. A younger man with a ready laugh. A smell of woodsmoke and a feeling of vast distance. Aeneva forced her eyes back to the wildflowers. As she bent over to pick them she felt a wave of dizziness overcome her. She sat down. She felt hot and she was sick to her stomach.

"Are you all right, *señora?*"

"Yes, Alfredo, I am fine. I am just a little tired. Maybe we should return to the rancho."

Aeneva and Alfredo rode back to the rancho at a slow pace. When Aeneva dismounted and walked into the hacienda, she was immediately trailed by Estella.

"Are you all right, *senora?* What is the matter?"

Aeneva shut the bedroom door, lying down on the bed. "I don't know. I feel strange. I feel sick to my stomach and I feel hot. Do you suppose I am coming

198

down with something?"

Estella shook her head. *"Señora*, do you suppose it is possible for a woman to *wish* herself pregnant?"

Aeneva looked at the woman. "What do you mean? I cannot be with child. It is not possible."

"Are you sure, *señora?* What about Ladro? You were with him for some time. The time would be right."

Aeneva sat up. "No, it cannot be." But she touched her stomach lovingly. "Do you suppose it is possible, Estella? Ladro's child?"

"When was your last time, *señora?*"

Aeneva shook her head in disbelief. "It was over two months ago. But I thought it was the running, the fear. I thought . . ." She looked up. "I am carrying his child, Estella." Her joy quickly turned to fear. "God, I do not want Cortez to have this child. He will destroy it!"

"Do not excite yourself, *señora*. You must take care of yourself now. You will find a way to take care of the child. Already the *Patrón* seems to care for you more. Perhaps in time he will learn to care for the child."

"Estella, you know him better than I. Do you think that is possible?"

Estella lowered her eyes, shaking her head. "No, I do not think the *Patrón* would ever care for a child. The only things he cares for are his possessions."

Aeneva knew what courage it took for Estella to speak out against Cortez and she took her hand. "Thank you, Estella, thank you for being such a good friend. I will think of something. I will not let him hurt this child."

Aeneva laughed at Cortez's joke. "I never knew you had such a sense of humor, Emiliano. You are very nice when you want to be."

Cortez raised his glass to Aeneva. "I might say the same for you, Aeneva." He sipped at his wine, staring at her over the rim. "You are looking especially lovely this evening. I think being pregnant agrees with you."

"I do feel good." She lowered her eyes in an uncharacteristic gesture. "Thank you, Emiliano, for making things so much easier for me. I know I have been difficult."

"Well, perhaps it was for the best, eh? It seems we are growing closer, you and I. One day we may even become lovers?"

Aeneva forced herself to meet Cortez's eyes. "Perhaps." She lifted her wineglass and sipped at the liquid. "What will you do with us after your grandfather gives you the land?"

"That depends on you and the child. I don't want a brat running around here. On the other hand, if you take good care of him and teach him how to behave properly, I may let you both stay."

"Thank you," Aeneva replied quietly. She wanted to throw her wineglass across the table at Cortez. She wanted to do a lot of things to him, but she would not. She had Ladro's child to think of now.

After dinner Aeneva accompanied Cortez on a walk around the grounds, growing more and more comfortable in the role as the *Patrón*'s wife. But she knew she could never trust Cortez. The man was like a rattler; if you disturbed him carelessly he would strike.

"It's a lovely evening tonight, don't you think?"

Aeneva looked up at the stars, a strange feeling coming over her. How many times in her past had she done the same thing? "Yes, it is lovely. The stars look like jewels in the sky."

"Yes, I suppose they do." Cortez led Aeneva to a bench where they sat down. "Tell me, Aeneva, do you miss your people?"

"No. I have no memory of my people."

"What do you mean?"

Aeneva told Cortez the story of her capture and subsequent injury. "I cannot even remember my own family."

"So, you do not even know if you have a family?"

"I have a husband and a son."

"How do you know that if you can't remember?"

"I know this because the wife of my brother told me after we were kidnapped by your men."

"And your husband? You remember nothing of him?"

"Nothing."

"Was he a Cheyenne?"

"Little Deer told me he was a white man, but I do not remember." Aeneva looked up at the stars, trying to lure Cortez into her trap. "I could not have loved him very much if I have forgotten him so soon."

Cortez took Aeneva's hand, kissing the palm. "Perhaps he was not worth remembering."

Aeneva nodded. "Yes, I suppose you are right." She sighed deeply, suddenly frightened by the way

Cortez was delving into her past. "I am so tired tonight. I feel as though I could fall asleep right here."

"And I would carry you up to your bed if you did," Cortez replied. She could hear the lust in his voice.

"Would it be all right if we went inside now, Emiliano?"

"Yes, by all means. We wouldn't want you to catch a chill."

Cortez walked Aeneva to her room, hesitating as she sat down on the bed to take off her shoes. When she bent over to unbutton the shoes, Cortez walked to her, kneeling beside her.

"Please, I want to help you." He unbuttoned each shoe, slowly removing each one from Aeneva's feet. He massaged each foot gently. "Does that feel better?"

"Yes, thank you." Aeneva tried to remain calm, but she was afraid that Cortez would not stop.

Cortez sat on the bed next to Aeneva, taking the shawl from her shoulders and slowly unbuttoning the back of her dress. He pulled the dress from her shoulders, exposing her bare shoulders. He ran his hand along her shoulders and back. "You have beautiful skin, Aeneva. Very beautiful skin." He leaned down and kissed her shoulder. "I would like to have you stay here with me, but I don't know if I can trust you."

"You can trust me, Emiliano. I have nowhere else to go."

"Yes, that's true. You have no one but me." His hand moved over her neck and down to her breasts. "You are very desirable, Aeneva. Do you know that?"

Cortez pushed her down on the bed. "You do want me, don't you, Aeneva?" He held her arms pinned to the bed. An urgent knock on the door interrupted them. Cortez sat up, angry and annoyed. "What is it?"

"*Señor,* it is very important. I must speak with you now."

"Not now, Alfredo. I do not wish to be disturbed."

"But *señor,* I think you will want to hear this."

Cortez stood up, striding over to the door. "What is it, Alfredo? If you have bothered me for nothing you will regret it."

"Not here, *señor.* Please, let me talk to you outside."

Cortez walked back to Aeneva, taking her hands in his. "I will be back soon. Wait up for me."

Aeneva nodded as he walked out of the room. She breathed a sigh of relief when he left but knew that his return was inevitable.

"What? I thought you told me he was dead!"

"That is what I thought, *señor.* I would have sworn it. I . . . Perhaps I was wrong."

"You yourself killed him. You told me he was dead. And now he's been seen? Are you sure it's Ladro?"

Cortez nervously ran his fingers through his hair.

"No, but one of the men said they saw someone riding on the land who looked like Ladro."

"What was he doing?"

"He was watching your wife as she and I rode, *señor.*"

Cortez banged his fist on the desk. "Damn it! He

can't still be alive." Cortez thought for a moment. "I don't want to be left unguarded, not for a moment. I want men at my door at all times and I want them around the house. And I don't want the *señora* riding anymore."

"*Señor,* if it is Ladro and he has come back for the *señora,* would it not be better to let her keep riding? Perhaps he will try to come for her."

Cortez bit on his lower lip as he thought. "Yes, perhaps you are right. If Ladro is here, he has come for my wife. The best way to get him out in the open is to use my wife for bait." Cortez smiled. "I can't wait to see the look on his face when he finds out . . ." Cortez stopped himself before he said any more. "Everything will be as before except we will be watching for Ladro. You are not to say a word to the senora about this. And if you catch him, I don't want him killed. At least not yet. I have a few things to say to him first. And if you do not catch him, Alfredo, you will die for your stupidity. I will have no more of your mistakes. Do you understand me?"

Ladro watched the hacienda as he had so many nights before. He had waited patiently. He wanted Cortez to know that he was around; he wanted him to worry. It was easier to wait now that he knew Aeneva was safe. The first time he had seen her riding he had almost ridden after her, in spite of the risk. But it was better to wait until Cortez got frantic and careless with fear. Soon Cortez would be jumping at shadows. Then he would get Aeneva and take her so

204

far away they would never have to worry about Cortez again.

Cortez banged his fist on the desk, shaking the wine decanter that sat on the edge. "Where is he, Alfredo? You told me he was here! First he is dead, then he is alive. Where is he?"

"I said it was someone who looked like Ladro, *señor*. We don't know for sure if it is Ladro."

"But you have seen him since, haven't you?"

"Yes, many times. He rides the hills and watches. He just watches us, *señor*."

"What is he waiting for? Why doesn't he try to come for her? I know that's why he's here."

"I don't know, *señor*. I only know that he is still around."

"Get out, Alfredo." Cortez poured himself a glass of wine. "Alfredo, wait. Come back here." Cortez downed the glass of wine and poured himself another. "Has she seen him yet?"

"No, *señor*. She sees nothing but the land when she rides."

"You are sure?"

"*Sí, señor*. She has even told me how happy she is now."

"She has said that to you?"

"*Sí, señor*. I think she is content to be with child."

"Good, good. You may go, Alfredo. And make sure the guards are alert. And send for my wife."

"*Sí, señor*."

Cortez walked to the window of the study and

peered out of the sheer curtains. Was Ladro out there watching him right now, or was Ladro just a figment of his imagination, just a vision out of the past? He walked back to the desk and poured himself another glass of wine. "Damn him! What the hell does he think he's doing? If he thinks he's going to get in here and take Aeneva away from me he's crazy. He'll be shot before he gets anywhere close to her." Cortez drank the wine and threw the glass against the wall. Aeneva was his now and no one would take her away from him, especially not when he was so close to realizing all of his dreams. Ladro would not spoil things now. There was a knock at the study door. "Come in."

Aeneva walked into the study wearing a deep blue linen dress. Her hair was pulled back from her face and she had a flower on one side. "Alfredo said you wanted to see me."

"Come here, Aeneva. You look so beautiful tonight."

"Thank you, Emiliano. I feel good."

Cortez took Aeneva's hands, leading her to the small sofa. "Sit down. Please." Cortez walked to the window, peering out of the curtains once more. "Are you happy here, Aeneva?"

Aeneva forced her voice to betray no emotion. "Yes, Emiliano."

Cortez turned from the window, penetrating Aeneva with his sharp gaze. "You would not lie to me? You are truly happy here? You want to stay here and have your child?"

Aeneva sensed Cortez's uncertainty. "Yes, if you want us to stay, I would like to raise my child here."

She looked around her. "This is a wonderful place for a child to grow up. I would not like to raise my child out in the open as it is said my people do." Aeneva knew she had said the right thing.

Cortez walked to Aeneva. "It pleases me to hear you say that. But what if something happened? What if someone came to take you away; would you go?"

"Who would come to take me away?"

"You still have a husband."

"A husband I cannot remember. And I think he must have forgotten me by now." Aeneva shook her head. "No, this is my home now. I want to stay here. I want my child to be raised as a Cortez."

Cortez sat next to Aeneva on the sofa, taking her hands in his, kissing them gently. "And what about Ladro?" His eyes searched hers.

"What about Ladro? He is dead now. He is part of my past."

"But what if he weren't dead? What if he tried to come back for you?"

Aeneva tried to still the beating of her heart. "You are being foolish, Emiliano. We both know that Ladro is dead."

"Humor me, Aeneva. What if Ladro weren't dead?"

Aeneva stared at Cortez, reaching up to touch his face. "Things are different now, Emiliano. Even if Ladro came back for me right now, at this very moment, I would not go with him."

"But you loved him; you are carrying his child."

"I did not really love him. I came to depend on him because there was no one else and I had lost my memory. There is a difference."

Cortez took Aeneva in his arms. "I believe that you are telling me the truth."

Aeneva tried to conceal the contempt in her voice as she spoke. "I am telling you the truth, Emiliano." She knew where this talk could lead and she wanted it to end before anything started. She caught her breath, bending over.

"What is it? Are you all right?"

"I don't know. I have been having pains all day. Estella says they are normal."

Cortez put his hand on Aeneva's stomach. "Why didn't you tell me? You should be in bed."

"It is nothing. I am fine."

"Come." Cortez stood up, offering Aeneva his hand. "I will take you up to your room and make sure you go to bed. We can't have anything happen to you or the child."

Aeneva took Cortez's arm and walked up the stairs, making it seem as if each step were an effort. When they reached her room, Cortez helped her to undress. She had to suffer through his lustful stares until she slipped on her nightgown and got in bed. Cortez pulled the covers up and leaned down to kiss her cheek.

"I will send Estella up with some warm milk. You rest now, my dear. I will see you in the morning."

Aeneva held on to Cortez's hand, kissing it gently. "Thank you, Emiliano."

Cortez nodded slightly and left the room, closing the door quietly.

Aeneva stared after Cortez, a look of anger and disgust coming over her face. God, how she hated the man. One minute he was a raving maniac, the next minute he played the caring, loving husband. She hated him, but she would play his game for as long as it took to find a way to escape. She shook her head. The man was even jealous of Ladro; he was jealous of a dead man. He had to be constantly reassured that he was the best man, the only man in the world. "I can do that," Aeneva said to herself. "I can do it as long as I need to, Cortez." She patted her stomach lovingly. "This is one life you will never take from me. Never."

Ladro watched from the side of the barn as the guards walked back and forth. He knew Cortez so well; he knew that he would have guards all over the place. He also knew that the guards were in the habit of drinking and taking naps. He could wait. Sooner or later one of them would relax for a moment and he could make his move.

Ladro waited for what seemed like an eternity until the guard in the front of the house walked around the corner to the back. He knew he'd have a few words and possibly a drink with his friend. Ladro moved quickly in the darkness, his movements unheard and unseen. When he reached the courtyard he hesitated. There was a guard by the front door. Ladro watched the man for a few minutes and saw that he was barely awake. Too many nights had passed without anything happening. Ladro moved slowly along the flower bushes surrounding the courtyard. When he came to the arched entryway in front of the door he took a pebble out of his pocket and threw it on the other side of the guard. The man stood up, walking toward where the pebble had hit. Ladro was behind him and had his arm around the guard's throat in an instant. He hit the man over the head with his gun and dragged him to the side. Knowing how suspicious Cortez was, Ladro was sure he would have men inside the house as well. He knocked, and when the door opened slightly he heard Alfredo's voice.

"What is it, Raul? You still have two more hours."

Ladro slammed his weight against the door, throwing Alfredo backward. He fell hard and sat up slowly. Ladro put his gun against Alfredo's temple. "Stand up, Alfredo. Put your hands on top of your head." Ladro pulled Alfredo's gun free of his holster and shoved it into his belt. "Where is the woman, Alfredo? Don't lie to me or you will die. I don't have time to waste."

"So you *have* come back."

"Where is she, Alfredo?"

"In the room at the top of the stairs. The room he has always used for his female visitors. The one with the bars on the window."

"You mean the room he uses to punish his women," Ladro replied with disdain. "How many guards are in the house?"

"A man by her door and one by his. Also one in the kitchen."

"Then I'm going to need you help, Alfredo. I don't want to hurt you, but I'm going to get Aeneva with or without you."

"I will help you, Ladro. But not because I care anything for you. The *señora* deserves a man better than Cortez. She will never be happy here. And I have come to respect her."

"He hasn't hurt her?"

210

"There were a few times. But since he found out about the child, he has been kind to her. He almost seems as if he cares about her now."

"What child?"

"She is going to have a child."

"No, that's not possible." Ladro's voice was filled with anger and despair. "Not his child."

Alfredo shook his head. "You were the only one who stood up to the *Patrón*. I, myself, have not been so brave because I have a wife and five children. I know the kind of man he is and I fear for their safety."

"You've done what you had to do, Alfredo. I don't blame you."

Alfredo was silent a moment. "I should never have let you live. Cortez will kill me when he finds out you have taken the *señora*."

"Not if I kill him first."

"You can't, Ladro. Just take your woman and go."

"I don't understand you, Alfredo. You know the kind of man Cortez is."

"Yes, I know. But no one deserves to be shot while they sleep. Not even Cortez."

"Then I'll wake him up."

"You owe me, Ladro."

"Why? For letting me live?"

"I could have killed you but I did not. Does that not count for something?"

Ladro looked toward the stairs. He was wasting time. "All right, Alfredo. I won't kill him. Where is the *señora*?"

"Ladro," Alfredo said firmly, "the child is yours. She is carrying your child."

Ladro gripped Alfredo's arm in the semidarkness.

"You're sure?"

"Yes. My wife told me. The *señora* was pleased that it was your child, but for its safety and hers she has let him believe that she did not love you. He now believes that she is happy here."

Ladro took a deep breath. "Will you help me, Alfredo?"

"*Sí*, but when you have the *señora* you must knock me out. He must not know that I have helped you."

"I understand. Let's go."

Ladro followed Alfredo to the stairs and waited as Alfredo went up to talk to the guards who were posted upstairs. Ladro heard Alfredo tell the men a noise had been heard outside. He sent them hurrying down the stairs and stood with his pistol drawn, as though he would guard the doors until they got back. When they had passed, Ladro stepped from the shadows and climbed the stairs.

"This door, Ladro. Here." Ladro went to where Alfredo was standing. Alfredo unlocked the door. "Hurry, Ladro. I will risk my life for her freedom, not yours. If anyone comes, I'll have to shoot you."

Ladro entered the room, closing the door silently behind him. He walked over to the bed. He stared at Aeneva, unable to believe that he was so close to her again. He put his hand over her mouth, leaning on the bed. "Aeneva, wake up."

Aeneva opened her eyes. She couldn't see anyone, but she felt a hand covering her mouth. She struggled to move, but she felt a body across hers. Then she heard his voice. It was Ladro. Ladro!

"Are you awake, Aeneva?"

She nodded her head and he removed his hand.

212

Aeneva sat up. "Ladro, is it really you?" Her voice was an astonished whisper. She threw her arms around his neck, reveling in the feel of his healthy body next to hers. She started to cry quietly. "I can't believe you are alive. Thank God."

"Come, you must get dressed. I have to get you out of here."

Aeneva got out of bed and went to the closet. She pulled out a shirt, some pants, and a jacket; sturdy clothes which Estella had gotten for her to ride in. She dressed quickly and pulled on some boots.

"Are you ready?" Ladro's voice was a tight whisper.

"Yes, Ladro." She took his hand, still trembling from relief and shock, as he led her out the door. She saw Alfredo and stopped, understanding that he had helped them. She kissed Alfredo on the cheek. "Thank you, Alfredo. Tell Estella that I will be fine. Thank her for everything. I will never forget you."

"Good-bye, *señora. Vaya con Dios.*" He turned to Ladro. "I've sent the guards outside to the back of the house. When they find nothing, they will be back."

Ladro nodded. *"Muchas gracias,* Alfredo. I will not forget what you have done." As Alfredo turned back to the door, Ladro hit him sharply across the back of the head, catching him as his body slumped against the door. "Let's go." He took Aeneva's hand and led her down the stairs to the entryway. Ladro reached into his belt and handed Aeneva a gun. "If I'm killed, you go on. My horse is in the cornfield beyond the barn."

"I will not leave you."

"I want you away from this place. Ride to Gonzalo

if you have to. Tell him you need help."

Aeneva nodded and they went outside. They reached the shadows of the barn just as they heard the guards run back toward the entryway. Aeneva flung the door to the barn open and fumbled in the darkness. The horse in the first stall nosed her calmly. Ladro's voice came from the shadows.

"Hurry up, Aeneva. I will get my horse. The guards will come out soon. Hurry." His footsteps moved into the night. Aeneva felt her way into the stall.

The horse had a halter on. That would be enough. Aeneva's frantic hands found a rope hanging outside the stall and she led the horse outside. She mounted quickly. Ladro rode from the shadows. Together they rode into the night, pushing the horses as fast as they could in the darkness.

Ladro and Aeneva galloped into the countryside. Voices rang out behind them but dimmed as they pressed the horses harder. Ladro followed the path he had laid out, avoiding the camps of the outriders. They rode through the night, putting as much distance between Cortez and themselves as they could. As the sun began to rise, Ladro found a place where they could rest. Aeneva dismounted and walked to Ladro, looking up at him.

"I still cannot believe that you are alive. You came back for me."

"Did you think I would leave you with him?"

"I thought you were dead; that's what he told me."

"Did he hurt you?"

"At first he kept me locked up in the room. When I would not do as he said he would beat me. He tried

214

to break me, just as one would break a horse." Aeneva reached up and touched Ladro's face. "And then he changed toward me."

"Why?"

"Because he found out that I was with child. Your child."

Ladro pulled Aeneva to him, cradling her in his arms. "God, I cannot believe it, our own child. And Cortez was willing to accept my child?"

"I think he liked the idea of having your child to raise. In his mind it was the best revenge."

"Did he touch you?"

"No, he tried many times but I pretended to be sick. He did not take any chances. He wanted the child to be born healthy."

Again Ladro took Aeneva in his arms. "I cannot believe that I am holding you in my arms, Aeneva. I was so afraid he had hurt you. Then I saw you riding one day with Alfredo and I saw that you were well. Your hair was blowing in the wind and you looked free; I knew then that I would get you back."

"Oh, Ladro," Aeneva rested her head against his chest. "I love you. I want to be with you always."

Ladro held Aeneva in his arms. But he could not get her husband out of his mind. "When we are safe, away from here, we have to talk about your husband."

"No, I don't want to talk about him. I only want to talk about us."

Ladro held Aeneva away from him. "I know why you don't want to talk about him, Aeneva. You are afraid."

"Why should I be afraid?"

"You are afraid because you might really love him and then you would have to choose between him and me."

Aeneva turned away. "No, that's not true. I don't even remember his face. I don't even know him."

"But you remember something, I know you do. Whenever we talk about him you try to change the subject." Ladro took Aeneva by the shoulders. "Listen to me, Aeneva. I love you. I will do anything for you. But if you get your memory back and you want to go back to your husband, I want you to go. I don't want you staying with me because you think you have to. I have learned that, in this time away from you. I want you—but more than that, I want you to be happy."

"I want to stay with you, Ladro, do you not understand that? You are everything to me, you and our child. Would you let anyone take me away from you now? Would you?" Aeneva stared up at Ladro, her eyes brimming with tears.

Ladro took her in his arms, knowing that he could never willingly send Aeneva away from him. No matter how much he felt he owed her husband, he could never give her up if she didn't want to go. He kissed her head. "We must go now. I'm not going to give Cortez the chance to catch up with us this time."

Cortez woke up to a pounding on his door. "What is it?"

Alfredo stumbled into the room, holding the back of his head. "*Patrón*, Ladro has been here. He has taken the *señora*."

216

Cortez sat up. "What? He got into this house through all of these guards?"

"*Sí, señor*. He made sounds behind the hacienda. I sent the guards out to catch him before he got inside, but he evaded them. I stayed here, to protect you and the *señora*."

"And how did he get past you? You would have seen him come up the stairs, Alfredo."

"I heard something on the stairs. I went to look. When I got to the top of the stairs he was on me. That was the last I remember. I am sorry, *Patrón*. The man is like a mountain cat."

"And my wife? He forced her to go?"

"We found her nightclothes on the floor of her room. He forced her to change and then he took her out of the house. No one saw them go. The riders are searching now."

"The bastard! I knew he would do something like this; I knew it. I want him brought back here. I don't care how long it takes or how many men it takes. I want Ladro!

"But *Patrón*, we have no idea which way they went. They are half a day ahead of us by now."

"We caught him last time, didn't we? We'll do it again."

"*Patrón*, we caught him only because they were on foot. I don't think he will be so careless this time. He was able to slip past all of the guards and into the house. I think we'll have trouble finding him this time."

Cortez walked to the window, looking out at the silhouettes of the mountains. "We need a professional tracker." He turned to face Alfredo. "And I know just where we can find one. I want a group of men handpicked by you, ready to leave in an hour."

"Where are we going, *Patrón?*"

"We are going to get our tracker, Alfredo."

Larissa walked into Trenton's room, pushing the half-open door all the way open. "What are you doing?"

Trenton didn't look up. He continued packing his things in his saddlebag. "I'm packing."

"But why? You said we would be together. Did I do something wrong?"

Trenton stopped for a moment, looking at Larissa. "I have to get out of here, Larissa. I have to get out of this Godforsaken country. There's no reason to pretend to be Cortez's man anymore."

"What will you do?"

"I'm going to search for my friend, Joe."

"Then I'm coming with you."

"No, Larissa. No. It's not the kind of life you're used to. I don't know where I'm going. I'll be riding every day, going from place to place, eating on the trail, sleeping on the ground. You've never lived that way."

"But I want to be with you, Trenton. I don't want to stay here. This place is like a prison to me."

"I can't take you with me. The trail is no place for a woman."

"But you traveled with your wife."

"She was used to it. She was born to it. You were not."

"Why don't you give me a chance, Trenton. I can

help you. I speak the language much better than you and I'm a good cook. And I ride very well. If you decide that I'm a burden then you can send me back."

Trenton sat down, running his fingers through his hair. "I haven't been honest with you, Larissa."

"Honest about what?"

"About why I really don't want you coming with me. I loved my wife very much; I don't know if I'll ever be able to love that way again. I'm not ready to be with someone else yet. It's too soon."

"But the other night . . ."

"The other night I was lonely. I had just found out that my wife is dead. I needed someone."

"And I was the most convenient?"

"I'm sorry, Larissa. I like you. I like you very much. I'm trying to be honest with you."

Larissa controlled her anger. "I know you are." She sat down next to Trenton, putting her arm around his shoulders. "I don't expect you to love me as you did your wife; I don't even expect you to love me. But I want you to give me a chance to be with you. We are both lonely people who have been hurt deeply. You need me, Trenton, whether you admit it or not."

"Larissa . . ."

Larissa put her fingers to Trenton's mouth. "Don't talk yet, let me finish. We can help each other. You can't tell me that you don't enjoy making love to me. We are good for each other, Trenton. Just give us a chance."

"I have a son, Larissa, a son who needs me very much. Someday I'll be going back to him."

"I can help you take care of him."

Trenton shook his head, resting his face in his hands. "I don't know. It's all happened so fast."

"I know and I'm sorry." Larissa leaned over and kissed Trenton on the cheek. "Let me be with you. Let me take care of you."

Trenton sat up, staring at Larissa with a fixed gaze. "I'll never forget Aeneva. She was everything to me. I don't want another woman in my life."

Larissa pulled away but she was resolved to win this battle. "All right, I understand. Just let me ride with you. I will not ask anything of you; I don't expect you to love me. I just want to get away from this place. I want to feel free again. I want to feel like a decent human being. You couldn't help your wife, but you can help me."

"All right, Larissa. All right. But don't expect anything from me because I can't give it right now."

"I won't expect anything from you, Trenton. I just want to be with you." Larissa watched Trenton as he finished packing his bags. She realized then the real hold that Aeneva had over him. She would lose him for good if he ever suspected Aeneva was still alive. They had to get as far away from this town and Cortez's name as they could. That, she knew, was the only way she could hold on to Trenton.

Aeneva reached out and touched him. She felt as if he would take her breath away. She was sure she had never felt this way before. She tried with all of her being to still the beating of her heart, for she was sure that all the world could hear it. He touched her face and she closed her eyes. His fingers caressed her lips

220

and she kissed his fingertips. His mouth touched hers and she ached inside; never had she felt such exquisite yearning. His arms came around her and their bodies touched—had she suddenly come alive with him? Was it he who stirred her very soul?

"Trenton." The name came to her lips with such ease and such love.

"I love you, Aeneva," he responded tenderly. "Don't leave me. Don't ever leave me."

She tried to hold on to his hand, but it slipped away. She looked, but she could not see him—there was an emptiness, a void where he once had been. She called for him but he was gone.

"Trenton! Trenton!" She screamed his name but he was gone.

"Aeneva, it's all right. You were dreaming."

She heard a voice, but it wasn't his voice. She looked for him, but out of the fog she saw another face. It was a good, kind face, but it wasn't the face she wanted so desperately.

"Aeneva, I'm here."

"Ladro," she said softly, almost sadly. She sat up, looking around here. "Where are we?"

"We are resting for a while. Calm down, everything's all right."

Aeneva looked around the loft and she suddenly remembered. Ladro had taken them back to the farm where she had been captured. "I must have been dreaming."

"You called someone's name in your sleep. Do you remember who it was?"

Aeneva closed her eyes and tried to remember. "I do not know. I remember that I had a dream about

221

someone, a man. He was . . ."

"He was what?"

Aeneva shook her head in embarrassment. "It does not matter."

"Please, Aeneva, I want you to be honest with me."

"I had a dream about a man. He had golden hair and light eyes. His skin was dark and he looked . . ." She stared into the darkness.

"What?"

"He looked good. He had the face of a good man."

"Do you know who it was?"

Aeneva shrugged. "I do not know. Just a man." She lay back down on the hay, turning onto her side. She felt Ladro's hand on her shoulder.

"Was it your husband, Aeneva?"

She shut her eyes, afraid to find out the truth; afraid to face the truth. "I do not know."

"Are you beginning to remember?"

"I cannot remember anything. It was only a dream, Ladro."

Ladro took Aeneva's shoulder and turned her face to him. "Sometimes dreams are the tellers of truth. You are starting to remember, but you're afraid."

"No, it was just a dream. I don't know who he was. He was just a white man."

"I think it was your husband. You even called his name."

"No!" Aeneva sat up, burying her face in her hands. "Do not do this to me, Ladro. Please."

"I'm not trying to hurt you, Aeneva. I'm trying to help you."

"You want me to go back to a man I do not even know?"

222

"No, I want you to stay with me. But I want you to stay with me because you love me, not because you can't remember him."

Aeneva leaned against Ladro, her head falling on his shoulder. "It was just a dream, Ladro. You are the only man I love, the only man I want to be with. Do not push me away."

Ladro put his arms around Aeneva, wondering how long it would be before he lost her. "I want you with me, Aeneva. I love you."

They lay together in silence, each wondering what the future held, each knowing how uncertain it was for them both.

Ladro had made his decision early that morning, while watching Aeneva as they worked in the fields together. She stood up, rubbing her lower back. As she bent backward he could see the roundness of her stomach, proof that his child was alive inside her. He knew then that he could never let her go, even if it meant forsaking his sister.

It had seemed best to come back here to Gonzalo's. Cortez wouldn't think of looking for them here. He would assume they had headed for Guadalupe del Sol to find Larissa. But he couldn't take the chance. Coming back to this place might fool Cortez for a time, but not for long. He would be somewhere around. He wouldn't give up.

It was time to take Aeneva far away from here. But could he give up Larissa after all the years he had searched for her? He had no choice. He had a child to consider now. Aeneva and the child had to come first.

223

They would have to leave very soon.

He walked over to Aeneva, who was resting under one of the shade trees. "Here, drink some water. Gonzalo doesn't want you to work. You should take better care of yourself."

Aeneva smiled as she reached for the cup. She drank greedily. "I did not know you knew so much about having babies, Ladro."

"I know enough for you to stop working so hard in the hot sun. You don't drink enough water and you hardly eat enough to keep a bird alive."

"I eat well and you know it. Do you want me to be so round that I cannot even walk?"

Ladro sat down, pulling Aeneva to him. "I wouldn't care if you were the roundest woman in the world. I would still love you."

Aeneva reached out, gently touching his face. "I think you would love me no matter what." She sighed contentedly, placing her head on Ladro's chest. "Oh, Ladro, I am so happy."

"I'll always take care of you, Aeneva. Trust me."

"I trust you." She took his hand and put it on her stomach. "Do you feel it?"

Ladro felt the firm thump against Aeneva's stomach and his heart soared. "God, it's incredible. I've never felt anything like it."

"It is a life that we created."

"Yes, a life that I am responsible for."

"You sound so serious. Take pleasure in this—our child will give us much joy."

"I just want to do the best thing for both of you."

"You will. I know you will."

Ladro wrapped his arms around Aeneva as she lay

224

back against him and the urge to protect her and his child grew even stronger. It didn't matter that she had a husband and a child somewhere else; it didn't matter that she had had a life before they met. All that mattered to Ladro now was that he keep Aeneva with him, no matter what happened.

Chapter VIII

Trenton held up, looking back at Larissa. He shook his head impatiently; he had known it would never work. Why the hell had he taken her with him anyway? Larissa finally came riding up to Trenton, her face flushed and sweaty, her expression one of anguish.

"Are we resting now?" she asked hopefully.

"We've only been riding for three hours, Larissa. If we rested every time you wanted to, we'd never get anywhere."

"But it's so hot. Don't the horses need to rest?"

"We'll rest them during the hottest part of the day. We'll keep riding for now." He kneed his horse and rode off leaving Larissa to follow along behind.

Trenton didn't know where Joe was. The only thing he knew for sure was that Cortez had recently sold some Indian women and children to a man named Hernandez, who owned a large rancho in southern Mexico. Ramon had told him that this Hernandez might be able to help him. If he couldn't find Joe, maybe he could find some Cheyennes or Arapahos. It was about time he did something to help someone.

He looked back at Larissa and slowed his pace a little, allowing her to catch up. Larissa was different from the sweet girl he had first met. When he had met her she seemed vulnerable, young and naive; now suddenly, she seemed calculating, cold, and very grown up. He had known that she was in love with him. That should have warned him against taking her with him. But he couldn't help feeling sorry for her, too. She had never had anyone to care for her. It would do him good to think of someone else.

They stopped at midday to rest. Larissa looked as though she would faint; Trenton took care of her horse while she lay down. When Trenton was through with the horses, he brought Larissa a piece of dried meat and let her drink some water.

"Easy now, just small sips."

Larissa gulped hungrily at the water. "Please, Trenton, just a little more."

"No, that's enough for now. If you drink too much you'll get sick."

"Oh, I don't care," Larissa responded listlessly, lying down on her side. "I don't care. I hate it out here."

"I'm sorry, but I warned you. Just a few more days and we'll reach a town. You can stay there."

"No!" She sat up, leaning back against a rock for support. "I want to go with you."

"You can't make it. We've only been on the trail four days now and you can barely keep up with me. This isn't the kind of life for you, Larissa. I told you that before."

"Please don't make me go back there, Trenton. Please." Larissa leaned her head on Trenton's lap, covering her face with her hands. "I am doing the best I can."

"I know," Trenton said with as much patience as he could, "but you can't go any further with me. I need to find my friend and you'll just slow me down. I'm sorry, but that's the way it is."

"I understand," Larissa responded coldly, sitting up. "I'll do as you say."

"Please try to understand, Larissa . . ."

"I understand completely. You are just like every other man I've known in my life. You have used me, gotten what you wanted from me, and now you have no more use for me. I do understand, Trenton, more clearly than you think."

Trenton tried to touch Larissa, but she pulled away from him. "When I head north I'll take you with me."

"Do not make me promises. I know how you feel about your wife, even though she is dead. I will never be able to take her place. So just take me with you to the nearest town and I will find my own way from there. You do not have to worry about me anymore."

Trenton didn't argue. What Larissa had said was true. No woman could take Aeneva's place. He had tried with Larissa, but he could not forget Aeneva because in the deepest part of his heart he couldn't yet admit that she was dead. He couldn't believe it because he didn't feel it. The way he felt about Aeneva was as alive as the sun shining on the ground before him. She couldn't be dead. He would

229

know it. He shook his head. Someday he would have to accept it. Someday he would be able to accept it without wanting to die. But for now, he would hold on to the feeling that his wife was still alive somewhere.

Aeneva walked slowly to the edge of the fields. She smiled down at the tiny child who held her hand. He was the youngest of Gonzalo's and Elena's children. His name was Pablo and he always had a smile on his face.

"Do you want to climb the rocks, Pablo?"

"*Sí, sí!*" the boy answered excitedly, scurrying up the rocks well ahead of Aeneva. When she got to the top of the rocks she sat down, looking at the valley below them. It was a beautiful place, one that was perfect for raising children and having a good life. She watched Pablo as he scampered up and down the rocks, laughing as he did so. She smiled at the dark head and the shining face; it reminded her of other dark faces. She stared out into the distance, motionless. She saw two young boys and a young girl climbing over rocks, holding small bows and arrows, fierce looks on their faces. She saw the blond-haired boy and she knew his name was Trenton. She knew it as surely as she knew this was the boy she had loved, the boy who had grown into manhood and married her. She shut her eyes, trying to remember, but nothing was clear, nothing except his face and his smile.

"Aeneva, watch!"

Aeneva heard Pablo's voice, but she saw Trenton's

face and the faces of her brothers, Brave Wolf and Coyote Boy. Tears came to her eyes. Her brothers. They had always been so close; they had always protected her and taken care of her. They had always loved her. She felt a rush of warmth as she recalled the many times they had played together as children, and fought side by side as adults. She remembered the time they were caught in a snowstorm as children, and Brave Wolf had walked into a pack of wolves and took some of their meat for food. She remembered a tall man, a man who sat high on a horse, a man so handsome and strong and proud that she knew it was her grandfather, Stalking Horse. She remembered his voice and the way he had loved her so fiercely. And she remembered her grandmother, Sun Dancer, the woman who had taught her everything that was important. The woman who had always stood by her and loved her. The woman whom everyone had loved. Aeneva remembered; could not stop remembering. Her past rushed into her mind, into her heart.

"Grandmother," Aeneva whispered, tears streaming down her cheeks. "Oh, Grandmother, what have I done?" She wrapped her arms around her stomach and just as she did so, the life from within responded with a sharp kick, as if to let her know of its existence. "What have I done, Grandmother? I am carrying Ladro's child inside of me. This should be Trenton's child."

And she remembered the child that she had lost, the child that she and Trenton had wanted so badly. Now she was carrying another man's child, the child of a man she loved, or thought she loved. Now that she remembered Trenton, she was unsure of how she

231

felt about Ladro. He had been good to her, he had helped her and protected her, he had loved her, but now she couldn't know whether or not she loved him. She looked out across the fields and saw a figure walking toward the rocks and she knew it was Ladro. She sank to the rocky ground, forcing herself to breathe slowly. Should she tell him that she remembered everything about her past? Should she tell him that she was unsure of her feelings for him?

Trembling under the weight of her confusion, she watched him as he came up the rocks. He climbed easily, smiling. Pablo called to him and he grinned, waving the boy homeward. "Your mama needs you, Pablito." The boy scampered away. Aeneva saw the look of love on his face when he looked at her. When he held out his hand to her she took it, unable to deny him. He pulled her up to him and kissed her passionately.

"You looked so beautiful sitting here. I just wanted to take you in my arms."

"Ladro . . ."

"No, don't talk." He pressed his mouth to hers, stopping any words she might have spoken. He held her to him. "You are my life, Aeneva. I saw you here on the rocks and I knew it. I want to say it. I will never let anything happen to you or our child. I will always take care of you."

Aeneva smiled weakly at Ladro's words, fighting the tangle of her feelings. She buried her head in his chest, unable to look into his eyes.

"Are you all right? You're not ill?"

"No, I am not ill."

"What is it? Something is bothering you."

Aeneva shook her head, pulling away from Ladro. "It is nothing. Perhaps I am just tired of running. I wish I had a home and a people. I wish . . ."

"You wish you had a husband, is that it?" Ladro smiled, taking Aeneva's face in his large hands. "If that is all that is upsetting you, let's get married. We will find a priest and get married as soon as possible."

"But our marriage would not be real, Ladro, just as the one with Cortez was not real."

"But the feelings we have for each other, they are very real, aren't they?" Ladro stared into Aeneva's large, dark eyes and for the first time he saw them waver. "What is it, Aeneva?"

Aeneva pulled away, trying to control the tumult of feelings that threatened to explode inside her. "I am beginning to remember, Ladro." She looked up at him, pleading for his understanding, but she could see the look on his face change immediately. She watched as he turned away and walked to the edge of the rocks, looking down at the small valley.

"You remember your husband?"

"Yes," she responded quietly.

"And do you love him as much as it was said you did?"

Aeneva started to reach out to touch Ladro but quickly withdrew her hand. "Yes," she said simply.

Ladro continued to stare, unmoving, at the valley below them. His anger grew until he felt as if he could destroy the world. He turned to Aeneva, his black eyes burning with anger. "So what do we do now? Do I take you back to him? Or do I keep you here for myself?"

"Do not be angry, Ladro. I did not plan this. I never wanted . . . We knew that this could happen."

"Yes, we knew, but we never believed it would happen, did we? You were the one who asked to stay with me, remember? You didn't want to go back to your husband even when I spoke of him. You wanted to stay with me. You said I was your only love, your only man."

"And you were."

"But not now." Ladro kicked at the rocks. "So, Aeneva, what will you tell your husband about me? Will you tell him that you loved me for a while until you could remember him, or will you tell him that I forced you to stay with me the entire time?"

"I will tell him the truth."

"And what is the truth? Tell me, Aeneva, because I'm not sure anymore."

"The truth is that I do love you. I do love you, Ladro. You helped me when you could have sold me and forgotten about me. You risked your life for me; and you loved me more than I deserved to be loved." Aeneva sat down, rubbing her hands over her skirt. "Try to understand, Ladro. This is not easy for me. I have loved my husband since I was a child; I loved him from the first moment I saw him. We have been through so much together and yet we have always managed to keep our love strong. He is a good man. I know he is probably looking for me. He will not give up until he finds me."

"Is this supposed to make me feel better?"

"No, I just have to tell you how I feel."

"Well, tell me, Aeneva, how do you feel?" Ladro walked to her, pulling her up, holding her shoulders tightly. "Can you spend the rest of your life with me? And what about our child? Will you take it from me and go back to your husband? Or will I take it from you and let you go back to your husband?"

"Please, Ladro, do not do this to me."

"Do what?"

"Torture me. You want to punish me for remembering."

"No, I don't want to punish you, I want to love you. I want you to have our child and feel that you can't live without me. I want you to love me beyond all else."

Aeneva turned away. "You will not let me go, will you, Ladro?"

"I will not hold you against your will, Aeneva."

"You will not?"

"No. But the child will stay."

"No, you cannot do that to me. It is my child."

"It is our child. I have as much right to it as you do. If you leave, then at least I want the only part of you I can have."

Aeneva nodded slowly. There was no way out, then. "I will not leave you, Ladro." Her eyes stared into his. "I will not leave my child."

"And if your husband comes for you?"

"I cannot say what will happen if he comes. I cannot say." She turned away trying to control the tears that filled her eyes. How could she refuse to go with Trenton if he came for her? How could she look into those eyes that were so clear and blue and tell him that she was carrying another man's child? She felt Ladro's hands on her shoulders and she tried to pull away from him, but he turned her to face him.

He gently wiped the tears from her cheeks.

"I love you, Aeneva, and I thought you loved me. Do you think I want to keep you as my prisoner? I do not. I want you to stay with me because you love me. I want us to raise our child together in love."

"But how can I do that when I remember the man I loved before I loved you? My mind is racing with memories and it will not stop. Just because I stay here with you and have your child, it does not mean I will forget my husband."

"Then go back to him. It is your choice."

"There is no choice when you tell me I must give up my child as well. You know that I will not do that."

"If you love your husband as much as you say you do, then you will do anything to be with him." Ladro shrugged his shoulders. "What does it matter, Aeneva? It is only one child. You can have many others with your husband."

"But this is *your* child," Aeneva cried before she could stop the words. "Oh, God." She buried her face in her hands.

"You do love me," Ladro said gently, putting his arms around Aeneva. "I don't want you to suffer, Aeneva. We will wait. There is nothing else we can do. We will see how things work out."

Aeneva nodded feebly, holding on to Ladro, as if afraid to ever let him go. She did love him, more than she had imagined she could; but she also loved Trenton, and her love for him was the kind of love that could never die.

Cortez screamed at Ramon. "What do you mean

he's gone? I have to find him. Where did he go?"

"He and Larissa left a few days ago."

"But where did he say he was going, you imbecile?"

"I told him of Hernandez and his ranch. I told him that there was a possibility that some Indian women could be there. He is a man who is lost, Cortez. I think he just wanted to be gone from here. He asked many questions about Hernandez and his family. I know he's headed there."

"Good, good. That is at least a week's ride and Larissa is not used to that kind of traveling. It will take them longer." Cortez turned to one of his men. "Pedro, I want you to ride as quickly as you can to Hernandez's rancho. Tell the gringo that Ladro is alive and has stolen money from me. I need him to track the thief. He will ask about the woman. Tell him nothing. And talk to him alone, Pedro. Make sure Larissa does not hear."

"*Sí, Patrón*. Anything else?"

"No." Cortez walked to the window that overlooked the garden he had enjoyed for so many years. The gringo would be shocked to find out that he was tracking his own wife, but by the time he found out it would be too late. He and Ladro would be dead. Aeneva and Larissa would be taken back to the rancho. He laughed, thinking of the fun he would have with the two women. This time he would be assured of an heir. "Ah, Emiliano, sometimes I think you are too smart for everyone." He smiled wider, knowing that soon he would have it all.

Trenton waited impatiently as *Señor* Hernandez

237

finished his business and called him into his study. He had left Larissa in the kitchen, exhausted and weak. Trenton had already decided he was going to leave her here with Hernandez.

"*Señor*, the *Patrón* will see you now."

Trenton stood up and followed the man into the study, a room that was not unlike Cortez's in its richness and earnestness to please. Trenton waited. Hernandez held his hand up to signal that he would be finished writing in a moment. He was middle-aged, graying, but lean and strong. He did not look like the kind of man who would deal in slaves.

"Yes, can I help you, *señor?*"

"I am looking for some Indians. I was told that you had just bought some Indian women and children."

"And from whom did you hear this rumor, *señor?*"

Trenton stood up, walking over to the man's desk. "Look, I'm not here to play games. I've ridden a long way. Now either you tell me of your own free will or I'll find a way to force it out of you."

Hernandez laid down his pen, folding his hands on the desk in front of him. "I do not like threats, *señor*, especially in my own home."

"And I don't like people who deal in slaves, especially women and children."

"Who are you, *señor?*"

"My name is Trenton Hawkins. I was married to a Cheyenne woman. She was taken by a Comanchero. I came to Mexico to get her back . . . but I was too late. It's possible I know some of the women you have. I'm going north soon. I have money. I'll buy them from you if I have to."

"Is that all, *señor?*"

"No, I'm looking for a black man. He's tall, taller than me, and he's smart."

"Well, I am sorry, *señor*, but I have seen neither this man nor the women and children of whom you speak."

Trenton stepped close. "Let's be honest with each other, Hernandez. You will deal in anything that will make you money."

"That is not quite true, *señor*."

"I want these people, Hernandez, and I'll do it with or without your help."

Hernandez took a thick cigar out of a box, rolling it between his fingers and sniffing it. "Now, I will be honest with you, *señor*. I have no Indians, but others near here buy women and children. I can find out. I have many sources."

"Could you do that for me?"

"But why *would* I do that for you, *señor*?" Hernandez bit off the end of the cigar and lit it.

"I hear you are the father of three daughters, *señor*. What would you do if one of them were taken away from you to another country? Wouldn't you do everything in your power to get her back?"

"Of course I would."

"Then I want you to do this for me because it is the right thing to do."

"I do not always do what is right, *señor*. Do not mistake me for a saint."

"I would never do that, Hernandez." Trenton walked around the room observing the portraits of Hernandez's three daughters. "Very pretty girls."

"Yes, they are."

"And they are all at school in Mexico City?"

Hernandez sat up suddenly. "What are you saying, *señor?*"

"I'm saying that if you don't get me the information I need I have friends in Mexico City who are ready to kidnap one or all of your daughters." Trenton silently thanked Ramon for all he had told him about Hernandez. The bluff might work.

Hernandez stood up, banging his hand on the desk. "No! That is impossible!"

"Your oldest daughter, Yolanda, goes to the school of the Sacred Heart, your second daughter, Josephina, goes to the School of Saint Veronica, and your youngest . . ."

"No, you cannot be serious." Hernandez came out from around the desk. "My daughters are innocent. They have done nothing."

"Neither had my wife. Neither have any of the other women or children."

Hernandez nodded. "I understand." He walked to the portraits of his daughters, looking at each one lovingly. "And how do I know that you are telling me the truth, *señor?* How do I know you can do what you say?"

"You don't. But do you want to take the chance?"

"I could send someone to warn them."

"You could but it wouldn't do you much good. My men are good at what they do."

"You must have loved your wife very much. You said you were too late to help her. She is dead then?"

"Just as you love your daughters, *señor,*" Trenton said, ignoring the question. Somewhere deep inside he was still unable to believe Aeneva was gone.

"All right, I will find out what I can. You can stay

240

ZEBRA HOME SUBSCRIPTION SERVICES, INC.

P.O. BOX 5214

120 BRIGHTON ROAD
CLIFTON, NEW JERSEY 07015-5214

Get a Free
Zebra
Historical
Romance

*a $3.95
value*

─── FREE ───

BOOK CERTIFICATE

ZEBRA HOME SUBSCRIPTION SERVICE, INC.

YES! Please start my subscription to Zebra Historical Romances and send me my free Zebra Novel along with my first month's Romances. I understand that I may preview these four new Zebra Historical Romances Free for 10 days. If I'm not satisfied with them I may return the four books within 10 days and owe nothing. Otherwise I will pay just $3.50 each, a total of $14.00 (a $15.80 value—I save $1.80). Then each month I will receive the 4 newest titles as soon as they come off the press for the same 10 day Free preview and low price. I may return any shipment and I may cancel this arrangement at any time. There is no minimum number of books to buy and there are no shipping, handling or postage charges. Regardless of what I do, the FREE book is mine to keep.

Name _____

(Please Print)

Address _____ Apt. # _____

City _____ State _____ Zip _____

Telephone ( ) _____

Signature _____

(if under 18, parent or guardian must sign)

Terms and offer subject to change without notice.

10-89

MAIL IN THE COUPON
BELOW TODAY

GET FREE GIFT

To get your Free **ZEBRA HISTORICAL ROMANCE** fill out the coupon below and send it in today. As soon as we receive the coupon, we'll send your first month's books to preview Free for 10 days along with your **FREE NOVEL.**

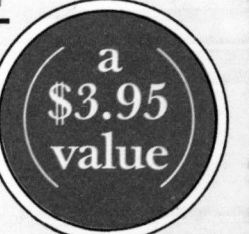

here in the guest room of my home. But what if I cannot find out anything?"

"Do the best you can. I want to find my friends, Hernandez, and my wife's people."

"I will do my best, *señor*."

Larissa bent down to pick some flowers. "Aren't they lovely. I could live on a place like this for the rest of my life."

"Why don't you talk to Hernandez? I hear he's a widower."

"Be serious, Trenton. We could live on a place like this together."

"Larissa, I told you before . . ."

"I know what you told me, but there is something I haven't told you. I have money, a lot of money. Cortez gave me many expensive jewels."

"I don't want your money, Larissa. And I don't want a ranch like this."

"What do you want then?"

"I want to find my friend, and my wife's people."

"And after that?"

"I'll head north. I still have a son waiting for me."

"So you will go on with your life. You are beginning to accept that your wife is dead?"

"I won't believe that until I have proof."

"What proof do you need? Cortez would not lie about this."

"I think he would do anything that would serve his own purposes."

"But why?"

"I don't know that yet, but I'll find out." Trenton

started to walk away but stopped when he saw a rider coming. It was one of Hernandez's men.

"*Señor,* the *Patrón* wants to see you immediately. He says it is very important." He looked at Larissa. "You go on ahead. I will ride with the *señorita.*"

Trenton nodded and rode in the direction of the rancho. He rode fast, hoping that Hernandez had finally found out about Joe. When he reached the rancho he dismounted and ran up to the hacienda. He went in and a servant led him to Hernandez's study.

"What is it? Have you found . . ." Trenton stopped when he saw the man standing next to Hernandez. He looked familiar. "You are one of Cortez's men. Pedro, isn't it?"

"*Sí, señor.*"

"What do you want?"

"I have a message from Cortez."

"A message? What does he want?"

"He says he needs your help."

"What does he need my help for?"

"He needs you to track someone."

"Who?"

"Ladro."

The room was intensely silent until Trenton spoke. "Ladro is alive?"

"*Sí, señor.*"

"And the woman?"

"I know nothing of the woman, *señor.* I just know that Ladro came into Cortez's hacienda and stole some of his money, a lot of money."

"How does he know it was Ladro?"

"He left a message telling Cortez that he was using

the money to find his sister. He said he would come back for Cortez. Cortez is scared. He is afraid Ladro will kill him."

"And he wants me to track him? Why me?"

"Because you told him you are one of the best, *señor*. He will do anything to find Ladro."

"You're sure he said nothing of the woman who was with Ladro?"

"No, *señor*."

"When will Cortez be here?"

"He should be here in two days."

"How do I know he is telling me the truth, Pedro?"

The man shook his head. "You don't, *señor*, you never know with Cortez. But I do know that he is scared. Ladro is alive and he wants to find him."

Trenton nodded. If Ladro was alive he would be able to tell him about Aeneva. He knew she wasn't dead, he knew it. But if she wasn't with Ladro, where was she?

Aeneva felt Ladro's hand move down her hip and she closed her eyes. He moved close to her, kissing her shoulder, sliding his hand under her arm to her breasts. She tried to pull away but he held her in a way that was not physical; he held her in emotional bondage. His hand went to her slightly rounded stomach and she knew the pride and possessiveness that he felt. She knew that she could never leave him willingly, because to do that would also be to leave her child.

Her mind could not stop thinking of Nathan—she

243

wondered how he was and what he was doing. He was such a beautiful child, so loving, and so used to being loved. She missed him. She wondered if she would ever see him again.

Ladro's arms went around her and he held her to him. She rubbed his hands, knowing how much he loved her, knowing that he needed her.

"Are you all right, Aeneva?"

"Yes," she responded quietly, knowing that she would have to be all right. She could not live in the past now that she had regained her memory. Her life was the present and the future was with Ladro and their child. She could only hope that Trenton and Nathan were together and that they would find a new life for themselves. Without her.

Larissa blossomed in the days that she spent at Hernandez's rancho. As Trenton had suggested, this was the kind of life she was used to, not the life of traveling and being on the trail. She enjoyed being pampered and being waited on. She assumed that she and Trenton were staying at the rancho for a while. She had no idea that Cortez was coming to the hacienda until the day he arrived. She was sitting in the courtyard watching the fish in the small pond when she heard the riders approach. She was not particularly interested; people came and went all of the time. She did not look up from the pool until she heard Cortez's voice.

"Take me to Hernandez immediately!"

Larissa turned, startled upon hearing the familiar voice. "Emiliano, what are you doing here?"

244

"Ah, Larissa, I am surprised you lasted this long." Cortez walked up to her, taking her hand and kissing it in a most ungentlemanly manner.

Larissa pulled her hand away. "What are you doing here, Emiliano? What if Trenton sees you?"

"I hope that he does, my dear, because it is he that I have come here to see."

"No! You promised me. You promised me, Emiliano!"

"I am sorry about that, Larissa, but sometimes promises have to be broken. Things have changed."

"What has changed?"

"Your brother is alive and he has taken my wife. I want her back and I want your brother dead. It's all very simple."

"Ladro is alive?"

"Yes, but not for long."

"And you expect Trenton to lead you to them? Do you actually think that he will hunt down his own wife for you?"

"He won't know that his wife is with Ladro."

"You're crazy, Emiliano, the man is not stupid."

Cortez grabbed Larissa by the shoulders, squeezing them so hard tears came to her eyes. "I've told you before not to call me crazy. I know exactly what I am doing. The gringo just needs to know that Ladro stole some money from me. He does not need to know more. And you, dear Larissa, will not tell him, do you understand?"

Larissa stared at Cortez. "Yes, I understand."

"Good, because if you tell him anything, I will kill you. If you are good, I may spare him for you. But if you don't do as I say, he's a dead man for sure."

"You'll have to kill him anyway when he sees his wife. He'll never let her go back to you."

"He won't have a choice. He is only one man against all of my men."

"You are a hateful person, Emiliano. I cannot believe that there was a time when I actually thought I cared for you."

"Do not fool yourself, Larissa, there is no such thing as love. The only thing that matters is power. And I have power. Love is a foolish, useless emotion that turns men like the gringo and Ladro into little boys."

Larissa pulled away from Cortez, walking stiffly back to the pool. She watched the fish swim around in the clear water and waited for Cortez to leave. When he did not, she looked up and found him staring at her. "What do you want, Emiliano? Haven't you done enough already?"

"Do not cross me, Larissa, or you will pay for it. You will pay for it dearly."

Larissa's eyes met Cortez's and she did not lower her gaze. When he left, she sat down by the pool, reaching into the cool water. She had never done anything admirable in her life; she had never taken a chance on being honorable. Her life had been easy compared to Ladro's. He had never given up searching for her, never. Now there was a chance that she could save him. She remembered Trenton telling her how important honor was to the Indians and to him. Well, for once in her life she would do something honorable, even if it meant losing the only man she had ever loved.

* * *

"So, Cortez, why do you think Ladro only stole money out of your house? If he hates you so much, why didn't he just kill you and have it over with?" Trenton sat across from Cortez at the table, carefully cutting his thick piece of meat.

"If I knew that, I wouldn't have to find the man. I only know he has what belongs to me and I want it back."

"What else did he take from you, Cortez?"

Cortez tried to evade Trenton's piercing blue eyes; the man was too smart. He had to come up with a better answer. "He took something that was even more precious to me than my money."

"What?"

"My family ring. It has my family crest on it; it belonged to my great-grandfather. It is a very valuable ring, but it is more than that—it gives me my name and my heritage. Ladro knows what it means to me. The bastard knows."

Trenton looked at Cortez, and seeing the glazed look in his eyes, he believed him. Nothing mattered more to Cortez than pride and legitimatizing his name. The ring would mean a lot to him. "So, he knows you'll come after him to get the ring."

"Yes. We believe he's gone east but we don't know where. There is rough country east of my rancho. It is all rock and brush, mountainous. And beyond that is the desert. That's why I need you."

"And what happens when we find Ladro?"

"I will kill him of course."

"And what about the woman who was with him?"

"But I told you, she is dead."

"You also told me that Ladro was dead." Trenton took a sip of wine. "I want to talk to Ladro first, then you can do whatever you want with him." Trenton got up from the table. "I'll be ready to leave at dawn. Have your men ready."

Cortez watched Trenton as he walked from the room, an evil smile appearing on his face. It would be interesting when the gringo and Ladro met. He was going to enjoy this.

Trenton opened his eyes when he heard the light knock on the door. Before he was able to get up, the door opened and Larissa walked in.

"Trenton, I must talk to you."

"What is it, Larissa?"

"When are you going to look for my brother?"

"You know about Ladro?" Trenton sat up and ran his fingers through his hair. "We're leaving at dawn."

"Trenton, I must know something." Larissa stood, rubbing her hands together. "Is there a chance that you will ever love me?"

"What do you want from me, Larissa?"

"The truth. I want the truth, Trenton."

Trenton looked at the beautiful young woman, holding out his hands to her. "Sit down, please. I don't know what to tell you except how I feel. I don't feel that Aeneva is dead, Larissa. We have been a part of each other for so long now that I'm sure I would know it if she were. I have loved her all of my life. We have shared things that only we can understand. Even if I found out that Aeneva were dead, I don't think I could love another woman, Larissa. Not even you."

"But you made love to me, Trenton. You said you cared for me."

"I do care for you. I'm sorry if I hurt you, but I was honest with you from the beginning."

"Yes, you were honest. That is more than I have been with you."

"You've been honest with me. You told me all about your past with Cortez."

"But there are some things I chose not to tell you."

"What are you talking about?"

"I am now going to be honest with you, because I know how important honor is to you. You have given me that much, Trenton. Honor." Larissa touched Trenton's face, leaning over to kiss his cheek as if for the last time. "Your wife is alive. She is with Ladro."

Trenton stared at the floor, his heart pounding. "I knew it. I knew she was alive. How long have you known?"

"I've known since Emiliano first came to Guadalupe del Sol. I wanted you so badly, Trenton. You were the only man who had ever treated me decently. I made a deal with Emiliano. He would tell you your wife was dead and I wouldn't tell you that he had married her."

"Damn him!" Trenton pounded his fist into his leg. "And what about your brother? Didn't you care about him? Didn't you care that he's been searching for you all of these years?"

"Of course I cared, but I hadn't seen him for twelve years. To me, Ladro was just a boy, just a memory. But you were real and you made me feel clean inside. You did not make me feel like a whore."

"Why are you telling me this now?"

"Because I realize that you will never love me. We could never have the kind of love you and your wife have. And I want to do something good. I am not a bad person, Trenton."

Trenton pulled Larissa to him, stroking her hair. "You have done an honorable thing, Larissa. I will always be thankful."

"You must leave tonight, right now, before Cortez gets up. When you are gone he will have no way to find Ladro or your wife. But I must ask two things of you."

"What are they?"

"I must ask that you take me with you."

"I can't do that. You'll only slow me down."

"Please, Trenton. I want to see my brother. If you take me to him, he and I can go away somewhere, somewhere far from Cortez."

"What's the other thing?"

"Do not kill Ladro. I know you are angry with him, but he has taken care of your wife."

"You're asking a lot, Larissa."

"I don't think so. I think you already respect my brother; you and he are much the same."

"I won't kill him, but will he kill me? If he is in love with Aeneva, he might never let her go."

"He is a good man, I believe that. He will let her go if it is what she wants."

"All right. I'll take you with me. But if you fall behind, I'll leave you. I don't have the time to wait for you."

"I understand." She stood up. "I can be ready in minutes."

250

"No, wait. We'll travel with Cortez."

"No! We cannot do that. The man is a murderer. He will kill you once you have led him to Ladro. Trenton, this is crazy."

"Once I get close enough to your brother I'll go on ahead and warn them."

"But why travel with Cortez at all?"

"Because I want to be there when he sees Aeneva. I want to see the look on his face before I kill him."

"This is the wrong time for pride, Trenton. You must forget about Emiliano and get your wife."

"I'm not being proud, Larissa, I'm being practical also. Cortez has lots of men and equipment. We'll be traveling through rough country at first, and desert after that. We'll be safer with a large group. When we're close enough to Ladro and Aeneva you and I will find a way to get to them. Then I will go back to Cortez. I imagine Ladro would like to go back with me."

Larissa smiled. "Yes, I'm sure he would." Larissa put her arms around Trenton, hugging him fiercely. "You are a good man, Trenton. I will always love you."

"And I'll never forget what you've done for me tonight, Larissa. You would make your parents proud."

Larissa's eyes filled with tears. "Thank you. I will be ready to travel in the morning. You will be proud of me this time." She walked to the door, stopping as she put her hand on the handle. "What if Emiliano does not want me to come?"

"How can he argue? I am his guide and he needs me. I will tell him that I need you to keep me warm at night."

Larissa smiled broadly. "Be careful or I will act the part. Sleep well."

"Sleep well." Trenton got up from the bed, putting on his clothes. When he was completely dressed he checked his pistols and two rifles, making sure they were clean and loaded. He packed his saddlebags and put them by his guns. He lay down on top of the bed, his hands behind his head. So, Cortez had known about Aeneva the entire time. And Ladro had stolen Aeneva away from Cortez. Where would a man like Ladro go to keep from being found?

He closed his eyes and he thought about Aeneva. He wanted her so badly his body ached, and he needed her more than he had ever needed anyone in his life. He wondered what Ladro would do when he found them? Surely, a man who had risked his life to save a woman wouldn't just turn her over to another man, even if the man was her husband. But Trenton had a feeling that Ladro was a man of honor. He was counting on that honor to make Ladro realize that once Trenton found Aeneva, he would never give her up again.

Chapter IX

It had been hard to leave Gonzalo and Elena. Gonzalo had tried to persuade them to stay, but Ladro had explained why they could not. "Cortez will come looking for us soon and I don't want you and Elena and the children in any danger. You've done too much for us already."

"But where will you go?" Elena had asked Ladro.

"There is a place." Ladro's eyes had narrowed as if recalling the place in exact detail. "It is called El Circulo. Few have heard of it. It is beyond the desert."

"What kind of place is this?"

"It is a place where people who are in trouble can go."

"You have people there?" Gonzalo had asked in a concerned voice.

Ladro smiled. "Yes, Ignacio and Marcela. They took care of me after my family was killed. They will be happy to see me and Aeneva. Do not worry, we will be safe."

Aeneva smiled with pleasure at the memory of

Gonzalo's face when Ladro had given him the spirited mare they had taken from Cortez's barn. A man like Gonzalo could never have hoped to own such a fine animal. Aeneva stroked the neck of the sturdy mount Gonzalo had given her. She looked up at the sky, shielding her eyes from the glaring sun.

"Is there never a winter here in Mexico?"

"Yes, there is winter, but the weather stays warm almost all year. It's late fall now."

"In my land it is beginning to get cold now. We may have already had the first snow."

"Do you miss it?"

"Sometimes. I liked the snow. Perhaps that is why I was named after it."

"Come on, we better keep riding."

Aeneva kneed her horse. She tried to keep her mind off Trenton, but she found that almost impossible to do. Daily, things came back to her about her past, things that she hadn't recalled in a long time. But as she felt the life inside her move, she knew she had to forget about Trenton.

They rode until well after dark, Ladro pushing Aeneva hard. Ever since they had left Gonzalo's farm the week before, Ladro had become surly and taciturn, usually speaking only when spoken to. If Aeneva mentioned anything about her past, he changed the subject immediately or wouldn't respond. Aeneva wondered how long it would be like this between them.

As they sat around the small fire drinking the precious coffee that Gonzalo had given them, Aeneva looked over at Ladro. He was staring into the fire, his strong face betraying no sign of emotion.

"What is it, Ladro? Have I done something to make you angry?"

"No," Ladro responded coldly, not turning to look at Aeneva.

"Please talk to me, Ladro. I cannot take this silence."

When Ladro turned to Aeneva, there was a certain sadness in his expression. "I cannot keep you with me, Aeneva."

Aeneva put down her cup and moved to Ladro. "I am going to stay with you. We are going to raise our child together."

"No, you don't understand."

"I do not understand. I thought you loved me."

"I love you more than you will ever know, Aeneva. I love you more than I thought it possible to love another person. I thought I would do anything to keep you with me, even threaten to take our child away from you, but I can't do that."

"Ladro . . ."

"I love you too much and you don't love me enough. You will always be thinking of him. When I am holding you in my arms and I am making love to you, how do I know you won't be thinking of him?"

Aeneva rested her head against Ladro's shoulder. She could not answer his question because she knew he was right. "I do love you, Ladro. I want to stay with you."

"But you want to be with him more than you want to be with me. That is the truth of it, Aeneva."

"I do not know. I am so confused. Never did I think it was possible to love two people at the same time."

"It is possible. But usually one love is stronger

than the other. Your love for your husband is stronger than your love for me." Ladro stood up, throwing the rest of his coffee into the fire. He walked to the edge of the camp, his hands tucked into the back of his pants. Aeneva walked up behind him, putting her arm through his.

"I do not want to leave you, Ladro."

"But you will." He turned around, cupping Aeneva's chin in his hand. "In time you will think of me as your captor instead of your lover. I don't want to be like Cortez; I don't want you to be my prisoner."

"I will never be your prisoner. I can leave with you now and never turn back."

"And could you be happy?"

"Yes, I could be happy."

"Could you be as happy as you were with him?"

"I cannot compare these things, Ladro. There were times even with Trenton when I was not completely happy. It is not the nature of human beings to be happy all of the time."

"God, Aeneva." Ladro took her in his arms, holding her tightly to him. "I want you to be with me. I want you to be happy."

"Then trust me, I will be happy with you."

"And your husband?"

Aeneva turned away, not wanting Ladro to see the tears in her eyes. "My husband will be fine without me. As long as he has his son to go home to, he will build a new life."

Ladro walked up behind Aeneva and hugged her fiercely. He wanted to tell her that he'd take her back to her husband, but he could not. He loved her and he wanted her with him. He did not possess the kind of honor of which she had so often spoken, the kind of honor that would force him to do the right thing. Aeneva had that kind of honor. Someday, perhaps he would, too. But not now, not while he could hold her in his arms and love her. Honor did not matter to him now.

Larissa walked out of the camp, sitting down by the small stream. She dangled her legs in the water, relishing the feel of the cool water on her swollen feet. She leaned back on her hands, looking up into the sky. She looked at the thousands of stars. Her parents had often told her, when she was a child, that the stars were all beloved people who had gone to heaven.

"Tired, my dear Larissa?"

Larissa stiffened at the sound of Cortez's voice. She had been expecting him to confront her ever since they had started three days ago, but Trenton had always managed to keep them apart. "Emiliano. What do you want?"

"I want nothing from you, Larissa." Cortez sat down next to her, running his fingers through her hair. "I hope you have not said anything to our friend."

"If I had, do you think he would be leading you to his wife?"

"Probably not, but one never knows. Perhaps he has a plan in mind."

"A plan? Don't be silly. He thinks he is leading you to Ladro because Ladro might know something

257

about his wife."

"He has not asked you anything?"

"Yes, he asked me if he could trust you."

"And what did you tell him?"

"Of course not. What did you think I would tell him?"

Cortez laughed, nodding his head in approval. "Ah, Larissa, I have taught you well. I should never have doubted you. You have always served me admirably."

"You have not done the same for me."

"Yes, regrettably I had to lie to you. There was no other choice. Ladro stole something that was mine."

"Aren't you forgetting something, Emiliano? She is not yours."

"It's a minor problem."

"You told me you would not kill him."

"I cannot make any more promises to you, my dear. I will do what I have to do to get the woman back."

"Including murdering my brother and my lover."

"If it is necessary, yes. But it is up to you to change the outcome."

"How can I change the outcome?"

"You can make Trenton fall in love with you before we get there. He has not seen his wife in a long time. Perhaps his feelings for her aren't as strong as they used to be. And I have seen the way he looks at you; he can't stand to have you out of his sight."

"I don't know."

"You can do anything you set your mind to, Larissa. If you want your man to remain alive, I suggest you make him fall in love with you before we find his wife."

"And what about Ladro?"

"What about Ladro? He should have been dead a long time ago."

"I want to see him, Emiliano. I want him to live. Please, do not kill him."

"I cannot make any promises about Ladro. If I don't kill him, he will kill me." Cortez reached over and patted Larissa's cheek. "Do not be so sad, *querida*. At least you will have one of the men you love."

"Larissa, are you out there?"

Cortez turned at the sound of Trenton's voice. "Ah, it is your lover coming to search for you. How sweet." Cortez stood up, dusting off his pants. "I should leave before he shoots me." Cortez walked by Trenton, lifting his hand in a small wave.

Trenton went to Larissa. "Are you all right? He didn't hurt you?"

"No, I am fine. He wanted to talk to me."

"About what?"

"About you. He wanted to know if I told you anything." Larissa laughed. "I told him that you couldn't trust him. He liked that."

"Did he believe you?"

"I think so." She looked back over her shoulder. "He plans to kill Ladro immediately. He might let you live if you act as if you are in love with me."

"So, I'm supposed to lead him to Aeneva and act like I don't love her anymore when I see her?" Trenton threw a rock into the stream. "The man is crazy."

"He's not just crazy, Trenton. He is defending his land. Nothing else matters to him. I'm afraid of what

259

he will do once we get to Ladro. I still think we should leave him now, while we can."

"No, we need him for now. We'll find a way out when the time comes. Don't worry, I'll do everything I can to help Ladro. I owe you that."

"Thank you, Trenton." Larissa stood up, leaning on Trenton as she did so. "I love you." She kissed him on the lips, then took his arm. "Come, we better get back to camp and start looking like passionate lovers. I don't want Emiliano to get suspicious."

"He won't get suspicious." Trenton mussed Larissa's hair, pulling her blouse out of her skirt. "He'll just think we've been making love away from camp."

Larissa laughed, putting her head next to Trenton's as they entered the camp. Cortez glanced at them as they passed. Trenton put his arm around Larissa. They went to their blankets and lay down. Larissa put her head on Trenton's chest. Across the camp, Cortez played poker with some of his men.

"Is he still looking?" Larissa asked quietly.

"No, he's concentrating on his cards."

"He doesn't have to concentrate. He cheats. He used to have me stand behind the other players and signal to him what they had in their hands. If the men got nervous with me standing by them, he'd just pull a card out of his boot or sleeve."

"The man doesn't do anything straight, does he?"

"No, and he'll pay for it someday."

"Go to sleep now, Larissa, we've got a long day ahead of us tomorrow."

Larissa closed her eyes. "I wish it could always be like this," she said softly, snuggling against Trenton.

"I wish you loved me, Trenton. I wish . . ." Her voice trailed off into sleep.

Trenton felt Larissa's breath against his chest. She was a beautiful girl; he was crazy not to love her. But he knew that love didn't come that easily, certainly not just through the physical act. Larissa deserved something more; she deserved a man who would love her for more than what she could give him physically. She deserved to be loved for herself. "Sleep well, Larissa," Trenton said affectionately, closing his eyes and wondering what Aeneva was doing at that minute.

Aeneva stretched out her cramped legs. "How much farther is it?" She looked out over the vast desert.

"On the other side of this desert. It's just a small place. The people there are mostly men who are on the run. Some of their families are there. The people there won't tell outsiders anything."

"What is it like there, Ladro?"

"El Circulo? It's a strange place. It has desert on one side and mountains on the other. There's a little arroyo that runs through the village. It floods in the winter and spring and usually dries up in the summer. But there are small springs in the foothills where you can usually find water. It's not the kind of place that most people would find beautiful but I like it there." Ladro thought for a moment and smiled. "I've told you about Ignacio and Marcela, but I haven't told you about old Maximo."

"And who is that?"

261

"Maximo was the one who first found El Circulo. He was Ignacio's uncle. He had been an artisan in the city. He worked in iron and he was very good. He had been designing iron bars for the home of a wealthy hacendado. Maximo put the bars in the hacienda and left, but he was later accused of stealing some jewels from the hacienda. Maximo was innocent, but no one would believe him. So, with the help of a friend who had loaded up a wagon with Maximo's tools and iron, Maximo escaped where no one would ever find him."

"El Circulo."

Ladro nodded. "He stopped there for a few days to rest, but decided he liked it. It was a natural fortress, almost. Maximo decided it needed something more. He planted cactus all around it except for a small opening on the desert side. That made it hard to get in. Now it's impossible. There are guards day and night. He built a hacienda with the help of other men like himself, who had come to El Circulo for help. He liked the hacienda, but he spent most of his time in a little shack outside of the village. He set his tools up in there. He worked there most of the time, especially in his later years.

"When Ignacio got in trouble with the law, he and Marcela went to El Circulo. Marcela very quickly took over the hacienda and Maximo felt more and more out of place. He spent almost all of his time in his little shack. When I first came to El Circulo I was frightened of Maximo because he seemed gruff, but I soon found that it was just his way. I began following him around and I would often go to his shack." Ladro had a puzzled expression on his face. "I always thought he was magic. Sometimes I would see him and I would follow him to his shack and then he would be gone. Marcela said he was crazy. But I never believed that.''

"You are fond of this place.''

"It's the only place I've been happy since I lost my family. It's the only other home I've ever known.'' Ladro took Aeneva's hand. "We'll be safe there, Aeneva, I promise you. It is getting near your time and I don't want to be riding. I want you to rest. You're looking too tired.''

"I am fine. Do you not know that Indian women are as strong as horses?''

"I don't care. I want you to rest. We'll stay in El Circulo until you have had the child and you are rested. When we are sure that Cortez has given up, we'll look for a place to settle down.''

"You have a place in mind?''

"Yes, the farm where I grew up. The land still belongs to me. It's good soil and we could raise crops. That would be a good place to raise a child.''

Aeneva nodded, wiping her hand across her forehead. "How long will it take us to cross the desert?''

"Two, three days maybe. We'll take our time. Rest now. I'll wake you when it's time to ride again.''

Aeneva nodded, looking out at the vast, barren land in front of them. Ladro was right—she was tired. It was close to her time. It would be good to have the child in a place where they could stay for a while. She only hoped that she didn't have any difficulty. She thought of the child she had lost. Protectively she clutched her rounded belly, wishing that her grandmother were with her. She was frightened; she was afraid she would lose this child also. She was afraid of a lot of things lately. She had changed so much; she was hardly the same person who had been taken from her husband and people almost a year before. What would her grandmother think if she knew that she was having the child of a man who was not her husband? She would never have approved, but she might have understood. And what of Trenton, what of her husband? How would he take the news that she was having another man's child? She felt the sweat roll down her face. It was hotter today, much hotter than yesterday, she thought. She closed her eyes. Her body felt heavy. She felt . . .

"Wake up, Aeneva. We have to go."

Slowly Aeneva opened her eyes. What had she been thinking about? She sat up and looked around her. She looked for the sun and saw that it was not at its highest point. She had fallen asleep and not even realized it.

"Are you all right?"

"Yes," Aeneva responded quietly, taking Ladro's hands. It was such an effort to get up.

"Drink some water." Ladro held the bag to her lips.

"Thank you." The water tasted warm, but it was a welcome taste. Ladro helped her on to her horse and they rode into the desert. She tried to think of things, pleasant things, but none came to mind. The heat was pervasive and she found it difficult to breathe. The sun was so bright she couldn't see. She squinted, trying to see Ladro, but all she could see was the sun.

"Ladro," she said, her voice trembling.

Ladro stopped. Aeneva was swaying on her horse. He spurred his horse closer and caught her. "It's all right, Aeneva. I'm here. I want you to ride with me. I'm afraid you'll fall." She nodded and tried to help him as he pulled her from her horse. He caught the reins of her mount and tied them to his saddle.

Aeneva leaned back against Ladro, closing her eyes. "It's so hot."

Ladro put his arms around Aeneva, making sure that she didn't move. He knew that she was weak; he had seen signs of it the day before. But they had to go on. To stop now would mean suicide or death at the hands of Cortez. They had to keep going. He took the bandana from around his neck and doused it with water. He tied it around Aeneva's forehead. She slept, her body resting limply against his as they rode.

As night approached, Ladro stopped to rest the horses. He lifted Aeneva from the horse and laid her on a blanket. He decided to rest a few hours and continue riding that night. They could rest again in the heat of the next day. He was afraid that Aeneva wouldn't make it and he didn't know if there was anything he could do to help her. He wet the bandana again and dabbed at the back of her neck and face. She slept soundly now; perhaps she would feel better when she woke up. But Ladro knew that Aeneva was not just weak in her body, she was torn inside. As much as she didn't want to admit it, having his child and being with him was against everything she believed. Honor was important to someone like Aeneva, and what honor was there in having a child by a man who was not your husband?

He felt her forehead; she was still hot. She mumbled things in her sleep, Cheyenne words. He knew that the only thing he could do to help her now was to get her to El Circulo as soon as he could. There she could rest, have the child, and begin to heal the wounds that didn't show, the wounds that were so deeply embedded she was afraid to even admit they were there.

Ladro held Aeneva against him and looked out into the darkness. The reins were loose and the horse walked with his head low. He was sure El Circulo wasn't more than forty miles away. They should be there by the next night. Aeneva moaned in her sleep. She had a high fever and Ladro knew she was getting weaker with each passing hour. He'd been a fool to put off crossing the desert until she was so near her time. If he could only get her to El Circulo, she would be all right.

They rode until the hottest part of the next day and rested in the shade of some rocks. Ladro saw to the horses and made sure Aeneva was comfortable. They slept until the late afternoon and went on again. A few hours after sunset, Ladro saw the lights of El Circulo. Ladro expected guards. They were stopped before they even reached the circle of cactus.

"Who is it?" A voice came out of the darkness. Ladro couldn't see the man.

"My name is Ladro. I have come with my woman. She is very ill."

"Can anyone here speak for you?"

"Yes, Ignacio Perez knows me. Tell him Ladro is

here and needs help."

"Wait here, *señor*. Do not attempt to enter. You are being watched."

Ladro held on to Aeneva tightly, stroking her hair. "It is all right, Aeneva. We are safe now." He kissed the top of her head. She didn't respond. At last Ladro heard the guard approach.

"*Señor*, Ignacio says you are to come to his house. I will show you the way." He followed the guard. He smiled when he saw the cactus. It was the cheapest and most loyal sentry a man could have. Old Maximo hadn't been so crazy after all. "Be careful, *señor*. The cactus is all around."

"Yes, I know," Ladro responded, guiding the horses carefully through the path that led to the town. The darkness was broken only by the lights that came from the houses. Ladro tightened his hold on Aeneva as they reached Ignacio's two-story adobe. The guard reined in his horse. He dismounted.

"This way, *señor*."

Ladro dismounted and lifted Aeneva from the horse. He followed the guard up the stairs to the porch, waiting as the man knocked on the door. Ladro looked through the window that was to the left of the door. Marcela and Ignacio sat at the wooden table that was their favorite place. He watched Ignacio rise when he heard the knock. The door opened and Ignacio stood looking out into the darkness.

"Ladro?"

Ladro stepped forward, holding Aeneva in his arms. "Hello, Ignacio."

Ignacio gripped Ladro's shoulder. "It is good to

see you, my boy. Come in." He turned to the guard. "It is all right, Jesus. Good night." Ignacio pulled the door shut behind them.

Ladro smiled at the woman. "Marcela, you are still as beautiful as I remember."

"And you are still as good a liar, Ladro." Marcela picked up a lamp, barking orders to the two men. "Ladro, take her upstairs to your old room. Ignacio, bring me water and fresh cloth." They walked up the stairs to the room. Ladro laid Aeneva on the bed. "When is her time, Ladro?"

"Any day now. She started feeling feverish about two days ago. She won't eat, but I've made her drink water."

"I think she is just exhausted. I will try to help her."

"Thank you, Marcela. It is good to see you."

"And you, my boy." She hugged him. "Go downstairs. There's nothing you can do here."

Ladro smiled wearily and walked downstairs. He saw Ignacio at the table and sat down. He drummed the table nervously with his fingers, watching as Ignacio went to the cupboard and brought out a bottle of mescal, pouring a glass for Ladro.

"Drink this, my friend, you look as though you need it."

Ladro downed the hot liquid, feeling the sting in his eyes and the burn in his throat. It felt good; it made him feel alive. "I'm sorry, Ignacio, but this was the only place I could go. I was afraid she would die."

"You don't need to apologize to me, Ladro. Never. You are a friend for life." Ignacio poured another drink for Ladro and sat down, picking up his cup of

268

coffee. "Now, tell me what happened."

"It's a long story, Ignacio."

"Start with this woman. Is she your wife?"

Ladro stared down at the glass in his hand. "No, she is not my wife."

"She is carrying your child?"

"Yes." Ladro stood up, walking across the room. "I don't think you want to hear this."

"But I think I must hear it, Ladro."

Ladro nodded wearily. Ignacio leaned forward and refilled Ladro's glass. Ladro began talking. The candles burned low before Ignacio interrupted him.

"So, Cortez is looking for you because of the woman?"

Ladro nodded. "I went back for her and we have been running ever since. The man is a bastard, Ignacio. He will stop at nothing to find us."

"You know you will be safe here."

"But we can't stay here forever."

"Why not? She is going to have your child. It is a nice enough place here. These are good people, people who look out for each other."

"I know that, Ignacio, but we have to leave after the child is born."

"Why? Why would you let that man have a chance at you?"

"I don't have a choice, it is something I must do." Ladro sat down at the table, folding his hands in front of him. "She is married, Ignacio." Ladro searched Ignacio's face for some sign of disapproval, but there was none. "Her husband is searching for her, I know it. He loves her very much. She told me that once he searched over a year until he found her. I

269

told you she had lost her memory. Her past with this man made little difference when she could not remember. But now she does. More than she will admit, I think."

"It sounds like you respect this man."

"I suppose I do. I understand what it is like to care for someone so much that you never stop searching for them."

"So, after the child is born you plan to take her back across the border to her husband?"

"I have to, Ignacio. It is tearing her apart."

"Does she love you, Ladro?"

"I think so. That's why she's staying with me. But she also loves him; she has loved him all of her life. I cannot have her staying with me because she thinks I need her. I must do what is right for her."

Ignacio reached out and pressed Ladro's hand. "You are a good man, Ladro, I always knew it. When you came to us as a young boy, lonely and afraid, I knew you were different from most of the people who came through here. I had always hoped you would find some land of your own and settle down."

"I thought I would with Aeneva, but I can't."

"Would she stay with you?"

"Yes, she would stay out of loyalty, a sense of honor. But I don't want loyalty. I want love."

"Have you asked her how she feels?"

"Yes, but I know she is not saying how she really feels. She is telling me what I want to hear."

"And you don't trust her enough to believe that what she tells you is the truth?"

"You don't understand, Ignacio. She is a good

person. She will do what she thinks is the honorable thing."

"But you don't think she does it out of love? Excuse me, Ladro, I have known a few women in my lifetime, as you know, and I have not known many who would stay with a man because it was the honorable thing to do. Most women are governed by their hearts; they are not as cold as we men."

"Do you know what I feel, Ignacio? I feel the pain that her husband must be going through knowing that she is with another man. Loving her as much as I do, I can understand what it would be like to have her taken from me."

"Yet you are ready to give her up willingly. I do not understand."

"There is a difference. When Cortez stole her from me I almost went mad not knowing if she was dead or alive, or whether she was being mistreated. But if I had known that she was safe and where she wanted to be, it would have been easier. When I take her back to her husband, I will know that it's what she wants. I will know that he will love her and take care of her. He is the only man who could love her as much as I do."

"And what of your child?"

Ladro stared down at his hands, clasping and unclasping his fingers. "The child will go with her."

"You could give up your own flesh and blood to another man, Ladro?"

Ladro looked up at Ignacio, his dark eyes betraying his sadness. "If I must."

Marcela came down the stairs and into the room,

271

sitting down at the table with the men. "Have you eaten, Ladro? You look terrible."

"Of course he looks terrible, woman. He has been traveling for weeks trying to care for his sick woman."

"Shut up, old man." Marcela took a sip of her coffee and stood up. "I have some beans and tortillas. You must eat."

"Don't, Marcela. I'm fine."

"Don't argue with me, Ladro."

"Don't argue with her, Ladro. You will never win."

Ladro attempted a smile. "Thank you, Marcela. How is she?"

Marcela went to the fire, spooning some beans on to a plate and quickly warming some tortillas. She walked back to the table handing the plate to Ladro. "Eat." When she was sure that Ladro was settled comfortably, she sat down. "She is feverish, but she will recover. I think she is just very tired. She keeps saying things in a language I don't understand."

"She is Cheyenne. What about the child?"

"There are no signs that she is ready to deliver. She just needs to rest."

"Tomorrow I will look for a place for us to stay."

"You will do no such thing. You will both stay here where I can look after your wife."

Ladro's eyes touched Ignacio's for a brief moment. "Thank you, Marcela, but I . . ."

"Don't argue with me, Ladro. Don't you remember that you can never talk me out of something I want to do?"

"Yes, I remember well. Ignacio has always told me not to waste my breath."

Marcela feigned an angry expression and shrugged her shoulders. "The old man knows me well. Now, how long do you plan to stay with us?"

"Until after the child is born and then we must go."

"Why? Why not stay here for a while? You will be safe here. You do not want to take your newborn child and travel in this country."

"Do not interfere with Ladro, Marcela. You are not his mother."

Marcela waved her hand impatiently. "This has nothing to do with being his mother. I only want what is best for him and his family."

"Then let him decide what is best. He is a grown man now."

Marcela looked at Ladro, as if noticing for the first time that he was different. "Yes, you are a grown man now, not the scared young boy who first came to us. My heart broke the day you left here."

Ladro reached over and took Marcela's hand. He held it gently. "You were like the mother I lost, Marcela, and I am grateful for that. You and Ignacio took me in when I had no one or nothing. You helped me to survive the pain of losing my family. You helped me to love again."

"Oh, Ladro." Marcela reached into her dress pocket, dabbing at her eyes with her handkerchief. "You have never found your sisters?"

"I found Manuela. She would not come with me. She had . . . accepted her life. I was told Larissa was in a town called Guadalupe del Sol, but I haven't had a chance to go there. Aeneva and I have been on the run ever since I found out."

"Aeneva. That is a beautiful name."

"Yes, it means winter. She was born in the wintertime." Ladro's face showed pride as he spoke of Aeneva.

"What is it, Ladro?" Marcela reached for Ladro's hand. "You look so troubled."

"Nothing is wrong, I'm just tired."

"You never were a good liar, you know. Even as a boy I would see you out in the desert, sitting by yourself on a rock and I would ask you what you were thinking about. You would tell me nothing. But I knew you were thinking about your family. The sadness was always written on your face. It is written there now."

"A lot has happened in my life since I last saw you, Marcela. I will tell you about it sometime but not now. Right now, I'd like to sleep." Ladro stood up. "Do you mind if I lie with Aeneva? I want to be there if she wakes up in the night."

"Why would we mind if you lie with your woman?" Marcela stood up, walking over to Ladro. Although she barely reached his chest, she stood on her toes and kissed his cheek. "Yes, you be with her, Ladro. Go now."

"Thank you both. Good night."

"*Buenos noches, hijo.*"

Marcela sat back down at the table, looking over at her husband. "Whatever it is, it has him greatly troubled."

"Yes, but he will have to work it out himself. We

274

can do nothing for him except love him as we did before."

"That I will gladly do." She glanced upstairs. "I wish I could make it easier for him."

"You know we cannot do that, Marcela. Ladro is a strong man. He will survive."

"I know he will survive, but I want him to be happy. Is that so much to ask?"

"You are too romantic, woman. You always want everyone to be smiling and happy."

"And you would have me no other way."

"Yes, you are right." Ignacio took his wife's hand, squeezing it tightly, wishing with all his heart that Ladro could have the kind of enduring love that he and Marcela had.

It had been weeks of work. The ragged brush country hid tracks well. Trenton had finally resorted to riding wide sweeps, hoping to cross a trail he could follow once they were through the mountains.

He ran his hand over the hoof prints. They were old, probably weeks old, but at least they were there. Two horses, side by side, and one had the hoof shape that matched Ladro's tracks in the cornfield. He squinted and looked out at the desert beyond. So, he had taken her across the desert. God, he hoped that they had made it.

"Well, what did you find?" Cortez asked impatiently.

Trenton stood up, stretching. "It's them. They were here three, four weeks ago. They've gone into the desert.''

"Why would he do something like that? It's a godforsaken place."

"It's also a place that most people won't go into. He's smart."

"Not so smart. What if they die out there?"

"I'm sure he was prepared for this. What's on the other side, Cortez?"

Cortez shrugged, looking over at one of his men. "What is that place, the town where the *bandidos* live?"

"El Circulo."

"What's it mean?"

"It means 'the circle'. The village is built in a circle so that they can protect each other. They have men guarding it all the time. No one can get in unless they know of you."

Trenton nodded approvingly. Ladro was smart. If he hadn't stolen Aeneva away from him, he could almost like him. "So, is there any way a person can get into the village?"

"If someone knows you. That is the only way."

"This is ridiculous. We'll just sneak in there while it's dark and find Ladro."

"Don't be stupid, Cortez. The place is guarded all the time, probably even more at night."

"Well, we have enough men. We'll fight them."

Trenton noticed the crazed look in Cortez's eyes; he was frantic to find Ladro. "I'll think of something before we get there. We'll rest up here and ride again tonight. We can't push the horses too hard."

Trenton walked over to a shady place by the rocks and sat down, observing the desert below them. From what he knew about the area, they would be crossing the narrow part of the desert. They should be able to cross it in a few days.

"Will it be difficult to cross the desert?" Larissa sat on a rock next to Trenton.

"It'll be hard, but you can do it. You've done well so far."

"The desert frightens me."

"It can be frightening, but you must respect it also. We'll travel mostly at night and in the morning and late afternoon. We'll rest in the hottest part of the day."

"I'm afraid I won't make it."

"You'll make it, Larissa. Don't forget what's on the other side of that desert—a brother who has been looking for you for many years."

"Yes, I will think of seeing Ladro."

"You have to be strong. I will help you."

"You have already helped me, Trenton." Larissa sighed, leaning back against the cool rock. "What will you do about Cortez now that you are so close to Ladro? He is so dangerous."

"When we're close enough to the town, I'll sneak away and warn them. It's the only way."

"Cortez will be watching you."

"I know, but I'm counting on the heat to make him miserable. He'll be more worried about himself than he will be about Aeneva and Ladro."

"I hope you're right. He frightens me, Trenton. He's like a snake. He sneaks around and strikes when you least expect it."

"Don't worry about Cortez. Better rest now. We'll be riding through the night."

277

Larissa settled back against the rock and within minutes she was asleep. Trenton crossed his arms over his chest, looking out over the desert. Before long he would find Aeneva and Ladro. He didn't know what would happen after that. He could only hope that she still loved him. He didn't want to face what would happen if she didn't.

Aeneva walked into the room, finding Marcela at the counter next to the fireplace. "Good morning."

Marcela turned around, a smile lighting her face. "Oh, you look much better. Very rested. Come, I want you to sit down. I am fixing something to eat."

Aeneva glanced around the room. There were dark wooden counters built on either side of the adobe fireplace. It filled one corner of the room, the whitewashed adobe rising smoothly to the ceiling. On either side of the stairs there were rough barrels and shelves for storage. Aeneva breathed deeply. The familiar odor of herbs brought a smile to her lips. Marcela had drying racks all along one wall and the smell of the herbs filled the room.

Marcela brought a plate of food to the table. "I am Marcela. I and my husband have known Ladro since he was a boy."

"Ladro has told me. You are very kind to take us in. Thank you for helping me."

"I am always glad to help people in need, especially those I love."

"Ladro cares very much for you and your husband."

"He has told you how he came to live with us?"

Aeneva nodded. "What was he like then?"

"He was young and very sad. It was months before I even saw him smile. But he was a hard worker. He helped me around here and he was always doing things for Ignacio. He helped build parts of this house."

Aeneva looked around the neat, clean adobe house. "It is a good house. It is easy to tell it is a house that has been filled with love."

"Yes, it has been filled with love. Even though my children are all grown up and gone, I still have the memories. Here, I want you to eat this."

Aeneva looked at the plate before her. It was filled with meat, beans, tortillas, and fruit. "Thank you, Marcela."

"And I have some fresh milk. It is good for the baby."

Aeneva smiled her thanks. "How long was I asleep?"

"For two days. You were feverish. You have much on your mind, eh?"

Aeneva looked down at the plate of food. "You know that Ladro is not my husband?"

"No, but I guessed. He loves you very much, you know."

"Yes, I know. There is something else, Marcela. I am already married."

Marcela sat down at the table, pouring herself some coffee. "I am sure there is a good reason for this."

"I hardly understand it myself." Aeneva saw the concern in Marcela's eyes. She took a deep breath and began talking quietly.

"You forgot everything?" Marcela asked. "Even your husband?"

"Yes. I had no memory of him or my people. The only thing I knew was that I was frightened and Ladro took care of me. And when Cortez found us, they kidnapped me, leaving Ladro for dead. But he was not. He risked his life to save me. We have been running ever since."

"When did you regain your memory?"

"Before we crossed the desert." When Marcela didn't speak, Aeneva went on. "It frightens me, Marcela. I have loved my husband all my life. But I feel a different kind of love for Ladro and I am confused. I am carrying his child; it only seems right that I should stay with him."

"Would you only stay with him out of loyalty?"

"No, I love him. I do. Oh, Marcela, I do not know."

"Aeneva." Marcela reached over and took her hands. "It seems to me that you do love Ladro and you are grateful for what he has done for you. But can you live with him the rest of your life knowing that you love someone else more?"

Aeneva leaned back in her chair, pressing her hands to her stomach. "I do not know. I am afraid, Marcela. I do not know what to do."

"It is a difficult decision, my dear, but it is one only you can make. And you must do what is right for you."

"I know."

"Eat. You are too skinny for a woman who is about to have a baby."

"I do not want to take Ladro's child from him,

Marcela. I cannot do that to him."

"Then you must decide who is more important to you, your husband or Ladro. Only you can decide, Aeneva."

Aeneva avoided Marcela's eyes, looking past her into the room. The racks were hung with drying herbs. Their sweet smell reminded her of her grandmother's lodge. She stared at them, trying to fit her past into her future. If she returned to Trenton, things would not be the same. She would have Ladro's child and there was no guarantee that Trenton would accept it. And if she stayed with Ladro, could she willingly leave behind the man she had always loved, the man who was part of her soul? There was no simple answer; it was something she would have to think long and hard about. She knew only that she loved them both in different ways, and right now, aching inside, she wished she had never met either one of them.

Chapter X

The man sat in the chair in the shade, watching as the children played. He smiled broadly, enjoying their exuberance and their youth. One of them yelled to him.

"Look, *Negro*. Look now I play your game."

"Yes, that is very good, Pepito. *Muy bueno.*" He laughed as the young boy tried to hit the rock with the stick, knocking it from one goal to the other. It was a game he had seen the Cheyenne children play often; it was a game he had often played with Nathan.

He stood up, waving to the children as he limped past them, flashing a brilliant smile. He loved them and he enjoyed being with them. He walked along the trees, sitting down under his favorite one, taking care not to aggravate his injured leg. He hadn't seen Aeneva and Trenton for almost a year and he still couldn't accept that he would never see them again. He tried to believe that Aeneva and the others had made it to the Arapaho camp. He had even prayed for their safety.

When the Comancheros had attacked them, Joe had been prepared to die defending the women and children. But the Comanchero hadn't killed him. They had taken him captive. When he overheard that they were going to sell him to work in the mines, he had decided he would rather die trying to escape than die in some dark tunnel under the ground.

He sighed deeply, carefully stretching his bad leg. He was lucky even to be alive. The night he had attempted to escape, he had been caught. In a drunken fury, the Comancheros made sure he wouldn't try to escape again—they broke one of his legs. For two weeks they had dragged him along, forcing him to ride and to work. Then, at the edge of the desert, his leg swollen to twice its size, they had left him. Driven into a rage by their parting taunts, Joe had lunged at one of the men, dragging him to the ground. He tried to grab for the man's gun, but he was hit from behind. When he regained consciousness, the Comancheros were gone. They had left him on foot, in the middle of nowhere, with no food or water.

Refusing to simply wait to die, he forced himself to walk, the pain in his leg growing ever worse. When he had no strength left, he sat down in the shade of a large cactus. He had decided that this was his place to die. He had hoped he could accept death with as much dignity as the Cheyennes had. But death hadn't come. Joe shook his head at the memory, grinning.

He thought he had died and gone to heaven when he felt the water on his lips. He had grabbed the water bag and drunk it almost dry before the man could pull it away from him. Riding hurt almost as much as walking, but they had made it to El Circulo in a couple of days. Ignacio had listened to Joe's story, while Marcela had tended his leg. She hadn't been able to do much, but at least he could get around now. And the old shack they had given him to live in might be the last home he would ever have.

He reached down and rubbed his leg, wincing as he touched it. He knew he would never be able to ride again. He would never be able to go back to the Cheyennes. It hurt him to admit that he would never see Aeneva, Trenton, or Nathan again.

He stood up, leaning on his stick. He walked away from the trees toward Ignacio's house. He saw the old man sitting in his chair on the porch, whittling on a piece of wood. Ignacio loved to whittle.

"Ola, Ignacio. *Cómo está?"*

"Bueno, Negro." Ignacio glanced up, observing that Joe was leaning heavily on the stick. "And how is the leg?"

"It's fine, just fine." Joe eased himself down on one of the porch steps. "What're you making now?"

"A doll."

"A doll out of wood? I never heard of such a thing."

"It is a special kind of doll." Ignacio looked around him, making sure no one overheard him speak. "It is a doll that will bring good luck to the child who carries it," Ignacio whispered. "It's a magic doll."

"A magic doll?" Joe repeated, rolling his eyes. "And who's going to carry this doll?"

"A child."

"What child? A boy or a girl?"

"I do not know that. It has not been born yet."

Joe scratched his head. "You are acting very strange today, Ignacio."

"Perhaps it is the heat. It does strange things to a person."

"Or perhaps it is the people who rode into the town last night."

Ignacio narrowed his eyes. "What are you talking about?"

"A man and a woman. They're staying right here."

"Who told you such a thing?"

"Pepito."

Ignacio shook his head. "Ah, I should have known. A man has no secrets around here. Yes, it is true. I have two people staying with me."

"I won't ask you more, Ignacio. I know the importance of silence in this place." Joe looked around. "Where is Marcela? It's too quiet without her."

"Yes, I know. Isn't it wonderful?"

"She is a good woman and you know it. You would be lost without her."

"Yes, you are right. But sometimes the silence is blessed." Ignacio stopped whittling for a moment. "You speak the language of the Cheyenne, *sí?*"

"Yes, why?"

"The woman who stays here is Cheyenne. She keeps saying words in her sleep. There is one word she repeats over and over."

"Can you remember the word?"

"It is something like Tenton or Treton."

286

"Trenton? Is it Trenton?" Joe felt his stomach tighten.

"Sí, that is it. Trenton. What does it mean?"

Joe stood up, grabbing his stick for support. "It means husband." He looked up at the house. "Where is the woman, Ignacio?"

"She went with Marcela to the house of Pancho. His daughter is very ill."

"Thanks, Ignacio."

"Where are you going, *Negro?* I thought we would have time for a game of cards."

"Later," Joe mumbled anxiously, walking as quickly as he could to the small house where Pancho lived. He waited outside, telling Pancho that he had to talk to Marcela about something. It seemed like an eternity until he heard voices and saw Aeneva.

"Aeneva," he said softly, aware of the emotion that choked his voice.

She turned, looking somewhat weary but beautiful. Tears filled her eyes as she walked down the steps. "Joe." She walked to him without hesitation, going into the safety of his large arms. She cried as she had not cried in all the long months since she had been kidnapped. When Marcela tried to see if she was all right Aeneva waved her away, smiling. She held on to Joe until she felt better. She smiled up at him, standing on her tiptoes to kiss him on the cheek. "It has been a long time, has it not?"

"Too long." He took her arm. "Come, let's walk. I know how you like the trees. I have a perfect spot for us." They walked past white adobe houses toward the arroyo that ran through the center of El Circulo.

Women with water jars smiled at Joe, their children running and laughing. Aeneva walked close to Joe, slowing to match his uneven step, but she said nothing. He would tell her when he was ready.

The path dropped into the oaks. Joe went slowly, easing himself down in the shade. The little spring-fed creek trickled over the rocks below them.

They both began to speak at once and laughed. Joe grinned. "You go first, you're the lady."

"I have so much to say. I do not know where to begin." She touched her stomach and looked up, meeting Joe's inquiring eyes. "It is not Trenton's child."

"I didn't figure it was."

"It belongs to the man who kidnapped me. His name is Ladro."

"I've heard the name before. Ignacio has spoken of him."

"He is a good man, Joe. He loves me."

"What are you trying to tell me, Aeneva? That you don't love Trenton anymore?"

"Of course I love Trenton. I will never stop loving Trenton."

"Then why in God's name are you going to have another man's baby?"

"I fell in love with Ladro along the way." Aeneva was at a loss for words. How could she explain the depth of feeling she had for Ladro? "I do not expect you to understand, Joe. But it has happened and I am going to stay here with him."

"And that's the end of it? What about Trenton? And Nathan? And your family?" Joe shook his head in anger. "This doesn't sound like you, girl. There's

288

something you're not telling me."

"When I was first kidnapped I tried to fight. I suffered a wound on my head. I was unconscious for a while and when I woke up I had no memory of my life."

"What? You couldn't remember anything?"

"No, my memory was completely gone. I did not remember Trenton, or you, or Nathan . . . I knew nothing except what Little Deer told me before we were separated."

"When were you kidnapped?"

"After we reached the Arapaho camp. They attacked before sunrise. A group of women and children was taken. Little Deer was among them. Nathan was not. I think he is safe."

"So what happened after that? I can't believe you fell in love with the bastard who kidnapped you."

"We were all tied together and it was almost impossible to escape. But one day while we were by a river, I did escape. The Comancheros came after me and I hid up a tree. Ladro found me but didn't tell the others. He decided he would take me as his own captive and sell me to a man named Cortez."

"And you fell in love with this man?"

"Joe, please do not judge me. You do not understand."

"No, I guess I don't." Joe stretched his leg out, wincing as he did so.

"What happened to your leg?"

"It got broke when I tried to escape. Never healed right."

"Let me take a look at it."

Joe pulled away. "No, leave it. It's all right."

Aeneva ignored Joe, reaching down to feel the leg. "Hand me your knife." Joe complied and Aeneva slit the pants leg. "No wonder you are in such pain. This has healed terribly. The bones are crooked and pressing on tender areas inside of your leg."

"Well, there's nothing you can do about it." Joe shook his head in disgust. "And look what you did to my pants."

"You are an old woman, Joe. I can fix your pants later, it is your leg I am worried about." Aeneva stared thoughtfully for a moment. "I saw my grandmother fix someone's leg before. She told me once that Horn, the great healer of our tribe, had helped a man whose leg had been badly broken. Horn broke the leg again and then made it straight with two flat sticks. He made the man stay still for weeks and eventually the leg healed. The man could walk almost as well as he could before he was injured."

"You're not going to break my leg again. Once was enough."

"But I think I can help you, Joe. Let me."

"No! I don't want you touching my leg."

"Ah, you are so stubborn! No wonder you and Trenton get along so well."

"That sounds kinda funny coming from you. You're one of the most stubborn people I've ever known."

Aeneva smiled, leaning against Joe. "Yes, you are right. Oh, I have missed you Joe. I have missed you so much."

Joe put his arm around Aeneva. "I'll figure out some way to get you home if that's what you want."

"I do not know what I want right now, Joe. First, I must have my child. After that, I will decide what to do."

"All right, I won't push."

"What about you?"

"I'd go home if I had a choice, but I don't. I can't ride."

"Let me help you."

"I don't know, what if I'm worse afterward? What if I can't walk?"

"I think I can help you. Do you not trust me?"

"Of course I trust you. It's just been a long time since we've been together. I haven't been able to trust anyone that way for a while."

"I understand, Joe. That is how I felt when I was kidnapped. But then I came to depend on Ladro and he treated me well. When I could not remember anyone or anything from my past I was frightened, but he did not take advantage of me. He talked to me and he grew to respect me."

"And to love you?"

"Yes, and to love me."

"But you don't love him as much as you love Trenton? I know you couldn't."

Aeneva looked away, not able to meet Joe's eyes. "That is not important. What is important is that he needs me, and I carry his child."

"Trenton needs you, Aeneva. And so does Nathan."

"Don't do this to me, Joe. Please, I just need you to be my friend."

"I am being your friend. What happens when Trenton finds you? What will you do then?"

"He does not know where I am. He will never find me."

"Do you really think he will give up searching for you? You know he will find you, Aeneva."

Aeneva nodded, dropping her head. "I do not know what I will do, Joe. I do love him so much. But there is the child to think of." She covered her rounded stomach with her arms, a protective gesture not lost on Joe.

"You really want this child, don't you?"

"Yes. I do not want to lose it as I lost Trenton's."

Joe was silent for a moment. "What if Trenton comes, Aeneva, and you decide you want to go back with him? Do you think he'll accept the child?"

Aeneva's eyes met Joe's, a piercing look. "I accepted his child from another woman, did I not?"

"Yes, you did, and you loved him as if he were your own."

"Perhaps Trenton would do that with my child."

"Maybe." Joe put his arm around Aeneva, smiling as he did so. "What would your grandmother think if she saw you now?"

Aeneva laughed. "I am sure she does see me now. She is probably defending me and Grandfather is angry with me. And Naxane Jean is laughing at them both." She laid her head on Joe's shoulder, feeling the comfort and security that only a true and close friend can provide. But their closeness did not last long.

"Aeneva, are you all right?" The voice was impatient.

Aeneva and Joe turned. Ladro was standing behind them, his face betraying no emotion.

"Ladro, I want you to meet my friend Joe. He lived with my people. I never expected to see him again."

Ladro didn't move, only nodding his head slightly to acknowledge Joe's presence. "It is time we went back to Ignacio's. Marcela is worried about you."

"I am well, as you can see. I am with my friend."

Ladro barely glanced at Joe. "Are you coming with me or not?"

Aeneva looked at Joe and then at Ladro. "Ladro, I asked you to meet my friend. Why do you not sit down and talk with us?"

"Maybe he's scared," Joe said in a low voice, looking steadily at Ladro.

Ladro approached, standing in front of Joe and Aeneva. "Why should I be afraid of you, eh, *Negro?*"

"Because I'm from Aeneva's past and I don't think you want anyone to remind you of that."

Ladro shook his head, ignoring Joe and looking at Aeneva. "I am going back to Ignacio's. I will see you when you return."

Aeneva's eyes followed Ladro as he left. "He is a good man," she said defensively.

"Yeah, I can tell. Does he always order you around like that?"

"He does not know you. He was afraid for my safety." She started to get up but couldn't. "Can you help me up? I am finding it more difficult to move these days."

Joe attempted to stand, but had a hard time with his leg. "Maybe we can help each other." He helped to push Aeneva up and then she helped him gain his balance as he stood on his good leg.

"I want to look at your leg again tomorrow, Joe.

293

Do not argue with me."

"If you say so." They walked back past some of the small houses, barely large enough to house the families that dwelled inside, but clean and white-washed. Smells came from everywhere; it occurred to them both that it was very similar to a Cheyenne camp. When they reached Ignacio's house, Aeneva turned to Joe.

"Thank you for your concern, my friend. I know this is difficult for you to understand. But I must do what I think is right."

"You mean what is honorable."

"I am not so sure that Trenton would regard this as honorable."

Joe pulled Aeneva to him, patting her on the back. "Don't worry. I'll be here if you need me. This will all work out somehow."

"I hope so, Joe." Aeneva watched Joe as he walked away, feeling as though she was being torn in two. Ladro came out and stood beside her.

"He is a friend of your husband's?"

Aeneva nodded without turning. "He is also my friend."

"And what does he think about us?"

"It does not matter what he thinks, it matters what we think." She turned and started up the stairs, stopping suddenly as she felt a sharp stabbing pain. She reached out to Ladro.

"What is it?"

"I do not know. Help me into the house, please."

Ladro helped Aeneva into the house, sitting her down at the small table. Marcela immediately rushed to the table.

"Is it time?"

"I do not know, Marcela. I just had a sharp pain for a moment. It is gone now."

"If it comes back in a few minutes we will know that it is your time."

"Isn't there anything we can do?" Ladro asked.

"There is nothing we can do now, Ladro. We must wait for the child to come in its own time."

Ladro stooped next to the chair, looking into Aeneva's eyes. "I'm sorry, Aeneva. I didn't mean to upset you. Your friend was right—I didn't want to meet someone from your past."

"Ladro, it's all right."

"No, I want you to know that I love you. I will bring your friend here if that's what you want."

Aeneva reached out and touched Ladro's face, running her fingers up to his thick, dark hair. "I am only going to have a baby, Ladro. I am not going to die."

"Don't say that, Aeneva." He hugged her, putting his face in her stomach. "Don't ever say that."

Aeneva held him, putting her arms around his shoulders. "It is all right, Ladro. Everything will be all right." And she knew at that moment that she had no other choice but to stay with Ladro.

"This is enough! We are not going any further!"

Trenton, well ahead of the others, could still hear Cortez's voice. He kept riding, ignoring the man.

"Stop, gringo, or I will have you shot. We don't need you now. I can find Ladro without you."

Trenton kept riding, the others following.

"Stop, gringo! Stop!" Cortez pulled out his rifle and fired alongside Trenton.

Trenton pulled up, waiting for Cortez to get close enough. He threw all of his weight into the swing and when his fist slammed into Cortez's jaw, the force knocked him from his horse. "The next time you fire a gun at my back, Cortez, you're a dead man."

Cortez staggered to his feet. "I'm tired, don't you understand? I can't ride any further!"

Trenton looked at the men around him and at Larissa. "Everyone else seems to be doing fine. Even Larissa is not complaining."

"I don't care. The heat is tearing my skull in two. I want to stop."

Trenton shrugged. "If you don't care about finding Ladro that's fine with me. We can set up camp right here."

Everyone dismounted, building makeshift lean-tos from the sparse brush to protect them from the unrelenting rays of the sun. No sooner had Alfredo built the shelter for Cortez than Cortez was asleep on his back. Trenton and Larissa stayed well away from the others.

"He could have killed you, Trenton. I told you he is crazy. He's been drinking, too."

"Yeah. He acts like he doesn't want to find Ladro."

"I don't know, Trenton, I think he's scared. He gets crazy when he drinks sometimes."

Trenton thought a moment. "I brought a bottle of mescal. When we get close enough to the town, we'll make sure Cortez gets plenty to drink."

"Don't worry, I can make sure he drinks. I am still

able to reach Emiliano in ways other people are not."

"You may not need to do anything." He looked at Cortez asleep under his lean-to. "He may do it for us."

"When will you go, Trenton?"

"Tomorrow, while he is sleeping. I'll tell the others that I'm going out to check the trail. You're going to come with me, Larissa."

"Are you sure?"

"I don't want to leave you here with him. There's no telling what he'll do when he wakes up and finds me gone."

"I'm afraid, Trenton. I am so close to finding Ladro. I'm afraid I won't see him, that something will happen."

"Be patient, Larissa. You'll see him soon enough."

Ladro paced the room, stopping abruptly every time he heard a noise from the upstairs room.

"Sit down, my friend, it could be a long time."

"How can you stand this, Ignacio? I'm about to go crazy."

"I have been through this many times before, my friend. I have learned it does no good to pace. Come, sit down." Ignacio poured Ladro a cup of mescal. "Drink this. It will help you to remain calm."

"I hate this stuff," Ladro said as he downed the fiery liquid. "Pour me another one."

Ignacio laughed as he poured Ladro another cupful. "You will be fine, my friend. These women, they are as strong as work horses. I would die if I had to have a child. You know that I watched my youngest be born?"

"You watched? What was it like?"

Ignacio poured himself a drink. "It was like nothing I have ever seen. I have seen the birthing of cows and pigs and horses, but the birth of a human being, of one's own child, is truly a miracle."

"I'm not sure if I could watch."

"Of course you could watch. It is beautiful, Ladro. I tell you, my friend, you should be in there with her."

Ladro shook his head defiantly. "No, only if she calls for me. I know her, she will want to do this alone."

"They all want to do it alone, but why should they, eh? After all, it is the least we can do to be with them, *si?*"

Ladro nodded absently, getting back up and pacing around the room. Twice he started upstairs but stopped, deciding to wait until Aeneva called him.

"You will not make it if you keep on like this. Please, come and sit down."

"I guess you're right." Ladro sat down again, nervously running his fingers across the table. "Tell me about *El Negro*. What is he like?"

"I thought you talked to him today. What did you think?"

"I didn't talk to him very long."

"He seems to be a good man. We took him in here as we have so many others. He is very good with all of the children."

"Did you know that Aeneva knew him?"

"I know nothing of his past, Ladro. You know that

we do not ask such things of a man here."

"He is a friend of Aeneva's and also of her husband. She and *El Negro* seem to be very close."

"Are you jealous?"

"I suppose I am jealous of anyone who knew her before."

"So how can you give her up so easily?"

"I never said it would be easy, Ignacio." Ladro jumped when he heard Marcela's voice calling him. He rushed up the stairs, taking them three at a time. Cautiously he walked into the room, kneeling next to the bed on which Aeneva was sitting. She was panting and she was covered with sweat. Her swollen belly seemed to dominate her entire body. "Aeneva," he said quietly, gently touching her face.

Aeneva feigned a smile when she saw him, but immediately the smile changed to a grimace as the next wave of pain overcame her. She bent forward, hugging her knees to her chest and breathing heavily. When the pain passed she put her head back and Marcela wiped it with a cool cloth. Ladro started to stand up, but Aeneva grabbed his hand. "Do not go, Ladro. I want you to be here."

Ladro took Aeneva's hand in his, kissing it gently. "I'll stay here as long as you want me to."

"Hold me up, Ladro."

Ladro pulled Aeneva up from the bed, holding her by the shoulders as the next pain came.

"Sit behind her on the bed. It will be easier for both of you that way."

Ladro did as Marcela ordered and Aeneva relaxed against him as the pain passed. He rubbed her shoulders and arms, talking to her in a calm voice. "It will be fine, Aeneva. You are doing well."

She pressed her back against him as the next pain hit her and she moaned. Ladro caught Marcela's eyes.

"Isn't there anything you can do, Marcela?"

"Believe me, Ladro, there is nothing I can do. But you can be with her and comfort her. She has to do the rest on her own."

"But the pain . . ."

"She will survive the pain."

"Oh, Ladro," Aeneva pleaded, leaning forward, holding onto her knees as tightly as she could. "I want this baby to live."

"It will live, Aeneva. I promise you."

"Lie back. Let me check you," Marcela ordered in a firm voice.

Ladro held Aeneva against him as Marcela felt Aeneva's stomach, praying silently as each pain came and went. "How long, Marcela?"

"Not long now. The pains are very close together and it feels like the child has moved down. It will be here soon."

"Ladro, will you do something for me?" Aeneva whispered, as she lay against his chest.

"What?"

"I want you to get my friend. Get Joe. Ask him to come here. Please."

"But I don't want to leave you."

"Please, Ladro, he is like my family. I want him here."

"All right." He kissed her cheek and helped her to sit up. He stood up. "We'll be back as soon as possible."

"Thank you."

Ladro hurried down the stairs. "Where does *El Negro* live, Ignacio?"

"Why do you want to talk to him at this hour?"

"Aeneva wants him here."

"I will take you to him."

Ladro and Ignacio moved through the night, skirting the arroyo. They passed the last adobe and Ignacio stopped. A small hut, barely big enough to hold a bed and a table, stood in the moonlight, lit from within by a candle. Ignacio started to the door, but a voice stopped him.

"What do you want, Ignacio?"

"I did not see you, *Negro*. You blend in so well with the darkness."

Joe smiled to himself. "I'm just enjoying the cool air. What's wrong?"

Ladro stepped forward. "Aeneva wants you. She is having the baby now."

Joe stood up immediately, knocking his stick over in the darkness and almost losing his balance. Ladro reached out, holding Joe so he didn't fall.

"Thanks."

"It's all right." Ladro bent down for the walking stick and handed it to Joe. "Are you ready?"

"Yeah."

When the three men returned to the house Aeneva was holding on to her legs, pushing as hard as she could.

"Come, Ladro, sit behind her. Hold her up. She is using up all of her strength."

Ladro sat behind Aeneva, supporting her gently. "It's all right. It's almost over."

"Where's Joe?"

"I'm right here, darlin'," Joe said soothingly, moving to Aeneva's side, kneeling as if it pained him not at all. "You are doing just fine."

Aeneva reached out and took Joe's hand. "Thank you, Joe." She squeezed his hand and leaned forward, pushing as hard as she could.

"I see the head!" Marcela exclaimed excitedly. "Don't ease up. Keep pushing."

While Ladro supported Aeneva from the back and Joe held her hand, Aeneva used all of her will to push the child from her womb. With one final effort, using all of the strength she possessed, she pushed as hard as she could and she felt instant relief as the small body came out of her. She looked down at the tiny brown body on the bed. Marcela was quickly wiping the blood away from the eyes and mouth, sticking her fingers inside the mouth to remove any mucus. The child was silent.

"Hand him to me, Marcela." Aeneva held out her arms and received the small boy. His tiny eyes opened and he made sounds, but he didn't cry.

"Is he all right? Why doesn't he cry?" Ladro asked, glancing up at Marcela.

"He is fine, Ladro. Not all babies have to cry when they are born."

"But he's so small."

"Don't worry."

"He's a fine-looking boy." Joe smiled as he reached over and touched the new life. "He's real happy; no need to cry."

Marcela stood up, wiping her hands on her apron. "I will be back in a minute to clean up. We'll leave you alone for a few minutes. How would you like a drink, *Negro?*"

Joe stood up on his good leg, leaning on his stick. "I'll talk to you later, Aeneva."

Aeneva nodded, resting against Ladro. She closed her eyes for a moment. "I cannot believe that it's over and that he's here. He is so beautiful. He is wonderful."

"Yes, he is." Ladro tentatively touched his new son. "I can't believe he's so small."

"Why don't you hold him?"

"I can't. I don't know how to hold a baby."

"You can learn." Aeneva moved forward, handing the baby to Ladro. "You see, all you have to do is support his head and he will be fine. He likes you, Ladro."

Ladro looked down into the face of his tiny new son. The dark eyes stared back at him. The baby made sucking sounds and squirmed around in Ladro's hands. "My son," he said solemnly.

Aeneva's eyes filled with tears and she kissed Ladro. She felt such extreme happiness at this moment that she was sure it would never end.

Trenton looked from underneath his hat to see if Cortez was asleep. The man was actually sitting up and gambling with some of his men. He seemed to be feeling fine. Larissa sat down next to Trenton.

"I will have to get him drinking somehow. He doesn't look like he will go to sleep."

"No, it's too dangerous. He'd suspect something now. We'll have to wait until tonight."

"But we'll be approaching the town tonight."

"I know. I'll just have to think of another way."

"I don't like it, Trenton. I feel as if he's been toying with us all along."

"Maybe he has, but I know he won't take a chance with his own life. He'll want me to ride into El Circulo first. I just have to figure out a way to have you come with me."

"Don't worry about me. Just get into the town and warn Ladro."

Trenton rested fitfully, trying to push Aeneva from his mind yet unable to, knowing that she was so close. It had been so long since he'd seen her, almost a year. He wondered if she would have changed much. His mind raced with different thoughts until he fell asleep and awakened as the sun was going down. He sat up, stretching his arms. He looked around him; everyone was asleep. The sun had done its work. He took a drink from his water bag, making sure there was enough for Larissa. He shook her gently, putting his finger to his lips. She sat up, taking the bag and drinking from it. They both pulled on their boots and rolled their blankets. They walked to the horses and quietly saddled them. Trenton led the horses out of the shelter and away from the camp. Once he and Larissa mounted, they rode toward the town.

Cortez sat up and watched as Trenton and Larissa rode away. He nodded his head. He would let them get into the town, let them all be together. Then he would come and he would make them all pay for what they had done to him.

*　　*　　*

304

Riding in the heat of the day was hard on the horses, but Trenton pressed on. Larissa followed silently behind. When the sun set, the horses lifted their heads and traveled faster across the sand. When the shout came out of the darkness, Trenton stopped.

"Do not go any further, *señor*. What is your business here? Do you know someone in El Circulo?"

"My name is Trenton Hawkins. I want to go into El Circulo. There is a woman there who knows me. Her name is Aeneva. And a man called Ladro will know about me."

The man told Trenton to wait while he checked. Trenton's guns were taken and he was guarded by three men. The man was back quickly.

"You will follow me, *señor*."

Trenton and Larissa followed the man into the darkness. They could see the outlines of adobe roofs and the lights still burning in some windows. The man stopped in front of a small shack that was completely dark.

"You can dismount here, *señor*."

"What about my guns?"

"You will get them back later."

Trenton and Larissa dismounted.

"Well I'll be. What took you so long, boy?"

Trenton jerked around in the darkness, recognizing Joe's voice immediately. "Joe? Where are you?"

Joe stepped out of the darkness of the small porch. "It's been a long time."

Trenton walked up to his friend, putting his arms around him. "I'm glad you're safe, my friend. I didn't know where you were."

"I'm all right."

"What about Aeneva? Is she here?"

There was an awkward silence. "She's here, boy."

"Is she all right? She's not hurt, is she?"

"No, she's fine."

"Well, where is she? Take me to her."

"I can't do that, Trenton. She's staying with an old man named Ignacio. He's the one who told the guard to bring you to me. Come on in here and sit down. We have to talk."

"What is it, Joe? What's wrong?"

"Just be patient, boy, and come on in here. Bring the girl too."

Trenton and Larissa followed Joe into the small shack. Joe struck a match and lit the lamp. The room was slowly revealed. It was all adobe and very cool inside. It had an ornate iron bed that filled most of the room and barely left room for the table and chairs.

"Smells good in here."

"I got some beans left from dinner. Pretty good, too. Got some meat thrown in. You and your friend sit down and I'll get you some."

"Please, let me help." Larissa went to Joe. "Go talk with Trenton."

Joe nodded his thanks and went to the table, sitting down. "I knew you'd get here someday."

"How long have you been here?"

"Quite a while. How's Nathan? Is he safe?"

"He's fine. He's with my people. What happened to your leg?"

"Had a run-in with the Comancheros."

Trenton thanked Larissa as she poured them coffee

306

and served them plates of beans and meat. "What about Aeneva? She's okay, isn't she?"

"That much I'm sure of. There's an old man here named Ignacio who is helping her." Joe looked at Larissa, who was sitting on the floor by his bed eating. "Come here and sit down. You must be tired."

"I am fine, thank you. Please talk with your friend."

"What is this lady's name, boy? You never did have proper manners."

"Sorry. Larissa, this is my friend, Joe. Joe, this is Larissa."

"I'm pleased to meet you, Larissa." Joe turned to Trenton. "You've got real trouble, boy."

"Aeneva?"

Joe nodded. "She's here but she's not alone."

"I know. She's traveling with a man named Ladro."

"Yeah. How'd you know that?"

"I know a lot. How is she, Joe? She's not sick, is she?"

"No, she's well."

"But?"

"I think she should tell you the rest."

"The rest of what? What is there to tell? She has been traveling with the man who kidnapped her and she grew to care for him. I can understand that, but it doesn't mean anything. It's not like anything we had together."

Joe stared at the table, running his finger over the grooves in the wood. "It's not that simple, boy."

"Well, just tell me, for Chrissakes."

"I can't. It's not my place to. You have to talk to her."

Trenton stood up, not masking the anger that was on his face. "Where is she? I'll talk to her now."

"You can't talk to her now. People around here go to bed real early. You'll have to wait until tomorrow."

"All right, then I'll talk to her in the morning." He glanced over at Larissa. "Can we sleep here tonight?"

"You know you don't even have to ask. Larissa can have my bed. You and I can sleep outside. Just like old times."

"No, please, I don't want to take your bed away from you."

"Don't argue with me. You sleep in here. My friend here and I are going to sleep outside under the stars." Joe stood up, going over to the corner and grabbing a rolled-up blanket. "I'll meet you outside, boy."

Trenton walked over to the fireplace, leaning against it and staring at the fire. He felt Larissa next to him, but he didn't turn.

"Don't worry, Trenton, it will be all right."

"There's something wrong and Joe won't tell me. Either she's hurt or your brother's done something to her."

"I don't think he'd hurt her."

"I just want to know, damn it!" He walked away from the fireplace, pacing around the room.

Larissa walked up to him. "Be patient, Trenton. You will know soon enough. At least you know she is safe and away from Cortez."

Trenton looked at Larissa.

"You really have become a friend to me, haven't you?"

"I had no choice, did I?" She smiled and went to the bed. "Don't worry. You'll see your wife tomorrow, and I will see my brother."

Aeneva sat straight up in bed. In her dream she had seen Trenton standing in front of her, a look of hatred on his face so strong that she could barely look at him. He had seen the baby. She shook her head to clear it.

"Ladro?" she asked in the darkness.

Ladro sat up next to her, his arm immediately around her. "Did you have a bad dream?"

"Where is the baby? Is he all right?"

"He is sleeping well. Don't worry."

"I want to see him." Aeneva got out of bed and walked to the cradle, looking down at her sleeping son to reassure herself that he was fine. She walked back to the bed, sitting down on the edge. "Something is wrong. I can feel it."

"What? The baby is healthy. You're worrying too much."

"No, it is something else."

"Your husband?"

"I do not know. Perhaps it is Cortez. I would not feel this kind of danger from Trenton."

"Even if he knew you had a son by me?"

"He would never hurt me, Ladro. Never."

"Are you sure?"

"Yes, I know him as I know myself."

Ladro touched her shoulders, urging her back into bed. "Come back to bed now; you're tired. You need to sleep."

Aeneva lay back down, unable to still her racing mind. Trenton was near; she could feel it. And he would be here soon. What would she tell him when she saw him? What could she tell him? She closed her eyes and forced her body to relax. Sleep overcame her, rescuing her from her own thoughts until the morning.

Chapter XI

Trenton sat on the front steps, sipping at the coffee. He watched the colors of the sunrise as they lit up the sky. It was a sight he had always loved as a boy.

"What you up so early for, boy?" Joe ambled down the steps, leaning against the wooden rail. "Nice sunrise."

"It reminds me of the prairie. I miss it, Joe."

"I do too, boy."

"Why didn't you go back? Why did you stay here?"

Joe patted his leg. "I can't ride. This leg has kept me from doing most everything."

"Why don't you go to a doctor? Is there one here? Maybe something can be done about it."

"I don't think anything can be done about it. I think it's as good as it'll get. Besides, aren't too many doctors around here."

"If Sun Dancer were here . . ." The name had passed through his lips so naturally that Trenton could hardly believe he'd said her name. "I miss that lady, Joe. She was good to me and she sure knew how to handle her granddaughter. Much better than I ever could."

"Yeah, she was something, wasn't she? She had an answer for everything."

"And she was usually right." Trenton turned to Joe. "I want to see Aeneva. Tell me where she is."

"It's still early in the morning, boy."

"Tell me where she is, Joe, or I'll find out myself."

Joe nodded. "Just let me get a shirt on and I'll take you."

Trenton stood up. He was close now. So close.

"You ready, boy?"

Trenton nodded. Joe led him around the backs of the adobe houses and turned away from the houses onto a path that ran downhill into an arroyo. Ancient oaks arched above them. At the bottom they crossed a trickling stream and started uphill. When they came out from under the oaks, Trenton saw an adobe house larger than all the others. Ornate ironwork railings surrounded the porch. An old man sat in a chair carving on a piece of wood. He didn't look up when they approached.

"*Buenos días,* Ignacio."

"*Buenos días, Negro.* It's early for a walk, no?" He looked at Trenton. "You are the man who came last night. You are her husband."

"Yes, I'm her husband."

"You will not cause trouble, *señor?*"

"I don't want to cause any trouble. I just want to see my wife."

"You understand she is with another man, a man who is like a son to me?"

"I know about Ladro."

"But there is more, *señor*."

"I think Aeneva should tell him, Ignacio. It's not our place."

Ignacio nodded in agreement. "You are right, *Negro*." Ignacio stood up. "I will get Marcela and we three will go for a walk while you talk to your wife, *señor*. Please remember that this is my home. I want no trouble in it."

"I give you my promise that I won't cause any trouble, Ignacio."

"All right then." Ignacio returned in just a few minutes with Marcela, who eyed Trenton warily. "She is upstairs, to the right. She is sleeping . . ." She hesitated, but Ignacio took her arm firmly and the three of them walked away.

Trenton took a deep breath and walked up the steps to the house. He walked into the large room where he could smell coffee brewing and something cooking in a pot over the fire. He looked around and walked up the stairs. He hesitated before the closed door. He knocked lightly.

"Who is it?"

Trenton froze at the sound of a man's voice. His hand went to his gun, but he knew. It was Ladro. He pushed open the door, moving quickly to one side.

"I want to talk to my wife."

"So you have come. I knew you would." There was a moment of tense silence. "Step into the doorway, Hawkins. Do you think I'd risk gunfire with her so close?"

Trenton went into the room. He looked at the bed. Aeneva was asleep, her long hair spread out around her. Ladro was sitting, his arm thrown protectively across her. Nothing could have prepared Trenton for this.

"I should kill you, Ladro."

"This is not the place to talk about it. Let's go downstairs."

Trenton started to protest, but Ladro got up, quickly putting on his pants and walking out of the room. Trenton followed, his anger growing with every passing second.

The two men regarded each other in silence before Trenton spoke. "Why the hell did you take my wife away from me?"

"I needed her."

"You used her. Why her? It could have been any woman."

"She was beautiful. She was just what I needed for my purposes."

"You mean she was just what Cortez wanted."

"You know of Cortez?"

"I'm riding with him." Trenton let the words sink in. "You see, I know all about you, Ladro."

"You don't know anything about me." He stared at Trenton, his black eyes glaring. "Why are you riding with Cortez?"

"Because I thought it was the safest way to keep an eye on him."

"So he is behind you?"

"He won't get through here. Goddamn you." Trenton walked up to Ladro, his face only inches away from the other man's. "I should kill you right now."

"But you won't because you want to find out about Aeneva. You want to know if I love her."

314

"Do you?" Trenton's blue eyes challenged Ladro's dark ones.

"Enough to do what she wants."

"What does that mean?"

"That means if she decides to go with you I won't stand in her way."

"That's very gallant of you, considering I am her husband."

"Yes, but she's been with me for almost a year now. You weren't there when she needed someone to care for her, or to protect her, or to love her. And you haven't asked if she loves me. She does."

"You bastard!" Trenton smashed Ladro in the face, knocking him to the floor. He jumped on him before he could get up, hitting him again. Ladro pushed Trenton away and the two men squared off, circling slowly. The sound of a baby crying came down the stairway. Ladro looked up. Trenton straightened, staring at Aeneva as she came down the stairs, the baby at her breast. She saw Trenton and stopped.

"I want to talk to him alone, Ladro."

Ladro didn't move, looking from her to Trenton.

"Please, Ladro."

"Will you be all right?"

"Yes, I will be fine." Ladro hesitated, then spun, slamming the door behind him.

Aeneva walked to one of the chairs and sat down, cradling the baby in her arms. She smiled down at him and then looked up at Trenton, her eyes taking in how thin and tired he looked.

Trenton walked over to Aeneva, staring at her and then down at the baby. He reached out to touch her, but instantly she pulled back, as if regretting the gesture. "It's Ladro's child?"

"Yes."

He nodded slightly, turning away. "I don't understand, Aeneva. I thought you loved me. I thought we loved each other."

"We did love each other, Trenton."

"But apparently it wasn't enough." He shook his head in anger. "All of this time I thought you were being held against your will. I thought unspeakable things were happening to you. There were times I ached for want of you and for your suffering." He glanced at the newborn child. "It doesn't look like you suffered very much at all."

"Please, Trenton, I want to explain to you."

"What is there to explain, Aeneva? You have a child by another man and you act as if you don't even know me." He kicked at one of the chairs, knocking it over. The baby jerked, crying at the noise. "You couldn't have our child, but you can have the child of a complete stranger." He walked back to her, squatting down to stare into her eyes. "I don't imagine you've even thought about Nathan. Or Little Deer. Or the others."

"Little Deer is safe?"

Trenton nodded.

"I think about Nathan every day. I love him."

"I bet you do, between raising your new child and making love to your captor."

"Please don't, Trenton. I want to explain. I want to make you understand."

"What is there to understand? God, Aeneva, how would you feel if I were gone for almost a year and you found me with another woman and a child? Could you understand? Do you think I would expect you to understand?"

"No," she replied quietly, trying to still the emotions that were rising in her. "Perhaps none of this can be explained. I do not blame you if you hate me."

"That's an easy way out for you, isn't it? If I hate you it's much easier for you to take, isn't it? Jesus, woman!" He slammed his fist down on the table. The baby cried until Aeneva soothed it into nursing again. "Just tell me one thing and, please, be honest. Did you ever love me at all?"

"I have always loved you, Trenton," Aeneva replied honestly, seeing the pain in his eyes as she answered.

Trenton said nothing, but looked at her a moment and walked out of the house. Aeneva watched him leave, unable to stop the flow of tears as they poured from her eyes. She held her baby to her, wishing with all of her heart it were Trenton's son and not Ladro's. She held the baby tightly, trying to find peace from the warmth of its tiny body. She would never see Trenton again. Her love was gone, and with him, part of her soul. She cried until there was nothing left but emptiness and a sense that her life would never again have the kind of simple joy she felt when she was with Trenton. When he had walked out the door, he had taken part of her with him.

Joe found Trenton behind the shack, just sitting, staring up at the mountains. "You crazy, boy? This

317

heat can kill you." Joe walked up to Trenton, shaking his head. "You just going to sit out here and hope you'll die from the sun? Seems pretty stupid to me."

"I don't remember asking for your opinion."

"Well, you're gonna get it anyway." Joe cussed while trying to ease himself down on the rock next to Trenton. "What makes you think you're so special anyway?"

Trenton looked over at Joe. "What're you talking about?"

"What makes you think you're better than Aeneva?"

"I never said I was."

"Oh, but you're thinking it, aren't you?" Joe lifted his hat, wiping the sweat from his brow. "You can hardly stand the fact that she went off and had another man's child, can you?"

"What am I supposed to do, like it?"

"I never said that."

"Don't play games with me, Joe. I'm not in the mood."

"I'm not playing games, boy. I was just thinking your point of view has narrowed a bit."

"For an educated man, you don't speak English very plainly, Joe." Trenton picked up a rock and threw it.

"All right, how's this—did you ever let her explain?"

"She didn't have to explain. She was holding his child in her arms."

"You didn't answer me, boy."

"No, I didn't let her explain."

'Do you suppose she might have a side to the story, a side you don't know about?''

"What could she say that would make any difference?" He shook his head, laughing derisively. "No, the truth is she fell in love with someone else and had his child."

"And you could never accept that child, could you?"

"Why should I be expected to?"

"Because you expected her to accept the child of another woman."

The words were like a blow to Trenton. It was true. He'd brought Nathan back to the Cheyennes after his wife had died. Although he had never loved Lydia and had been forced into the marriage, he had stayed because of his child. It had seemed the honorable thing to do. Maybe that's what Aeneva was feeling now. "I feel like a fool."

"You should and you will when you hear all of the story. Unlike you, she had no choice. When you chose to marry Lydia, you knew exactly what you were doing. Aeneva didn't have that choice for a long time."

"You mean because she was kidnapped."

"Yes, and because she lost her memory for a long time. She didn't even remember you or her life until a little while ago."

"She didn't tell me . . ." Absently he ran his fingers through the dry sand.

"Did you give her a chance to tell you?"

"No." He leaned forward, his elbows resting on his knees. "She didn't say a word to defend herself."

"She feels badly enough about what happened.

319

She didn't intend to fall in love with this man; it just happened. She had no one, not even her memories, and he became everything to her." Joe pressed Trenton's shoulder. "She never stopped loving you, boy, but by the time she regained her memory she was carrying Ladro's child and they were being chased by Cortez. The only thing that mattered at that point was protecting the life of that unborn child." Joe reached over and pressed Trenton's shoulder. "I was there when the child was born, boy. She kept saying over and over that she wanted it to be healthy."

Trenton nodded. "I should have been with her. It should have been our child."

"But it isn't and you have to accept that."

"It doesn't matter now anyway, Joe. She's already decided she wants Ladro."

"What're you talking about?"

"She is staying with him because she thinks it is the right thing to do, the honorable thing."

"I do understand. I did the same thing with Lydia."

"But it doesn't mean you have to give up on her."

"She's already made up her mind, Joe. You told me she loves Ladro. What can I do to change that?"

"Yes, she loves Ladro, but not in the way she loves you. I'm willing to bet on it."

The corners of Trenton's mouth curled up in a slight smile. "And what do you have to bet with?"

"I've got a few coins put away. What about you?"

"I've got some of Cortez's money I'd just love to gamble with."

"Well, then, why don't you remind Aeneva of how much you had together? Don't be cruel and don't be forceful. Take your time, show her that you care. In time she'll want to be with you."

Trenton shook his head doubtfully. "I don't know. You should have seen her holding that baby. I've never seen her look so content. I would've given anything if it were mine."

"I forgot to tell you something, boy. When she was giving birth to the child, she would occasionally doze off. Once, while she was resting, she called your name. I heard it and so did he."

Trenton's eyes met Joe's, then slid past him to the mountains above El Circulo. He hadn't lost her yet.

Trenton walked up the stairs to Ignacio's porch. The old man was sitting in his chair. "I'd like to speak with you, Ignacio. It's very important."

"If it's about Aeneva and Ladro . . ."

Trenton held up his hand. "No, it's about Emiliano Cortez. May I sit down?"

Ignacio nodded, waving with the knife in his hand for Trenton to sit down on the step next to him. "What about Cortez, the *cabrón?*"

"He is right behind me with twenty men. They're well armed and Cortez is desperate. He wants Aeneva and he'll fight to get her back."

"As you will, eh, gringo?"

Trenton avoided the trap. "I thought you'd want to know about Cortez."

"Yes, it is good you have come to me. I will alert the men of the village and all of the guards. We will be prepared for Cortez." Ignacio held up his piece of wood, squinting as he looked at it. "What do you think? It is going to be a doll for Aeneva's baby."

"You are good with the knife and wood, Ignacio,

almost as good as you are with your tongue."

Ignacio smiled, nodding his head in appreciation. "I think I like you, gringo. You are not stupid." Ignacio rubbed the wood with his finger and continued carving. "How do you feel about your wife having Ladro's child?"

"How do you think I feel?"

"Angry, deceived, as if your heart were cut out."

"That's a good description."

"Yet you come here and do not ask to see her. Why?"

"You tell me, old man. You are the smart one."

"I think you plan to win her back, no?"

"I would be stupid not to, wouldn't I? I have known her almost all of my life and I feel I have loved her even longer. I don't plan to give her up so easily."

"I was hoping you would say that, gringo."

"Why? I thought Ladro was your friend."

"He is my friend, but she is your wife." Ignacio shrugged his shoulders. "I would not be willing to give up such a woman."

Trenton stood up. "Cortez will be here soon. When he finds out he can't get through the guards or the cactus, he'll try to think of another way to get in. Make sure your men are prepared."

"We will be prepared, don't worry."

Trenton nodded and started to walk away but stopped. "Tell Ladro I want to see him at *El Negro*'s place. It's important."

"I will tell him. Good luck, gringo. You will need it against such a worthy opponent as Ladro."

* * *

322

Larissa went to Trenton. "I am sorry, Trenton. Joe told me everything."

"Don't be sorry, I haven't given up yet."

"I did not think my brother would do such a thing. Another man's wife."

Trenton smiled. "Larissa, you are ready to take another woman's husband away from her. There is no difference."

"I suppose you are right. Does she intend to stay with Ladro now that you are here?"

"She says it is the right thing to do, especially now that she had Ladro's child."

"But what does she feel, Trenton? Does she still love you?"

"I don't know."

"I know how you can find out."

"I'm not going to force her, Larissa."

"I didn't say to force her, not in that way, anyway." Larissa put her arm through Trenton's. "But if you let her know you were interested in someone else, maybe she would realize how important you are to her."

"Aeneva's not like that."

"Every woman is like that, Trenton. Believe me. If she wants you badly enough and still cares for you, she won't like seeing you with me."

Trenton looked down the road and saw a tall figure walking toward them. "We'll talk about it later. Someone is coming to see you."

Larissa turned and looked down the road. She shielded her eyes against the sun, but as she saw the tall, dark figure approaching, she knew instantly that it was her brother.

"Ladro!" She ran until she reached her brother, throwing herself in his arms. He turned, lifting her from the ground. "Oh, Ladro, I can't believe it's really you."

"It's really me, little sister. Let me look at you." Ladro gave an appraising eye. "You are all grown up, Larissa. And so beautiful."

Larissa reached up and caressed her brother's face, hardly able to control the rising emotion in her throat. "I knew you would come for me someday. I knew it."

Ladro pulled Larissa into his arms, looking past her to Trenton, who stood in front of Joe's shack. It was strange. Both of their searches were at an end, but at least he had the satisfaction of holding Larissa. He felt he owed Trenton something for bringing Larissa to him. He even respected the man. But not enough to give up Aeneva.

"Let's walk, Ladro."

Ladro pulled his eyes away from the door and smiled at Larissa. "Yes, I think the last time we walked together we got in trouble for going so far away from the house."

"We did. And Papa said that we didn't do our chores. He called us lazy."

"But he smiled too, remember?"

"They were good to us, Papa and Mama."

"Yes, they were. They gave us a good start in life. We can always be grateful for that."

"I was so frightened that day, Ladro. I do not think I have ever been so frightened in my whole life."

Ladro tightened his arm around Larissa. "You don't have to be frightened anymore. I will never leave you again."

"I am not a little girl anymore, Ladro. I don't need your protection now."

"I don't ever want you to be alone again, Larissa. Not ever."

"What happened to you, Ladro? I have always wondered."

"I wandered from place to place, trying to find work and trying to find clues about you and Manuela. I finally found two of the men who kidnapped you. I shot them both. Their friends came after me and I wound up here. A family took me in and I stayed here for a long time until I felt ready to leave again."

"And then you worked for Cortez?"

"Yes. What do you know of him, Larissa?"

"He was the man I was sold to, Ladro."

Ladro stopped, a look of astonishment on his face. "You were sold to Cortez?"

"Yes."

"How long were you with him?"

"I was with him from the time I was twelve until I was twenty. Then he sold me to a whorehouse in Guadalupe del Sol, where I was given only to the richest men. And I was always to be ready if Cortez came into town." She watched his face, terrified his look of love would change to disgust. But his dark eyes filled with anger.

"He knew where you were all the time? The bastard!"

"He was not bad to me, Ladro. He gave me nice clothes and presents and he taught me to read and write."

"And what else did he teach you?"

Larissa turned away, ashamed to face her brother. "You don't want to know, Ladro. Please."

Ladro gripped Larissa's shoulder, his dark eyes boring into hers. "What else did he teach you?"

"He taught me many ways to please a man."

"*Dios!*" The curse came from so deep inside him, it hurt. "He did this to a child?"

"Yes. But he did not hurt me, Ladro. He was kind to me in a strange sort of way."

"Why are you defending this man? Don't you realize that what he did to you was against the laws of God?"

"I know more than anyone what he did to me, Ladro. So please, do not tell me about God." Larissa wrapped her arms around herself, feeling chilled in spite of the sun. "I have known men who were crueler. At least he took care of me."

Ladro made an effort to control his temper. "Did you know that I was looking for you?"

Larissa nodded and lowered her eyes, unable to face her brother.

"Then why didn't you tell Cortez you wanted to see me? If he cared for you as you say, he would have let you."

"I was ashamed. I did not want you to see what I had become."

"So you let me go on searching for you." Ladro let go of his sister, staring at her in disbelief. "Do you know how many innocent women I sold to Cortez to try to find out where you were? And all the time you knew I was looking for you."

"I know it sounds horrible, but please do not hate

me, Ladro. I would die if you hated me." Her voice broke.

"I don't hate you, Larissa. I could never hate you." Ladro pulled his sister to him again, stroking her hair and kissing the top of her head. "I am just so sorry that you ever had to feel ashamed enough to hide from me. I wish I could have helped you."

"You are helping now. It feels so good to be with you."

Ladro held Larissa for some minutes until he gently pushed her away from him. "What about the white man?"

"Trenton?"

"Why are you with him?"

"We have been traveling together. He has taken care of me."

"And what else?"

"There is nothing else. He is my friend. That is all."

"I don't believe you. I don't trust him."

"You are not one to talk of trust, brother." Larissa pulled away from him, her hands on her hips, her dark eyes blazing with anger. "Trenton is a good man and you have no right to judge him."

"I don't want you staying here. I want you to come with me."

"And stay with your woman, Trenton's wife?"

"I want to explain about her."

"You do not need to explain about her. You kidnapped her and fell in love with her. I am glad for her sake that you did not sell her to Cortez."

"I didn't mean for it to happen, Larissa. I was going to sell her to Cortez but I couldn't. Once I got shot by some Kiowas. Aeneva took care of me. She had lost her memory by then and she was frightened and unsure of herself, but she took care of me when she could have run away. She was brave and she was never once frightened of me."

"Did you know all along that she was married?"

"Yes."

"And yet you let yourself fall in love with her. Oh, Ladro." Larissa sighed deeply, bending over to pick a small red wildflower. She brought it to her nose, breathing deeply, then opened her hand and let it drop to the ground. "I am guilty of the same thing, only what I did was worse. I knew that Cortez had Aeneva and I didn't tell Trenton because I was afraid to lose him. I would have done anything to keep him."

"I understand why you did it."

"No, I don't think that you do. I also knew all about you and I was willing to risk never seeing you again so that I could have Trenton. I cannot believe that I would do such a thing. But he made me feel clean again, Ladro. Like a woman worthy of love." She trembled, pleading with her eyes.

"Don't do this to yourself, Larissa. You were afraid to lose him. He was the first person you could hold on to since you were taken away from our parents."

"You do forgive me, don't you, Ladro?"

"Yes, I do." Ladro held Larissa again, shutting his eyes to push away thoughts of what he had done to Aeneva. He spoke, his lips brushing Larissa's hair. "We have done what we had to do. You have held on to Trenton, just as I am holding on to Aeneva, out of love and need. I understand you, little sister. Better than anyone else could."

Larissa rubbed Ladro's cheek. "I am glad I have you, Ladro."

"I will protect you, Larissa. You will never again have to depend on a man like Cortez."

"Oh, Ladro, we will never be free of Cortez. He is coming here."

"I know. Ignacio told me. Why were you and Trenton traveling with him?"

"Because he knows what a good tracker Trenton is. And because it gave him a perverse pleasure to have Trenton track his own wife without even knowing it."

"But he did know. You told him."

"I couldn't go on lying. I had to tell Trenton the truth."

"And you haven't lost him, have you? I saw the way he looked at you. He cares for you."

"Yes, he does care for me. He took me with him. He didn't want to leave me with Cortez."

"I owe him for that. Why hasn't Cortez given up?"

"He needs her and the child to show his grandfather that he is married and has an heir. He won't give up." Larissa grabbed Ladro's arm. "And it kills him that she is with you. He hates you, Ladro, and even more, he fears you. He will do anything to stop you."

"Don't worry about me, Larissa. I can take care of Cortez."

"Enough of Cortez. I won't let him spoil my happiness now."

"Have you heard I have a son?"

"Yes."

"You aren't happy for me."

"I am happy for you, Ladro. But I am sad for Trenton."

Ladro turned away, his face angry. "Why must it always come back to him?"

"Because he is her husband. It should be his child, not yours."

"I didn't expect this from you, Larissa." Ladro's eyes pleaded with his sister's. "I know what I have done, but I cannot give her up. I cannot."

Larissa put her arms around her brother's neck, knowing exactly how he felt, yet not knowing how to comfort him. They both loved people they could not have. The difference was she had accepted it but Ladro had not.

Aeneva put her head back against the tree, feeling the cool breeze blow against her face. Her body was beginning to regain some of its old strength; she was beginning to feel good again. She opened her eyes and watched as the sun danced on the surface of the little stream. It soothed her and brought back pleasant memories of her childhood. Memories that included Trenton.

"You look happy."

Aeneva was startled by the familiar voice that seemed to come in answer to her thoughts. She looked up at Trenton. He looked like a boy. She was afraid to open herself to him. "I am content."

"Can I sit down?"

"Yes."

Trenton sat down next to her, playing with the

plants on the ground. "I came to say good-bye."

"Good-bye? You are leaving?"

"I think it's the best thing to do under the circumstances, don't you?"

"But why so soon?" Aeneva could not contain the note of desperation in her voice.

"There is no reason to stay now, is there?"

Aeneva could not meet Trenton's eyes and she turned away. "I do not want to drive you away, Trenton. I did not mean for this to happen." In spite of herself, Aeneva began to cry. She covered her face with her hands, trying to hide from him. She felt his arm go around her.

"It's all right, Aeneva. Don't cry."

"Why are you doing this?" she asked suddenly, anger apparent in her voice.

"Doing what?" Trenton asked innocently.

Her anger grew. "I know you, Trenton Hawkins. I know the way your mind thinks."

Trenton smiled openly, wiping a tear from Aeneva's cheek. "Then you know that I can't be angry with you. I just want to be friends."

"You do not. You are trying to change my mind."

"Aeneva." He ran his hand lightly across her mouth. "I don't want you remembering me the way I was yesterday. I was angry and hurt. I don't want you to hate me."

"I could never hate you."

"Good." Trenton looked out at the water, knowing that what Joe had said was true. Already Aeneva was warming up to him. But he knew he had to take it slowly. "Do you remember the time you and I and your brothers out-hunted Gray Fox and the other boys? How many rabbits did we get?"

"Many more than they did. They were so angry."

"I remember. Gray Fox tried to hurt you."

"But you helped me. You almost killed him, you were so angry." She looked into his eyes. "You have always been there for me." She could feel herself getting lost and she quickly looked away. "Will you be leaving alone?"

"I don't know. It depends on what Larissa wants to do. She may want to stay here with you and Ladro."

"Is she very beautiful? I have not seen her yet."

"Yes, she's beautiful."

"Where will you go from here?"

"I'm going back to Nathan."

"He must miss us terribly."

"I want Joe to come with me, but he can't ride the way his leg is."

"I think I can fix his leg, Trenton."

"Did you tell him that?"

"Yes, but he will not let me try to fix it. I once watched Grandmother do it. It would not be easy, but I think I could do it. I would have to break the leg again, then I would set it so that the bones grow back the right way."

"Are you sure it would work?"

"No, I am not sure, but I think I can do it. He can barely walk the way he is now."

"I know and he really wants to go north with me. I'll talk to him about it. If he agrees to do it, I'll stay until his leg heals."

"All right." Aeneva felt excitement rise inside her, just knowing that Trenton would be around for a while longer.

"How is your son?"

"He is well," Aeneva said, avoiding Trenton's eyes.

"Have you named him?"

"No, not yet." She was feeling acutely uncomfortable at Trenton's ease in discussing her son.

"Well, I should go back and check on Joe. He's in a lot of pain."

"Talk to him today, Trenton. I can do it as soon as he wants me to. I just have to find some plants around here that are good for healing."

"Sun Dancer would be proud of you."

"Why do you say that?"

"Because no matter what happens to you, you always survive and you never lose your heart."

"Trenton, don't . . ." She turned away, but his hand on her shoulder stopped her.

"It's true, Aeneva. I understand why you did what you did; you had no real choice. Just as I had no choice with Lydia. It's all right."

"It was easier when you were angry with me."

"I can't be angry with you. But I can let you know that I'll always love you."

"Oh, Trenton." Aeneva leaned against him, feeling his arms go around her. It felt so good to be with him. It felt so right.

"The baby is waiting for you, Aeneva." Ladro's voice startled Aeneva. She quickly pulled away from Trenton. She noticed that Trenton seemed to enjoy her discomfiture. She stood up, glaring at Trenton as she took Ladro's arm. He guided her back to Ignacio's.

"Was he professing his love for you?" Ladro asked sarcastically.

"No, he was telling me that he doesn't hate me. He

333

says he understands why I did what I did."

Ladro nodded. "Yes, I bet he does."

"Do not be angry with him, Ladro. He did nothing wrong."

That was just the point, Ladro thought. The man was smart. He was playing on Aeneva's emotions and already she was defending him. Yesterday he had walked out on her, today he was holding her in his arms. "I'm not angry," Ladro replied calmly. He could play the game too.

"Good." She squeezed Ladro's arm. "How is your sister?"

"She is wonderful. She is so beautiful and so grown up, I can't believe it. We talked of the things we did as children and all of the trouble we used to get into."

"Yes, it is special when you share a part of your life like that with someone." Aeneva thought back to her childhood and of all the things she and Trenton had done. She smiled inside.

"She is in love with Trenton. Did you know that?"

"No." Aeneva tried to force any emotion from her voice. "But she is so happy to see you, she will stay here I am sure."

"I don't think so. She says she wants to go north with him. She wants to help him care for his son."

"She will help him care for Nathan?" Aeneva felt the pull inside her. How could Larissa care for Nathan? She didn't know him like she did—she didn't love him like she did.

"I think she just wants to be with Trenton."

"But how can she care for a child she doesn't even

334

know?" Aeneva stopped, realizing she had said too much. She continued toward the house, but Ladro took her arm.

"Do you want to be with him, Aeneva? I will not stand in your way if that's what you want."

"I did not say that I wanted to be with him. I merely asked if your sister was able to care for a child." She yanked her arm away, walking up the steps. Marcela met her on the porch, holding the baby in her arms. She handed him to Aeneva. "Thank you, Marcela. Was he crying long?"

"He is a good boy. He only cries when he is hungry."

Aeneva held her son to her breast, sitting down on one of the chairs. She watched Ladro as he walked across the yard to the corral. He was a good man, a handsome man. He would be a good father. Still . . .

"What is the matter, Aeneva? Are things not going well between you and Ladro?"

"Things are well enough."

"You don't lie well. Is it your husband?"

Aeneva continued to watch Ladro until he was out of sight and she turned to Marcela. "Yes, it is my husband."

"You still love him, don't you?"

"I have never stopped loving him, Marcela. He is a part of me, just as this child is a part of me."

"Then why do you stay with Ladro? You will only hurt him more if you stay with him out of pity."

"I am not with him out of pity. I love him."

"Then I am the one who does not understand."

"I am not quite sure I understand either." She

kissed her son on his small head. "Ladro is strong, but he needs me. We are tied together through this child."

"So you will stay with him because of the child? That would be a mistake, my dear. The children do not stay little and cute forever. What happens when they get bigger and you find that Ladro has not fulfilled you as you thought he would?"

"I do not know, Marcela. I want to do the right thing."

"You want to do the right thing for Ladro, but what about for you?" Her hand squeezed Aeneva's shoulder. "I did not love Ignacio when I married him."

"But you love him now. I can tell by the way you look at each other."

"Yes, I love him now for different reasons. He is a good man, he will deny no one help, he has been a good father. But he is not the man I loved when I was young. The man I loved was sent to prison and Ignacio married me because I was carrying the man's child."

"But you learned to love Ignacio. I already love Ladro and our love will only grow stronger."

"Why do you lie to yourself, girl? I have never forgotten my first love. There were nights when I thought I would die for the want of him. I even thought of taking our son and running away to him."

"But you did not, you stayed."

"I stayed because I found out he had died in prison. If he had been alive, I probably would have gone to him."

"I am sorry, Marcela."

"Do not be sorry for me, girl. I just want you to learn from my mistake. You have a chance to be with the man you truly love. Do not throw that chance away." Marcela watched Larissa as she walked with Ladro across the yard. "Do you see that girl, Ladro's sister? She is young and beautiful and she wants your husband. Do you want to give him up to her?"

"I do not have a choice," Aeneva replied coldly, watching the beautiful young woman as she held on to Ladro's arm and laughed gaily. She was darkly beautiful and full of life. She was the kind of woman that Trenton would be attracted to. "She is beautiful. She resembles Ladro."

"Yes, and like Ladro, she will not give up."

"Ladro has been good to me, Marcela. He has not forced me to stay with him."

"Aeneva, I love Ladro like a son. What I am going to say comes from my heart because I hurt for you. Ladro is a clever man. He will not force you because he knows you are already tied to him through the child. He knows he can tell you to leave at any time but you will stay."

Aeneva didn't argue because she knew what Marcela said was true. "I know that what you tell me is true, Marcela, but I still do not know if it will change anything. Trenton is strong, much stronger than Ladro. He will be fine without me."

Marcela stood up, patting Aeneva on the shoulder. "It is your decision, girl, but make the right one. Sometimes the nights are unbearably long and lonely when you are not sleeping next to the one you love."

Aeneva held her child up to her shoulder, patting

337

him on the back. She had her son now, but what would happen when he was older and did not need her so much? Would her yearning for Trenton tear her apart? Would the nights without him be so lonely that she would want to die? She stood up, looking out at Larissa once more. Could she give Trenton up so easily to another woman? She didn't know. She knew only that when he had held her in his arms again it had felt so good, so right. She had never felt that way in Ladro's arms and she wasn't sure if she ever would.

Chapter XII

Cortez tried to get through El Circulo, but he found it more difficult to penetrate than he had anticipated. He tried to bluff his way through the guards, saying he was on the run. The guards cut him off before he could finish. They told him to go back the way he had come or die where he stood. Cortez considered trying to break through the guards, but the cactus looked like a solid wall and there was no way to know how many guns were behind it. When he was sure the guards could no longer see them, he turned, riding a wide arc toward the foothills behind El Circulo.

"Tell me again about El Circulo, Pedro."

"As I said before, there is a way through the cactus, if you know it. But it is almost impossible to get through unless you know the way."

"How many people live there, do you think?"

"I don't know, *Patrón.*"

"Guess!"

"One hundred, two hundred at the most."

"But there are women and children, no?"

"Yes. And many old ones. Men who have been there many years."

"And is there a central place, a place where they all meet?"

"I don't know, but there's an old man named Ignacio. He decides who can enter."

"He won't decide this time, Pedro. Is there a path through the cactus from this side?"

"I don't know, *Patrón*. The stories say there is only one way in."

Cortez brushed some sand from his sleeve. "Then we will have to make another one, won't we, Pedro? I want those people. Understand that. I will stop at nothing to get them."

Aeneva threw the plant down. "This will not do, Marcela. I do not recognize any of these plants. We have a plant that, when it is cooked and made into a tea, will make a man sleepy. Joe must be completely asleep before I try to fix his leg."

"Well, that is easy. I can just give him mescal."

"What is mescal?"

"It comes from these." Marcela pointed to a large, deep green cactus.

"What is it called?"

"The maguey. We take the juice from its leaves and make it into a liquor. It can make men crazy if they drink too much, but it can also put a man to sleep if he drinks the right amount."

"All right, we will use this mescal." Aeneva looked into her basket. "I hope these plants you've given me will work, Marcela. I must have a poultice that will keep the swelling down."

"I have used these many times. They will work."

Aeneva put her arm around Marcela. "Thank you, Marcela. I do not mean to doubt you. I am just worried. I have never done this myself. I only watched my grandmother do it."

"*El Negro* told me you could do magic things with your hands just as your grandmother did. He trusts you."

"But what if I fail? What if he is more crippled than before?"

"You cannot doubt yourself, girl, or it will never work. Come, he is waiting for you."

They walked to Joe's small shack. Trenton and Larissa were sitting outside. Aeneva tried to ignore them, but Trenton stood up.

"Aeneva, I want you to meet Larissa."

Larissa stood and the two women appraised each other silently. Finally Aeneva spoke.

"Your brother is happy to have you back. He loves you very much."

Larissa put her arm through Trenton's. "It appears you have made my brother very happy. He loves his new son." Aeneva forced herself not to look at Trenton. She smiled past him at Joe, who stood in the doorway. "Are you ready, Joe?"

"I guess I'm as ready as I'll ever be. What've you got in the basket?"

"Some herbs I need to boil up. I need a pot." Aeneva went into the shack.

"Do you still have that bottle of mescal I gave you?" Marcela stood with her hands on her hips.

"Yeah. It's over on the shelf. Why?" Joe eyed Marcela suspiciously.

"That is what you will drink." Marcela went to the shelf for the bottle.

"I hate that stuff. I thought you were going to make me some of that nice sleeping tea, Aeneva."

"I do not know the plants around here, Joe. Drink this cactus juice. Marcela tells me it will make you sleep."

"Yeah, it'll make me sleep all right and when I wake up I'll wish I was dead."

Aeneva looked at Trenton, who had just stepped into the shack. "Where is Larissa?"

"She went to see Ladro."

Joe cursed loudly. "I'm not drinking this *mierda!*"

Aeneva shook her head. "Please talk to him."

"Come on, Joe, after a couple of glasses you won't even notice the taste. I'll drink with you."

"All right, but I'm not crazy about this. I don't like it one bit." Joe walked over to the table and sat down heavily.

Marcela poured. "Drink, drink, *Negro*, it will not kill you."

"That's what you say, woman. I don't see you drinking any of this poison."

Marcela took the glass out of Joe's hand and downed the liquid without hesitating. "There, *Negro*, would you feel better if I drank along with you?"

Joe laughed loudly, pounding his hand on the table. "Now I see why old Ignacio hangs on to you, woman. You're a tough one, all right."

"Yes, I am tough and do not argue with me. Now

drink up."

Aeneva smiled as she listened to the two banter back and forth. She put the different plants and herbs in the pot and poured water over them, hanging the pot over the fire. She leaned against the fireplace, watching the flames dance around. She couldn't stop thinking about Larissa and the possessive way she had looked at Trenton. She hated to think of him in the arms of another woman.

"Hey, Aeneva, what you doing over there? Come over here." Joe waved his hand toward Aeneva. "And you too, boy. I'm not getting my leg broke by no savage without you for protection."

Trenton shook his head. "Are you drunk already, Joe? I thought you could hold your liquor."

"Don't start on me, boy. I'm still bigger than you are."

"Yeah, I know, Joe. How's the leg feel?"

"What leg? I don't feel any leg. In fact, I don't need nothing done now. I feel fine."

"Don't argue with Aeneva, Joe. She can be mean, remember?"

"Yeah, I've seen her angry before. She's like her grandmother. They're both witches."

"Drink up, *Negro*. You are doing fine." Marcela refilled his glass.

Joe emptied the glass, pounding it on the table for more. "This isn't bad stuff. I kinda like it." He looked from Aeneva to Trenton, his eyes narrowing. "Why aren't you two together, huh? You belong together. I never seen two people who belong together more than you two."

"Don't, Joe. You're drunk." Trenton tried to quiet

his friend.

"Why? I can say what I want; this is my house." Joe waved his glass around the room, spilling some of the drink. "Why don't you just steal her away, boy. By God, if you had any sense that's what you'd do."

Trenton ran his fingers through his hair. "Aren't you tired, Joe? Wouldn't you like to rest for a while?"

"No, I feel fine. In fact, I feel like dancing." Joe stood up, knocking over the chair behind him. He stood on his bad leg, seemingly unmoved by the fact that it was badly mangled.

Aeneva stood up, attempting to walk to the fire, but Joe grabbed her and pulled her into his arms. "Did I ever tell you how beautiful you are?"

"No," Aeneva replied patiently, a smile on her face.

"I think you're almost as pretty as your grandmother was."

"Thank you, Joe. Can you let me go now?"

Joe bent over, making a sweeping gesture with his arm. "By all means, my lady, do your work. I'm not going anyplace."

Aeneva stirred the pot, sniffing at a spoonful of the smelly concoction.

"That smells terrible," Trenton volunteered as he walked up behind Aeneva.

"I don't care how badly it smells as long as it works." She looked over at Joe. "Will he be tired soon? Marcela told me this was strong drink."

"It is strong and it will work fast. He'll drop any time now." Trenton had barely uttered the words when Joe started to slump, quickly losing his balance. Trenton ran to him, catching him before he

344

hit the floor. He half carried him to the ornate bed and laid him down. Joe was unconscious before Trenton had even removed his pants. He covered him with a blanket and for the first time really looked at his leg. "Christ, his leg looks bad, Aeneva."

Aeneva kneeled next to Trenton. "Yes, I have seen it." She shook her head in doubt. "I am worried, Trenton. I do not know if I can help him. I was so sure that I could, but now I am afraid."

"Of what?"

"At least he can walk now. What if I make him a complete cripple? He will never forgive me; I will never forgive myself."

Trenton took Aeneva's hands, staring down at them solemnly. "These hands have so much knowledge in them, Aeneva. Knowledge that was passed from Horn to Sun Dancer to you. I am sure there were many times when they doubted themselves, but they went ahead and they did their best. Just as you are going to do right now."

"And if I fail?"

"You won't."

"But if I do?"

"You won't." He squeezed her hands, and bringing them to his lips, he kissed each one. "You will not fail, Aeneva. We all believe in you."

Aeneva could not take her eyes from Trenton's, feeling as though he had drawn her into the very depths of his soul. "Thank you." Reluctantly she withdrew her hands and turned to Marcela. "We will need a rock, heavy and rounded."

Marcela walked to the bed, opening the chest that stood beside it. She pulled out a huge hammer, using

345

both hands. "Old Maximo's tools. I thought of them last night." Out of her basket she pulled some clean cloth, some pieces of flat board, and some padding made from mattress filling.

Aeneva examined Joe's leg and felt the ugly lump where the bones had mended poorly. She took the padding and wrapped it around the leg. She put one of the boards underneath the leg for support and she picked up the hammer. She looked at Joe's serene face and again she was filled with self-doubt. Perhaps she wasn't strong enough to do it; perhaps he would be better off without it being done.

"Do you want me to do it, Aeneva?" Trenton asked in a gentle but firm tone.

Aeneva took a deep breath and shook her head. "No, I can do it." She held the hammer tightly in her hands. "Hold him down, Trenton. Hold him tightly." She waited until Trenton nodded, then raised the hammer high. She struck the leg with a hard, sharp blow. She heard the crack of the bones as they broke. She felt the leg. The bones had broken cleanly. She took Joe's foot in her hand, gripping it firmly and pulling the leg straight. She heard the bones crack again as she pulled. "I will need the poultice now, Marcela." Aeneva dipped pieces of cloth in the mixture and wrapped them around the leg. Then she placed the boards on both sides of the leg to keep it stiff and immobile. She covered Joe with the blankets and leaned back, pushing the damp hair from her face.

"He will sleep for a long time now, Aeneva. You sit down and rest. I will send Ignacio with some food and coffee."

Aeneva took Marcela's hand with both of hers. "Thank you, Marcela. I could not have done this without your help."

"Yes, you could have." Marcela looked at Trenton. "Make sure she rests for a while. She has not been sleeping well lately."

"Here, sit down." Trenton pulled out a chair, but Aeneva shook her head. "I'd rather sit outside." She walked to the steps and sat down. "He will be in much pain when he wakes up. I wish I had my tea."

"Joe's strong, he'll be all right."

"I am worried, Trenton. What if the leg does not heal? What if . . ."

"No more what ifs. Joe will be fine. It took a lot of courage to do what you just did."

"It took a lot of courage to do what Joe did. He trusts me more than I trust myself." Aeneva tried to look at Trenton but she could not.

"Where will Larissa sleep now that Joe needs the bed?"

Trenton shrugged. "Out here with me, I guess. She got used to sleeping on the ground. She won't mind it."

"Is she going north with you?"

Trenton looked at Aeneva's large round eyes. "It's up to her."

"She does not know Nathan. He will need someone who knows him." She stopped suddenly, realizing what she had said. She felt like a trapped deer that had nowhere to flee.

"He will be all right, Aeneva. I will take care of him. Your family will help me."

"I know you will take care of him. I am sorry." She

turned away, unable to look at Trenton. His presence was so overwhelming that she felt as if she couldn't breathe. She felt as if her chest would break open and her heart would be exposed for him to see. Only Trenton had ever made her feel this way.

"I miss you, Aeneva." She felt the warmth of his hand on her shoulder. "I am empty without you."

"Please do not, Trenton," she said in a choked voice. She stood up. "I must go back to Ignacio's house to feed my baby. I will be back to check on Joe in a while."

Trenton didn't try to stop Aeneva. He watched her as she walked away, her tall frame striding along the trail, the brightly colored skirt barely covering her ankles. She looked like a girl who was about to go picking wildflowers instead of a woman who was on her way to feed her newborn baby. He had seen her begin to weaken and he had taken advantage. He knew that she still loved him; he could tell by the way she continually avoided his eyes. He also knew that she was confused right now and that he couldn't push her. If he did, he might push her away from him forever.

Aeneva was nursing the baby when Ladro walked in. She looked up at him. "I know what I want to name the baby."

"What?"

"James. It is a good strong name."

"Why James?"

"I like the name."

348

"I was hoping we could name him after my father, Roberto."

"What about James Roberto?"

"I don't like it. My son is Mexican, he should have a Mexican name."

"*Your* son is *my* son. I like the name James."

"I will not argue with you about this. His name will be Roberto."

"You call him what you like. I will call him James." Aeneva stood up, placing the baby in the cradle. "I am going back to check on Joe."

"Is the gringo there?"

Aeneva turned, her eyes narrowed in defiance. "Yes, he is there."

"What do you think when you see him, Aeneva?"

"I do not think anything."

Ladro strode across the room and grabbed Aeneva. He kissed her hard on the mouth. She tried to pull away, but Ladro held her. "I want you to think about that when you see the gringo."

Aeneva threw him an angry glance and left the room, stopping only to get a container of soup from the counter by the fireplace. She walked back to Joe's shack using the path that crossed the shady part of the arroyo. Laughter sounded as she neared the front steps of the shack. The door stood open.

"Oh, Trenton, you make me laugh."

Aeneva paused on the steps, clearing her voice as she went up. Trenton and Larissa were sitting on the floor, their backs against the wall, their heads close together, laughing.

"Can I come in?" Aeneva asked. "I have come to

check on Joe."

"Sure," Trenton answered easily. "He hasn't been awake yet."

Aeneva walked over to Joe, kneeling by the bed. She felt his forehead, then unwrapped the leg to check for swelling. The skin was swollen and discolored but the leg looked good.

"That you, Aeneva?" Joe asked in a tired, weak voice.

Aeneva wiped the sweat from Joe's brow. "It's me, Joe. How do you feel?"

"I feel like my head's been run over by a herd of buffalo."

"How does your leg feel?"

"It feels better than my head."

"Good."

"How's the leg feel?" Trenton asked, squatting next to Aeneva.

"Like I told Aeneva, my head feels worse than my leg."

"Well, you should be recovered in no time then."

"I hope so."

"Are you in much pain, Joe? If you are I can find something to take the pain away."

"No, I'm not in much pain. Couldn't be any worse than what you had to go through having that baby. God, I never seen anything so incredible in all my life." Joe looked at Trenton. "You should've seen her. You would've been proud of her."

"I am proud of her."

Aeneva ignored Trenton's reply. "Are you hungry? Marcela sent over some good soup."

"No, I'm not hungry. Say, did you name that boy

350

yet? Every child needs a name. You can't go too long without naming him."

"In my tribe many times parents will wait until their children earn names before they are given, or they wait for signs. My grandfather was named Stalking Horse after it was found that he could hunt wild horses better than anyone. And Grandmother was named Sun Dancer because it seemed as if she danced in the sun every day she was alive."

"And you were named Winter because you were born in a snowstorm and you survived. Your strength and your beauty shone through even when you were first born."

Aeneva didn't avoid Trenton's eyes this time. "And you were called Swiftly Running Deer because never was a boy fleeter of foot. I used to watch you, your light hair shining in the sun, running next to my brothers. You were unlike anyone I had ever seen. I asked my grandmother if the sun had kissed your hair because it seemed to shine like gold."

Joe cleared his throat. "Well, you never did tell me what you named your boy."

Aeneva turned her eyes away from Trenton's and she spoke in a low voice. "I will call him James."

"James," Joe repeated. "Isn't that . . ."

"My father's name," Trenton interrupted. "You named him after my father?"

"It is a good name. That is why I chose it."

"Yes, it is a good name," Trenton agreed. "What does Ladro think of it?"

"He wanted a Mexican name. But he is my son also. I will call him James."

Joe took Aeneva's hand and squeezed it. "You look

tired. Why don't you go home and get some rest. I'm doing just fine."

"Just let me wrap your leg back up." Aeneva rewrapped the boards so that Joe's leg was held straight. "Do not move. I want you to be still so the leg can heal properly this time. If you need anything, have Trenton get it for you."

"I'll be good, don't you worry."

Aeneva stood up, walking to the door. "If you need anything or you have any pain, have Trenton come for me." She nodded politely at Larissa, who was seated at the table. "I will be here in the morning." She walked out the door to the trail that led back to Ignacio's. She heard footsteps behind her and she knew it was Trenton.

"Aeneva, wait!"

Aeneva stopped without turning. She didn't want to look into his face, into those clear blue eyes that threatened to engulf her.

"Why did you name your son James?"

"I told you why." She still wouldn't turn around.

Trenton put his hands on her shoulders, turning her to face him. When she wouldn't look at him, he put his hand on her chin and forced her to look up. "Why did you name him after my father?"

She felt her resolve drain away. "Because I could not let you go. At least this way we would still be tied in some way."

"Aeneva." Trenton put his arms around her, holding her as gently as he would a china doll. "Come back with me."

"I cannot."

"I will take care of your son. I will learn to love him."

"No, Trenton. Please! Please!" Aeneva tried to pull away but Trenton stopped her.

"Ladro will never make you happy the way I make you happy. He can never love you the way I do." He touched his mouth to hers. He kissed her gently at first, and then more passionately. He felt her body stiffen. Before she could pull away, he released her and quietly walked away.

Aeneva closed her eyes and relived the kiss. Her body trembled. It wasn't like Ladro's kiss—forceful and demanding—it was a soft, gentle, loving kiss. It was the kind of kiss that would never lose its excitement to her. It was the kind of kiss that could remind her when she was old how wonderful it had been to be young.

Tears welled in her eyes and she started back toward Ignacio's. She envisioned her grandparents and how much in love they had been. She remembered how much her grandmother had loved Trenton. It was he who had taken her grandmother to her dying place and stayed there with her until she was gone. It was he who had placed her grandmother on her burial platform next to her grandfather. And it was Trenton who had rescued her from Crooked Teeth when no one else could. Trenton loved her as no one else ever would.

She wiped the tears from her eyes and looked up at Ignacio's house. She saw the room where she slept with the man who was the father of her child, the man who loved her and cared for her, the man who had risked his life for her. This was the man she had chosen to stay with not out of love, but out of loyalty. He needed her, and as long as he needed her she would stay. And like Marcela, the nights of her future would be long and lonely. She would never again have the passion she had had with Trenton. But she would survive, because it was meant to be so. In her heart she would always carry the memories of the man she truly loved, the man who had taken her heart as a child and never given it back. The man she would love until she died.

It had taken Cortez and his men over a week to backtrack through the foothills. Now they were hidden in the rough country behind El Circulo.

Pedro approached Cortez. "What do we do now, *Patrón?* There are no guards, but there is still the cactus."

"We wait. I want to watch these people for a while. Once we see what they do and where they go, where the guards are located, then we can begin our work. The men have their machetes and we have plenty of time."

"What if Ladro and the others have escaped?"

"They have not escaped. They feel safe there. They will not leave for a while." He smiled when he thought of Aeneva alone with her husband and lover. He wondered if one of them was dead by now. It didn't matter to him, as long as he got Aeneva back. No one deceived him and got away with it. He took a drink from his bottle and closed his eyes as the mescal burned his throat. It would be worth waiting, now that he would soon have Aeneva. And Larissa—she would pay, too, for her deceit. Well, it only proved that he could trust no one but himself. As soon as he showed Aeneva and the child to his grandfather, he would have it all. He would be one of the richest men in Mexico. No one would ever deceive Emiliano Cortez again.

Ladro reached over, running his hand along Aeneva's hip. He kissed her on the neck. "You feel so good."

"Please, Ladro. It is too soon. I am still healing from the birth."

"I can't wait, Aeneva. It has been too long." He kissed her deeply, holding her hands against the mattress of the bed. "I want you, Aeneva."

"Ladro, please. I am not ready yet. Please."

Reluctantly Ladro let her go and rolled onto his back. "You liked me to touch you before. What has changed?"

"I have just had a baby, Ladro. I am tired and my body is not ready yet. Give me time."

"How much time? Until the gringo leaves?"

"It has nothing to do with him."

"Why do you lie to me, Aeneva? Do you think I am stupid? I know how you feel about him. I can see it every time you look at him."

"I do not want to talk about it."

"Well, you are going to talk about it because I want to be sure you know something. I won't give you up to him. He will never raise my son."

Aeneva felt a stabbing pain in her stomach. "I am not going to take the baby away from you, Ladro."

"That's right, you're not. Because if you do, I'll come after you. I would rather die than have my son raised by a white man."

"What is wrong with you? I thought you loved me. But now you are making threats. You sound like Cortez."

"No, Aeneva, I sound like me. I have never had anyone in my life. You are the first person I have ever loved besides my family. I will not let you go. I cannot."

Aeneva turned onto her side. He didn't sound like Ladro; he sounded like a stranger. "I am sorry if I have hurt you, Ladro. I will not see him again if that is what you want."

Ladro's arms went around her and his face was close to hers. "See him if you want to, but I will be watching. I won't let you take the baby when you go over there. I believe you care for me, Aeneva, but I also believe that when you are around him you cannot think clearly. He bewitches you."

"You make him sound like an evil person. He is not. He is my husband."

"Then go back to him. Go back to him, Aeneva, but you will never see your son again."

Aeneva bit her lip to keep from crying. She knew that Ladro was telling her the truth. He would never let her see James again if she went away with Trenton. She had been a stupid, foolish woman and she would pay for it the rest of her life. She had a child whom she loved dearly, but a man whom she knew less and less every day.

Perhaps it was her fault that this was happening to Ladro. He was a good man. He was only doing what he thought was right. And she had driven him to it. Her grandmother would have told her it was fate and she could not change her fate. She felt Ladro's face against her neck and she closed her eyes tightly, fighting back the tears. She had been given her punishment—to be near Trenton but never to have him again. She felt as though her heart had been ripped from her body and thrown away. And without Trenton she was not sure if she would ever find it again.

Aeneva quickly checked Joe and started on her way out, but Joe called her to come back.

"I thought you were asleep. I did not want to wake you."

"All I've been doing is sleeping." Joe studied Aeneva's face. "You still look tired. Don't you sleep at night?"

"I have to feed the baby."

"What is it, Aeneva? This is Joe talking."

"It is nothing, Joe." She tucked the blanket around him, although the room was hot. "Your leg is healing well. You should be able to stand on it soon."

"That's good. Why are you tucking this blanket around me? It's already so hot in here I can barely breathe."

"I am sorry." She shook her head. "I have to go now, Joe. I cannot be here when Trenton returns."

"Why not? You've been in and out of here lately like a fly. I've hardly seen you."

"I just cannot." She stood up, smoothing out her skirt. "I will get you something to eat before I go." She walked to the pot and spooned some stew into a bowl and brought it over to Joe. She propped him up in bed with some blankets and she handed him the

357

bowl. "If you do not need me anymore, I must go."

"You're as skittish as a deer today. If I didn't know better, I'd say you were afraid of something."

"I am not afraid of anything."

"Is it Trenton? Is he forcing himself on you? 'Cause if he is . . .'"

"No, Trenton has done nothing. He has been kind to me." Her eyes stared out of the small window above Joe's bed. "The bad spirits are making me pay for all of the terrible things I have done, Joe. I will never be allowed to take the Walking Trail up into heaven and see my grandparents when I die."

"What is this foolishness? What's come over you? You've never talked like this before."

Aeneva's eyes became glassy. She appeared not to even notice Joe anymore. "They were testing me. When I was a child, my Uncle Jean would leave some of his pretty trinkets on a blanket outside of his lodge. My brothers and I would look at them and we were tempted to take them. Once we did, and Grandfather punished us for it. It is the same now. The bad spirits have found out what I have done and they are not pleased. I am being punished. I am the grand-daughter of a great chief, the granddaughter of a great healer. I have dishonored them both. I have dishonored my whole family."

"Aeneva, look at me. Look at me!"

Reluctantly Aeneva looked at Joe. "They put me with Ladro to see if I could be strong away from my husband, but I was not. I was weak." She blinked and tears rolled down her cheeks. "I have dishonored my husband in a way that I would not dishonor my enemy. I deserve to be punished."

"Damn it, Aeneva. Listen to me. You are talking nonsense. You're tired; you've been through a lot. Give yourself time. You've got to forgive yourself. Trenton has forgiven you."

Aeneva acted as if she didn't hear Joe. She turned away from the bed and walked toward the door. "I will return later to check on you."

Joe watched Aeneva as she walked away and he was frightened for her. Honor was so important to her people and she was convinced she had dishonored everyone in her family. She needed help or she would break apart. Joe remembered seeing one of the slave girls on the plantation when he was a boy. Her name was Jasmine and she was beautiful. One of the master's sons took her for his mistress. At first she was scared, but in time she grew to accept it, or so everyone thought. But the longer it went on, the more disgraced and sullied she felt. She began to lose touch with reality until one day Joe's mother found her hanging in the barn. She hadn't been able to live with the dishonor. No matter what happened, Joe swore to himself, the same thing would not happen to Aeneva. Not as long as he and Trenton were around to help her.

Trenton was on his way back to Joe's. He had spent the morning helping Ignacio repair the barn. He was happy to see Aeneva on the trail. He'd barely seen her for over a week.

"Did you just see Joe?" he asked, smiling easily.

"Yes." Aeneva answered nervously.

"He seems better today, doesn't he?"

"Yes." Aeneva avoided contact with Trenton's eyes. She looked toward the house. She couldn't keep her mind off James.

"Aeneva, are you all right?"

"I must go." She walked past Trenton without saying another word.

"Aeneva!" Trenton shouted after her, but she didn't respond. He wanted to run after her, but he was trying to be patient. He didn't want to force her. But she had been acting strangely lately. He walked back to Joe's shack, stopping to get some fresh water from the spring-filled cistern. He walked into the shack to find Joe sitting up, his bad leg dangling off the bed, in an attempt to stand up on his good leg.

"What in hell are you doing?" Trenton rushed to Joe, pushing him back down and gently lifting the leg and placing it back on the bed.

"What are you doing? Do you know how long it took me to get this far?"

"Aeneva told you to lie still and you're going to lie still if I have to knock you out. What the hell were you trying to get up for anyway?"

"I wanted to go after Aeneva."

"But why? Aeneva can take care of herself. You, on the other hand, cannot."

"That's where you're dead wrong, boy. Aeneva needs all the help she can get."

"Is she in some kind of trouble? I just met her on the trail and she was acting real strange. She acted as if she didn't even know me."

"She's in bad shape, boy. She's not sleeping and having you here is driving her crazy."

Trenton flashed a smile. "Well, that's what I

hoped would happen."

"No, it's driving her real crazy. All she can think of when she looks at you is how she has dishonored you and her family and herself by being with Ladro and having his child. She keeps talking about the bad spirits."

"Aeneva?"

"It doesn't sound like her, does it? I'm worried, boy. She needs our help but as long as she stays in that house with Ladro there's not a damn thing we can do."

"I can go to Ladro, I can confront him. I know she still loves me. If given half a chance, I know she'd come with me."

"And the child?"

"I want him to come too."

"And what if Ladro doesn't want him to come? That doesn't leave Aeneva much of a choice, does it?"

"Then she is trapped here by the baby. She could never leave him, not even for me."

"And Ladro knows it, damn his soul!"

"I could always take her and the baby with me without telling Ladro."

"Take it easy, boy, don't forget we're in hostile territory. Ignacio is being our friend now, but if we cross Ladro, who knows what he would do. We're going to have to be real careful. We have to wait for just the right time."

"Is she coming back here today?"

"She said she'd be back later to check on me. But if she knows you're here, she might not come."

"Then we just won't let her know that I'm here. I've got to talk to her, Joe. Maybe she'll listen to me."

361

"Maybe, but be careful. She's real scared right now, like a trapped animal. If you push too hard in the state she's in, who knows what she'll do?"

"I'll be careful. I just want her to know that I love her and that I'm here for her."

"I think she already knows that, boy. That's part of what's driving her crazy."

"I'll be careful with her. I'll ask Larissa to keep Ladro occupied."

"Are you sure you can trust her?"

"I don't know for sure, but there's one way to find out." Trenton went outside, looking for Larissa. He found her in the arroyo by the stream sitting on the edge, her legs kicking at the water. "I need your help, Larissa."

Larissa turned. "You sound very serious, Trenton. What is it?"

"I need you to go see your brother later today. I need you to keep him busy for a while."

"So you can see your wife?"

"I need to talk to her while she's tending Joe. Something is wrong with her, Larissa. I'm worried. I think Ladro's threatening to keep their son if she decides to come back with me."

"And why shouldn't he? He is his son."

"He should have been my son, damn it!" Trenton squatted next to Larissa, pulling at the grass on the ground. "When your brother raided the Cheyennes, Aeneva was already carrying my child. She and many of the women and children were forced to walk for weeks. She lost the baby. It was a boy."

"I'm sorry. I did not know."

"Your brother is using his son to keep Aeneva with

him. And it's killing her."

Larissa turned to Trenton. She started to protest, but she said nothing. She kicked at the water for a minute, watching as the droplets ran along her bare legs. "Ladro told me he has never loved anyone the way he loves Aeneva."

"Yes, I believe he does. But you, yourself, have learned that you can't get someone to love you by trying to possess them or force them."

"Ladro and I have been alone for so long . . . it doesn't seem fair."

"It doesn't seem fair to me or to Aeneva, or to my son, either."

Larissa looked at Trenton and her eyes were filled with tears. "Ladro told her that she can go back to you at any time, but if she does, she will never see her son again."

"Will you help me, Larissa? All I want to do is talk to her. If she wants to stay with Ladro, I'll leave as soon as Joe is well. But if I find out that she still loves me and wants to go with me, I will find a way to take her and her son out of here."

"Ladro will kill you first."

"He can try, but that doesn't mean he will." He took Larissa by her shoulders. "I don't want you in the middle; he is your brother and you love him. All I want you to do is give me some time with her so I can find out how she really feels."

"I will go after siesta. I'll tell Ladro that I would like to visit with him. Perhaps it would be a good time for her to check on Joe then."

"Thank you, Larissa. You are a friend."

"So are you." She watched as Trenton ran back

toward Joe's shack, looking more like a young boy than a man. She wished with all her heart that she was more than a friend to Trenton. But since she could never have his love, she would take his friendship. For in that, at least, she had something real, something honest.

Chapter XIII

Cortez sat under his lean-to listening to the men as they hacked away at the cactus. It was not an easy job, especially at night, but it had to be done. Pedro handed him a cup of mescal.

"When do you want to move, *Patrón?* We have been here for days now." The man's voice was impatient.

"There is no hurry, Pedro. They are not going anywhere. Everyone there feels so secure they would not dare to leave. And one of these very hot days, when they are all taking siestas, we will strike. We will take them all by surprise."

"Why during the day, *Patrón?* They will see us riding in."

"Because they will not expect anyone to attack them during the day. They will all be sleeping after their big meals."

"But the guards will be awake."

"The guards are on the other side. They will have eaten and they will be lazy. Besides, I am going to send someone in to take care of the guards. Then we will have the town to ourselves."

"Whatever you say, *Patrón.*"

"Yes," Cortez mused to himself, "whatever I say." He smiled as he thought of the surprise his visit would cause. All of them—Aeneva, Larissa, the gringo, and especially Ladro—would be surprised to see him. And what nice plans he had for all of them.

Cortez drank from the cup, immediately feeling relaxed as the liquid hit his stomach. He remembered his grandfather had once told him that the mescal would kill a man if he drank too much of it. But what did it matter what his grandfather said? He took another drink and lay down on the blanket, completely relaxed. He would soon be one of the richest men in Mexico, and he could do anything he wanted.

Aeneva held James, talking to him in a quiet voice. She kissed him, somehow afraid that every time she left him she would never see him again.

"Don't worry, Aeneva, we will be fine," Ladro said calmly, taking the baby from her arms.

Reluctantly Aeneva handed James over to Ladro. "I won't be long. I just want to make sure Joe is all right."

"Take your time. Marcela tells me that Larissa wants to visit with her new nephew."

"You will be careful with him, won't you?"

"He is my son, Aeneva. I will not let anyone hurt him."

Aeneva understood the veiled threat in Ladro's words and nodded slightly, walking to the door. She turned and her dark eyes seemed to glow black as she spoke. "He is my son too, Ladro. Do not ever think you can keep me away from him. Ever." Aeneva walked down the stairs and out of the hacienda, visibly shaking. For the first time, she was afraid of Ladro and that saddened her greatly. At one time she had loved him enough to give herself to him willingly, but now those feelings were gone. All she felt now was fear, anger, and bewilderment. She walked the trail to Joe's shack and she looked behind her, wondering for an instant if Ladro was having her followed. There was no one even looking at her, but it didn't matter. He had her son. As long as he had James, she would always go back to Ladro.

She walked up the steps to Joe's shack, praying that Trenton was not inside. She looked inside and saw Joe, asleep on the bed. It was dark and cool inside the adobe structure and she sat down on the floor by the huge bed, pulling her knees up to her chest and hugging them. The elaborate ironwork was cool on her shoulder. She was tired of feeling helpless. She laid her head on her knees, closing her eyes. She was so tired; she felt as if she hadn't slept in months. She told herself to get up, but she felt her body relax. She couldn't fight the sleep that overtook her. She liked being here with a person she felt close to, a person who was no threat to her.

Her mind drifted and she saw herself as a child, running through the trees. She looked back over her shoulder and saw Trenton coming after her, his long blond hair contrasting with his dark skin. She laughed as she ran. When she got to the river she jumped in. She felt the coolness of the water as she swam through it. And when she dove under, she felt a hand on her leg. She smiled to herself, knowing that it was Trenton. But when she came up, it was not Trenton who was holding on to her. It was Ladro. She screamed, but he wouldn't let her go. Her body jerked and she sat up, opening her eyes. Trenton was sitting next to her, staring.

"How long have you been there?" she asked angrily.

"Long enough. How long has it been since you've slept?"

"I sleep every night."

"But not well. You're plagued by bad dreams."

"You do not know what is in my mind when I sleep."

"I just watched you, Aeneva. Your body twitched and you moaned in your sleep. You're frightened of something."

"No, I am not!" She started to get up but Trenton held on to her.

"Talk to me, Aeneva, I can help you."

"You cannot help me, Trenton. No one can help me now."

"What are you talking about?"

"I deserve the punishment I am getting. I have brought dishonor to you and to my people."

"You're being ridiculous. You've brought dishonor to no one."

"How can you even stand to look me in the eyes? By the laws of our tribe, you can turn me away from you. You can shun me."

"I don't want to shun you, damn it. I love you."

"Do not love me, please. Do not waste your love on

me." Trenton reached out for her, but Aeneva pulled away. "You make me confused. You have always done that to me. I cannot think clearly when you are around."

"Then I'll leave."

"No!" Aeneva responded much too quickly. She looked at him, trying to control the trembling in her body. "I have always loved you." She leaned against him, her head touching his. "I am sorry that I have hurt you."

"You didn't mean to. I understand that now."

"But I still cannot go away with you."

"Why? I know you don't love Ladro."

"I do love Ladro. He was good to me. He never took advantage of me." She lowered her eyes, ashamed to look at Trenton. "I gave myself willingly to him."

"I understand, Aeneva. I do. But you don't have to do that anymore. I want you with me. I will take care of you, just like I've always wanted to do."

"But my son. He will take my son away from me if I go back to you. I cannot leave my son, Trenton."

"Then we'll take him with us."

"Ladro will not let me leave the house with him. He knows how I feel about you."

"We'll find a way. He's your son, too." He looked at her a moment, gently touching her shoulder. "What's bothering you?"

"He loves James. I do not know what he would do if I took him away from him."

"So you'll stay with a man you don't love?"

"What else can I do?" She turned away, getting up on her knees to examine Joe's leg. The silence hung

369

between them uneasily. She quickly changed the dressing and stood up. "I have no choice, Trenton. Just as you had no choice when you married Lydia. You would never have left Nathan." She looked at him once more and left.

Trenton didn't go after her; he knew it was useless. She had made up her mind. She would not leave her son, and there was no way Ladro would let her take the boy. He kicked at the wall in frustration, knowing that all too soon he might never see Aeneva again.

Ignacio gripped his cup tightly, looking out the window to the mountains beyond. He knew that Cortez and his men were outside El Circulo, and he knew that they would find a way to get inside. He had alerted his guards and had even doubled them, but he knew men like Cortez. It would not be enough. Daily, his men rode around the forbidding cactus barrier, but none had seen a sign of Cortez and his men. But Ignacio knew they were there.

He had already decided where he would hide his friends. He hadn't used the cellar in a long time, but it would serve as a safe refuge until Cortez was gone.

It was times like these when he wished he was not responsible for so many lives. These people had come to him for help and he had taken them in. They were all loyal to him; they would die for him. He truly hoped that they did not have to die. He heard the footsteps on the stairs and looked up. It was Trenton and Larissa.

"What do you want, Ignacio?"

"Sit down. Ladro and Aeneva will be here soon."

Trenton and Larissa sat next to Ignacio. He looked at them both, smiling, then raised his eyes back to the door. "Ah, here they are." He nodded at Ladro and Aeneva as they walked in. He could see the tense looks that Trenton and Ladro exchanged.

"Now is not the time for anger. I am glad you are both here."

"What's the matter, Ignacio?" Ladro asked, walking over to him.

"Cortez will be here soon. I can feel it. I want you all to hide."

"I won't hide from Cortez," Ladro responded adamantly.

Trenton stood up. "Neither will I."

"Would you rather be killed then?" Ignacio forced himself to lower his voice. "We don't have a chance against Cortez. When I came to El Circulo I thought it would be an impenetrable fortress; I thought people would be safe here. But I realize now how foolish I was to believe that. There is no fortress to keep out men like Cortez."

"Can't we leave, Ignacio?" Larissa asked anxiously. "Why can't we ride into the desert, back the way we came?"

"You would not have a chance, my dear. You would be out in the open, an easy target for Cortez."

"What do you want us to do, Ignacio?" Aeneva asked gently, holding her baby against her.

"There is a place, a cellar over there underneath the racks. It is not very big, but it is big enough for you four and *El Negro*." He looked at Ladro, then at Trenton, his eyes pleading. "You must understand that there is no shame in hiding. It would be foolish for you to be here when Cortez comes. He will kill you all instantly. This way, at least, you will have a chance, and perhaps so will we."

"I know Cortez, Ignacio, he's not going to look for us and then leave. Someone is going to be hurt and I don't want it to be you or Marcela." Ladro gripped Ignacio's shoulder.

"We are not afraid, Ladro. Everyone here is prepared to help all of you."

"I don't like it." Trenton shook his head. "I don't want anyone getting hurt because of me."

"For once, I agree with you, gringo." Ladro glanced over at Trenton. "It won't work, Ignacio. We can put the women and the baby down there, but I and the gringo will stay and fight."

"No!" Ignacio shouted, slamming his cup on the table. He looked at the two men. "There is no place for pride here. Pride will only get you killed."

"We can fight! We can get the men of the village together . . ."

"There are not enough men in this village to fight, Ladro. They are simple men, not fighting men."

"I thought a lot of the men here were bandits," Trenton said.

Ignacio smiled. "Most of the men here were falsely accused so they ran. That does not make them bandits. Many of them do not even know how to handle a gun. And many of them are old. They came here to rest, not to fight."

"But their lives are being threatened. They will want to fight for their families."

"You are stubborn, gringo. I am sure it has

served you well in the past but it will not now. Make no mistake, we are as prepared as we can be for Cortez. My guards are fighting men and they will do what they can to stop him. But if he gets through the barrier, we will not be able to stand against his men."

"I don't understand you, Ignacio." Ladro squatted next to him. "How can you give up so easily? The gringo and I could take the men into the trees, we could be waiting for Cortez and his men. You and some of the others could take the women and children into the arroyo."

"Ladro . . ." Ignacio was interrupted by gunfire and the screams of women and children. There was yelling in the yard and one of the villagers ran to the door.

"Ignacio, Cortez is here! There are many men. They are taking the women and children."

They all stood up. Trenton and Ladro started for the door, but Ignacio's voice stopped them. "If you go out there you will die right now. If you stay here you will have a chance at least."

"What about Joe?" Trenton asked.

"Do not worry about *El Negro*. Cortez is not looking for him." Ignacio didn't wait for a response. He moved to the drying racks and pushed them out of the way. He leaned down, prying his fingers into a small crack. He pulled up a door. "Here it is. There is a lamp and matches down there, and some food. Go, my friends. Please."

Aeneva and Larissa went to the trapdoor. Larissa went down first, steadying the ladder and helping Aeneva with the baby. Ladro and Trenton hesitated, eyeing each other.

"Don't argue," Ignacio said firmly. "You owe me this. Both of you. It is the only way."

Trenton started down, pausing an instant on the ladder. "Thank you, old man. *Vaya con Dios.*"

"*Vaya con Dios, gringo.*" Ignacio turned to Ladro. "Well, are you going to argue with me?"

Ladro stared at the old man a moment and stepped forward, pulling him into his arms. "I will never forget what you and Marcela have done for me. Never. *Muchas gracias,* Ignacio."

"Yes, yes. Go now." Ignacio dropped the door and moved the racks back into place. "Good-bye, my friends." He walked to the table, took a drink from his coffee cup, and walked onto the porch. He waited.

In the heat of the midday sun, the village slept. Cortez's men hacked away the last of the spiny cactus, shielded from view by rocks. The pathway through the cactus had grown each night, little by little, until only the inner plants remained. Cortez watched from above as his men confronted the guards on the desert side. The fight was quick and silent, and the mirror flash signal told him it had been won. He waved at the riders who waited near the cactus and they went through. They spread out quickly, according to plan. Astonished women and sleepy, crying children were rounded up, their men disarmed and tied. The heat shimmered on adobe walls. A few shots were fired, but it was too late. Cortez rode into the village, shouting orders to the men who had already secured everything.

He sat proudly on his horse until all of the village's people were herded to stand before him. He looked at them with interest until it became obvious that the ones he sought were not there. Anger clouded his face, and he wiped at the sweat that covered his forehead. "Where is the old man called Ignacio?"

Ignacio came down the steps to the yard, deceiving Cortez with his frail looks.

"So, old man, you are the leader here?"

"I am not the leader. People come to me for advice."

"So you are the sage, the adviser."

"Yes, I suppose you could say that."

"Then tell me, sage, I am looking for four people. A white man with light hair, a Mexican man who goes by the name of Ladro, his sister, Larissa, and an Indian woman who was with child."

"I know none of these people."

"I think you are lying, old man."

"I do not care what you think, Cortez."

"Ah, so you have heard of me? My name is known far and wide, I see."

"Just like the rattlesnake's is," Ignacio replied calmly, staring at the man on the horse.

"I would not talk like that if I were you, old man. I have the people of your town. I do not think you would like to be responsible for their deaths."

"I would not be the one responsible."

Cortez was clearly nonplussed by this calm old man. "Do you want me to have them all killed? I will."

"You will do what you want anyway. I cannot stop you."

"Don't you care about your own people, old man?"

"I care and they know it, but they are all at peace with their God. They will die if they must."

"What is the matter with you?" Cortez dismounted from his horse. "Are you crazy?"

"Less so than you, Cortez." Ignacio's clear, calm eyes challenged Cortez.

"Well, I will give you one hour to produce the people that I spoke of or you will force me to kill someone."

"Do what you must."

Cortez couldn't contain his anger any longer and he slapped Ignacio across the face. "I will start with your family first."

"Start with me if you like, but you will not force me to do what you want. I have known men like you all of my life, Cortez. You feed off of other people's fear because you are such cowards."

Cortez struck Ignacio again, this time knocking the old man to the ground. He stood over him. "You will regret talking to me like that," Cortez said angrily, kicking Ignacio in the side and in the stomach. Ignacio moaned but Cortez kicked him as if he were no more than a rag doll.

"Please stop!" Marcela came running forward, kneeling down to her husband. "No more. I will tell you what you want to know."

"Good. A woman with a brain, I see."

"Ignacio." Marcela turned her husband over on his back, gently placing his head on her lap. His eyes were closed. She looked up at Cortez. "What do you want to know?"

376

"I want to know about four people . . ."

"No!" Ignacio interrupted, coughing as he did so. "Say nothing, Marcela!"

"I suggest you tell me what I want to know, old woman, or I will kill your husband right now."

"Tell him nothing, Marcela. He is scum. His belly rubs at the ground when he walks."

Cortez kicked the old man in the head, ignoring Marcela's screams. "Tell me, woman. Or he is dead."

"All right. They were here. The man called Ladro came with the Indian woman. He stayed a few days and left with supplies. Then the white man and the Mexican girl came, looking for the other two. They left in search of the others. That is all I know."

Cortez took out the revolver, aiming it at Ignacio's head. "You are lying, woman."

"No, please, that is all I know."

Cortez put the barrel of the gun to Ignacio's temple, pulling back the hammer. "This is the last time, or I pull the trigger."

"All right, they . . ."

Ignacio pushed against Cortez's arm. "Go to hell, you bastard!" Marcela screamed, but it was too late. Cortez had pulled the trigger. Ignacio lay dead. Marcela wailed, holding her dead husband in her arms. Cortez took her by the shoulder.

"Tell me the truth, woman, or you will be next."

"Kill me if you like, I don't care. What have I left now?" She hugged Ignacio to her, ignoring Cortez's presence.

"Ah!" Cortez waved her away and strode toward Ignacio's house, three of his men following. The door was open. He pushed things off of the counters as he walked through. He went to the stairs, gun drawn, waving his men ahead of him. He waited until Pedro returned.

"The rooms are empty, *Patrón*."

Cortez checked each room and came out, his face distorted with rage. "Bring all of the villagers to the yard. Immediately!"

"*Sí, Patrón*."

Cortez went downstairs, eyeing the bottle of mescal that sat on the shelf. He walked over and picked it up, uncorked it, and brought the bottle to his lips, taking a large drink. His eyes stung and his throat burned but he quickly took another drink. He wiped his mouth with the back of his hand and walked to the door, watching as his men brought the villagers into the yard. He took another drink and walked outside, leaning against the iron railing. He looked out at the frightened people.

"Did you all see what I did to the old man?" He drank again, staring at the people. "I came here to find four people. You all know who they are. I will do anything to find out where they are." A child cried out and Cortez looked in its direction. "You people do not matter to me. I can kill you all as easily as I would swat a fly." He eyed them all, walking back and forth across the porch. "I am a generous man. I will give you all until sunrise to tell me where the people are. If you do not tell me, I will have you lined up in rows and shot." He took another drink and shrugged his shoulders. "I do not care." He nodded toward Pedro. "Take them away. And bring me a woman. A young one." Cortez went back up the stairs, weaving slightly as he did so. He went to the first room and sat down on the bed. He took off his boots and shirt. He set the bottle on the night table and started to take off his belt, but stopped. He saw a cradle. He walked over to it, pushing it so that it rocked back and forth. He laughed loudly. So, she had had the baby. Now all he had to do was find them. Footsteps sounded in the hallway and Cortez looked up. Pedro stood with a young woman, his hand grasping her arm tightly.

"Here, *señor*."

Cortez walked to the woman, pulling her inside and slamming the door behind him. He smiled as she cowered into a corner of the room. She was scared; he liked that. He took his belt off and wrapped it once around his hand, slapping it against his thigh. He walked toward the frightened girl, smiling. She would do until he found Aeneva.

Aeneva stood up, clutching her baby to her. "I cannot stand it anymore. I am going up."

"You can't do that." Trenton stood next to her. "He's crazy. You just heard what he said."

"He is right," Ladro agreed. "We don't know how many men are in the house."

"Once he has me and the baby he will leave."

"Don't be foolish, Aeneva, the man is a killer. He will stop at nothing." Ladro glanced over at Trenton. "I will go up. If I can get to him, I will kill him."

"No!" Aeneva pleaded with Ladro. "He will kill you, Ladro."

"She is right, Ladro." Larissa stepped closer to her

brother. "I know Cortez better than any of you. He is a cruel man. He will not just kill you, he will make you suffer first."

"I know that, Larissa, but I can't wait here while innocent people die. Already Ignacio is dead because of me. You heard the shot and Marcela's scream. And he will kill more people tomorrow if I don't go up."

"Ignacio died because of us all," Trenton corrected. "It wasn't your fault."

Ladro acknowledged Trenton with a slight nod. He looked around at the small, dark hiding place. Trenton leaned forward.

"What if you get caught? You won't have a chance."

"I will if I tell him I know where you and Aeneva are."

"What're you talking about?"

"I'll tell him you've gone to his grandfather's to tell him the truth. The old man suspects what his grandson is really like. All he needs is proof. Aeneva is proof enough."

"What's to stop him from killing you before he goes off on his wild goose chase?"

"I'll tell him that if I don't get to Mexico City within five days after you do, you'll tell the old man."

"I don't think he'll believe you, Ladro."

"Do you have any better ideas, gringo?"

Trenton's reply was cut off by the sound of bootheels on the stairs in the room above. Ladro stood up, walking over to Aeneva. "I'm going to go now. Can I hold James for a moment?"

Aeneva nodded, handing the baby to Ladro. Ladro

took the baby, smiling at him and holding him close to his cheek. He held him tightly, kissing him on the head, then handed him back to Aeneva. "He is a beautiful son, Aeneva. Thank you."

"I am sorry, Ladro."

Ladro reached out and touched her cheek. "It is I who am sorry, Aeneva." He pulled her to him, stroking her hair. "When this is over, I want you to take James and go back with your husband. It is where you belong." When she tried to protest he shook his head. "We both know you belong with him. You and I lived in a dreamworld for a little time, but now it's over. We both must face reality now."

"Ladro . . ."

"Don't say anything. Just remember that I love you." He kissed her softly and walked to the ladder. Larissa stepped forward.

"I am going with you. I know Cortez better than any of you. If anyone can convince him, I can. Do not argue with me. I will not change my mind."

Ladro stared into his sister's eyes, seeing his own determination reflected there. "I will not argue, little sister." He held out his hand.

"Ladro."

"What is it, gringo?"

Trenton spoke quietly. "I will take care of Aeneva. No one will ever love her more than I do."

"I already know that. Take care of my son."

Ladro climbed the ladder. He pushed the trapdoor open. He peered out of it, making sure that no one was in the room. The fire burned dimly, casting a pale shadow over the empty room. Ladro climbed out of the cellar, standing behind the fragrant racks of herbs. He put his hand down and helped Larissa out.

"Was it Cortez who came down?" she asked quietly, her voice trembling slightly.

"I don't know."

"How will we get out? We can't go out the front."

"There's a window at the end of the hall upstairs. We'll go out that way. You'll have to jump. Can you do it?"

Larissa smiled. "Of course I can jump. Don't you remember how I used to swing from the loft and jump down?"

Ladro hugged his sister. "Let's hope you can still jump as well." He took Larissa's hand and stepped out from behind the racks. They crossed the room silently and paused at the bottom of the stairs. Hearing nothing, they climbed the stairs quickly.

Ladro whispered, "No guards. Cortez is getting careless." Ladro pulled Larissa along to the end of the hall. He unlatched the window and climbed out onto the grillwork. "I'll jump first."

"I'll be all right, Ladro. Go."

Ladro hung on the outside of the railing, then let go, landing on the soft dirt. He looked around. None of Cortez's men were around. "Jump, Larissa."

Larissa climbed onto the railing behind Ladro and jumped, landing on the soft dirt next to her brother. "Where now?"

"We can go through the trees behind the house and circle around. I just don't want Cortez to think we were hiding in the house.'

Ladro followed one of the many paths that led

from Ignacio's house to the other houses. He and Larissa kept to the trees until they reached the top of the arroyo. They walked down into the arroyo, coming up out of the trees below the well. Ladro stopped, taking Larissa's shoulders. "Are you sure you want to come with me? You might have a chance if you stay here."

"No, I am coming with you. I won't be separated from you again, Ladro."

"I love you, Larissa," Ladro said fiercely, holding his sister tightly. He took her hand in his. "Let's go." He and Larissa walked out of the trees, into the yard in front of Ignacio's house. They were completely surrounded by guards before they had reached the steps of the house.

"Where is Cortez?" Ladro spoke firmly.

"Who are you? No one is to be in the yard."

"I am Ladro. I am the man Cortez is looking for."

The guard shouted to some of the men. One of them left and returned a moment later, followed by Cortez. Cortez looked at them, smiling.

"So, you could not escape. I knew you were here." He glanced at Larissa. "And you have found your brother, Larissa." He threw his head back and laughed loudly. "Too bad he won't be alive for much longer."

"Emiliano, don't hurt him."

"And why shouldn't I? What will you do for me if I don't?"

Ladro moved forward. "Don't touch her."

"I would not be so brave if I were you, Ladro." He reached past Ladro to touch Larissa, but she shrugged him away. "I could make you watch while I

383

torture your sister."

"You won't do that."

"And why won't I?"

"Because right now Aeneva and the gringo are on their way to Mexico City to see your grandfather. If Don Francisco doesn't see Larissa and me in Mexico City soon, you will never own your land."

Cortez looked unsure. He stared at Ladro. "You are lying. My grandfather would never listen to them."

"I think he would. The gringo can be very persuasive, as you already know."

"So what can he tell him?"

"He can tell him a lot. He knows your business, Cortez. You taught him yourself. How do you think your grandfather will feel when he finds out about you?" Ladro smiled. "I don't think he'll take it well."

"I should kill you for this right now."

"But you won't. You touch me or Larissa and you will never have that land that you love so much."

Cortez walked around them, looking at Larissa as he did so. "So, you think you have outsmarted me, Ladro. You think that my grandfather will believe what two strangers have to tell him? You don't know him at all. He is from the old country. Family is more important to him than anything." He laughed. "He will forgive me for anything, including murder, as long as I give him an heir and the line of Cortez is not broken."

"I think you're wrong. I saw him at your ranch once, Cortez. He seemed displeased by everything you did."

"Well, in any case, it will be my word against the word of a stranger. He will believe me."

"If you're so sure, then kill us all now." Ladro stared at him, his black eyes hard.

"No, that would take the fun out of having you with me. This way I can make you wonder each day if I am going to kill you."

Larissa stepped between them. "You are sick, Emiliano. I have always known it. Your mind is so muddled by your lust for wealth and power you cannot see reality for what it is. You are a sad, pathetic man. I feel sorry for you."

Cortez slapped Larissa, knocking her back against Ladro. Ladro started for Cortez, but Larissa pulled him back.

"Do not bother, Ladro. He is not worth it."

"Don't touch my sister again."

"You are my prisoners and will be treated as such. You will be held inside the hacienda until we leave for Mexico City."

"I can't wait to see your grandfather, Cortez, when he finds out about you."

"You will be dead by then, Ladro, so don't worry about it."

Ladro laughed. "You won't touch us, Cortez."

"We'll see. And just in case your friends are still around here somewhere, I'll search the entire area again. I'll rip everything apart. If they're here, I'll find them."

"You're wasting your time. They're on their way to Mexico City and they're laughing at you."

"Perhaps, but I am a prudent man. I will take every precaution to ensure that they are not here." He motioned his men to take Ladro and Larissa away. Cortez thought for a moment. What Ladro had said was true—his grandfather would never give him the land if he found out everything. He had to make sure he got to Mexico City before they did, if in fact they were on their way there. He had not seen them leave El Circulo. And if they had not, he would find them.

Cortez lay on his bed thinking. Where would he hide someone so they would not be found? This was a simple place, everything was as it appeared. Or was it? He remembered that as a boy he had hidden in the cellar of his grandfather's hacienda when he didn't want to be punished. Perhaps Ignacio had made just such a place here. But where? He sat up, looking around the room. The obvious place was downstairs. But his men had already looked there. But had they looked well enough? He got up and went downstairs. He looked around the main room for something in the floor but he couldn't see anything unusual. The planking met perfectly everywhere. The smell of sweet herbs hung in the room. He stared at the wood racks leaning against the wall. He turned up the lantern and pushed them aside. The boards appeared whole, there was no discernible trapdoor. He shoved the racks back in place, stumbling a little. His bootheel thudded as he caught his balance. He kicked the fallen herb racks away from the wall, slamming his boot into the floor over and over, a few inches apart each time. Finally he smiled.

"Pedro. Come here!"

Pedro came running inside the hacienda. "What is it, *Patrón?*"

"I have found them."

386

"Where are they?"

"In there." He motioned to the corner.

"Where, *Patrón?* There is no one there."

"Ah, but there is, Pedro. Follow me." He pointed down at the floor. "There is a cellar underneath here. Listen." He stomped his foot again. "Right about here, Pedro. Do you hear it?"

"*Sí, Patrón.*" Pedro knelt, running his fingers along the floor. "Here, *Patrón.* I have found it." He took out his knife, jamming it into one of the cracks. "I will have it open soon."

Cortez smiled to himself, quite pleased at his own cleverness. They were down there; he knew it. They were like trapped animals, unable to run away. He could just see the look on Ladro's face when he told him that he had found his friends. He walked back up the stairs to the bedroom and grabbed his bottle of mescal, taking a quick swallow from it. He felt it course through his veins and felt his strength grow. Now he had them all within his reach and he grew excited just thinking about what he would do to them. He drank some more and sighed deeply. Soon he would have it all.

Trenton and Aeneva listened to the sounds from above. Trenton looked over at her. She hadn't spoken since Ladro left.

"He knows we're down here, Aeneva."

Aeneva held her son to her breast. "He cannot have my son. He cannot."

"Be strong, Aeneva. Cortez will try to break you, but he won't kill you or James. He needs you both."

There were footsteps and voices above them. "They're coming." Trenton took his derringer out of his boot and gave it to Aeneva. "Put this somewhere. Do you have a knife?"

"Yes."

"Good, hopefully he'll see my weapons and assume you don't have any. If you have to use the gun or knife to defend yourself, do it."

Aeneva took the gun and put it inside her moccasin. The knife she strapped high up on the inside of her thigh. "Trenton, if something happens to me or to Ladro, will you take James?"

"Nothing is going to happen to you."

"Please, I have to know that he will be taken care of."

"Of course I'll take care of him. Don't worry."

She leaned against Trenton. "I do love you, Trenton."

The trapdoor opened. Trenton pulled Aeneva away from the door. He turned down the lamp.

"What if we try to fight them? Cortez will send someone down here to see if we are here. We can . . ."

"No, it won't work. Cortez can do anything he wants. He can even burn us out if he wants to. I won't take that chance with your life."

"But I hate giving in to him like this. I hate it." She held James close to her.

"We're not giving in, we are biding time. We're trying to figure out a way for all of us to get out of here alive."

"What about Joe? Do you think he is all right?"

"I don't know, but we can't say anything. If Cortez knows he's our friend, he'll kill him right away."

Aeneva held on to Trenton's arm. They waited in the darkness as the light streamed down from the room above. They heard Cortez's voice.

"I know you two are down there. Please come up." When Trenton and Aeneva didn't respond, Cortez spoke again. "I saw the cradle, Aeneva. I know you have a baby. If you don't want it to get hurt, you better come up. Now!"

Trenton gently pushed Aeneva forward. Carefully she climbed the ladder, holding her son tightly. Cortez took her arm when she came out of the cellar.

Cortez stared at Aeneva. She stood before him holding her child, her hair in wild disarray, her face flushed with fear. He had forgotten how truly beautiful she was. "As long as you do as I say, I won't hurt your child. But if you disobey me, well, need I say more?"

"I will do as you say," Aeneva responded in a placating voice, holding on to her son desperately.

Trenton came up the ladder after Aeneva and stood facing Cortez. He handed him his gun. "I suppose you'll want this."

"Yes, and anything else you might have. Search him." Pedro quickly ran his hands over Trenton and handed Cortez a knife. "You know, gringo, I'm very angry with you. You lied to me."

"I was only returning the favor."

"You can play all the games you want. But I have your wife now." Cortez walked over to Aeneva, putting his arm around her. He pushed the blouse from her shoulder and ran his hand along the soft skin. "Very lovely, don't you think, gringo?"

Trenton started to step toward Cortez, but Pedro

and another man held him back. "Don't touch her, Cortez."

"Or what? You'll get angry with me?" Cortez laughed loudly. "I'm sorry, gringo, but it seems I hold all the cards now. I have your wife and the new heir to my fortune. I also have Ladro and his sister. I have everything. There is nothing you can do about it."

"Don't hurt her."

"Why should I hurt her? She is the mother of my newborn child. And if she is good to me and proves she is worthy of me, perhaps I will let her and the brat live. But if she gives me trouble . . ."

"What is it with you, Cortez? You only seem to be brave when you are threatening women, children, or old men. But what about me or Ladro? Why don't you fight one of us alone?" Trenton looked around at the men in the room. "I'm sure your men would like to see you prove yourself. You're always boasting, but words are made of air, Cortez."

"I need to prove nothing to anyone!"

"You're afraid, Cortez, that's why you won't fight me or Ladro. You prove your worth by beating up on women; that's what excites you."

Cortez pulled out his gun and aimed it at Trenton. Aeneva grabbed his hand.

"No! Do not shoot him. Please!"

"And what will you do if I spare your husband, my dear?"

"Anything, I will do anything you want."

Cortez smiled, still aiming the pistol at Trenton. "Did you hear that, gringo? Your wife will do anything I want. Would you like to watch?"

Trenton threw himself across the room at Cortez, knocking him against the wall. He hit Cortez twice before he was pulled away. "You son of a bitch! You touch her and I swear I'll kill you."

Cortez wiped at the blood on his mouth. "Hold him!" He took the butt of his gun and hit Trenton across the face. Aeneva ran to Cortez, grabbing at his arm.

"Stop it, please. Please, Emiliano."

Cortez held the gun up for a moment, then put it in its holster and backed up. "I will see you later, gringo. After your wife and I have visited."

"Aeneva, don't." Trenton tried to pull away, but Pedro punched him in the stomach.

Aeneva didn't look at Trenton as she left the room. She didn't want to remember the look on his face as she left the room with Cortez.

"You know the way to the bedroom, don't you, Aeneva?" Cortez took Aeneva's upper arm in a viselike grip and led her to the bedroom, slamming the door behind him. He went up to her, taking her face in his hand and kissing her roughly on the mouth. James squirmed in his mother's arms and made a squawking sound. Cortez looked down at the child. "You should learn to keep him quiet or I will give him to someone who can."

"He is hungry. Once he has been fed he will sleep."

Cortez nodded in agreement, sitting down on the bed. "Well, then, feed him. I need him looking healthy."

Aeneva turned her back to Cortez, lowering her blouse and putting her son to her breast. She felt uneasy and she knew her son could feel it. He squirmed in her arms and cried until milk came from her nipple.

"Turn around," Cortez commanded.

Aeneva felt the color rise in her cheeks, but she did as Cortez commanded. She felt his eyes on her, devouring her. He clearly enjoyed watching her breast-feed her child. But she refused to be cowed by him; she had to keep a clear head and remain strong. She had to think of Trenton, Ladro, and Larissa. And there was Joe. Joe—why hadn't she thought of him before? Perhaps there was a way she could get to him. Trenton and Ladro were being guarded. It was up to her now. She walked over to Cortez and sat down next to him on the bed, letting him look all he wanted.

"What do you plan to do with me, Emiliano?" She looked him straight in the eyes.

"I have not yet decided. It depends on you, I think."

"And what of my son?"

"We will take him to see my grandfather. My grandfather will be pleased that I have such a beautiful Cheyenne wife and a fine son. He will gladly give me the land grant. Then I can do whatever I please."

"And after that, will you kill me and my son?"

Cortez stared at Aeneva, appreciating her unspoiled, natural beauty. Again he kissed her, this time more gently. He was surprised by her eager response and he was pleased. "I could give you a good life, Aeneva. I can give you everything—a big house, jewels, clothes, and my name. Your son could grow up a Cortez. He could be very important someday."

Aeneva looked thoughtful for a moment before replying. "I will not lie to you, Emiliano. I do not love you; I love Trenton. But I do not want my son raised in an Indian lodge. After seeing your house and all of the things that you have, those are the things I want to give my son. He will not grow up barefooted and ignorant. He will be smart, rich, and powerful." Aeneva said it with such conviction she surprised even herself.

"I can give those things to your son, but you must give me something in return."

"I do not know if I can ever love you, Emiliano."

"Ah, what is love anyway? I want your loyalty. If you ever deceive me again, I will have to kill you and your son. Remember that."

"I will not endanger the life of my son."

"Good. There is something else. You are to be my wife in every other way as well. When you come to my bed, you give yourself to me willingly. I don't care if you love me, as long as you are passionate with me. Can you do that?"

"Yes."

Cortez reached over, running his hand along her shoulder and down to her bare breast. His fingers caressed it lightly. "Are you sure?"

Aeneva didn't flinch. "Yes, Emiliano. I will be the wife you want me to be."

"Good." He pulled her close, kissing her deeply. "I want you to be ready for me tonight. I want you to prove to me that you can do as you say." He stood up, walking to the door. "I will have a bath sent in here for you. And try to find some other clothes. Those are not befitting the wife of a hacendado."

Aeneva nodded, watching him leave the room. She held James to her, closing her eyes as she thought of what the night held for her. But she had been through worse things and survived; she would survive this. People were depending on her and she had to find a way to help them. She put James on the bed and took the small derringer out of her moccasin, hiding it under the mattress along with her knife. As long as James was close enough to be endangered she couldn't do anything. But if she could get the weapon to Joe, perhaps there was something he could do. But first she had to prove to Cortez that she was loyal, that she would do whatever he asked. She took a deep breath and looked down at her sleeping child. She resolved to do whatever it took to save him and the others.

Marcela brushed Aeneva's long hair in silence. Aeneva had asked Cortez if Marcela could help her with James and he had agreed. Marcela was still grieving for Ignacio and Aeneva could say nothing to comfort her. They sat in silence, Marcela making Aeneva beautiful for the man who had murdered her husband.

Aeneva looked at herself in the mirror and she was shocked at what she saw. She looked older, more womanly than she remembered. Her face had thinned and she looked strange in the white nightgown that Marcela had given her. Marcela pulled her hair back and tied it with a white ribbon. Aeneva sat still, staring at her reflection, forcing herself to forget about Trenton and the others. Her eyes met Marcela's in the mirror and there was disgust in the other woman's eyes. Aeneva turned.

"Marcela, I want to talk to you."

"What is there to talk about? This is insanity. You are going to sleep with the man who murdered Ignacio. What about Ladro? What about your husband?" Marcela shook her head, wringing her hands together. "I do not understand you."

"Marcela, listen to me." Aeneva took Marcela's hands. "I will do anything I have to to save my son and my husband."

"And what about Ladro? He loves you with all his being."

"I know that, and I will do what I can to save him and Larissa. If Cortez wants me to play at being his woman, I will do that if it gives me time to save the others. You must understand, Marcela. I hate this man as much as you, but I will do what I must to save the people I love."

"You will never be clean if you sleep with this man. You will carry his filth with you forever."

"No, that is not true. Trenton helped me to see that. Once I was kidnapped by an enemy of our tribe, a Crow warrior called Crooked Teeth. He was evil and cruel and he treated me no better than he treated his dogs. I slept outside his lodge, tied with a rope around my neck to a lodgepole. I lost all dignity and honor; all I knew was that each day I had to find a way to survive, no matter what I had to do. And I did survive—Trenton found me. It took me many weeks before I would even speak to him. I hated myself for what I had done. But Trenton showed me that I did what I did to survive, and that nothing was worth dying for. I believe that, Marcela. Life is very precious and I will do anything I can to save the lives of the people I love and care for."

"But I could do nothing for Ignacio. Nothing."

Aeneva took the woman in her arms and held her. "It was not your fault. Cortez is an evil man. He could not stand a man like Ignacio who showed no fear; it made him look bad. He had to kill him to save face in front of his men. Ignacio was a brave man, Marcela, a good man."

"I did not love him enough. I told you of the other man that I had always loved. Ignacio knew it. He died knowing that I did not love him."

"He died in your arms, Marcela. He knew that you loved him." Aeneva held Marcela until she stopped crying. She wiped the tears from her face. "We must all be strong now, Marcela. I will need your help. I want you to take James for me. Cortez will have you guarded. He knows as long as he has James, I will do anything he says."

"You are so calm. I could not do what you are about to do."

"There is not much time, Marcela. Find out about Trenton, Ladro, and Larissa. We must help them." She hugged the old woman once more. "Be strong, Marcela. Soon we will be out of this."

Aeneva watched Marcela take her son and her heart sank as they left the room. But she forced herself to be strong. She went to the bed and pulled the derringer from underneath the mattress. She checked to make sure it was loaded and she put it back in its hiding place. When the time was right, she would kill Cortez.

She stood up straight and tall. She had had enough of being weak. It was time to be strong again. Her grandmother had always been strong, and her dear, sweet mother had been strong in her own way. And so she would be strong also. It was up to her to save the lives of the people who needed her. She would not fail.

Chapter XIV

Aeneva moved in the darkness, careful not to awaken Cortez. The little derringer was still in its hiding place and it would do her no good now. He had told her if anything happened to him this night he had given orders to his men to kill her son and the others. She had to see if James was all right. She moved slowly to the edge of the bed and stood up. She grabbed her robe and wrapped it around her. Cortez was sprawled across the bed, his heavy breathing echoing in the darkened room. Aeneva walked to the door, opening it slowly. The hallway was empty. Aeneva crept out of the doorway and down the hall to Marcela's room. Marcela was sitting in a rocking chair holding James. Aeneva touched her son's face.

"Did you find out where they are?"

"Ladro and Trenton are being held in the barn. Larissa is being held in a different place. Is he asleep?"

"Yes."

"Kill him now, while he sleeps. His men will do nothing without him."

"No, I cannot risk it. The gunshot would bring his men."

"Use the knife then."

Aeneva shook her head. "He told me that if anything happened to him his men have orders to kill James and the others. I cannot take the chance, Marcela. I must find another way."

"What way? It has to be soon. He has punished them all already. And poor Larissa . . ."

"What about Larissa?"

"He has given her to his men."

"Oh, God." Aeneva covered her mouth with her hand. "Tomorrow night. We must try to set them free tomorrow night. I need to know how many men are guarding the barn and how many men are surrounding the town. Also, I need to know where all the people of the town are being held."

"What do you plan to do?"

"I do not know yet, but somehow we are going to get weapons and we are going to free Trenton, Ladro, and Larissa—and hopefully the other people of the town." She bent down and kissed her son on the cheek. "I will talk to you tomorrow."

"Be careful. I do not trust the man. He has the devil inside of him."

"Yes, and too much mescal. It is much like a drug my people use in some of their rites, I think. Only he drinks it without the guidance of the spirits. But he also sleeps very deeply. We have so little time, Marcela. It must be tomorrow night."

Aeneva left. She walked back down the hall and into Cortez's room. She crept back into bed and lay next to him. In the morning she would find a way to get to Joe. He would help her. She would not let Trenton die.

Cortez put his arm possessively around Aeneva, holding her close to him. They walked into the barn. Once inside, Aeneva saw Trenton and Ladro, both tied to poles, their arms outstretched. Both had been badly beaten; they hung limply from the poles. Aeneva felt tears sting her eyes, but she forced her face to remain calm as she looked at the two men. She knew that Cortez was testing her.

"Well, what do you think?"

Aeneva looked at the two men. "I do not understand why you must torture them. What pleasure do you derive from it?"

"It gives me great pleasure to see them suffer. Both of them have deceived me and tried to take what is mine. They should suffer."

There were deep gashes in Trenton's chest and Aeneva longed to reach out and touch him. "Why did you bring me here?"

"Because I want to see how much you care for these men." An ugly smile appeared on Cortez's face. "In fact, I want to see which one you care for the most."

"I do not understand."

"You will." Cortez walked to Trenton, jerking his face up. He slapped him across the face. "Wake up, gringo! You have a visitor. You see, your lovely wife has come to say good-bye to you. Open your eyes."

Slowly Trenton opened his swollen eyes. "Aeneva . . ."

"Yes, it is Aeneva. She is beautiful, is she not? She also knows how to treat a man. But of course you know that, don't you?"

Trenton looked at Aeneva, his eyes saddened. "No . . ."

"Oh, yes. Your wife is mine now and as long as she is good to me, she will continue to be mine. She has beautiful skin, don't you agree? It's as smooth as a fine pearl." Cortez stood behind Aeneva, running his hands along her neck and shoulders. "You will never feel this skin again, gringo!" Cortez hit Trenton across the face with the back of his hand several times. Then he stopped and faced Aeneva. "He does not look so brave now, does he, my dear?"

Aeneva looked at the man she loved with all of her heart and she died a little inside. "No," she replied coldly, attempting to sound as if she agreed with Cortez.

"And look at this one, this snake who deceives me like no other." Cortez pulled Aeneva in front of Ladro. Cortez yanked Ladro's head up by his hair. "How does it feel, Ladro? Are you ready for some more?"

Ladro's black eyes shone with hatred. With as much strength as he could muster, he spit in Cortez's face.

"You bastard!" Cortez wiped the spit from his face and struck Ladro until his head hung limply on his chest. Cortez turned to Aeneva, rubbing his hand. "So, what do you think of your two heroes? Soon I will have them begging for mercy. Both will die, but one I will kill quickly. The other . . ." Cortez examined one of his fingernails. "The other will die very, very slowly. I know which one I would choose but it is not my decision. It is yours, my dear."

Aeneva's eyes widened. "No, I cannot." She turned away but Cortez held her so that she faced Trenton and Ladro.

"But you must pick, Aeneva, or they will both suffer horrible deaths. At least you can spare one of them." He shrugged his shoulders. "I thought it would be easy for you. You love your husband so let Ladro be the one to suffer. Ah, but Ladro was with you for a long time; you had his child. Perhaps it is he you would like to spare."

"Let me have some time, Emiliano. Please."

"Very well, I will give you until tomorrow. But I want your decision then, or they will both suffer more than they already have."

"I understand." Aeneva thought for a moment. "Emiliano, may I take a walk to think? Please. You can send one of your men with me."

"Yes, you can take a walk, but please remember that I have your son." He turned for the door. "The men will wait outside. Say good-bye to your two heroes, my dear. You will not see them alive again."

Aeneva walked to Trenton, gently lifting his head. She took her skirt and wiped some of the blood from his face. When he opened his eyes Aeneva could see the pain in them. She kissed him gently. "Trenton, you must listen to me." She looked around at the men who stood guard at the barn doors. "I am going to help you escape tonight."

"No, you can't do anything. Save yourself if you can. Leave me, Aeneva."

"I will never leave you." She held his head against her chest. "If I can get a weapon to you, do you think you can use it? Are you strong enough?"

"I don't know."

"Trenton, please. I am being strong for you, be strong for me."

His blue eyes sought hers. He saw the strength in her dark eyes and nodded. "I'll try, Aeneva. What about Ladro? How is he?"

"I do not know. I will find a way to get to you tonight. I love you." She kissed him on the cheek and walked to Ladro. She touched his face, her fingers trembling. He pulled away reflexively, thinking it was one of Cortez's men. Aeneva looked from Ladro to Trenton and she thought how strange it was that the two men she had loved in her lifetime were now being punished for loving her. "Ladro. Oh, Ladro, I am so sorry."

Ladro slowly lifted his head. "Aeneva. Are you all right?"

"I am fine. I am only frightened for you and Trenton."

Ladro tried to look over at Trenton but couldn't turn his head. "How is he?"

"He is suffering just as you are. Listen to me, Ladro. Tonight I am going to try to get you both out of here. Do you think you can walk?"

"I don't know." He looked at her, a strange calm in his eyes. "When we first kidnapped you I knew you were special. You were so different, so proud, so unafraid. I knew that I would never sell you to Cortez."

"Ladro, please listen to me."

He closed his eyes and spoke again, as if to himself. "I knew that what I was doing was wrong. I wanted you and I wanted you to love me. I knew that eventually you would love me because you were scared. You didn't know anyone but me and you came to depend on me. I remember the first time we made love . . ."

Aeneva leaned her face against his. "I am so sorry if I hurt you. I did love you."

"But not in the way that you love him," Ladro replied in a steady tone. "I understand now, Aeneva. It was wrong for me to try to force you to stay with me. I want you to go with your husband. You belong with him." His head sagged onto his chest.

Aeneva leaned close. "Ladro, you must listen to me. Tonight I am going to try to get you and Trenton out of here. Can you walk?"

"I want you to take James with you also. I cannot give him the kind of love that you can . . ." Ladro stopped, coughing loudly. "You must get yourself and James away from here. Kill Cortez if you can."

"I will not leave without you and Trenton and Larissa."

"Larissa? Have you seen her?"

"No, but I will find her. Hang on, Ladro. I will be back tonight."

"Aeneva." His voice was stronger and he had raised his head.

Aeneva turned to hear him. "I love you as I have never loved anyone. I want you to remember that."

Aeneva nodded, running from the barn, unable to look at either man again. Outside she started on the familiar path to Joe's, closely followed by two of

405

Cortez's men.

"I must go in here. There is a man who needs my help."

"The *Patrón* said nothing about this."

"I am going in to help this man. He is sick; he cannot walk. He cannot do anything to harm anyone. Watch from the door if you wish."

The man nodded his assent and Aeneva went inside. She found a bowl and went outside to the cistern, filling it with water. She went back to Joe's bed, unwrapping his leg.

"Joe," she whispered in Cheyenne, working at his leg. "Joe, wake up."

Joe opened his eyes. "I'm awake. I wondered when you'd get here."

"Is the guard still watching us?"

"No, he's turned around. He doesn't think I'm worth watching. I fell down a few times to convince them I couldn't walk. Cortez wanted everybody in front of Ignacio's but nobody really wanted to carry me. So they left the one guard. And he sleeps most of the time."

"How does the leg feel?"

"It feels pretty good."

"Do you think you can ride?"

"You plan on getting us out of here?"

"I am going to try. Tonight."

"Tonight? You don't believe in wasting time, do you?"

"Cortez has already beaten Trenton and Ladro. He will kill them soon. He has them tied up in the barn. I have to get them out tonight, Joe."

"I was afraid of that. What can I do?"

"I will try to sneak out of the house tonight, after Cortez is asleep. But there are guards outside of the barn. Do you think you can help me?"

"I'll find a way. Just find me my stick and leave it close."

"But I am worried about your leg. It still needs more time to heal."

"It'll be fine. Besides, if Cortez has his way, he'll kill everybody in this town anyway. A good leg isn't much use on a dead man. I'll mosey over to the barn when everybody's asleep. Always did like a good fight."

Carefully Aeneva reached into her moccasin and brought out the gun. She placed it under Joe's blanket. "You can use this. It is loaded."

"Good. What about you? Do you have a weapon?"

"I have my knife. It is enough."

"Good. I'll meet you there. Where are we going to go after that? We can't take on Cortez's whole army."

"We can worry about that later. First we must get Trenton and Ladro out of that barn." She wrapped Joe's leg tightly in the splint. "Be careful, Joe. If it hurts you too much, do not do it. I will find another way."

"Count on me. I will see you tonight."

Aeneva leaned down and kissed him on the cheek. "Thank you." She walked out of the shack, ignoring Cortez's men as she walked by. She started back toward the hacienda but stopped, turning to one of the men.

"Where is the girl?"

"What girl?"

"Larissa. I want to see her."

"What is she to you?"

"I am a healer. I want to see if she needs help."

"She is no concern of yours. Cortez gave her to us."

"Do I need to go to the *Patrón* and tell him that you would not let me see her?"

Unsure of Aeneva's influence over Cortez, the men gave in. "She is in the camp near the arroyo. Follow us."

Aeneva followed the men to the camp. It was hot and the camp smelled of sweat and alcohol. She discovered Larissa lying on one of the bedrolls. Her clothes were dirty and her hair was matted and tangled. Aeneva bent down next to her.

"Larissa," she said softly, touching the girl's face.

Larissa turned her head slightly, opening her eyes to look at Aeneva. "What are you doing here?"

Aeneva bent closer. "I want to help you. I want to get you out of here."

"You can't help me now," she answered, barely turning her head.

"Larissa, I am going to get you out of here right now."

Larissa looked at Aeneva. "How? Cortez will not let you take me out of here."

"Let me worry about Cortez. Sit up." She pulled Larissa's arm and tugged her to a sitting position. "Are you all right? Can you walk?"

"I think so." She smiled weakly. "They were not so cruel as Cortez."

"No woman should be treated like this."

Larissa nodded. "How is it with you and Cortez? I don't envy you, Aeneva."

"I will do what I have to do to save us all." She

pushed the hair back from Larissa's face. "They have hurt you. Are you sure you are all right?"

"I have been hurt before. Don't worry. I'll be fine. How are you going to get me out of here?"

"You are going to stand up and walk out of here."

"But how? They will never let me leave."

"Stand up." She took Larissa's arm and helped her up. "Walk with me." When they walked to the edge of the camp one of the men held his rifle up.

"Where do you think you're going with her? She's to stay here."

"I need her to help me. The *Patrón* said that I could get anyone I wanted to help me and I want her."

"But she is ours."

Aeneva stood up straight and tall, staring the man in the face. "She belongs to no one. She is not your slave nor is she mine. I am the *Patrón*'s wife and if he finds out that you have disobeyed me, you will have to deal with him." She narrowed her eyes at the man. "I am sure you have more important duties than arguing with me. Stand aside please." She took Larissa by the arm and dragged her along.

"Where are we going?" Larissa looked behind them at the guards who continued to follow them. "Emiliano will never allow me back in Ignacio's. He wants to see me dead."

"You are not going back to the hacienda. I am taking you to Joe's."

"But the guards . . ."

"Do not worry about them. I do not think they will question me. We have no other choice." They arrived at Joe's shack and before the guard could say anything, Aeneva turned to confront him. "I want her to stay here and look after this man. I will send for her tonight. Make sure she does not leave."

"I don't know. The *Patrón* said nothing about her."

"If you are unsure, ask him. But remember, I will have the final say."

"All right, all right."

Aeneva went to Joe. His eyes were open.

"What are you doing here again? You're gonna get yourself killed and none of us is going to get out of here alive."

"I've brought you Larissa. They will kill her in that camp. She can help you tonight, if you need anything," Aeneva said in Cheyenne.

Joe looked at Larissa. "You all right?"

"I'm well enough. What about you?"

"The same." He looked at Aeneva. "You going to be all right until tonight?"

"I'll be all right. Larissa can help you get to the barn and get those men out of the way."

"Don't worry about us, we'll take care of it."

"All right, I must go now. I will meet you at the barn as soon as Cortez falls asleep. If I am late, do not wait for me. Get Trenton and Ladro out."

"We won't leave without you, Aeneva."

"Please, Joe, it is important that you all get out if you can. Cortez will keep me alive for a while. He needs me to show to his grandfather. Promise me that if I cannot get to the barn you will go." Joe nodded. She took Larissa by the shoulders, whispering in Spanish, "Promise me, Larissa. If I am late, take the baby."

"I promise you, Aeneva. But nothing will go wrong. We will see you tonight."

Aeneva turned and smiled at her two friends. "Good luck. I hope the Maiyun are with us all tonight."

Joe waited in the shadows as Larissa moved silently ahead of him, checking to make sure there were none of Cortez's men walking around. They made it unhampered until they reached the trees close to the barn. Larissa held on to Joe's arm.

"Are you all right, *Negro?* Your leg must be very sore."

"I'll be all right. Let's worry about getting those two out of there." He handed Larissa the derringer. "It's loaded. You know how to use this?"

"I should. Cortez taught me himself." She stuck it behind her waist. "Aeneva told me there were three or four guards. But our plan should work even if there are more."

"You just keep the first one busy long enough for me to get there and borrow his gun. Be careful, pretty lady."

"I will." Larissa smoothed back her hair and pulled her blouse down. "Wish me luck, *Negro.*"

"You won't need it. I'll be right behind you."

Larissa walked casually out of the darkness and into the dim light from the barn door.

"Quién es?"

"Larissa," she responded in a deep voice, walking wantonly out into the open. "I was told you might want to see me."

One of the men approached her, looking around. "Where is Julio? He should be with you."

Larissa reached up and touched the man's chest, running her fingers up to his neck. "Julio is resting. He had too much to drink and he told me to come see you. What's the matter, are you afraid?"

The man looked around as if to check that Cortez wasn't around. "I'm not afraid, *bonita*. Come here." He pulled her to him, kissing her hard on the mouth.

"Wait. Not here. Cortez might come. Let's go over by the side of the barn."

The man nodded, taking her by the arm. He looked over at the other guards. "I am going over there for a little while. Make sure you keep an eye on things."

"Eh, Trino, why do you get to have all the fun? We deserve some too."

"When I'm done," Trino responded, waving away the men's objections. He literally dragged Larissa to the side of the barn, pushing her to the ground. He climbed on top of her and shoved her skirt up. Quickly Larissa pulled out the gun and put it to his head.

"Do not move, *cabrón*, or I will blow your head off."

"You wouldn't do that. The noise would bring Cortez running."

Larissa cocked the gun, pressing the barrel against his temple. "I would gladly die right now if I could take you with me," she responded coldly.

"But she won't have to," Joe added, coming out of the shadows. "Get off the lady," Joe ordered. While the man moved, Joe pulled his guns loose. "Now, lie on your belly with your hands behind your back. I

412

want you to call one of your buddies over here but don't try anything or you'll be dead." He pressed the barrel of the pistol into the back of the man's neck as assurance that he meant what he said.

"Naldo, come here."

"What's wrong, Trino? You need help?" Laughter sounded.

Joe pressed the pistol harder into the man.

"No, come here. I think you'll like this."

They heard some words as Naldo spoke to the other man and then they heard footsteps. Joe straightened up and Larissa took his place. Just as the guard came around the corner of the barn, Joe lifted the gun and hit him square in the face with the butt. The man grunted and fell to his knees. Joe hit him once more in the back of the head. He dragged the man over to the side. "Now call the other one."

"José, come here."

"What is it? What are you two doing over there?"

"Come here and find out, José. Hurry."

As José started to round the corner of the barn, Trino rolled over, grabbing for Larissa's leg.

"Watch out, José!"

José stopped as he reached the corner, holding his rifle out in front of him, but before he could do anything, Joe hit him. José's rifle fell to the ground as he dropped. Joe hit him again to knock him out and gathered his weapons. Joe whirled to help Larissa but she had already stopped Trino with a knife to the gut.

"Let's make sure they can't be seen." They dragged the bodies to the side of the barn, then went cautiously to the front.

"Are there any guards inside?"

"I don't know. I can check."

"No, stay behind me." Joe peered around the edge of the door and looked inside the barn. It was lit by only one lantern which hung on the pole above Trenton. Joe couldn't see any other guards. "All right. I want you to stay at the door and make sure no one comes in. Try not to shoot unless you have to." Joe walked over to Trenton. He took out his knife and cut the ropes which bound his friend. "Come on, boy, wake up. This is no time to sleep." He slapped Trenton on the face a few times until Trenton opened his eyes. "That's right, boy. Wake up. We got to get out of here right now." He left Trenton and walked to Ladro. When he cut the ropes, he caught the man in his arms, half dragging him to where Trenton sat.

"How is he?" Trenton rubbed his head and jaw.

"I don't know." Joe slapped Ladro's face until he lifted his head and opened his eyes. "Come on, Ladro. Larissa is right here waiting for you. We're getting out of here tonight."

Ladro slowly lifted his head. He looked first at Joe and then at Trenton, squinting his eyes as if to see more clearly. "What are you saying?"

"We're getting out of here right now. Can you stand up?"

Ladro nodded toward Trenton. "I can stand up if he can."

Trenton tried to smile but he winced. He took Joe's hand and stood up, rubbing his shoulders. Joe pulled Ladro up, pushing him toward the door.

"Come on. Out here. We borrowed a few guns.

We'll wait here for Aeneva and Marcela."

Larissa went to Ladro. He leaned against her for support. "I was afraid I would never see you again, Ladro. Are you all right?"

"I'll be all right as soon as we're away from here. And you?"

"I am better now that you are here."

"When is Aeneva coming?" Trenton asked anxiously, strapping on a gunbelt and picking up one of the rifles.

"Soon, boy. Real soon."

"She better be here soon or I'm going after her. I won't let her stay with that bastard another night."

"Take it easy. We promised her that we'd wait here for her and Marcela. Just be patient. She'll be here."

Marcela looked at the clock on the table. Ten o'clock. Where was Aeneva? She could wait no longer. She picked up the basket in which James was sleeping and tucked the blanket around his tiny body. She walked to the door and listened. There was no sound in the house. She opened it and moved down the hallway. She listened outside Cortez's door, but there was no sound. She turned the knob silently but it was locked. Reaching into her pocket, she pulled out a key and unlocked the door, setting the basket to the side. She opened the door and light from the hallway lamp shone into the room. Cortez was sprawled across the bed, his leg thrown over Aeneva. Marcela wanted to kill him, but any struggle would bring the guards and she would not take a chance with James's life. She walked to Aeneva, touching her shoulder, trying to see her eyes in the dim light.

Aeneva covered Marcela's hand with her own. She eased herself from under Cortez's leg and got out of the bed. She quickly got into the robe that Marcela handed her and walked outside, closing the door.

"How did you get the door open?" Aeneva asked Marcela as they walked toward the hall window.

"This is my house, remember?"

"You shouldn't be here, Marcela. You should have taken James and gone."

"And how was I to get a small baby out of here without you? I cannot jump from this window without your help, Aeneva."

Aeneva nodded. "All right. We must hurry. Cortez could wake up soon."

Marcela unlatched the window and pushed it open. "You go first, Aeneva. I am not sure that I can do it."

"You can do it, Marcela. I want you to go first. I will lower James to you. I will need your shawl."

Marcela breathed deeply and climbed out on the railing, handing her shawl to Aeneva. She took another deep breath, made the sign of the cross, and jumped. She fell to the side when she landed but she was unhurt. She looked up at the window. "All right, Aeneva. Now, the baby."

Aeneva quickly tied one end of the shawl around the handle of the basket and lowered it out the window. "Do you have him, Marcela?"

"Yes. Hurry, Aeneva."

Aeneva gathered up the hem of her robe in one

hand, then froze as she heard the bedroom door open. "Aeneva?"

She turned. Cortez stood in the doorway, his hair mussed, his face groggy with sleep. "What are you doing, Aeneva?"

She smiled, letting her robe down. "I was just getting a breath of air. It is so peaceful tonight." She pulled the window closed and walked back to Cortez, taking his arm. "I am ready to go back to bed now." Aeneva forced herself not to look back at the window. So close, she had come so close. But at least James was safe.

Marcela protested silently when she saw Aeneva close the window but she knew what had happened. She had heard Cortez's voice. There was nothing she could do to help Aeneva but get James to a safe place. She followed a little path that led around the hacienda and through the trees to the arroyo. She crossed the arroyo and came out behind the barn. She listened for the voices of the guards but there were none. She froze when she saw movement in the darkness.

"Ladro?" she whispered, praying that it was he.

"Yes, Marcela." Ladro went to the old woman, taking her hand and leading her to the small group.

"Where's Aeneva?" Trenton demanded.

"We were trying to get out of the hall window. I had jumped and Aeneva had just lowered the basket to me. But Cortez woke up. She had to go back to him."

"Jesus." Trenton kicked at the ground in frustration. "You mean she's still with him? I'm going after her."

"No." Ladro grabbed Trenton's arm. "Not yet."

Trenton yanked his arm away. "She's with that bastard right now and I'll be damned if I'll let her stay with him."

"You don't have a choice, Trenton," Ladro replied evenly. "If you go back there, you'll be killed before you even get to the hacienda."

"If Marcela can do it, I can. It can't be that hard."

"She latched the window, *señor*. You cannot get back in." Marcela touched his arm. "You must not take a chance. One shot will put all of Cortez's men on the alert. None of us will get out alive."

"I can't just leave her there."

"We'll get her out, boy. We just need some time to think," Joe said.

"I'm not waiting." Trenton started to walk away but Larissa grabbed his arm. "Trenton, wait. I know Cortez. He won't kill her."

"You mean not yet he won't."

"He is crazy but he is also smart. When he finds out we're gone he'll want to keep her alive even more. He knows she will bring you and Ladro back."

"And he's right."

"Yes, but not now, not when you are like this. You must be strong and have a clear head."

Marcela moved closer. "She is right, *señor*. Your wife asked me to tell you something. She said she would be all right as long as she knows all of you are safe. Please do as she asks, *señor*. She would be tormented if something happened to you or to her son."

Trenton turned away from Marcela, leaning against the side of the barn. "How are we going to get out?"

"There has to be some way, *señor*. Now that you are free, we will think of something."

"All right, I'll do as you say for now, Marcela."

"Good, now let's get going." Joe gave Trenton a solid pat on the back. "My shack would be a safe place to figure out a plan. Marcela, you know the trails around here. Can you lead us?"

Marcela nodded. She led the way. She knew paths through the adobe huts and the arroyo that were narrow enough to force them into single file, but they made it to Joe's shack without passing any guards. Trenton went in first with his gun drawn, then waved the others inside.

For a moment there was only the sound of breathing in the darkness, and the tiny contented sound of the baby. Ladro's whisper broke the silence.

"We've been fools."

Joe sat down heavily on the edge of the enormous bed. "We just outsmarted twenty ugly guards, and we're fools?" He brought his bad leg up and straightened it out with a groan. "All we have to do now is . . ."

"Figure a way out," Ladro finished for him. "And there isn't one. I know this place as well as anyone except Ignacio. That cactus would take us a week to cut through with machetes. And they are bound to have guards all across the entrance, and some out in the desert, too."

Marcela laid the sleeping baby next to Joe and sat down. "Crazy old Maximo. He built a place to defend, not a place to escape from." Her voice sounded weary and old.

."He wasn't ever crazy, Marcela." Ladro's voice was soft. "He was a crafty old man and his defenses have served many people very well."

"You always defended him, Ladro."

"And you always scolded him."

Marcela sighed. "If he were here tonight, I would do more than that. I would shake the old fool." She slapped the bed. "Only a crazy man would have made a bed like this in a shack. It is so heavy he had to leave it here."

Ladro laughed. "He did that on purpose so he could sleep here, away from your sharp tongue. I always thought he was magic."

Marcela made a sound of disgust. "He was the kind of man who could disappear whenever there was work to be done, if that's what you mean. I remember times he got out of that house . . . past me as I stood at the stove, and I never heard him."

Trenton leaned forward. "The hell with Maximo. If he wasn't smart enough to build an escape route out of this place, we'll just have to be smart enough to figure one out. I think we should go to the entry, right now, before anyone has a chance to see we're gone from the barn. We have three men. If we can surprise the guards . . ."

"Maybe he did." It was Ladro's voice, low and thoughtful. "Maybe his escape route is closer than you think."

"What are you talking about?" Larissa whispered. "Ladro, we have to get the child out, *now*. We haven't got time to sit around . . ."

Joe leaned forward. "Let the man think. I can

smell a good idea a mile away, and I smell one now. Let him talk."

Ladro pushed his hair back from his face, pacing the little shack. "He always worked here. I used to come and watch him. He could do anything with his hands. Anything. I watched him make that bed." He stopped, silent for a moment. "I asked him once, why he had made it so big. I remember telling him that no one would ever be able to move it." Ladro walked to the bed, gripping the ironwork. "He laughed and said that was what he had in mind. Then he told me a story and I forgot the strange answer. But I think I know what he meant now." Ladro pulled at Marcela's arm. She stood up, muttering, and lifted the baby. Joe got off the bed, using his stick for balance.

"Well, say it, Ladro. You more than got our attention, believe me."

"Help me move it."

"We're just wasting time," Trenton growled. "Aeneva is with that bastard and you want to see if we can move a bed that weighs as much as a horse."

Ladro spun to face him. "Then go, gringo, and fight Cortez's men alone. I am going to save my son." He stared at Trenton's face. "I am going to save him so that you can raise him, gringo."

Joe put his hand on Trenton's arm. "You never could beat me at arm wrestling, boy, but it's going to take a little effort to move that thing. Why don't you close your mouth and try."

The three men gripped the ironwork and pulled together. The silence was broken only by the sounds that the strain brought from their lips. Larissa

421

positioned herself near Joe and heaved. The bed slid a few inches. The men changed their footing and heaved again. It shifted another few inches. Marcela made a little sound and set the baby in the center of the bed, gripping the iron frame next to Larissa. They heaved again, making nearly a foot this time. Once more and they had to rest. Joe leaned forward, his face nearly touching the baby's blanket.

"Okay, you weak sons of bitches," he said between ragged breaths. "We do it this time or I'll kill you both. No more slacking off while I do all the work."

Larissa laughed quietly and Marcela made a choking sound. They took their positions and pulled again. The bed moved steadily away from the wall.

"That should be enough," Ladro panted. "Enough. If it's there at all he would have put it in the corner. He staggered around the bed and dropped to his knees on the planking. There were scratching sounds as he felt the floor. Then he straightened. "It's here. *Gracias a Dios,* it's here."

Marcela scooped up the baby. "A door, Ladro?"

"Either that or I'll flatten his head for him," Joe whispered.

"But I can't find . . ." Ladro began, then stopped. "Maximo was far from crazy," he breathed, as though he were talking to himself. "A piece of the floor comes up and beneath there is an iron ring, shaped to fit a man's hand."

There was a sound of hinges moving and Marcela whispered a prayer. The baby, at least, had a chance at safety. Joe had grabbed a bag, and was filling it with food and a water flask.

Ladro dropped into the tunnel. Joe passed a

lantern to Trenton. Ladro took it and a glow of light came into the room from below. "It runs both ways," he whispered through the trapdoor. "I can't see how far, but the air isn't stale. There is room for all of us."

"No." Marcela stood apart. "No, I will go back."

Larissa went to her and took her arm. "Of course you will hide with us. Cortez will kill you when he realizes the baby is gone. You have to come."

Marcela pushed the baby into Larissa's arms. "No. I will stay to help Aeneva if I can. And these old legs will only slow you down if you must run." She turned and was out the door before any of them could stop her.

"Come, Larissa," Ladro hissed from the trapdoor. "We have taken far too long already."

Trenton moved to let Larissa pass. "I'm not going to hide either."

Joe grunted. "He might be right, Ladro. If Cortez doesn't know we're gone yet, this could be our best chance to get Aeneva."

Ladro nodded slowly. "Maybe. And the baby will be safe with Larissa. All right, gringo. We do it your way."

Larissa lowered herself into the tunnel, handing the infant to Ladro until she was steady. Joe passed the bag down and stood clear as Ladro came up. "Move away from the trapdoor, and don't worry. We'll take care of you. Go easy on the light, there's matches in the bag, and food and water."

"And if I don't you'll flatten my head for me?" Larissa's whisper came up from the tunnel. Joe rocked with silent laughter. Even Trenton managed a smile. The baby was safe, at least for now. Aeneva would be next.

Joe leaned over the trapdoor. "Not likely. Yours is too pretty." He shut the door, carefully replacing the piece of wood that hid the ring. The three men shoved at the bed, inching it back toward the wall.

Trenton ran his hand over the planking, expecting it to be scarred from the heavy bedframe, but it was smooth. He ran his fingers along the base of the frame. Hidden pads masked the iron. He straightened up.

"Old Maximo has helped us about as much as he can. Now it's up to us. And I can't wait to get my hands around Cortez's throat."

Ladro looked at him. "And mine, gringo, but I don't think it is going to be easy."

Chapter XV

Aeneva tried to move, but she could not. Cortez had tied her to the bed, playing one of his sadistic games with her. She knew that time was running out, but there was nothing she could do about it. Soon Trenton, James, and the others would be gone and she would have to stay with this man whom she hated so much. She tugged at the ropes that held her, but she couldn't loosen them. The only thing that gave her comfort was knowing that they would all be safe away from Cortez. She didn't pull at the ropes anymore. Instead she closed her eyes and slept, knowing she would need all of the strength she had to survive.

Sleep came and it felt like cool water around her legs. She threw back her head, feeling her wet hair fall down to her waist. She felt free and she felt happy, happier than she had felt in a long time. She smiled to herself, knowing that he would be here soon. She felt the breeze touch her face lightly. And she felt his hands as they touched her shoulders, gently removing her dress. She kept her eyes closed, reveling in the feel of his hands as they moved over her bare back and shoulders. She felt his lips as he kissed her neck, moving her hair aside. She felt she would explode from the excitement within. She turned her head slightly and saw him, his blue eyes twinkling, his golden hair reflecting the sunlight. She had never known a man who excited her more than he did. With just a look he could make her feel weak. It had always been this way between them, even as children. He always teased her, but he had always loved her. But suddenly his voice grew harsh and his hands became rough as they pulled and tugged at her. She pulled away from him, but he pulled her back. What was he doing?

"No!" she exclaimed, trying desperately to get away from him but unable to move anywhere. It was as if she were his prisoner. . . . Aeneva came out of her dream, feeling Cortez touching her all over. Her dream had been so sweet but her reality was disgusting. She turned her face away from him as he tried to kiss her, but he held her head firm, probing her mouth with his tongue. He climbed on top of her, touching her in every way he could. She screamed within herself but she had to do just what he wanted, at least for now. She steeled herself, but just as he was about to take her there was a loud pounding at the door.

"*Patrón, Patrón!* I must see you. It's very important."

"Ah!" Cortez yelled, rolling off Aeneva and sitting up on the edge of the bed. He stumbled to the chair, quickly putting on his pants. "This better be

426

important, Pedro." He jerked open the door.

"They are gone, *Patrón.*"

"Who is gone?"

"All the prisoners. All gone."

"What? What happened?"

"We don't know, *Patrón*. I was on my way to the camp. Alvarro had come to relieve me. I passed the barn and didn't see any guards. I looked inside and saw the men were gone."

"Ladro, the gringo, both gone?"

"*Sí, Patrón.* So is the girl."

"Larissa?"

"Yes. I will send men to check on the black man."

"What black man?"

"He lives in a shack outside of the village. You saw him once. He was crippled. I didn't think he could even walk. Your wife was giving him medicine."

"They can't have gotten far. Where are the guards from the barn?"

"Dead, *Patrón.*"

Cortez's face had become a rigid mask. Only his eyes betrayed his fury. "Get all of the men together. Put the villagers in the barn and lock it. I will meet you there in a few minutes."

Cortez slammed the door shut and walked to the night table, turning up the lamp. He looked over at Aeneva. "Did you hear? They all escaped. I suppose you knew nothing about this."

"I knew nothing."

"And you did not help them?"

"How could I help them, Emiliano?" She tugged at her ropes, forcing the joy out of her voice. They had made it!

427

"Well, they won't get away from me," he said angrily, putting on his shirt. "They'll be even more sorry this time when I find them. I will stake them all out in the front yard of the hacienda for all to see. They will die slowly and painfully." He pulled on his boots and walked over to the bed, leaning over and squeezing Aeneva's face between his fingers. "If I find out that you helped them, you will be the first person I tie to the stake. Do you understand?"

Aeneva nodded, watching Cortez walk out of the room. She heard the door shut and the lock click behind him. She tugged and pulled at the ropes but to no avail. She heard yelling outside in the courtyard. She knew that Cortez was organizing a search. She thought she heard a knock on the door and she listened. The quiet knock came again. "Yes, who is it?"

"It is Marcela."

"Marcela, but I am tied up. I cannot come to the door." She heard the sound of a key in the lock and Marcela came inside.

Marcela frantically worked at the knots. "I was so afraid for you. I was sure he would discover that you were trying to escape."

"No, he thought I was just taking a walk." Aeneva sat up, rubbing her wrists. Marcela handed her clothes from the closet. Aeneva dressed quickly. She took the knife from underneath the mattress where she had hidden it. She strapped it on her thigh, pulling her skirt over it. "He brought me back here. I had to pretend that I enjoyed his game."

"He is a sick man, that one."

"I know, Marcela." Aeneva walked to the door and

peered out. "Let's go. Hurry."

They went to the hall window. Aeneva unlatched it and pushed it out. "Come, Marcela. You must jump one more time."

"This is too much for an old woman, Aeneva. Do you know what it took for me to climb back up here? *Dios!*"

"Go, Marcela."

Footsteps sounded below. Now they were on the stairs. "Hurry, Marcela. Cortez is coming." Aeneva tried to help Marcela out the window, but Cortez came up the stairs too quickly. The women stopped, helpless, turning to watch as Cortez walked down the hallway toward them. Behind him two guards stood at the top of the stairs. He stopped in front of Aeneva, staring at her for a long moment.

"You bitch!" He slapped her, knocking her against the window. "I should have known it was you." He looked around. "And you got the child out, didn't you?"

"Yes. You'll never touch him, Emiliano."

Cortez raised his hand again, but Marcela grabbed his arm. He shoved her away. "Get her out of here," he ordered. A guard forced Marcela down the stairs. "I told you that if you helped them to escape you would be the first one up in the yard."

"I do not care what you do with me now. My son, my husband, and my friends are all safe. And you will never find them."

"You don't give yourself enough credit, Aeneva. The men will come back for you. They love you."

"They will not come back."

"Oh, but they will." He stepped forward, his face

close to Aeneva's. "The old woman helped you. She will pay also."

"No, Emiliano. She did not help me. I forced her . . ."

"Do not waste your breath, my dear. You will need it later." He shook his head. "Ah, Aeneva, I wish you had not deceived me. I enjoyed our time together. You know how to please a man." His hand went to her neck, caressing it as a lover would.

Aeneva jerked her head away from his hand. "I hate you, Emiliano. I hate everything about you. You do not even know what it is like to make love to a woman; all you know is force and cruelty. The only thing I ever felt with you was disgust."

Cortez lashed out again, this time knocking Aeneva so hard against the wall that she hit her head. She leaned forward covering her face with her hands. "What's the matter? I thought Indian women were so tough." He reached down and pulled at Aeneva's hair. She moved to the side, getting her hand under the hem of her skirt. She pulled her knife from her thigh sheath and struck out at Cortez, slashing him in the side.

"Damn you!" he yelled. "Pedro, help me with this bitch. She has a knife."

Aeneva rolled to the side, striking out at both men. She stood up, holding the knife in front of her. She moved it from side to side as the men closed in on her. "Do not come near me, Cortez. I will kill you."

"You won't have a chance, my dear. You'll be dead before you can raise your arm. Put down the knife."

"No."

"Shoot her, Pedro."

Pedro pulled out his gun, aiming it at Aeneva. "Put down the knife, senora. I don't want to shoot you."

"Shoot her, Pedro. I command you!"

Pedro aimed the gun but didn't pull the trigger. "Put down the knife, please, senora."

Aeneva looked at the crazed look in Cortez's eyes and she knew that she didn't have a chance. If Pedro didn't shoot her, Cortez would. And she didn't want to die. Not this way. She dropped the knife on the floor where she stood. Cortez picked it up and pushed her against the wall, placing the point of the knife at her throat.

"How does it feel, Aeneva? Do you like it, eh?"

Aeneva stared at Cortez, refusing to let him frighten her. If he was going to kill her she would not give him the satisfaction of knowing she was afraid. Her eyes betrayed no emotion save hatred. "Do it if you must, Emiliano. If it will make you feel like a man."

Cortez pressed the point of the knife into Aeneva's throat. "I should cut your throat right now but I won't. That would be too fast. I want you to suffer first." He pulled her away from the wall and shoved her toward the door. "Take her outside, Pedro. I want her and the old woman tied to poles in the yard. I want all of the villagers to see them suffer. If any of them know anything, they'll speak up."

Aeneva was taken to the front yard of the hacienda and tied to a tall pole. She watched as Marcela was tied to another one. She expected to see all of the people of the town, but it was silent. Only Cortez and his men were there. Cortez walked to her, brandishing the knife in front of her face. He put the blade under the sleeve of her blouse and with one swipe ripped it from her arm.

"A very sharp blade," he said as if mesmerized, doing the same thing to her other sleeve. Again he pressed the point of the knife into her neck and slowly moved it down to the top of her blouse. With a swift motion, he cut the blouse so that it hung open exposing her breasts. He ran the blade between her breasts, to the top of her skirt. "You are a beautiful woman, Aeneva. It is too bad that you are so deceitful. People who are deceitful must pay." He pressed the blade of the knife into her belly, breaking the skin. "How does it feel?"

Aeneva continued to stare into his eyes, not betraying any sign of emotion. She knew that he wanted her to break but she refused to do so. She felt the warm line of blood from her neck to her belly where Cortez had cut the skin. It hurt. But not as badly as she was sure it would hurt when he was through with her.

Suddenly Cortez withdrew the knife. He looked at Aeneva, taking a handful of her hair in his hand and jerking her head back. He looked at her a moment, then pressed his mouth to hers. She wrenched away and spit in his face. She saw his rage but he didn't do anything. He took the knife and put it in his belt.

"We have lots of time for this, Aeneva." He wiped the spit from his face. "And Ladro and the gringo will be back for you. There is no doubt in my mind. And when they do come back, we will put on quite a show for them."

"They will not come back."

Cortez only smiled, walking back toward the hacienda. Aeneva looked over at Marcela. She seemed all right for now. She looked up at the star-filled sky and she wondered which one of the stars twinkling down at her was her grandmother. She knew that Sun Dancer was there somewhere and, wherever she was, Aeneva prayed that she would help her to be strong.

She took a deep breath and closed her eyes. She would have to draw from all her inner resources to survive Cortez's torments. She had the strength, it had just been a long time since she had had to use it. But she would be strong and she would not let someone like Emiliano Cortez dishonor her. He didn't know it now, but someday he would find that the Maiyun were not so forgiving. All of the torment that he had inflicted on others while on earth would come back to him in his next life. He might not pay for it now, but he would someday.

"You two aren't going without me." Joe walked over to the two men.

Trenton faced Joe. "I want you to stay here. Look at you, you're limping badly again. Besides, Larissa and the baby might need you."

"Please, *Negro*, I need you to guard my sister and my son. I need to know that they will be safe."

Joe nodded impatiently. "Yeah, yeah, of course I'll stay here. But you two be careful. That bastard would just as soon skin you two alive as look at you." Joe took a deep breath. "You know that he'll be waiting for you two. He knows how you both feel about Aeneva."

433

"But he doesn't know when we'll be coming, and he doesn't know from where. We have weapons and if we're careful we can get Aeneva out of there."

"And if we're lucky, we can kill Cortez and put an end to this. He has done too much to too many already."

"I just want you two to be careful, that's all." Joe hoisted himself into the bed, lying back slowly. He looked as though he'd never moved. "If something does happen to you, Ladro, I'll make sure your sister and your son get out of here safely."

"Thank you, *Negro.*"

Joe looked at Trenton. "If you can't get Aeneva out alive don't sacrifice yourself, boy. She wouldn't want that. Come back here. You still have a son waiting for you at home."

"I know that, Joe. I know." He grinned at his friend. "Wish us luck, Joe. We'll need it."

"As they say down here, *Vaya con Dios.*"

Aeneva heard a scream and she jerked her head up. The sun was already rising and she could feel the heat on her body. She heard a scream again and she looked over at Marcela. Cortez was standing in front of Marcela, a knife held in his hand, cutting her.

"Emiliano, do not!" Aeneva screamed. "Please, she is an old woman. She knows nothing."

Cortez didn't acknowledge Aeneva and Aeneva could see even from where she was that he was enjoying his sick game. Every time he cut Marcela he did something with his other hand which made her scream. Then it occurred to Aeneva what he was doing. The Indians had done a similar thing when they had tortured people. They would inflict wounds on their victims and then rub salt in them. She remembered vividly that Crooked Teeth had done the same thing to her dear Uncle Jean. And now Cortez, who was so obsessed, was doing the same thing to Marcela.

"Emiliano!" Aeneva screamed. "I can tell you what you want to know. Marcela knows nothing."

Cortez stopped, looking over at Aeneva for the first time. "It doesn't matter if she knows nothing. She is paying for your deceit." He yelled to his men and then untied Marcela and turned her around so that she faced the pole. Cortez ripped her blouse away from her back. He took a rope from Pedro, wrapping the end of it around his hand. He stretched the rope out tight, snapping it a few times. He stepped back. He lifted up his arm and the rope lashed Marcela's back.

"No! No!" Aeneva pleaded with Cortez but he wouldn't hear her. Marcela's screams tore at Aeneva. She was afraid he would beat her to death. But he stopped abruptly. She could hear him laugh as he rubbed salt into Marcela's wounds.

Aeneva's knees weakened. Marcela's screams rang in her ears and there was nothing she could do to help the old woman. She was sickened at the thought of someone suffering such pain because of her. And Cortez knew that. Suddenly the screams stopped. Aeneva looked over and saw Marcela hanging limply from the pole. Cortez turned and walked slowly toward Aeneva. He held his hand up in front of her face. She could smell the white crystals before she saw them.

"Do you know what this is, Aeneva?" he asked. He

435

was smiling.

She stared at him, refusing to answer.

"You are trying to be brave, aren't you? I like that. I have always liked that about you. Your people are strong. It would be dishonorable for you to show weakness, wouldn't it?" He ran his fingers down between her breasts, tracing the cut he had inflicted the night before. "I don't want to hurt you, Aeneva, but I must. Don't you see? I have to set an example. If my men see me being kind to you, they'll think they can get away with anything." His breath stank of mescal.

"Why do you not kill me then? Kill me and get it over with."

"I can't do that, Aeneva. You know me better than that. What fun is there in killing you right away? I want to see how really strong you are. You act brave, but when it comes down to it, I want to see if you really are strong enough to take what punishment I can give you." He ran his hand across her forehead. "You see, already you're sweating. Are you scared, Aeneva? Do you want to tell me something? If you tell me where they've gone, I may decide to be kind."

"Even if I knew where they were I would not tell you."

"Oh, but you will tell me, Aeneva. You will." Cortez took out the knife and cut the rope that bound Aeneva's hands. He motioned to Pedro and another of his men. They quickly turned her around so that she was facing the pole. They tied her hands high above her so that she was stretched out as far as possible. Cortez placed the knife under her blouse and cut it. It hung loosely on her bare skin. He ran his hand over the smooth skin. "Such a waste. You could have been with me. You could have lived."

"I would rather die," Aeneva said coldly.

"Do you feel the heat yet, Aeneva? The sun is rising steadily. Soon you will begin to sweat and your skin will burn and itch." He took the rope from Pedro, wrapping it around his hand. "And it will feel even worse when I am finished with you." The rope slashed downward, knocking her against the pole. Aeneva groaned but she said nothing. Cortez whipped her several times. He stopped, moving close to her. "How does it feel now, Aeneva? There is still time for me to save you if you tell me the truth."

Aeneva turned her face away from Cortez's, shutting her eyes. The pain was extraordinary, but she refused to give in to him.

"Well, I'm sorry but you asked for this." Cortez held up his hand and began rubbing the salt crystals into Aeneva's back. Her entire body arched but she held her screams inside her mind, pushing them deeper and deeper. "It will only get worse, Aeneva, unless you tell me where they are. I am the only one who can save you."

"I do not want to be saved by you," Aeneva uttered, biting her lip as the salt entered the wounds. The sweat poured down her face and she felt the bile rise in her stomach, but she bit her lip harder and closed her eyes. She thought of the river where she had grown up and how cool and refreshing it had been to dive into it. She remembered the games she and her brothers and Trenton used to play and a slight smile appeared on her face.

"What are you smiling for?" Cortez said angrily.

437

"Open your eyes and look at me."

Aeneva opened her eyes and looked but she did not see Cortez. Instead she saw the open prairie and the wildflowers that grew in the spring. She heard the snorts of the buffalo as they rolled in their wallows trying to cool off. And in the distance she saw the mountains that she loved so much. She would not let Cortez enter into any part of this memory.

"I will let you think about it for a while. But I will be back. It will get worse, Aeneva, and I don't think you'll be so brave next time."

Aeneva heard Cortez as he walked away. She had never known a person who so enjoyed inflicting pain on others. That was the one thing that truly excited him; that was his ultimate fulfillment. Aeneva knew that no matter what he did to her, she must not beg him to stop. She had to be strong. That was the only way to defeat Cortez.

As the sun rose higher in the sky, Aeneva felt the heat sear her skin. The wounds on her back felt as if they had opened and the sun itself was reaching inside them. The salt made it worse and she felt as if she would never survive. She thought of the long time she had spent with Crooked Teeth and all of the things he had done to her. She had survived him; she could survive Cortez. She looked over at Marcela. The old woman was still hanging limply from the pole. Aeneva had no idea whether she was alive or dead. She closed her eyes and tried to think of other times but this time the pain was too great. She could not clear her mind of it. It threatened to consume her. She heard footsteps behind her and she knew that Cortez had come again.

"Have you decided to tell me where they are, Aeneva?" His voice was thick and his words were slurred.

Aeneva was silent, trying to compose herself for what was to come next.

Cortez unscrewed the top to a canteen and drank greedily. "Ah, that is good." He held it by Aeneva's face. "Can you smell it? I have heard that a horse can smell water from a mile away if he is thirsty enough." He took another drink and poured the rest onto the ground next to Aeneva's feet, then dabbed at his face with a kerchief. "It's much too hot out here for me. I think I'll go inside and take a nap. It should be nice and cool in there." He wiped the sweat from Aeneva's face with the kerchief. "It must be painful, Aeneva. Why don't you tell me what I want to know and I'll untie you and bring you inside. I have a soothing medicine that I could rub on your back myself. You are making me do this to you."

"You are doing this because you enjoy it," Aeneva replied slowly, measuring each word. "You are a sick man. Hurting people is the only way you know of arousing yourself. You cannot do it otherwise."

Cortez slapped her hard. "I will be back later, Aeneva. I think by the time I return you will have changed your mind."

Aeneva opened her eyes and everything was blurry. She forced herself to stand up. The ropes pulled at her arms and made the pain worse. She took deep breaths and forced her thoughts to other things. She thought of Trenton and Nathan and James, and she wondered if she and Trenton would ever have a child together. She wondered what it would look like—

would it be light-haired or dark-haired, would it have blue eyes or dark eyes? She realized her mind was wandering but she didn't care; she needed to keep her thoughts from the pain. She was afraid it would consume her, and in so doing, she was afraid she would give in and tell Cortez everything. She heard a voice in her mind, a familiar voice. It was Sun Dancer, slowly repeating the chant for courage as though she were teaching it to a child. Aeneva did not question the reality of the voice. She simply clung to it, drawing from it the strength she knew she would need.

Trenton looked at Ladro. They stood in the shadows outside Joe's shack. "Are you ready?"

"I'm ready. I have two pistols, a knife, and a rifle. Joe's keeping two pistols. What about you?"

"The same as you have, and one extra pistol."

"Let's go."

"Ladro, wait. If something happens to me, get Aeneva out of here. She's suffered enough. Take care of her. Tell her that I loved her more than anything."

Ladro was silent for a long time, contemplating Trenton's words. "I had never even met you and I knew you were a good man. I knew that you loved her enough to search for her not once but twice. But I still tried to take her away from you. For that I am sorry."

"It's over now. I just want to know that you'll take good care of her if something happens to me. She'll need you."

"I won't need to. You will be fine."

"And if we both make it out alive? What then?"

"Just as before, you take my son. He will be better off with you and Aeneva. When he grows up, tell him that his father loved him."

"I will tell him." Trenton checked his guns. "Let's go. Cortez's men are probably searching by now."

"We'll go the way Marcela told us about—the path that goes to the back of Ignacio's house."

Trenton moved into the darkness, walking silently. He heard Ladro's steps behind him as he started down the narrow path. As they crossed the arroyo they heard voices, but none were close. Trenton walked carefully, his rifle held ready. As they started uphill, the narrow path joined a wider one. They heard voices. Trenton waved Ladro back into the trees and they ducked down low as some of Cortez's men passed them on the trail. When they were gone, Trenton led the way back onto the trail and toward the barn. They stopped in the shadows. The doors were closed and there were some of Cortez's men out in front.

"Why do you think the doors are closed?"

"I don't know."

Trenton thought for a moment. "Maybe they've got the villagers in there. It's about the only place big enough to hold them. If Cortez knows we're gone, he'll want to question them. If we get them out, do you think they'll help us?"

"I'm sure they will. How many men are out in front?"

"Three, maybe four."

"And there might be more inside."

"You have any ideas? Those guys are going to be a lot more careful now."

441

"Let's just surprise them."

"We'll have to use the knives, no guns. A shot will bring more than we can handle."

"We can do that. But we'll have to act fast. You can come from one side. I'll come from the other."

"All right. Ready when you are."

"Let's go."

The two men moved through the shadows until they were behind the barn. They nodded to each other and separated, one moving along each side of the building. Trenton waited until he could see where each guard stood and what they were doing. Two of them were talking, leaning close to the front doors. One stood farther away from the barn looking out toward the trees. Another was leaning casually against the barn, close to where Ladro stood in the shadows. Trenton took out his knife and put it in his teeth. He held the rifle ready in his hands. He crept around the corner. The two men who were talking stopped and turned. Trenton threw his knife; one fell clutching his belly. Just as the other was drawing his pistol, Trenton sprang forward and smashed the man in the face with the rifle. Trenton hit the ground and rolled. He saw the man in front hurrying back, gun drawn. Trenton raised his rifle and aimed, ready to fire, but he didn't have to. Ladro had already thrown his knife. It landed on target and the man went down. Trenton stood up, glancing around. Ladro had already taken care of the other guard.

"You're fast. If I'd had to shoot, we'd have been finished. Thanks."

Ladro nodded. "Let's get these doors open." They lifted the bar and opened the large doors. There were no voices, no guards inside. Trenton took a lantern and raised it high. The villagers were there, huddled in small groups.

"You talk to them. I'll get the weapons." Trenton ran back outside.

"Amigos, I need your help." Ladro gathered the men and older boys together, sending two of the men to help Trenton. "We have some weapons but not enough for all of you. You need to find any kind of tool you can—shovels, axes, pitchforks—anything that can be used as a weapon."

"What do you want us to do, Ladro? Do you want us to go up to the hacienda?"

"No. If you rush up there Cortez's men will shoot you down before you reach the hacienda. We'll leave four men here, two on the outside, two on the inside, to guard the women and children. The rest of you come with me." Ladro went outside to Trenton, who had passed out the rifles and pistols to the men.

Trenton faced Ladro. "How many do we have with us?"

"If we leave four here to guard the women and children, we'll have about thirty men and boys."

"And only weapons enough for about fifteen."

"I've got them searching for anything they can use as a weapon."

"You know this place better than I do, Ladro. Where do you think we should go in?"

"We'll divide up. I'll take half with me, you take the other half. You circle around the back of the barn. Take the path that Marcela used. It comes out behind the hacienda. I'll take the others. We'll go to the edge of the arroyo just inside the cover of the trees."

"Where do you think he has Aeneva?"

"I don't know. But I know Cortez and he's expecting us to come back for Aeneva. He'll find a way to bait us. We must be careful."

"If I see her, I'm going after her."

"That's what he wants, Trenton. He'll kill you before you even get close to her. You have to be patient. He won't kill her right away but he'll think of something. He needs her for the time being to draw us out."

"I can't watch her suffer again, Ladro. I saw what it did to her once before. I don't know if she can go through it again."

"She will if she must. She is a strong woman." Ladro put his hand on Trenton's shoulder. "She has you and her two sons. She will make it."

Trenton looked at Ladro. He reached for his hand and grasped it firmly. "You really do love her. I'm almost sorry that you have to lose her."

Ladro laughed. "If you feel that sorry for me, I'll gladly take her."

"I don't feel that sorry for you. But I do thank you. I understand now why she came to care for you."

One of the villagers ran up. "We are ready, Ladro."

Ladro nodded to Trenton. "Good luck, gringo. And remember, be patient. Be smarter than Cortez."

Trenton nodded and waved his men forward. He walked around the back of the barn and climbed the hill, followed by the small group of men. They moved quietly. He led them along the narrow path, trying to figure out what he was going to do when he got to the hacienda. He couldn't give Cortez time to kill Aeneva. The path wound through the trees, then opened out again. Trenton stopped, studying the back of the hacienda. The men behind him waited. There were none of Cortez's men in the back of the hacienda. He waved his men forward. He sent one to wait on each side of the hacienda. He and the others stayed in the back. There was a window on the second story. It looked like the grillwork would support his weight. Trenton signaled for the men to stay hidden. He looked at the wall. There was a decorative iron grill set into the adobe. He used it to hoist himself upward, clawing for handholds on the rough adobe. Finally he grasped the solid iron work around the window and pulled himself up. The window was open. He listened. Either no one was in the house or everyone was asleep. He climbed in, pausing an instant to listen again. Moving silently, he searched the rooms, then started down the stairs. Light came through the window. He squinted his eyes and his stomach knotted up so tightly he swayed. Aeneva and Marcela were tied to poles in the yard. Lanterns were hung high above, illuminating the entire area. He felt the hatred rise in him like a wave that he couldn't control. He wanted to kill Cortez. But he knew that Ladro was right; he wouldn't be able to get close to Aeneva. She was completely surrounded by Cortez's men. Cortez himself stood in front of Aeneva, a rope in his hand.

"Is everything all right, *señor?*"

Trenton spun. Two of the men had followed him in. They had seen what was outside as clearly as he had. Their faces were calm, but their eyes told him they would follow him to their own deaths.

"What's your name?"

"I am Enrique. My friend is called Pasqual. We were worried, *señor*."

"Cortez and most of his men are out there right now. He has my wife and Marcela. We have to get them out of there or he will kill them."

Enrique nodded his head. "Marcela was always so good to everyone." Enrique stared out at the light. "Have you ever robbed a bank, *señor*?"

Trenton looked at the man, puzzled by his question. "No. Why?"

"Well, I myself have robbed a bank. We used a diversion. You understand what that is, *señor*?"

"A diversion," Trenton repeated to himself, nodding. "What do you have in mind, Enrique?"

"Well, one of the best is an explosion. A big boom."

"And what better place than right here in the house?"

"*Sí, señor*, just what I was thinking."

Trenton patted Enrique on the back. "Pasqual, go back out and tell the men what we are going to do. Have them all get clear."

"*Sí, señor*. I will tell them and we will be ready to help."

"Thank you, Pasqual." Trenton stared back out the window. "Since you're so experienced at this, Enrique, you'll have to show me how."

"*No problema, señor*. Start emptying your bullets. We will need the gunpowder." Trenton tore his eyes away from Aeneva and climbed the stairs. Enrique followed. He spread his bandana on the landing.

"Here, *señor,* cut all of these open and empty them onto this. We will need some string. I will find something while you empty these. As soon as our friends are clear, we will light it. You and I will only have a few seconds to get out of here."

"I understand, Enrique." Trenton quickly cut open the cartridges and emptied the powder onto the cloth. In a few more minutes he would be holding Aeneva.

Chapter XVI

Aeneva jerked her head up, standing straight and tall. She opened her eyes, squinting at the light above her. She looked around. There were guards everywhere. She knew that Cortez was behind her, but she wasn't afraid. She had had a strange dream, a dream in which her grandmother had told her to be strong. She had actually yelled at her. Aeneva smiled to herself in spite of her pain—it was just like Sun Dancer to yell at her granddaughter when she was beginning to feel sorry for herself.

"So, you are awake."

Aeneva felt her stomach tighten at the sound of Cortez's voice. The man was like all bad spirits she had ever heard about. He was like the devil himself.

She turned her head to the other side to look at Marcela. The old woman was still hanging from the pole. "Emiliano, please cut Marcela down. She has done nothing."

"I will cut her down as soon as you tell me where your two lovers are." Cortez walked up behind

Aeneva. His breath was on her neck and face. "What was it like having two lovers, Aeneva? Was it good? Which one was better?" He rubbed his fingers along her neck, ignoring the fact that she jerked her head away. "Was Ladro a good lover? I bet he was. Ladro is a stallion, is he not?"

"Stop it!" Aeneva pleaded, knowing that she was reacting the way Cortez wanted her to.

"And what about the white man, eh? Was he good, too? Or did you just tell him that he was good? Eh, Aeneva?" He kissed her on the neck, holding her head still so that she couldn't move. "And what about me, Aeneva? You told me that I disgusted you, but I know the truth. I know that I am the only man who has ever excited you. I know that." Cortez pressed his mouth to hers, holding her head firmly in his hands. "You are in my power, Aeneva. You can't fight me."

"I hate you," she muttered, trying to pull her head away from Cortez's grasp.

"That makes it all the more exciting," he whispered, running his hands up and down her hips. "I can let you go right now. All you have to do is tell me where they are. You won't suffer anymore."

"You do not understand, do you? You are so sick you cannot see that I would rather die than tell you where they are. I would rather die." She practically spit the words out.

"Then it is your choice, my dear," Cortez replied angrily, pulling his knife out from his belt. He placed it next to Aeneva's head. "I have heard that it is painful to have the scalp removed. Have you ever scalped anyone, Aeneva?" He picked up some of her hair and pulled it straight out, placing the knife next to her head. "You have beautiful hair. It would be a shame to cut it off."

"I will not need hair if I am dead," Aeneva replied coldly.

"You are so brave, aren't you?" Cortez stuck the point of the blade into Aeneva's scalp. "How does it feel now?"

Aeneva closed her eyes, making her mind a blank. She refused to let this man reduce her to nothing. She would die with honor. She felt the blade move along her scalp but she remained motionless and emotionless. She tried to make herself be outside of herself. She tried to observe rather than participate.

Cortez stopped abruptly, letting Aeneva's hair fall back down. He reached up and wiped a trickle of blood that ran down her face. He stared at it a second, then put his finger in his mouth. "Your blood tastes no different from anyone else's, Aeneva. You are human. You can die." Cortez yanked her hair, jerking her head back as far as it would go. "I think it is time for you to pay for deceiving me. I have been patient long enough." Cortez reached up and cut the ropes that held Aeneva. He pulled her away from the pole. "All of you, come here. I want you to watch," he yelled at his men. The men formed a circle around Aeneva and Cortez. He stood behind her, holding her arms, exposing her breasts through the torn blouse. "What do you think? Do you men think she is beautiful?"

The men were silent. They knew that Cortez was raving. When he was like this, any answer could be the wrong one.

Cortez held Aeneva with one arm, and with the other he reached around and touched one of her breasts. "Do you men like this? If you do, you can have her." He shoved Aeneva forward. "You can have her when I am through with her."

Aeneva turned to face Cortez. Her legs felt weak but she forced herself to stand up straight. "You are a coward. *Cobarde!*" she screamed.

Cortez was angry and he lunged forward striking out at Aeneva. But she saw him coming and she moved to the side, staggering on wooden legs. She clenched her fists. She would fight him. It didn't matter if he killed her. At least she would not die the way he wanted her to, scared and begging for mercy.

"You are too afraid to face anyone, Cortez. You can only fight women, and even then you have to tie them up and beat them. You have no courage."

Cortez raised the knife, his eyes going wild. "I will show you what kind of courage I have, *cabrona.*" Cortez lunged for Aeneva but she dodged to the side. He swiped at her with the knife, cutting her in the side. "How does it feel now, Aeneva?" He held out his hand. "Bring me the rope, Pedro." Pedro ran for the rope and brought it back to Cortez. Cortez stuck the knife back into his belt and slowly wrapped the rope around his hand, leaving the knotted length hanging down. "I think you need to learn more about respect, Aeneva. You are an Indian. You would not know about such things." He swung the rope toward Aeneva. It caught around her neck. He yanked her toward him, unwrapping the rope. "Pedro, do not let her move from this circle. All of you! If she tries to run, push her back." Cortez lifted the rope and struck Aeneva across the chest, knocking her backward. The men pushed her forward and he struck her again with the rope. She fell to the ground from the force of his blows.

Aeneva huddled on the ground, trying to cover her head. It felt as if her entire body was being torn apart. The firelit faces of the men standing around Aeneva became blurred and unreal. Pain became her only reality. Cortez's voice came to her, as if from a great distance.

"Now you are ready to be taught a real lesson." He pushed her to the ground. "You men, hold her arms and legs. I don't want her to move." Cortez lowered himself to Aeneva, an evil smile on his face. He straddled her, his weight pushing her into the ground. "You will die wishing you had not deceived me, Aeneva." Cortez pushed Aeneva's skirt up to her waist, enjoying her discomfort. He ran his hands along her thighs and stomach. "I will miss you, Aeneva." He leaned over her, his mouth touching hers. An explosion ripped the night. Cortez rolled away from Aeneva, jumping to his feet.

"What is it? What has happened?" Cortez screamed. Some of his men scattered, running toward the hacienda. "Come back here!" he ordered, but the men would not listen.

Aeneva pushed down her skirt and pulled her blouse together. She stood up slowly. Pedro stood near her, staring at the fire, his knife strapped to the back of his belt. Aeneva reached forward, carefully pulling the knife from its sheath. She held it down by her side, gathering her strength. As soon as Cortez came at her again she would kill him. She knew she

453

could not stand to be touched by the man again. She would rather die first.

Enrique ran up the stairs. "They are clear, *señor*." He looked at the curtains that Trenton had pulled down and put in a pile. He wrinkled his nose. "Kerosene. Good, that is good. In case the explosion is not a big one, hopefully the fire will catch. Here, I have this." He took out a length of twine about three feet long. He unraveled it and placed it in the middle of the gunpowder. The other end he ran to the end of the hall. He looked at Trenton. "When you are ready, *señor*."

"You told the others to get back?"

"*Sí.* They will wait for us in the trees next to the house."

"Let's go, Enrique."

Enrique took a match from his pocket. He bent down. "Be ready to run, *señor*." He struck the match on the floor. The small flame lit up the room. He held it to the end of the twine. It sizzled for a second, then caught, inching steadily toward the gunpowder. "Go, *señor*."

Trenton shoved Enrique toward the window, then followed him. He hit the ground rolling, then was instantly on his feet running. He followed Enrique into the trees. They hit the ground and covered their heads. Seconds later the gunpowder went off. It was a loud explosion and the ensuing fire lit up the entire area.

Trenton got up yelling. "We move now, *now*, while they are looking at the fire!"

They ran out of the trees and into the yard where Cortez's men milled in the eerie orange light from the fire. Just as Trenton and his men began firing into the yard, Ladro came from the other side. Some of Cortez's men broke and ran. The others looked for cover, firing on the run. Trenton shot one man, then another, but still he couldn't see Aeneva. A man came at him with a knife, but Trenton turned in time and shot him in the chest. The roar of the flames muted the gunfire and the shouting. Trenton looked wildly around, but he couldn't find Aeneva or Cortez. He felt a shove from behind and turned. One of Cortez's men had backed into him, trying to get away from Enrique. Enrique shot the man in the leg and pulled his guns free, handing them to a man fighting with a pitchfork. Enrique grinned.

"Have you seen Cortez?" Trenton yelled at Enrique.

He shook his head.

"My wife?"

"No, *señor*. I am sorry."

Trenton fought his way toward the pole where Aeneva had been tied, but she wasn't there. He spun around, his rifle ready, waiting for some of Cortez's men to come his way. But the men of the village seemed to be controlling the fight. Trenton strained to see through the dust and smoke. Where was Aeneva?

"Over here, gringo." Trenton turned, hearing a voice from the trees. "If you want to see your wife again." He started for the trees. He knew that Cortez would shoot, but he couldn't stop himself.

"No, Trenton!"

Trenton heard Ladro's voice behind him. He slowed for a moment, but continued running.

"No, you fool!" Ladro ran in front of Trenton, pushing him to the side. Trenton hit hard, rolling. Ladro pounded past. "I am coming, Cortez, you bastard. I am coming."

Ladro ran toward the stand of trees, his pistol in front of him. A gunshot rang out and Ladro stumbled but kept going. Another shot rang out and this time Ladro fell.

Trenton crawled along the ground to Ladro, pulling him back away from the trees. Shots hit the ground next to him, but he was able to get Ladro away from the line of fire. "Goddamn you, Ladro. You did just what you told me not to do."

Ladro held his stomach and lifted his hand up to look. "A lot of blood, gringo. It does not look good."

"You'll be all right if you stop running straight at people who're shooting at you."

"You would have done it, gringo. I had to stop you."

"No, you didn't." Trenton took off his bandana and pressed it inside Ladro's shirt against the wound. "Damn you! Now I'm going to owe you."

Ladro laughed painfully, coughing as he did so. "I like you, gringo. You are different from most white men."

"Yeah, well I never thought I'd wind up liking the man who stole my wife away from me." Trenton felt Ladro's leg. "Where else were you hit?"

"My left leg. It doesn't feel bad." Ladro tried to look toward the trees. "You have to go around. Leave me here. Cortez is going crazy now. He will do anything to get out alive." Ladro felt around on the ground. "Where is my gun?"

Trenton put Ladro's gun in his hand. "Hold onto this and shoot anything that moves."

"Be careful, gringo. Cortez is a coward. He will probably use Aeneva as a shield."

"Don't worry about me. I'll be back." Trenton crawled along the ground until he made it to the trees along the path. When he knew he would no longer be silhouetted against the fire, he stood up, moving as quietly as he could. He walked silently through the trees, going wide, hoping Cortez would still be looking toward the fire. He came out by the barn. The villagers who were guarding it raised their guns until he spoke. "Be careful. Cortez has my wife. He may come out here somewhere."

"We will watch, señor."

Trenton turned back into the trees, nearly crouching as he had been taught to move when he lived with the Arapahos. He measured each step carefully until he thought he was close. Then he stopped and waited, standing next to a tree, his rifle down by his side. He waited for what seemed like an eternity, listening, praying silently that Cortez hadn't already taken Aeneva and left. He was about to move toward the yard when he heard a sound. He heard a branch snap as though it had been stepped on, then another. Cortez was coming toward him. He pressed himself against the tree, knowing that Cortez wouldn't be able to see him in the darkness. He waited patiently, knowing that soon his enemy would be within his reach.

Cortez held Aeneva from behind, shoving her

ahead of him, his pistol pressed into the small of her back. He stopped every few steps to listen, looking frantically around him. He heard sounds everywhere. He used Aeneva as a shield, turning her in the direction of each sound. If someone was going to shoot, they would hit Aeneva first.

At least he had shot Ladro. Now only the gringo would be after him. Somehow he had to find a way to get away from the man. Cortez knew that if Hawkins found him he would be made to pay dearly. He leaned close to Aeneva's ear. "Don't utter a sound or I'll shoot you."

"If you shoot me, Trenton will know where we are."

"I don't care if he knows. Once you're dead, he'll go crazy. He'll make a mistake and come at me like he did before. Then I'll have him. Move." He pushed Aeneva ahead of him.

Aeneva felt as if she would drop. Every part of her body burned. It felt as though the flesh had been ripped from her. But she wouldn't give up. She knew that Trenton was somewhere near. She could feel it.

"Stop!" Cortez hissed, holding her arm while pressing the pistol to her back. "This way." Cortez knew he was almost to the barn now. The villagers had probably killed the guards, but if he could get inside, the gringo would have no choice but to come in the wide door. He didn't have far to go now. The only thing he regretted was that he didn't get to see Ladro die. But he would see Aeneva die and he would take time to make sure she suffered just a little more.

Suddenly one of the shadows leaped in front of him. Cortez faltered and Aeneva was pulled away from him. He was slammed back against a tree. He tried to recover, but Trenton hit him in the face, knocking him down. Cortez lost the pistol and futilely tried to reach for it in the darkness.

"Forget it," Trenton said coldly, reaching down and pulling Cortez to his feet. "You son of a bitch, I've waited for this for a long time." Trenton slammed his fist into Cortez's face over and over again until Cortez fell to the ground moaning.

"Trenton, that is enough." Aeneva reached out for Trenton, taking his arm.

"God, are you all right?" He pulled her to him, feeling her cringe as he touched her. "Can you walk?"

"I will be all right. What about Ladro? Is he alive?"

"He's alive, but he's wounded badly."

"We must go to him then."

"Not until I've taken care of Cortez."

"Trenton, no. You will be just like him if you do."

"He can't live, Aeneva, or he'll come after you. The man is crazy. He'll never stop."

"You just can't shoot him."

"What's the matter with you? I've seen you kill lots of people and it never bothered you. This man had you, Joe, and many of your people kidnapped. He murdered Ignacio and probably Marcela. Do you think he deserves to live?"

Aeneva was silent. "It is not for me to decide. But I understand what my grandfather once told me. If you kill out of hatred, wanting only to destroy, then evil is not ended. It lives on in you. I do not want to be like Cortez. We are not like him, Trenton."

Trenton sighed deeply, then reached down and

pulled Cortez to his feet. "All right. We'll take him back. Maybe the villagers would like to have a say in what happens to him."

Trenton pushed Cortez along ahead of him, while Aeneva followed. When they reached the yard the villagers had overcome Cortez's men. Most of them were dead; just a few had been taken prisoner. Trenton took Cortez to Enrique.

"Hold on to him, Enrique, until we decide what to do with him."

"Gladly, *señor*," Enrique replied, pushing Cortez so hard that he fell forward onto his face.

"Trenton, is James safe?"

"Yes, he and Joe and Larissa are safe. We'll go to them soon. Do you want to see Ladro?"

"Yes, take me to him."

Trenton held on to Aeneva as he led her to where Ladro lay. Ladro's eyes were closed and his breathing was labored. His arm was spread out, still holding on to the gun that Trenton had put in his hand.

Aeneva stopped. "Can you bring him into the light? I cannot help him if I cannot see."

"I don't think you can help him, Aeneva."

"Please, Trenton."

Trenton reached down, picking Ladro up in his arms. "Hold still, Ladro. I'm carrying you into the light. Aeneva wants to take a look at you." Trenton laid him down gently in the yard. The light of the dying fire flared and dimmed.

Aeneva knelt close to Ladro. She unbuttoned his shirt and looked at the gaping wound. This time she knew she couldn't help him. "Ladro, how do you feel?"

Ladro slowly opened his eyes, trying to focus on Aeneva. "I knew you would come."

Aeneva leaned forward, running her hand over Ladro's sweaty brow. "Why did you do it, Ladro? You could have been safe."

"I had to do it, Aeneva. I couldn't live with myself after what I did to you."

"It wasn't all your fault. Do you remember when I begged you to let me stay with you? I forced you."

"Ah, Aeneva." Ladro reached up and touched her face. "Do you really believe that? Don't you know that I made you dependent on me? I made you fall in love with me."

"No, I fell in love with you on my own. You were good and kind to me. I wanted to stay with you."

"What choice did you have? You had no memory, no place to go. You were away from everything and everyone you knew. I was the only person in your memory and I knew it. I took advantage of you, Aeneva. I knew all along what I was doing to you."

"No," Aeneva said in a sad voice, putting her head on his chest. "You are good, Ladro. That is what I saw in you. That is why I loved you."

Ladro's arm came around Aeneva. "I wish I could make love to you one more time. Just one more time." He started coughing, groaning as he did so.

Aeneva sat up, closing the shirt over the wound. "What is your real name?"

"What?"

"What is your real name? Your birth name."

"Why do you want to know that?"

"Please, Ladro. I just want to know."

"My name is Roberto Silvan. I was named after

461

my father."

"It is a beautiful name. It is what I will call our son."

"No . . ."

"Yes, I will call him Roberto Silvan James Hawkins. I think it is a beautiful name."

Ladro squinted, trying to see Aeneva clearly. "I can die content, Aeneva. I know that you will take good care of our son. I know that Trenton will be a good father to him. Thank you."

Aeneva leaned down, kissing Ladro. Tears ran down her face. "I am sorry, Ladro. You deserved better than me."

"There could never be anyone better than you, Aeneva." With a great effort he wiped the tears from her cheeks. "Don't cry for me. You should know that it's better to die like this, like a warrior. There is no honor dying old in your bed."

Aeneva lifted his hand to her mouth and kissed it lovingly. "You are an honorable warrior, Ladro."

"Kiss me one more time, Aeneva. I want to feel your kiss for all time."

Aeneva leaned down again, not able to still the tears that flowed. She touched her lips gently to his, feeling the warmth of his kiss. His arm came around her, holding her tightly for a moment, and then it fell away. Aeneva pulled slowly away, touching Ladro's face. His eyes stared blankly up at her. He was dead. She closed his eyes and laid her head on his chest. She cried deeply, knowing that he was a good man and that she had indeed loved him. She cried silently until she felt Trenton's hands on her pulling her away.

"Come on, Aeneva."

"I do not want to leave him."

"You can't help him now."

"He died so bravely, Trenton."

"He lived bravely, Aeneva. Come on. I'll take you to James."

"His name is not James anymore. His name is Roberto Silvan James. That was Ladro's name."

"It's a good name." He put his arm around her, leading her away from Ladro.

Aeneva stopped, looking at Trenton. "It is strange to love you as I do yet still love Ladro. I grieve so much for him."

"It's not strange. He took care of you and he loved you in his own way. When you couldn't remember me, he took my place."

"I will never forget him, Trenton."

"I don't want you to. He was a good man. An honorable man."

"Yes, an honorable man." She leaned against Trenton feeling more tired than she had ever felt in her life. Her legs suddenly weakened and they buckled. She stumbled but Trenton caught her. He picked her up in his arms. He walked away from the yard and headed toward Joe's shack. He held on to Aeneva tightly, feeling that if he didn't hold her, he might lose her.

Joe got up as they entered. "Guard duty was getting pretty dull, boy. All that noise and smoke got me pretty nervous. How is she?"

Trenton laid Aeneva on the bed. "She'll be better when she sees the baby. I'll go get some of the villagers to help us move this thing."

Joe shook his head. "We won't need them."
Trenton looked at him.

"You plan to move it yourself after all that rest?"

Joe shook his head, touching Aeneva's cheek. She opened her eyes and smiled at him. He picked her up gently and put her in Trenton's arms. "Hold your wife, boy, and watch this."

He rolled the mattress back off the bed. A lever was set into the frame, hidden by the bedding. "I got to thinking. If old Maximo was so darn smart, he would have been able to figure out that a hidey hole isn't much good if you need four men to get into it." He leaned forward and pulled the little lever. The frame clicked neatly into two pieces and slid apart, leaving a pathway to the trapdoor. Joe chuckled. "I'd even bet there's some way to close it up from down there." He walked to the trapdoor and lifted it. Larissa climbed out, her face anxious. Aeneva reached for her child and pressed him against her breast. Joe pulled another lever on the near side of the bed and the frame closed. Trenton laid Aeneva down gently again and faced Larissa.

"I'm sorry, Larissa. Ladro was killed."

She spun away from him and ran into the night. Joe hobbled to the door. "I'll try to find her. I expect you two can find something to talk about. I'll sleep in the barn, or somewhere."

"Trenton?"

"I'm here, Aeneva. I'll always be here for you."

"Yes," she replied in a tired voice, knowing that what he said was true. Although they had been separated many times in their lives, they had always managed to find their way back to each other.

Always. She closed her eyes, knowing that she was finally safe. Her body ached but she couldn't think of anything but Trenton and her child. She felt as if she were finally home and she realized that it didn't matter where she was as long as she was with Trenton. She held on to his hand. The baby slept quietly and soon she was asleep.

Aeneva held on to the sheets, wincing as Trenton rubbed the grease onto her back. She had slept through the night peacefully, not feeling the full extent of the pain until she had awakened. Gently Trenton turned her over and applied the grease over her chest, careful not to aggravate the wounds. When he was through, he covered her with a sheet. He sat down on the bed, taking a cloth from a bowl of water. He pushed Aeneva's hair away from her face and wiped at the blood that had dried along the scalp. When he had cleaned the blood away, he applied the grease.

"How does it feel?"

"Better, thank you, but I smell like a bear. My medicine is better."

"Nothing is better than this for a whipping. I took care of you once before, remember?"

"I remember."

"I'm sorry he did this to you. I swore that no one would ever hurt you again. I'm sorry."

"It is not your fault, Trenton. We cannot control everything that happens to us; I learned that from my grandmother."

"We got in a fight that day. I should never have let

you go for a walk by yourself into the hills. I knew that there was danger with the Comancheros so close but still I let you go off alone."

"It does not matter. You know that I will do as I please no matter what. You cannot change that." She reached out for Trenton's hand, bringing it to her mouth. "Once I made you promise that you would never leave me. You told me that you could not keep such a promise and it was then that you had to search for Nathan. I was angry. It took me a long time to understand that we cannot make those kinds of promises. We do not know what will happen in the next moment of our lives to take us away from each other. All we can do is love each other the best way we know how. If we were separated tomorrow, I would know that you love me. Nothing else would matter."

"Aeneva," Trenton said softly, kissing her cheek. "I do love you. More than anything in this world."

"And I you."

"I'm sorry about Ladro. He loved you very much."

"It is strange to hear you say that."

"It's not so strange. Look at Sun Dancer. Most of her life she was loved by more than one man. Stalking Horse and Laughing Bird loved her when she was a young girl and a young woman, and Jean and Stalking Horse loved her all through her older years. And she loved them all. The human heart has a great capacity for love."

Aeneva nodded, staring past Trenton. He kissed her on the top of the head. "Will you be all right? I want to check on Cortez."

"Yes, I will be fine. What will you do with him?"

"I don't know. The people of the village want to

hang him. He deserves it after all he's done."

"What do you want to do?"

"I don't know. I can't just shoot someone in cold blood. I should make him fight me. I hate him enough to want to kill him. It would be fair, much fairer than he has ever been to anyone."

"Let the fighting be over, Trenton. Cortez will never fight fairly. I do not trust him."

"Don't worry about me." He kissed her one more time. "Rest now, I'll be back later. I want to find Larissa."

Aeneva nodded, watching Trenton walk out the door. Her heart was full; she loved him more than she could imagine.

Larissa walked up the stairs to the small house that served as Cortez's jail. Enrique was standing guard in front. "May I see Cortez?"

"No one is supposed to see him, *señorita*. Not until we decide what we are to do with him."

"Is he tied up?"

"*Sí*, he is tied up." Enrique smiled. "Very much like a pig ready for the slaughter."

"Then he cannot hurt me."

"No, he can't hurt you."

"I want to talk to him. He killed my brother. I want to ask him some questions."

"I don't know, *señorita*. Senor Hawkins says that no one is to see him."

"Senor Hawkins told me that I could come here. If you don't believe me, ask him."

Enrique thought for a moment and shrugged his

shoulders. "I suppose it will be all right. You can go in for a few minutes."

"Thank you, Enrique." Larissa walked into the house. She stared at Cortez, who sat tied in a chair, unable to move. His eyes were closed and his head tilted to one side. Larissa walked over and stood in front of him. She stared at him for a long time, then suddenly, with a swift, hard motion, she kicked the leg of the chair.

Cortez jerked his head up, staring at Larissa in surprise. A sly smile came over his face. "You have come to help me, haven't you? I knew you would, Larissa. We have been through much together."

Larissa remained silent; only her eyes moved as they looked him up and down. She stepped closer, hovering over Cortez.

"What are you doing?"

"I am looking at you, Emiliano. Do you like it?"

"No, I don't. Cut the ropes, Larissa."

"But that is what you did to me all the time. Do you remember? You used to make me undress and stand naked before you. I was so ashamed but you threatened to beat me if I didn't listen to you. How old was I then, Emiliano? Fifteen?"

"You enjoyed it as much as I did. I never had to force you."

"God, you are so evil. You knew how frightened I was, that I had no family. You knew that I was afraid you would sell me to one of those friends of yours, or send me away on one of your ships, so I did anything you asked me to do. You forced me, Emiliano. In many ways."

"Let us be honest, Larissa. You are a whore and

you always have been. I never forced you to do anything you didn't want to do."

Larissa struck Cortez hard across the face, knocking his head backward. "Does it feel good, Emiliano? Do you like it?"

"Are you trying to scare me, Larissa? You forget that I know you. I know you better than anyone in this world. You wouldn't hurt me; you couldn't. I am the man who took you in when you were just a child. I am the man who took care of you."

"Yes, and you are the man who made me into a whore. That is something that I can never forgive you for."

"I don't care about your forgiveness, Larissa. I don't care about you at all, in fact. You were fun and amusing for a while but then you grew tiresome."

"So you sold me to a whorehouse."

"Yes, and you made me good money there. I'm grateful for that." Again Cortez smiled.

"Have you ever thought about dying, Emiliano?"

"I have never thought much about it. Why should I?"

"Because you are going to die very soon."

"The people of this village are cowards. They won't kill me."

"Maybe they won't but I will." Larissa reached under her skirt and pulled out a knife, pressing the point to Cortez's throat. "Do not scream, Emiliano, or I will slit your throat right now."

"You can't do this, Larissa. The guard is right outside the door."

"The guard does not care. Everyone around here wants you dead, Emiliano." She ran the blade of the knife lightly back and forth across his neck. "How does it feel, Emiliano, now that you are powerless?"

"I don't think you can do it, Larissa. You were never very brave. If you had been, you would have left me a long time ago."

Larissa's eyes filled with tears and her hand began to shake. "You are right, Emiliano. I have never been brave. I was never like Ladro."

"Ladro was foolish. He died for nothing."

"No, you are wrong. He did not die for nothing." She stood behind Cortez, holding the knife firmly to his throat. "Take your last look at the world, Emiliano, because you are going to die." Larissa closed her eyes, running the blade across Cortez's throat. She heard a choking sound, but she refused to look. Instead she took the bloodstained knife and turned it to her stomach. She had nothing to live for now. Ladro was dead. Killing Cortez had not brought her the satisfaction she thought it would. She felt empty inside. She pressed the knife to her belly.

"Larissa, no!" Trenton ran across the room, knocking the knife from her hand.

"No, let me be, Trenton. I want to die!"

"No, you don't want to die." He held her arms to her side and hugged her tightly. "You don't want to die, Larissa."

"I killed him, Trenton. I murdered him like he has murdered so many others."

Trenton looked at Cortez, the blood running from his neck. "I suppose if anyone deserved it, he did. But it won't do any good if you kill yourself."

"But I have nothing to live for. I have nothing and

no one."

"That's not true." Trenton cupped Larissa's face in his hands. "You have a nephew, your brother's child. Don't you want to see him grow up?"

"Roberto," she muttered quietly. "But you will return to your people soon and I belong here."

"No, I want you to come with us. You can build a new life there."

"You want me to come with you? After everything I did to you?"

"I am not blameless, Larissa. I made love to you; you believed that I loved you. You did what you did because you were desperate. You have changed. You are my friend; you are Aeneva's friend. Come with us."

"But will Aeneva want me to come with you?"

"She loved your brother, Larissa. She will want you to come."

"Oh, Trenton." Larissa clung to him, crying in huge sobs. "I did not have enough time with Ladro. I wanted to know him better."

"You knew him well enough. You knew that he was loyal and good. He loved you very much."

"Does it bother you that you have Ladro's child?"

"No, I will be proud to raise his son. It is the least I can do for a man who gave his life for mine."

"Thank you, Trenton. Thank you. I hope that you and Aeneva will be together always."

"I hope so too, Larissa. I hope so too."

Three weeks had passed since the villagers had overcome Cortez and his men. Ignacio's house had not completely burned and the villagers were rebuilding it. Marcela recovered in spite of her injuries, and Joe's leg healed better than before. A fiesta was planned to celebrate Cortez's defeat and all of the villagers were excited. The women had been cooking for days, the men making plenty of mescal. Aeneva had almost fully recovered, enough to help Marcela cook.

"Do you have anything to wear to the fiesta, Aeneva?"

"Just what I have on."

"We must make you something. I have some white cloth. We can make a pretty dress for you. And for Larissa."

"I would like that, Marcela. Larissa and I can use something new to wear."

"Come with me. I will show you the material." Marcela took some white linen out of a trunk that was taken from the hacienda. She held it up. "What do you think?"

"It is nice," Aeneva replied absently.

"Nice? Is that all you can say? We are in the middle of nowhere and I bring out beautiful cloth for a dress and all you can do is say how *nice* it is?"

"I am sorry, Marcela. It is beautiful." Aeneva walked to the window and looked out into the yard.

"What is wrong with her, Larissa? She seems far away."

"I know what's the matter with her." Larissa leaned closer to Marcela. "Tomorrow we will leave."

"I thought you would stay for a while."

"No, Trenton has decided to leave tomorrow. He

472

has not seen his son in over a year, Marcela."

"And you will go with them?"

"Yes, I am frightened but I am excited, too. Perhaps I can find a man someday, and have a child. I would like to have a love like theirs."

Marcela hugged Larissa, then walked over to Aeneva. "Are you sad because you are leaving tomorrow?"

"I am just . . . I would like a time of peace. I am tired of being forced away from the people I love."

"Now you are being foolish, Aeneva. Love is not stopped by distance. I have come to learn that it is not even stopped by death." She put her arm around Aeneva's shoulders. "Go to your husband. He needs you. He feels what you do. You have been through much together. It is time to rediscover your love."

Aeneva looked back out at the yard. Trenton had his shirt off and was digging feverishly at the hole. His back was lean and hard and his skin was brown. She felt a growing sense of excitement as she thought of being alone with him. "All right, I will go to him. You must both promise me to take good care of Roberto. It frightens me to leave him, even for a few hours."

"Do not worry about Roberto. He is safe now. We have much to do before the fiesta begins tonight. Go."

Aeneva smiled at Larissa and Marcela. She felt content as she had not felt in a long time. "I will wait until the party. First, I am going to make a beautiful dress from the wonderful cloth in your trunk. How did you ever get such beautiful cloth out here in the middle of nowhere?" She smiled mischievously and the three women laughed together.

Trenton took another gulp from the cup, wiping his hand across his mouth. "God, this stuff tastes terrible."

"I don't know, I've grown to like it myself."

Trenton glanced at Joe, an eyebrow raised. "So what do you think?"

"I think this is going to be some party." Joe looked around. "Where is Larissa?"

"Probably with Aeneva. Why? You interested?"

"No, I was just thinking it would be nice to dance with a pretty girl now that my leg is back to normal." He patted the leg. "Aeneva did a good job. She's a prize, boy. Don't let her get away from you again."

"I don't plan on it."

Joe started to speak but stopped. Larissa walked up to the two men. Her long hair was pulled back and she was dressed in a white dress that Marcela had made that day.

"Good evening." She curtsied to both men and turned to Joe. "Would you like to dance with me, Joe? Aeneva told me that you grew up in the city and you know how to dance."

Joe stood up, winking at Trenton. He held out his arm for Larissa. "Yes, it's true. I am a man of many talents."

"Good." She took Joe's arm and the two walked away talking and laughing.

Trenton leaned over, his arms resting on his knees. He lifted the cup to his mouth but stopped. He saw

Aeneva's bare feet in front of him. Slowly, he looked up. She was dressed in a white skirt and a blouse that was pulled off the shoulders. Around her waist she wore a bright blue sash. She wore her hair straight and it hung to her waist. Trenton stood up, looking down at the woman he loved so much. She seemed to have grown more lovely with age or perhaps it was just that he had grown to love her that much more.

He touched her face lightly. "You are so beautiful."

"Thank you." She took his hand and kissed the palm, holding it to her cheek. "I remember when I first saw you running along the prairie. I thought you were the most beautiful boy I had ever seen. I thought the gods had made you especially for me." She kissed his hand again, rubbing it along her cheek. "I thought I would die when you returned to your people. We were so young but I knew even then that I wanted you to be my friend for life. I wanted us to be together forever."

"In our hearts we always will be together."

"Yes," she said softly, leaning forward. She touched her lips to his, barely moving them. She felt his body tense as he wrapped his arms around her, pulling her closely to him.

Trenton took her hand and led her away from the fiesta toward the trail that led to Joe's shack. They walked in silence, each savoring the moments leading up to their lovemaking. When they went inside the shack it was dark and cool. Trenton reached out for Aeneva, touching her bare shoulders. He pushed the blouse farther down, running his hands back and forth along her skin. He kissed her shoulders and neck, breathing in her scent, never wanting to forget how it felt to hold her. He untied the sash that was around the skirt and slowly pushed the skirt down Aeneva's hips. Then he pulled the blouse over her head. He took off his shirt and pants and they stood together in the cool darkness, not in any hurry.

Aeneva reached out and touched Trenton's chest, running her fingers through the coarse hair, enjoying the feel of his muscles under her fingers. It was as if they had never made love before. It was as if this was for the first time.

Trenton sat down on the bed, pulling Aeneva down next to him. He held her face in his hands, covering her mouth with his. He kissed her in a way he had never kissed her before; he consumed her with his desire. He lay down, pulling her to him, running his hands over her bare skin, enjoying the feel of its softness.

Aeneva closed her eyes, feeling as if she had never loved before. She heard herself moan as Trenton caressed her body, and her legs wrapped around his as he lay on top of her. His mouth covered hers and when he entered her she cried out, unable to contain her joy. She lifted herself up, giving herself entirely to him. It was a fierce, intense lovemaking but their desire was coupled with a great love, a love they both knew would last a lifetime.

As they lay in each other's arms each knew a completeness they had never known before.

"Thank you," Trenton breathed against her skin.

"I have never felt like that before. It was wonderful."

"Maybe we won't go. Maybe we'll stay here forever. We'll lie in this magic bed and make love until we die."

"And the world will pass us by."

Trenton smiled to himself. "At least we have now. No one can ever take this away from us. This is our time."

"Yes." Aeneva turned, resting her arms on Trenton's chest. "We are leaving tomorrow. I will never be separated from you again. We will return to our people and live together forever."

"You're sure? You're ready to leave?"

"Yes, I am ready. But there is something else."

"What is it?"

"I want to get Brave Wolf's horse. He loved that animal. It meant so much to him because it is descended from my grandmother's marriage horse."

"Yes, I think Brave Wolf would rather lose his scalp than his horse."

"We can get him then?"

"Yes, we can get him. Brave Wolf will be happy to have you and the horse back."

Aeneva smiled. "Nathan will be so happy to see us."

"And his new brother. They won't fight until they're older." He pulled her on top of him, kissing her, her long hair falling over them both. "You are part of me, Aeneva. Don't ever forget that."

"I will not forget it." She laid her head on his chest. "Do you think my grandparents can see us? Do you think they know how happy we are?"

"I am sure of it."

"I hope they are together. I have never seen two

people who loved each other more than my grandparents."

"I cannot imagine anyone loving anyone more than I love you." He stroked her hair. "We are lucky, Aeneva. We are young and our lives have been full."

"Yes, and our lives will continue to be full. We have a lot to give to each other and to our children. Someday I will give you a child, Trenton. I promise."

"No more promises. Let's just live each day the best we can." He pulled her to him, kissing her deeply. "I love you, Aeneva."

"Yes," Aeneva said softly before Trenton's lips touched hers again. And she knew that no matter what happened, she would always have him with her not only in her mind, but in her heart as well.